POWERTOOLS
COMPLETE SERIES

KATE'S CREW * MORGAN'S SURPRISE *
KAYLA'S GIFT * DEVON'S PAIR * NAILED TO
THE WALL * HAMMER IT HOME

JAYNE RYLON

HAPPY ENDINGS PUBLISHING

Contains Kate's Crew, Morgan's Surprise, Kayla's Gift, Devon's Pair, Nailed to the Wall, and Hammer it Home.

Six ménage romances about a crew of bisexual construction workers who take pride in pleasuring the women they love with the help of their friends.

ADDITIONAL INFORMATION

Sign up for the Naughty News for contests, release updates, news, appearance information, sneak peek excerpts, reading-themed apparel deals, and more. www.jaynerylon.com/newsletter

Shop for autographed books, reading-themed apparel, goodies, and more www.jaynerylon.com/shop

A complete list of Jayne's books can be found at www.jaynerylon.com/books

KATE'S CREW
POWERTOOLS
JAYNE RYLON
NEW YORK TIMES BESTSELLING AUTHOR

For everyone who has been told an idea they had was crazy.
Sometimes those turn out to be the best kind.

1

———

ate wiped her palms on her paint-splattered cutoffs before adjusting her grip on the rebuilt window casement. A flash of tan skin drew her attention to glistening muscles. They rippled over five sexy frames as the crew renovating the townhouse next door hammered nail after nail into their first-story roof, just a few feet below her perch.

From inside the bedroom where she worked, she inched to the edge of the ladder rung then craned her neck through the opening in front of her for a glimpse of the intricate tattoo spanning Mike's broad shoulders. Instead, she caught him reaching up to their stash of supplies for another pack of shingles. When her gaze latched onto the drop of sweat that slid along his neck, she forgot to breathe. She watched in fascination as it journeyed over his defined pecs and six-pack abs. After it was absorbed in the ultra-low-riding jeans snugged to his trim hips by a bulging tool belt, she heaved a sigh of relief.

Kate swiped at a blob of paint that had plopped onto her wrist unnoticed while she'd ogled Mike. Her tongue moistened her lips as she imagined licking a similar trail down his body. The edge of the fresh trim gouged her thigh as she strained for a better view. The gasp she made busted her. His head lifted, catching her spying. Great, now she'd never convince him to take it easy with his persistent innuendo or date invites. And, no matter how much she wanted to, she couldn't indulge either of their desires.

Mike threw her a dazzling victory grin. The anticipation sparkling in his cocky stare blasted a shockwave through her, screwing with her balance. The ladder wobbled then tipped. She probably could have righted herself if she hadn't been standing on tiptoes to maximize her view of the scenery. In slow motion, she watched his expression morph from flirtatious to horrified.

Kate flung out her arms in an attempt to catch the frame before she tumbled through it but the momentum swung her around. Her temple grazed the custom-made pewter latch she'd installed the day before. She hung, suspended in midair, as Mike rose from his crouch. The other guys began to turn toward her, but he was already sprinting for the edge.

Terror froze her insides when he launched himself across the ten-foot gap between their houses. Then she spun away, losing sight of him. She braced for imminent impact.

Shit, this is going to hurt.

Everything happened at once. Air whooshed from her lungs when she slammed, on her side, onto the roof. She rolled, flexing her ankles in an attempt to find purchase that would halt her skid toward the brink. But her knee wrenched at an awkward angle while she continued to rake over the slate. Her hand caught the ridge of an attic vent, slowing her descent, but gravity overcame the tenuous hold. Her frantic fingers recoiled from the sharp metal edge.

The gutters rushed closer, her last hope. After that, she'd have to pray the evergreen shrubs would cushion her, preventing any broken bones. The heels of her work boots hit the aluminum edging but kept going. Her legs dangled in thin air.

Then a strong hand banded around her wrist. Her arm nearly jerked from the socket as she lurched to a stop. Kate shoved on the edging shingles with her free hand, fighting to stay on the roof.

"Son of a bitch!" Mike hauled her the rest of the way up.

"Sorry, been eating too much fast food on this job." She surprised herself by squeezing false bravado past the thudding of her heart and the constriction of her throat. Mouthing off beat bursting into tears of relief in front of the construction-chief-turned-action-hero she'd lusted after for months.

"Now's not the time to be a smartass. You could have gotten yourself killed."

"It was your damn fault." She didn't wait for him before scaling the slope toward the safety of her window.

"*My* fault? We told you that ladder's a piece of shit. You're too stubborn to get a new one."

"My grandfather's ladder works just fine." She ignored his helpful boost. The way his hand spanned her ass, cupping her, would pitch her off the precipice again if she wasn't careful.

Mike climbed in so close behind her the heat of his defined chest scorched her bare arms. She attempted to leap away from the temptation of his security, but a spike of agony rolled up her ankle, buckling her knees.

His solid biceps banded around her, molding her to his chest as they sank to the floor together. "Jesus, I've never been that scared before."

No kidding.

"You shouldn't have pulled that stunt, Mike. Who do you think you are? Jackie Chan?" She struggled to break his hold before her adrenaline rush coerced her into doing something stupid, but the weak attempt didn't budge him. Unable to fight them both, she surrendered, resting her forehead on the side of his neck. She bit her cheek to keep from licking the pulse pounding within reach of her lips. "But thank you."

He framed her face, lifting it to his scrutiny. His forest green eyes widened at her automatic compliance. He stroked wisps of hair from her cheek with the knuckles of one hand. Mike's hunger etched into the rugged set of his full lips, igniting a flame of longing in her core. They leaned into each other, mouths parting, when the clomp of work boots shattered the moment.

Bulky forms honed by years of manual labor invaded all the free space in the spare bedroom. Then a chorus of testosterone-laden cheers stifled her hushed conversation with Mike.

"That was awesome!"

"Way to go, Mike! Dude, when you nailed that slide I thought for sure you were going over the edge with her." Joe leaned down to give Mike's back a solid clap. The impact jostled Kate, making her wince.

"Careful, she's hurt." James knelt beside them, running his capable hands over her arms, verifying she hadn't broken anything. She flinched from his touch but not because it hurt. Of all the guys, he seemed the most reserved—quiet, confident and sensitive. She'd been tempted to spill her guts to him on more than one of their shared breaks. But she'd never figured out how to phrase her longing without coming off like a slut. What would he have thought of her decadent curiosity?

"No, I'm fine. Really." As long as you didn't count the throbbing in her head, the zing racing up her leg every time she moved or the lust saturating her nerves at every place she made contact with Mike.

"I'm going to take her over to St. Anthony's. It looks like clear skies. We'll finish the roof tomorrow."

Though the five men were partners, Mike seemed to make the majority of the decisions. He had a knack for business, handy for managing their house-turning enterprise. They'd bought the brownstone next door not long after her grandfather had passed away, bequeathing his home to her. She couldn't count the number of times they'd sacrificed progress on their project to give her a hand with the minor renovations she'd taken on, or lent her their tools. Sometimes she suspected they hung around longer than necessary when they'd sensed her melancholy at roaming the big house alone.

She'd also lost track of how often she'd found herself daydreaming about one—or more—of them bending her over a sawhorse, their tools clanking together as they sought payback for their assistance. Or spread her out on the lush grass under the oak tree for an entirely different kind of refreshment at the end of the day.

Kate had stopped counting the depraved permutations at a million and one. But how could she watch their sexy bodies in motion, share lunch and beers after a hard day's work, or observe their camaraderie without wanting to be a part of it? Wanting them?

"Come on, Katie." Neil gave her shoulder a tiny shake that broke her from her reverie. "You're zoning on us. Let's get you checked out."

"Not necessary." She tried to smother their objections but one versus five weren't good odds.

In the end, Dave sealed her fate. "If you're not going to the doctor then you better decide who'll be camping out here tonight."

"What?" How could she choose Mike and risk leading him on or offending the others? How could she spend the night locked in here with any of them and avoid making a fool of herself?

They misjudged her alarm for outrage.

"You just took a header out the window, you're bleeding all over Mike and you're hardly able to focus. No way are we leaving you here by yourself, babe."

And no way could she control herself through a sweltering summer night with a fantasy or five hovering nearby.

"Fine. Let's get this over with. But you're only wasting your time."

They might have taken her grumbling more seriously if she hadn't blacked out the moment she struggled to her feet.

2

———

Sure hands travelled the length of her exposed back. A heated torso slid across her pebbled nipples. She closed her fingers around a pair of straining erections while someone smacked her ass then kissed away the sting.

Kate reveled in another steamy dream about Mike and his crew. Practice made perfect because this time she swore the heat of an intimate embrace seared her skin while she writhed on the cool sheets of her bed, half-awake. When she rolled her hips, her slick mound nudged a rock-hard shaft larger than any she'd imagined.

Her eyelids flew open to confirm her suspicions. Mike!

He was sprawled across her bed, making the queen mattress look like the rickety cot she'd slept on when camping as a kid. She remembered now. He'd escorted her home from the emergency room then refused to leave, though she'd been given the all clear.

Holy shit, she'd practically humped his leg. Attempting to hide it would be futile. His nostrils flared as he blinked against the golden glow streaming in the east-facing window.

"Morning." The sleep-roughened greeting accompanied by his sexy smile sent her heart into overdrive, but he only made it worse when he said, "Don't let me stop you. Sounded like you were having a good time."

She would have rolled away, locked herself in the bathroom for a week then ignored the whole fiasco, but he refused to let her flee. Faster than she thought possible, he flipped her to her back, pinned her wrists to the pillows with his forearms and trapped her ankles beneath his shins. The coarse hair on his legs abraded her as she struggled to escape. Every delicious rasp teased her sensitive flesh.

The weight of his cock thudded onto her belly as he closed the space between them to stare into her eyes. "Tell me now if you don't want me."

How could she lie like that? He'd be buried inside her within sixty seconds if she didn't object, but the greedy part of her screamed for her to take what they both needed now and sort out the consequences later. With a moan, she lunged up then covered his wicked mouth, devouring his stunned smile.

Mike groaned, sinking onto her. Her bruised hip protested, but she forgot all about the minor pain when he settled against her, skin on skin, from head to toe. Her instincts ran wild. She wrapped her thighs around his waist, crossing her ankles at the base of his spine.

Their tongues tangled, stroking, thrusting, licking. Her nails raked the length of his back until she grabbed his ass. The thick muscles there tensed beneath the pressure that left ten miniature crescents in the perfect globes.

When he broke the contact of their lips then rested his head on the pillow beside her for a moment, his harsh breaths buffeted the curve of her neck. "Now you...want... to rush? Damn it, Kate. I don't have any condoms."

"I'm on the pill," she whispered. "And I'm safe. Tell me you are, too?"

"I promise."

She nodded and sighed.

He dipped his head to suck on her tight nipple but she squirmed, angling her pelvis until the head of his cock bumped the mouth of her pussy. They moaned in unison. He teased her with tiny rocks of his hips that tapped the full head of his erection against her ultra-responsive tissue. After a few passes, her dripping slit transferred enough lubrication that he began sliding instead of nudging her.

The ridges of his heavily veined shaft stroked her clit while he rode the furrow of her labia. Dark hair feathered over his brow as he wandered lower, engulfing the tip of her other breast in moist suction. Her legs trembled. Each glide buffeted nerves already on edge.

Months of anticipation had made her needy. Nights of masturbation hadn't eased her desire. She didn't want to come again without him filling her.

"Fuck me, Mike." She shifted one hand to tug on the silky strands of his midnight hair, forcing him to look into her eyes. The instant he recognized the scale of her appetite, he lost all restraint.

"Shit, yes. I need you, too." He scooped his arms between her and the mattress, curving his hands so they cupped her shoulders. When his ass rose beneath her feet, gravity caused the head of his cock to sink. It dipped into her entrance.

They paused to take a synchronized breath. Then his arms flexed, the bulging sinew cushioning her as he impaled her with his erection. She screamed at the simultaneous pleasure and pain. His monstrous flesh spread her, stretching even as it fanned the raging inferno in the pit of her stomach.

He clasped her tighter, drawing her down while he thrust up until he worked his full length into her welcoming sheath. A shudder ran through her when his balls tapped her ass.

"You fit me perfectly. I knew you would." The satisfied possession gleaming in his eyes caused her pussy to clamp around his embedded hard-on. He nuzzled her neck, alternating biting with licking. When she'd adjusted to his intrusion, he began to thrust.

For the first few strokes, her swollen passage clung to his cock as though afraid he would abandon her. But his skilled mouth, roaming fingers and the circular motion of his hips teasing her clit coaxed more wetness from her until his entire girth was coated. Slick and hot he tunneled inside her, driving her to pleasurable heights she'd never before experienced.

Lasting more than a few minutes when subjected to such ecstasy would be impossible. The liquid fire spreading through her surpassed even her wildest dreams. Kate bit her lip, struggling to resist the primal urges encouraging her to crash into the best orgasm of her life. She didn't want it to be over so soon.

"Let go. I've got you."

She resisted the blanket of pleasure suffocating her.

"There's more, I promise. I'll give you more. Let go." She opened eyes. When had she scrunched them shut? Generous yet commanding, Mike left her no choice. His lips latched onto hers, drawing her tongue into his mouth, sucking in time to the rapid lunges of his hips. She had to obey.

Mike swallowed her scream when she shattered around him. She bucked, grinding her pussy into his waiting abdomen. She expected him to come with her, to end their long-awaited bout yet he preserved his restraint.

Not without effort.

She came hard, the orgasm clenching her channel. For each squeeze, she swore his jaw gave an answering clench as he gritted his teeth. He tipped his head back then groaned but held on.

His motions slowed until she wondered if she'd missed his climax. Still, the length of his shaft twitched inside her, triggering aftershocks of delight. She stroked her hand over his sculpted chest, fingers flexing in time with the periodic squeezes of her pussy.

The relief suffusing her didn't last long. In place of the mindless hunger she'd surrendered to, an undeniable yearning built within her. She had to return the pleasure this man had given her. At least this one time. Kate knew what he needed. After all, she'd refused to let him win for weeks.

With a sigh of regret, she separated their bodies. His cock abandoned her pussy with a slurp. Instead of evacuating the bed, she rolled. She presented her ass for his enjoyment as she knelt before him, shoulders flush with the mattress.

He growled. Then his hands gripped her hips as though he held on for dear life. "You trust me?"

"Of course." She trembled when she thought of all he could do to her in this position. When something nudged her rear passage, she jumped before she realized the digit was far too thin to be his cock. He swirled his thumb around the pucker before coating it with some of the juices that had spilled onto her thighs.

Kate rested her cheek on the sheet once more. She moaned when the thrill of his taboo touch sparked her lingering arousal. What would it be like to take a man there?

"Relax."

Mike teased her until her anxiety transformed into pleasure, allowing her muscles to go slack. Then his thumb sank into her virgin hole. She didn't expect it to feel so damn good. Just when she'd started to embrace the novel sensation, the bulk of his rigid cock prodded her pussy once more.

This time he glided in to the hilt. The combination of his thick shaft and his thumb in her ass had her undulating beneath him in minutes. When he leaned forward, resting his forearm across her shoulders, lightning bolts of desire struck her nervous system. Pinned under his bulk, she embraced his desires only to find she had adopted them as her own.

"Yes. Please, Mike. Take me." He answered her cry, riding her hard and fast. The knowledge that she could make him wild drove her higher. She craved the ultimate proof. The grunts he made as he slammed into her indicated she'd have her wish before long.

The thought made her muscles contract, hugging him tighter. The constriction of her pussy increased her own pleasure. She hovered on the cusp of another huge orgasm. "Mike!"

Her urgency broke through his pounding rhythm. "Yes? Tell me, Kate."

"I want you to come on me."

"Fuck!" His groin smacked the back of her thighs as his thumb rotated in her ass. Three, four more times, he pounded into her before he yanked his cock from her with a roar. The searing splash of his come on her spine triggered her own release. When her ass seized his thumb, the sensation amplified her orgasm. She came in his arms as stream after stream of his semen marked her.

She drifted in a haze of bliss with him on top of her, his heavy presence comforting. Eventually, he reached to the floor beside the bed to grab his discarded T-shirt. He wiped the evidence of their debauchery from their skin before turning her to face him. The tenderness mixed with contentment on his face spurred her to confess.

"I'm sorry, Mike. You can't stay."

He flinched, but refused to budge. When she tried to avert her face from his persuasive gaze, he captured her lip between his teeth then nipped her. "Enough. Enough running, Kate."

Her brain struggled to catch up to this alternate reality where she finally had what she wanted, but she couldn't keep it. If she could just get dressed maybe she could usher him out with a modicum of pride intact.

"What happened to our clothes?" Her question came out a bit garbled since he maintained his hold on her lip a few seconds longer. "I remember falling asleep with pajamas on."

"It's fucking hot up here at night. I'll have James take a look at the air-conditioning later. You stripped after you'd been asleep for five minutes." His eyelids drooped at the memory. "Now quit stalling. Why are you fighting what's between us?"

He dusted her mouth with his even as he left a sticky trail of arousal in the wake of his half-hard shaft, which traced a shallow arc across her abdomen. She forced her hips to stay glued to the bed instead of tipping up to align her aching pussy with the head of his cock. Even as endless passion threatened to obliterate her better judgment, guilt corrupted her bliss.

"It's not fair to do this to you," she whispered.

"To tempt me until I swear blue balls isn't some high school myth? To rile me up with those sweet smiles and naughty looks, then bolt whenever I get within arm's reach? To refuse me all damn summer until I end up fucking you like an animal before I've even taken you out to dinner? What? What exactly isn't fair about this bullshit?"

He'd never shown her even a hint of impatience before. It left her no choice but to be honest. To be direct.

"It's not fair to start something serious with you when I want to fuck your partners, too."

Heat crawled up her chest then progressed onto her cheeks at the admission. She'd never had these kinds of urges before. Well, maybe once or twice. But only in an abstract way. She'd never had anyone specific in mind, and she'd certainly never admitted the fantasy to a lover.

Kate had tried to discount her constant hunger for her new neighbors as a product of the steamy season, their often half-naked bodies or, even, her hormones kicking in as she got older. None of the lies held water.

Something about this man drew her like a bear to honey. And his friends sweetened the deal. Fear of his rejection had her mind racing so out of control, she didn't realize he'd started laughing until he flopped to his back on the mattress beside her.

He flung his contoured arm over his eyes, burying his once-broken nose in the crook of his elbow. The tribal armband ringing his biceps jerked as he tried to stifle his amusement but failed. Kate's face flamed even as her stomach cramped.

She slugged his shoulder. "What the hell are you laughing at? I know I'm nothing special, but I've seen the way your friends look at me when they think I can't see. Hell, I can feel their eyes undressing me every time I bend over. It's driving me insane!"

When she shifted—tucking her legs under her to scurry out of the bed—he rolled to his side, propped his scruffy jaw on his hand then grabbed her around her waist and refused to let go.

"There's no need to get your pretty panties in a bunch, doll."

"Good thing, since I'm not wearing any." She thrust her chin in the air.

"True, that." His pupils dilated. "But you're missing my point."

Mike coaxed her to recline beside him with languorous strokes of his fingers on her waist. Then he shook his head as if remembering what he'd been saying. "I can't believe you made me chase you like a rabid dog because my crew turns you on."

"It's not just that they're smoking." She cleared her throat.

"No worries. I caught you the first time around, babe. You want to get it on with them."

Kate clamped her bottom lip between her teeth then gave a reluctant nod. "I'm sorry."

"Stop it. Stop assuming you know what I want."

How had he ended up above her again? His laser stare sliced through the flimsy denials she'd hoped to construct.

"Ever hear the saying, 'Work hard, play harder'?" Mike encroached on her personal space, filling every gap with his scent, his heat and his challenge.

"What about it?" She gulped like a fish out of water.

"I've known the crew for ten years, ever since we suffered through trade school. There's not much we haven't done together. I'm a pretty open-minded guy. Would it surprise you if I said you wouldn't be the first woman we'd shared?" He traced the ridge of her collarbone with the tip of his middle finger.

She tried to answer but couldn't, her throat had gone dry.

"You think about it, Kate. Where's your feisty spirit now? Do you have the guts to go after what you want? All you have to do is ask."

Just when she thought he would steal her inhibitions with another kiss, he sprang over her then headed for the shower. On the vintage-tile threshold to the bathroom, he turned. "And, one more thing, sweetness... You're plenty special. Never doubt that."

WHERE THE HELL had Mike disappeared to? Kate shouldn't care, but she did. She scolded herself when she scanned the yard for the tenth time that minute. She'd spent the morning trying to ignore his insufferable smirk, as he strutted around the site, while mentally reciting all the reasons she couldn't accept his unconventional proposition.

Despite this morning's wake-up call, affairs weren't her style. The unwise urge to prevent him from walking away after one sweaty liaison had almost overwhelmed her sense of self-preservation. Instead, she'd driven her hand beneath her thigh to keep from reaching out to tug him into bed for another romp following his shower. She couldn't risk getting any more involved. No matter how she prayed she could change, she would always want more—something lasting.

The *thunk* of her forehead hitting the sheetrock patch she'd finished installing an hour ago almost drowned out her sigh. Her cell phone vibrated, alerting her to an incoming text message. Every hypersensitive nerve in her body jumped to attention.

She flipped open the phone. Mike.

Meet me in our laundry room. Come in through the garage. Quiet. Quick.

Ignoring his command would be prudent. Also impossible.

Kate sprinted along the hall then took the stairs two at a time before racing out the rear entrance. She hopped the low stone wall dividing their properties then snuck into the neighboring garage like a cat burglar working a world-class heist.

Her hand brushed the doorknob leading from the car bay into the house, where the washer and drier would one day go, but she got drawn inside before she could turn it. Mike's powerful arms surrounded her, pressing her spine to his taut abdomen. The ridge of his constant hard-on fit in the valley of her ass, covered only by the thin material of her Capri sweats and her thong.

"What—"

The astringent odor of sealant wafted up from his hand, which covered her mouth. In the pitch-black, the brush of his lips on the shell of her ear startled her. She flinched at his raspy whisper. "I want to show you something. Everyone lusts. Everyone fantasizes. When your lover respects you, you should feel free to explore your desires. No matter how extreme."

Her eyes began to adjust to the darkness. Slits of light

gleamed through the louvers on the interior laundry-room door, which faced into the kitchen of Mike's fixer-upper. Now that she could hear past the galloping of her heart, she froze. A masculine moan echoed off the tiled surfaces of the vacant living space. No, make that several moans.

"Want to see what it could be like?" The plane of Mike's chest cradled her as he inched them closer to forbidden delights with shuffles of his steel-toed boots. His hands encircled her waist. The tips of his fingers teased the hem of her tank top. Then they slid beneath it to rub irresistible circles over the skin on either side of her belly button.

Kate shivered in his hold.

"Go ahead, take a peek." He bumped her with his pelvis, grinding against her.

She worried her lip between her teeth as she debated. But the next primal grunt of pleasure dissolved all traces of resistance. Before she knew what she intended, her fingers tucked in the slats at eye level and her nose smooshed against the cool, painted wood.

Oh. My. God.

From this angle, she caught the strong profiles of both James and Neil. Tall and lithe, Neil leaned on the end of the countertop for support, his jeans unbuttoned. Framed in worn denim, his cock jutted from the vee of his fly. James hovered a mere half inch away from the head. His lips parted, glistening with saliva, as though waiting for permission.

"Suck it." The gruff command reverberated through the space, causing a trickle of wetness to run onto Kate's thighs.

In the kitchen, Neil buried his fingers in James's sun-bronzed hair, using the grip to tug the kneeling man closer still. With two fingers, he aimed his erect shaft straight for James's open mouth. When he slid inside, balls-deep with a single stroke, the look of rapture on both men's faces stole her breath.

From behind her, Mike's hands travelled lower, dipping beneath the waistband of her pants. He shoved them over her hips until they pooled on the floor. "Mmm...you smell delicious. Wet already? I thought you might enjoy the show."

He cut short her whimper when he tilted her face for a scorching kiss. But he didn't steal her concentration from the other men for long. When she turned her head back, they had paused. Had they heard her?

Please, don't stop!

As though they read her thoughts, the two men resumed their rough play. James's stout throat worked around Neil's embedded cock. She almost cried out again when his jaw slid forward, dragging his lower lip over Neil's tight sac.

"Fuck! Where did you learn that trick?" Neil panted.

"From me."

Kate's eyes widened as Dave strolled in from the living room. An impressive bulge tented the front of his cargo shorts. His hulking frame and towering stature might have been intimidating if he weren't so quick to joke or lend a helping hand when needed.

"Son of a bitch. Can't you two go five minutes without getting off?" Joe followed a step behind Dave. "We have a deadline..."

He should have saved his breath. James continued to give Neil what looked like a world-class blow job. She thought Neil's gaze flickered toward her and Mike's hiding spot, but he didn't say anything.

Joe grinned, then shrugged at Dave. "Now's as good a time as any for a break. We need them to concentrate when we snap the chalk lines for the patio or everything will be out of square, and we'll spend all afternoon fixing it anyway."

The easygoing partner stripped his shorts off in two seconds flat. His cock, bare beneath the khaki, sprang free. He put one hand on the counter then hopped up beside Neil with animal grace. When his balls rested on the cool marble they'd upgraded to, he hissed.

"Come on, Dave. I see you checking out James's ass. What are you waiting for?"

4

J ames raised his hips in clear invitation. Each man embraced his sexuality without inhibitions. Every desire they expressed met with acceptance and trust from the others. The display caused a surge of hope and desperation in Kate.

What would it be like to explore her yearnings without fear of recrimination? The mere idea of such freedom had her arching into Mike's roaming caresses, craving something more.

"Shh, babe. I've got what you need." His fingertips completed their circuit around her swollen folds before retreating. The pause, filled with the faint rustle of him shedding clothes, gave her a moment to refocus on the scene before her.

Joe had braced one arm behind him. He reclined with his weight on his straight-locked elbow to give Neil the room needed to reach over and surround his hard-on with one fist. Neil had joined him on the countertop. Their thighs pressed together from hip to knee. As she watched,

Neil turned his head to claim Joe's mouth in an aggressive exchange.

She'd never seen two men make out. Their whisker-stubbled jaws rasped together as their tongues clashed. They devoured each other. Meanwhile, James continued to feast on Neil's cock. His head bobbed with sure strokes on the other man's tool, eliminating the hesitancy she sometimes experienced when she wondered what her ministrations would feel like. Should she suck harder? Use more tongue?

James made short work of the fasteners on his torn jeans. Dave had positioned himself behind James, who bent at the waist between Neil's lightly furred legs. His meaty hand rubbed his crotch through his work clothes as he took in the trio of lovers before him.

The tendons in Dave's neck protruded when the golden skin of his partner's back gave way to the lighter flesh of his ass beneath his low tan line. Dave scrounged in his utility belt. When his hand landed on what he sought, he grinned.

"I was just about to start coating the bolts for the railing so they wouldn't rust." He held up a jar so Joe and Neil could see, then gave it a shake. "Let's hear it for petroleum jelly, huh, James?"

James moaned around Neil's erection then widened his stance. His steely cock bobbed between his legs. He ran his hands up Neil's thighs then cupped the other man's balls in his palms, nuzzling them with his chin. The confident massage of his stained fingers had Neil's hips bucking, driving his shaft farther into James's eager mouth.

"Put your hand on me, Neil." Joe grabbed Neil's wrist then guided it to his stiff flesh. Kate didn't blame Neil for being too distracted to function without assistance. James lapped the dripping head of Neil's cock before returning to his enthusiastic sucking.

Kate followed the line of Neil's toned arm to the juncture where it encased Joe. The flared tip beneath Neil's fingers left a trail of pre-come that glistened in the afternoon light. While Neil's lips travelled along the column of Joe's neck to tongue his pebbled nipples, Joe's gaze riveted to Dave, who swirled his index finger in the open jar.

Lost in her observations, Kate gasped when Mike's throbbing cock nudged her swollen pussy. Then she rocked against him, clamping her teeth shut over a whine when he retreated on the cusp of entering her.

"With James, babe. Imagine it's you out there, the center of all that attention."

Her pulse spiked at the thought.

Dave scooped a generous dollop of the lube onto his cock. He stroked the substantial length until it made squishy sounds against his greased palm. Then he wiped the excess jelly over the clenching pucker of James's ass.

Mike mimicked the sensation, swirling his fingertips across the mouth of her pussy, spreading her ample arousal over every exposed surface of her labia. The pleasure had turned to torture. She struggled to force him inside but he evaded her then pinched her ass.

Luckily, the men seemed oblivious to her squeak.

"No cheating." To silence her protests, he circled her mouth with two fingers until her lips parted to admit them. The sweet taste of her own arousal burst over her tongue. She realized his intent when he used the intrusion to tip her head forward, blanketing her back.

Kate sucked on his fingers as though they were Neil's

long, lanky cock. She swirled her tongue over his short nails then nipped the thicker, work-roughened pads.

"Yes, that's right." He adjusted her so she could see out a lower slat. The sensual recreation in front of her blazed to life once more.

Neil and Joe stared at Dave's cock as he set the head against the tissue ringing James's asshole. Dave's hard-on, though proportional to his mammoth frame, appeared out of scale compared to James's compact build.

How will he take all that?

Dave wrapped his fingers around the base of his shaft then bounced the heavy head against James—sensitive flesh on sensitive flesh—in a series of quick slaps. The contact initiated a chain reaction. James moaned then swallowed Neil's erection, his lips circling the root. Neil cursed then squeezed Joe's cock, pumping faster.

She swore Mike trembled behind her with the effort of hovering on the brink. Almost penetrating. Yet he refused to bury his length in her.

Dave gripped one of James's hips then used his other hand to guide his hard-on through the initial resistance of his partner's ass. It seemed as though all six of them gasped in unison when the tip plunged past the broadest point to drive several inches deep.

Mike's cock burrowed inside her before she'd recovered from the delicious vision. The shock of being filled to capacity obliterated rational thought from her mind. Both her and James writhed together beneath the assault of overwhelming pleasure.

"It's been a while, my friend. Your ass is nice and tight."

"No, Dave, you're just fucking huge. Don't hurt him." Neil gritted his teeth but whether he held back pleasure—

or some sort of possessiveness—at the sight, Kate couldn't tell.

A strangled groan drew her attention to Joe. "Oh, fuck. I can't watch, or I'll have to put up with you shitheads ragging on me for coming in seconds again."

The group laughed together despite the sexual tension arcing between them.

Joe bolted from his spot. He got to his feet on the countertop, straddling Neil's splayed thighs. The motion presented his crotch—at chest level—to Neil, and averted Joe's gaze from the other three guys' carnal display.

Dave chuckled as his hand snuck around James's waist to cup the man's dangling cock and balls. "Open to me. We'll go slow."

"No!" James protested around Neil's cock.

At the same time, she begged Mike. "Fuck me. Now."

Without waiting for either Dave or Mike to move, James and Kate rocked backward, taking their lovers balls-deep.

"Shit, yes!" Dave bellowed when his flat abs slapped James's ass.

On the counter, Neil surrounded Joe's cock in a double-fisted hold. He didn't offer to suck the standing man. Joe didn't push beyond Neil's limits. Instead, his hands clamped onto Neil's shoulders, braced for the ecstasy generated by the firm touch. He thrust into the grip, which hugged his shaft.

Mike spread his fingers along her pussy on either side of his cock, now shuttling in and out of her. She forgot to stay quiet when his palm rubbed circles over her clit, matching the way Dave began to jerk James in time to his steady thrusts.

The force of Mike's penetration shoved her forward.

She continued to lave his fingers in her mouth while she studied James's throat working around Neil's cock. A quartet of desire filled the space with a symphony of masculine grunts and moans that sounded like music to her ears.

Kate ground her clit against Mike's other hand. The contact compounded sensations pouring through her from the thrill of witnessing such honest passion. She could've come in an instant but, somehow, it didn't feel right to climax without James and the rest of the crew. The throb in her teeth alerted her to how hard she tried to hold on—to wait for them to join her.

"Good. Girl." If his gravelly tone was any indication, Mike struggled, too.

The rapid flex of Joe's ass grabbed her attention. Despite his attempt to block out the irresistible display, he seemed like he would be the first to cave. He hammered his cock into Neil's tense grasp.

"Almost worse." Joe groaned. "Can hear you guys. Smell you. Good imagination."

Kate had to disagree there. Nothing could surpass watching this fantasy come to life.

Dave grunted as he plowed into James's ass with measured strokes that Mike imitated one for one in her pussy. "Are you gonna shoot already, Joe? You know how it turns James on to see a dude come. He'll probably squeeze my cock in half if you give him such an up-close-and-personal show."

The dirty talk nearly destroyed her resolve. The walls of her pussy began to undulate, stroking Mike's cock.

"Not. Yet." Mike tweaked her nipple with his free hand. The pain should have helped her regain control, but it shoved her closer to the brink instead.

"Shit! Yeah, I'm coming." Joe's thighs bunched as he stood rooted to the counter. His pelvis jerked repeatedly, slamming into the side of Neil's hands. His head dropped back, exposing the prominent bump of his Adam's apple, which bobbed in time to the contractions of his muscles.

Neil angled his fists toward his lower abdomen, braced when the first hot rush of Joe's semen splashed across his belly button. All of them moaned at the contrast of the white strands decorating Neil's olive skin. When Joe collapsed onto the cool counter, Neil had a direct line of sight to the pure ecstasy etched on James's face.

"Son of a bitch! You do like that, don't you?" Neil clenched his jaw.

James's cheeks hollowed as he answered with a renewed show of enthusiasm.

"Want more?"

From her vantage point, Kate knew James's response to Neil wouldn't matter. Neil had no hope of stopping himself now. Mike and Dave increased the tempo of their fucking—whether because their partners had reached the breaking point or because they couldn't help themselves, she would never know.

She welcomed the powerful lunges, watching how Dave's hips forced James's cock through the circlet of the bigger man's waiting fingers. Their tensing balls tapped together on every stroke.

James lifted his gaze to the trail of Joe's come dripping toward Neil's hard-on. He reached his tongue alongside the shaft, scooping up a hint of the viscous liquid. The hum of approval he made around Neil's cock proved to be Neil's undoing.

Neil grabbed James's hair then rode his mouth hard as Dave slammed into his ass. Neil bucked against James's lips as he released with a shout. James sucked him dry before lifting his well-used mouth from his partner's wilting cock to clean the come from Neil's abdomen with soothing strokes of his tongue.

Dave groaned as he watched James lap up Joe's semen. He rode James harder and harder until the smaller man's grip on the edge of the counter slipped. James's cheek crashed into Neil's slick abs.

Kate bit her cheek as Mike used both hands to anchor her against his violent fucking.

"Get. Ready," he uttered between clenched teeth.

"Fuck. Yes!" Dave groaned as he continued to ram inside James. "Come now. Do it."

The first jerk of James's straining cock flung a jet of cream to the floor. It also shattered her restraint. All rational thought disappeared as sensation overruled her mind. Her torso went rigid in Mike's secure grip. Her pussy milked him, begging him to join her.

By the time James had finished coming, a string of pearly fluid dangling from the tip of his spent cock, her orgasm had picked up steam once more. Mike refused to let her off so easy.

Dave pounded James. The base of his erection throbbed in time with his hoarse shouts. He filled James's ass with spurt after spurt. Mike broke the parallel, about to pull out of her pussy. She chased him with her pelvis, refusing to let him free.

"Come. Inside me." The ripples of pleasure amplified into another full-blown orgasm when he stiffened behind her then poured his seed into her welcoming grasp. He shifted his hands to her chest, cupping her breasts in his calloused palms. He continued to fuck her through his climax, setting off waves of unrelenting pleasure with the liquid fire filling her.

Either from the position, or the physical effects of her release, she grew dizzy. In the kitchen, the guys had started to clean up when Mike obscured her vision by settling her against his chest. Aftershocks continued to contract her pussy when he picked her up. She tried to focus on taking deep breaths as he dashed across the yard with her cradled in his arms, buck naked.

Mike deposited her in the antique, bent-pine chair in her breakfast nook. Somehow, he'd managed to get redressed before whisking her away from detection. He reached behind his back, grabbed a handful of his black T-shirt then hauled it over his head. The supple cotton radiated his warmth when he threaded her arms through it.

The fabric that had hugged his muscular shoulders draped around her like a baggy dress. He crouched on the linoleum by her feet then patted her knee. "Fun, right?"

Fun? Blood rushed through her veins even minutes later. It throbbed in the engorged tissues of her pussy and fluttered beneath the flushed skin of her wrists.

She stammered, "That was—" *Rough. Free. Primal. Hot. Generous.* "—beautiful. But no wonder you laughed at me this morning."

"What the hell are you talking about, Kate?"

"They're gay." She wanted to sink into the earth. How conceited could she be? "I must have imagined the guys hitting on me because I was so attracted to them."

Mike's palms cupped her flaming neck. His thumbs tipped her face up with slight pressure on her jaw. "The universe has more shades than black and white. Believe me, they want you almost as much as I do. I'm no jealous prick, but I've had to watch my temper lately. You make me break all my rules, babe."

"Rules?" She couldn't imagine someone so uninhibited imposing self-restrictions.

He grimaced then shook his head. "Sorry, brain's not firing on all cylinders yet. Massive blood flow diverted."

She blinked when she confirmed the tent in his crotch. How could he be hard? She would have feared she'd never again see an orgasm the likes of the ones he'd given her if just thinking about the dirty deeds they'd exchanged in the laundry room hadn't fired her libido once more. Maybe their encounter hadn't satisfied all his needs?

"Um... Do you... Have you ever..."

He laughed, "Are you trying to ask if I'm bi, too?"

She nodded.

"I've tried just about everything once, but it's not really my thing. I'll admit, though...I've accepted more than one blow job from the crew members." He shrugged. "I'm a guy, I like getting head. For me, if it's just about having a good time, then a mouth's a mouth as long as I respect the person it's attached to."

Her knees went weak imagining his come spraying down another man's throat.

"But, I definitely like your parts best." He winked then laid his lips on hers with aching tenderness.

She bowed into his hold, soaking in every modicum of sweetness he was willing to impart. All too soon, he broke the embrace. He dusted butterfly kisses over her checks and eyelids before rising to his feet.

"Sorry to fuck and run, but we really do need to get the patio laid today if we're going to finish up by tomorrow night."

"Finish the patio?" Panic twisted her guts. Their skills had guaranteed their progress on the complete overhaul would be ten times faster than her snail's pace for even the simplest tasks, but they couldn't be done already.

"Yeah, it's the last thing on our list. The longer we hold the house, the less profit there is in turning it. So, before we start every job we set a date. If we make our deadline, we throw ourselves a wild party. Definitely keeps us motivated." He waggled his eyebrows.

It figured she'd discovered the perfect way to expand her horizons right before she lost the opportunity.

Kate pasted on a phony smile to cover the dread freezing the lingering heat from her core. If she felt anything other than disappointment over the lost opportunity, she forced herself to bury it. There would be plenty of lonely nights to examine her foolishness later.

"The pool inspector cleared our upgrades this morning so we're planning a cookout. You know, we'd love to have you as our guest of honor." He picked an imaginary piece of lint off his paint-splattered jeans.

She might have laughed if his sudden vulnerability hadn't stunned her silent.

"If you're still interested after today..."

"I'll think about it."

"That's all I can ask, babe." Mike brushed his lips over her forehead then turned away. "Stay off that ladder."

The wooden blinds tapped against the window as he shut the door tight behind him.

THEY'D SLAVED beneath the beam of spotlights until nearly midnight, then picked up again at the first light of dawn. Kate cursed the weather gods who hadn't answered her call for rain. Instead, the thermometer had spiked close to a hundred degrees by lunchtime. The crew dragged ass for the first time since they'd carted their equipment onto the lawn next door.

Before she could consider the consequences, she squeezed a dozen lemons into her grandmother's pitcher then grabbed a tray. As she arranged store-bought cookies on a plate, she wished she'd thought to make some from scratch.

The rays of the afternoon sun scorched her cheeks. She squinted, catching sight of James indulging in a timeout under the dense canopy of the massive oak in their yard. When he saw her coming, he patted the ground.

"As if I didn't already crave your goodies." He beamed. "Pour me some of that lemonade, and I'll be your slave for life."

She sat cross-legged beside him but didn't laugh. Somehow, their games had turned serious in the past twenty-four hours. As usual, James tuned in to her mood in a flash.

"Ah, sorry, Kate. I'd give you a hug but sweaty doesn't begin to describe me right now."

He accepted the glass she handed over then drained it in one long slug.

"What? Do I have concrete dye on me?" James scrubbed at his neck.

Thank heaven for the bright light. The heat climbing her cheeks had nothing to do with the thinning of the ozone layer. Still, she couldn't meet his curious gaze. Why hadn't she considered the guys' privacy before she spied on them?

"Oh. I see." He cleared his throat. "I didn't think you'd judge me."

When he began to rise, she grabbed his forearm. "What? James! It was the hottest thing I've ever seen. But how did you know I was there?"

"Oh shit, were you feeling guilty?" He plopped onto the lush grass with a chuckle. "For a second there you really worried me. Katiebug, you couldn't keep quiet to save your life. Plus, you forgot these..."

From one of a dozen pockets on his cargo shorts, he withdrew her favorite thong. Mike must have gone back to grab the rest of her discarded clothing.

"So you're okay..."

"Honey, knowing you were watching turned me on beyond belief. Couldn't you tell?"

"Well, you did look like you were enjoying yourself." She rested her head on his shoulder, sweaty or not.

"Sounded like you were, too." He rubbed his cheek over her hair. "So, you'll be there tonight then?"

"I...I haven't decided. Do you want me to be?"

"Hell, yes." He didn't hesitate even a fraction of a second before answering. "In my mind, sexuality is a continuum. Let's take Mike. Based on the ten years I've known him, I'd say only one out of a thousand people he finds attractive are men. And I'm not talking go-to-bed-with-them attractive but, you know, some kind of spark. For me, it's the opposite. I don't want to lose the chance to act on that rare opportunity."

It seemed so simple when he put it that way.

"I guess I just don't know how to do this. How do you know what everyone wants? Each of you must fall somewhere different. Like Neil... I could tell he wasn't into sucking Joe." Her curiosity pushed her beyond embarrassment.

"Yeah, each of us has boundaries. We respect everyone's right to do or not do as they please. No one would ever hurt you or force you to go further than you want."

Kate feared she would be the one who needed to go further than the rest. Beyond physical pleasure. At least when it came to Mike.

"But aren't there rules? Mike said something about breaking his rules?" She'd be mortified if she violated some principle out of ignorance, but Mike had dodged her follow-up questions.

"He only has one rule that I know of." James grinned. "And it's stupid. If he's in danger of breaking it, I think we're all in for a treat. He refuses to mix emotions with pleasure. Or, at least, he has in the past."

Hope blossomed in her soul, but she was scared to let it run rampant. "If he wanted me as something more than a plaything, why would he want to share me?"

"There's a difference. Do you know Neil and I consider ourselves life partners?"

"You do?" Could she really have it all?

"Yep." His grin faded as he became serious. "I'd give anything for that man. I love him unconditionally, and so I accept that he likes both men and women. He accepts that I enjoy sex with multiple partners. We never have sex without each other but, sometimes, we like to indulge in the pleasure that only comes from sharing."

They sat in silence for several minutes as he allowed her to absorb the possibilities.

"Look, Mike deserves to be as happy as I am. You two

are great together. Please, Kate, I'm begging. Come tonight." James winked. "Come a lot."

6

———

Kate paced the squeaky hardwood planks in front of the bay window. She took another pull of the Corona with lime she'd intended to take over to the crew's barbeque. Not like those guys would drink light beer anyway.

So why am I still inside? Chicken.

As she watched, Dave and Joe roughhoused. They wrestled, attempting to dunk each other in the crystal blue waters of the refinished pool. James and Neil huddled together on the sidelines while Mike tended the grill. She reminded herself that he couldn't actually see her every time he glanced in her direction.

After today, the manscape outside her window would disappear forever. The soft orange hues generated by the dusk blurred. She'd let herself get used to their laughter, but now they were leaving. Tonight was her last chance. If she didn't take it, they'd be gone when she woke.

Regret would destroy her.

Before she could harp on every possible disastrous repercussion—and Lord were there plenty of those—she grabbed the remainder of her six-pack, squared her shoulders then sashayed across the lawn in her best imitation of a supermodel swagger.

Five smoldering stares latched on to the bared skin between the strings and diminutive cloth panels of the itsy-bitsy bikini she'd bought this afternoon. Water drops trickled from the statuesque bodies of the men in the pool. Neil's jaw dropped open and James nodded at her. But only Mike's reaction could capture her interest for longer than a glance.

Kate inhaled then held her breath as she raised her gaze to his. How she kept from stumbling when the force of his hunger hit her dead-on was a mystery.

The silence stretched a little longer than comfort allowed so she raised the carton in her hand. "Brought some beer."

So lame.

He eyed the half-empty container and grinned. "Nervous?"

She gulped around a lie, "Not a bit."

"You're safe with us." He took the liquid courage from her then set it aside. His thick arm banded around her waist as he drew her into his sheltering embrace. The scent of charcoal and hot man made her mouth water. Puffs of air danced over her temple a moment before Mike's lips pressed against it.

Then he whispered in her ear, "All you have to do is tell me it's too much and I'll take you out of the game in a second. No questions, no hard feelings. Understand?"

Light fur brushed her cheek when she nodded against his chest.

"Good girl." He separated them just enough to catch her chin then tip it up. His lips caressed her mouth, which curved in a smile. The prodding tip of his tongue coaxed her mouth to open. A wave of desire made her forget her worries as she got lost in sensation. "Damn, I've wanted this since the moment I met you."

His strong hands landed on her waist, lifting her until her toes dangled several inches above the new flagstone pavers. She flung her arms around his neck, matching the intensity of his kiss.

Mike carried her to the edge of the pool. As he stalked closer, the motion bumped their hips together. The solid length of his erection singed her bared abdomen through his swim trunks.

A cool breeze washed over her feet as it danced across the water below. Then slippery fingers encased her ankles, guiding her descent. Water engulfed her calves then her knees. The refreshing relief from the blistering heat of the man holding her didn't last long. Kate squirmed when Dave's teeth scraped her ass. It passed before his face as Mike lowered her into the pool. Then Dave took hold of her beneath her left arm while Joe grabbed her right.

She whimpered when Mike untangled her fingers from his nape then transferred her weight to the other men. The soft protest transformed into a squeal at the icy caress of the tiny waves on her pussy. Instinct had her draping one arm around Dave's massive shoulders and the other around Joe until she tread water between them.

Half her torso had been submerged when Neil and James joined Mike poolside. Her two supports headed into deeper water, causing her to rely entirely on them to keep her afloat. She wouldn't be able to reach the bottom here.

"Look at how hard you make them." Joe cupped her breast, the nipple peaking in seconds beneath his dripping fingers. He painted cool droplets over her satiny bathing suit until it adhered to every ridge and contour of the puckered flesh.

It became a lot easier to see what he meant as the three men shucked their trunks. Mike crouched, put one hand on the intricate tile work then leapt gracefully into the pool with minimal splash. He inched toward her, never taking his eyes from her.

James sat on the edge, dipping his feet, stroking himself as he scanned the men bracketing her. "I'm so glad you decided to join us, love."

Neil brushed James's hair away from his face. He smiled when James kissed his palm then said, "What are you waiting for? Go play. I want to watch for now."

The graceful arc of Neil's arms as he raised them above his head drew James's attention as well as hers. His muscles rippled as he leaned forward to dive into the pool. She followed his progress beneath the glassy surface as he torpedoed toward her. When he was just a few feet short, he slowed, his hair swirling around his head.

Kate didn't realize his intentions until Dave jerked the string at her hip. A moment after the panels floated away from her bare skin, Neil's lips scorched her pussy. She didn't have time to feel awkward about being touched so intimately by more than one man at once.

Dave and Joe each hooked a wrist beneath one of her knees then spread her like an offering for their submerged crew member. Neil braced one hand on each of their thighs, then buried his face in her pussy. Her eyes widened at the sensation of his hot tongue licking her followed by the cool water rushing behind his touch.

Mike's groan had her searching for him. He swam closer, taking in the decadence before him. "That's right, babe. Let them give you pleasure. It turns me on to watch you burn. They can give you so much more than I could alone. I want you to take all you can."

Neil's lips closed over her clit. He sucked with gentle pulls that had her sighing before he placed one last tender kiss over her mound and surfaced. He flung his head back, sending water arcing from his Roman features in a glistening spray. Visions of erotic mermen filled her mind. James gasped behind them, apparently as impressed by Neil's primal display as she was.

"Sweet," he panted against her lips, sharing the taste of arousal tinged with chlorine.

Mike appeared over his shoulder. Her ability to focus on anything but the raging need in his eyes dissipated. He nudged Neil to the side as he claimed her lips. She sucked on his tongue, the hammering of her pulse going double time. While he occupied her, nimble hands untied the remaining strings of her bikini, baring her.

Then he, too, sank beneath the surface to tease her swollen folds with his mouth. She tipped her head back, sparing a fleeting thought for the spectacular sunset, almost as brilliant as the way the crew made her feel. The motion exposed her neck to Dave's tongue. Neil latched onto her breasts—licking, nibbling and squishing the globes together to nuzzle between them.

Just when the swirls of Mike's mouth instigated the pre-orgasmic clenching of her pussy, he swam between her legs to surface behind her. She groaned at the loss, her head now resting on his chest. The two men holding her tipped her, raising her feet out in front of her. Mike cradled her neck and head, kissing her with leisurely swipes of his lips.

Kate's toes curled as touch after touch drove her

higher. Dave and Joe slid their massive hands along her body until they supported her back and legs. She floated on the surface, her breasts heating in the humid air while the rest of her bobbed, held steady by the light grasp of her lovers.

"I need to taste more of you. I want to make you come." Neil groaned when his friends adjusted her thighs. He swam between them, inviting Dave and Joe to drape them over his shoulders. He homed in on her core. She sighed when he stopped just a fraction of an inch away from fulfilling the promise of ecstasy.

"Would you like that?" Mike's harsh breathing assured her that he would like to see it.

"Yes! Please." Her fingers dug into the thick pads of muscle covering Dave's and Joe's shoulders. The restless movements urged them to bend over her, to soothe the ache in her breasts. They complied with her wishes. Dave bit her lightly while Joe sucked her nipple tight against the roof of his mouth. The variations in their touch drove her wild.

"Relax, babe." Mike took her mouth in another scorching kiss. "We're going to give you all you can take."

Neil spread the lips of her pussy. Mike released her mouth, allowing her to watch the awe on the other man's face as he probed her saturated flesh with the tip of one blunt finger. She shook beneath the eight masculine hands stroking her. But the pleasure that raced up her spine when Neil's finger penetrated her burned brightest.

He worked her open, adding another digit to her greedy pussy. She savored the grimace of passion on his face when her muscles clamped around him. When he'd lodged his fingers in to the second knuckle, he bent to flick the tip of his tongue around her clit before kissing his way up her thigh.

She gasped then bucked so hard she nearly jerked away from his fingers. Dave's, Joe's and Mike's muscular arms banded around her, securing her in place when Neil's touch returned.

"I think she liked that, buddy." Joe's gravelly hum of appreciation ratcheted her need higher. "Do it. Make her come on your face."

This time Neil consumed her with less preparation. Neither one of them could wait for pleasantries. Mike tipped her face up. "Watch him. Look at his expression when you explode."

Three of Neil's fingers slid inside her. He pumped them with liquid glides. "You're so soft."

He groaned before transferring his mouth from the inside of her knee to her clit. He sucked the bud between his lips, sending pulses of pleasure through her body. Kate's eyelids drooped, but someone pinched her nipple. Hard.

"Keep your eyes open. Watch." Mike's command seemed impossible to obey.

Neil's rapture escalated her own. She moaned as every muscle in her body tensed, straining for release. When Neil added the slightest rasp of his teeth on her pussy she couldn't resist. She spiraled over the edge into a mind-shattering climax. He continued to eat at her until the pleasure renewed, cresting again and again.

Still, he refused to let her rest.

"You can take more, can't you, babe?" Mike pet her even as he demanded she go further.

"Yes." She would have begged him to show her how to if she could have formed the words.

"I gotta fuck her, Mike. Let me fuck her," Joe begged as he and Neil switched places.

"Do you want his cock in you?"

She nodded up at Mike, hoping he wouldn't be upset. Of course, he wasn't.

He took a deep breath then kissed her. The second their lips fused, he sank below the surface of the pool. The rush of water filling her ears sounded surreal. She should have panicked, being cut off from oxygen, but they would never let anything happen to her.

She opened her eyes. The water burned a little but couldn't overpower the renewed sense of wonder saturating her. Mike met her gaze, completely in control. He continued to kiss her, doling out his supply of air between nips of his teeth and the soothing rasp of his tongue.

After several long seconds, he squeezed her hand then rose. A tiny prickle of unease sent even more adrenaline pumping through her system but—before she could freak —he returned, kissing another breath into her lungs. They fell into a rhythm of fulfillment that left her head spinning.

Just when she grew accustomed to remaining submerged, a few inches below the surface, the men lowered her another foot or so. Dave's and Neil's cocks bobbed against her hips. She surrounded the stiff flesh with her fists, loving the way they jerked in her grasp. Before she could gloat, Joe appeared between her spread legs. His hard-on looked huge through the distortion of the water.

Mike fetched another breath of air just as Joe set his erection against her still-throbbing flesh. She moaned, surrendering the last of her reserved oxygen. The instant the bubble broke on the surface, Mike returned. He claimed her mouth as Joe buried himself inside her then began fucking her in short, fast strokes that had her poised on the edge of another orgasm in minutes.

Kate squeezed her fists around Dave and Neil. She tried to stroke their cocks but sensory overload left her uncoordinated. Instead, they began to thrust between her fingers in time with Joe. His cock shuttled in and out of her pussy. She arched her spine, trying to rub her clit against his pelvis but the harder she pushed, the farther away he got.

Dave's hand plunged into the water, landing low on her belly. His fingertip teased her clit as Joe began to fuck her faster. Mike braced her shoulders against the motion, keeping her still to accept his partner's pounding thrusts even as he continued to feed her oxygen at regular intervals.

When Dave's finger circled her engorged flesh, she knew she couldn't last long. If the quickening pace of Joe's thrusts were any indication, she realized she wasn't alone. When Mike returned, she bit his lip, trying to tell him how close she was.

He smiled and nodded before rising once more. Then Dave's finger tapped her clit in an irresistible pattern. She exploded around Joe's pistoning erection. Contractions milked his cock. She couldn't tear her gaze away as he whipped out of her. His shaft flexed. Spurts of fluid jetted from the tip to float in the liquid before her.

As though she'd triggered a chain reaction, Dave's cock bulged in her grip. Then he too sent ribbons of pearly come spiraling into the whorls and eddies made by their writhing bodies. She trailed her fingertips down the two cocks in her grip—one spent, one not—to fondle their balls.

The men raised her to the surface. Their harsh breathing, groans and awed compliments were distant in her ears. She curled into Mike's outstretched arms, seeking refuge for a moment, trying to catch her breath.

"Don't tell me you've had enough already?" he teased against her soaked hair.

7

————

Though she could hardly believe it, her body roared to life at the promise of having Mike—the man she craved—inside her. James stood at the edge of the pool, watching as their lovers abandoned the depths for dry land.

"That was the hottest thing I've ever seen." His dilated pupils and throbbing cock reminded her of the way she'd felt the day before, watching him take the three men with them now. He crouched down then extended his arms to her. She wrapped hers around his deceptively strong shoulders, clinging as he stood, lifting her from the pool.

Torrents of water sheeted off her, drenching James, but he didn't seem to notice.

Mike levered himself up, following two steps behind as James carried her toward a cluster of deck chairs near the grill. Mike lowered the seat until it became horizontal then lay out on his back. "Yo, Neil, toss me the lube."

When he snatched the tube of gel arcing toward him, she shivered in James's arms.

"It's okay, love. You'll see. It's not so difficult to take him in your ass. He'll make sure you enjoy it."

James's calm reassurance helped her battle the nerves trying to protest louder than the adventurous side of her spirit. After all, she'd already had two amazing orgasms. She turned to him, hesitating, to gauge his reaction a moment before her lips met his. The way he touched her melted her heart. Gentle. Sweet. Still hungry.

"Stay with me?" she begged against his lips. "Help me."

"Of course." James lowered her into Mike's waiting arms.

Mike cradled her back and shoulders against his torso. His cock, already greased, slid across her damp skin at the base of her spine. He leaned forward to nip her earlobe then his arms bracketed her ribs as he cupped her breasts from behind. "Are you sure you're ready for this?"

Kate glanced up into James's steady eyes. He nodded.

"Yes. Please, take me."

Mike groaned. He slipped his finger between her cheeks, teasing her as he had the morning before. This time she barely flinched when he pressed inside her tense hole.

James knelt on the chair between their spread legs. He covered her face in dozens of light kisses that had her relaxing into his touch. Mike's finger sank deeper as her muscles loosened.

Kate licked a line across the seam of James's lips when he paused to look into her eyes. He took the invitation to capture her mouth, this time with more force.

At some point during the kiss that reheated her blood to boiling, Mike had added a second digit to her ass. The forbidden touch sent a shaft of pleasure ricocheting around her body.

"Keep breathing, love." James drew her attention back to him.

She matched his measured inhalations and exhalations as he coached her through extracting every ounce of delicious sensation from Mike's ministrations.

"Son of a bitch, that's sexy," Dave praised them from the place he'd taken at her side. She realized that Neil and Joe had joined them as well. They stood in a semi-circle around the head of the chair, watching as Mike and James prepared her.

"I need you inside me." She wriggled her ass, trying to align with the head of Mike's cock. His erection felt so hot and hard against her lower back, she couldn't believe he hadn't exploded yet.

"Not like that." James nipped her lip. "Let Mike lead."

She went completely slack in their hold.

Mike moaned as the other men cursed or sighed at her submission. He tucked his cock against her ass then began to burrow inside.

Kate shrieked as the intrusion sent a lick of fire up her spine. She tensed, her pleasure receding.

"Relax, love." James resumed his passionate kisses as Neil took her hand in his, petting her until the first wave of pain passed. The tiny circles Mike made with his pelvis began to flood her with pleasure, obscuring her discomfort.

Mike pushed in farther, stretching her bit by bit, until —somehow—he'd filled her. Once inside, he raised her until just the head of his cock remained buried then lowered her until she sheathed him completely.

"Fuck, yes," he growled in her ear. She angled her

head to kiss him, snuggling into his chest now that no space remained between them. His hands cupped her hips, lifting and dropping her as he continued to rock. How did he keep showing her new things, taking her higher than she imagined?

Any lingering unease flew from her mind when his long fingers cupped her pussy, then spread her labia. Bare, open to the men's perusal beneath the now-dark sky, she shivered though she didn't think she'd ever be cold again.

"So pretty."

She'd almost forgotten James, who knelt between her legs, staring at her pussy.

"Can you take us both, love?" The muscle in his jaw jumped as he waited for her to respond.

Kate held out her arms, welcoming him into her embrace.

"It's been a long time since I've made love to a woman. I don't want to hurt you. You seem so delicate." He circled the purple head of his cock around her opening, collecting her wetness. His hard-on brushed Mike's where it lodged inside her.

"You couldn't hurt me. Please, James." She gathered him close, tilting her hips as far as she could with Mike buried to the hilt. When James pressed into the slick heat of her pussy, they both groaned.

"So tight, love. So hot." He began to move, tucking into her farther with each twitch of his hips.

Kate couldn't believe how packed she felt. Her pussy practically strangled his cock. The way her two lover's erections caressed each other through the thin membrane separating them fueled her desire. Soon she bucked between them, loving the way one would retreat as the other tunneled deeper.

When he had stuffed her pussy with the length of his throbbing cock, James rested his forehead on her collarbone. She stroked her fingers through his hair then down his back. Her nails dug into his ass, trying to force him closer.

"Oh, shit. Do that again, Katie." Neil's harsh rasp reminded her they had an audience. "Spread his cheeks for me."

She did as he commanded. When James's cock flexed, triggering a massive constriction of her muscles, he and Mike groaned together.

"That's right. That's the way." Neil appeared over James's shoulder. "How would you like to try fucking and being fucked?"

James's cock flared inside her. When he turned his head to engage Neil's mouth, Kate's head dropped onto Mike's shoulder. She could only go along for the ride. She knew the instant Neil had penetrated James's asshole. The man between her thighs cried out then shuddered with pure pleasure. Neil began to drive inside James, causing the cock buried in her pussy to grind into her.

Mike stayed still, allowing the motion of their lovers to sway her on his erection. The subtle fucking stroked hypersensitive nerves, providing more than enough friction to elicit a response from them both.

"Babe, I think Dave has a present for you." Mike's suggestive tone had her gaze flicking to the side. Though he'd come in the pool, Dave's hard-on oozed pre-come from the flared head.

She gladly accepted his offering, her lips surrounding the thick shaft, reveling in the taste of his pleasure. Knowing the sight of the four lovers turned Dave on spurred her to take as much of him as she could. Pinned in place, she accepted his assistance when he cradled her head in his huge hands and fucked her mouth with gentle strokes.

"Joe, why don't you feed James some of that meat. Don't let it go to waste." Something about the position seemed so right, harmonious. Mirror images, perfectly balanced. Mike fucked her ass while she lay on his chest. James fucked her pussy while Neil fucked his ass. She sucked Dave from his position on one side of the chair, and James did the same for Joe on the other.

Ragged breathing, grunts and the squeaking of the poor abused deck chair filled the night air. Surrounded by pure desire and honest ecstasy, none of them had a chance of lasting very long. Neil drove them all higher by riding James faster, harder.

When James's tight abs stroked her clit, she tensed.

"Oh, yeah. Kate's going to come." Mike's reverent whisper cut through the group. Each man picked up the tempo, shoving her beyond restraint.

She shattered around Mike and James. After a moment, they both followed, filling her with pulses of their come. Neil shouted at the same time Dave shot into her mouth. She swallowed reflexively until he slipped from between her lips. She continued to explode, her orgasm endless.

James groaned when Neil deserted his clenching hole. "She's still coming. Yes. Yes!" James's cock flexed in time with her contractions.

Her mouth latched onto his when his orgasm crested again. A second, weaker round of come spurted from his cock, searing the lining of her pussy.

After a minute, he bussed her forehead. Then he, too, withdrew.

"Thank you, love."

When Mike pulled out, Kate pivoted. She wanted to kiss him but was afraid of his reaction when another man's seed glistened on her lips. She shouldn't have worried. He cupped her neck then drew her head to his for a searing kiss. She shared the taste of Dave's come, of all the ecstasy that had filled her, then drooped against his heaving chest.

She felt his chuckle when one of the guys said, "I'm hungry but I think you charred the burgers, dude."

KATE BOLTED UPRIGHT IN BED. Disoriented, she checked the clock on her nightstand. Two a.m. The delicious soreness in her joints at least relieved her that she hadn't been dreaming about Mike's crew again. She'd really done it. She'd taken them all and loved every second of it.

So why did she feel like crying? Why did she feel more alone than ever?

"Everything okay?" The tender question from her right terrified her. If she looked, and he was just a figment of her imagination, she didn't think she could survive. "Babe, are you all right?"

Mike.

She sobbed in relief. To hell with hiding her feelings any longer. He'd shown her the beauty of trusting your lover enough to bare your soul. Your desires. And what she desired most was lying in bed with her right now.

"Oh God. Were we too rough? Where does it hurt?" Mike knelt beside her, cupping her cheeks in his palms.

She shoved his hands away, not wanting to give in to the temptation they would surely bring once he realized she hadn't been injured.

"It will only hurt if you leave me," she whispered, surprised at the scratchy tone of her voice, hoarse from her earlier screams.

"Leave you? Kate, why the hell would I leave you?" He flipped on the bedside lamp, then returned to peer into her eyes. "You don't get it, do you? All the time we've spent together this summer—laughing, working and wanting each other—only dug me deeper. I wasn't asking you out just to sleep with you. I'm not going anywhere...unless you make me."

"Never." Her heart raced ten times faster than it had by the pool. She wanted to give him the world. "So, what's *your* wildest fantasy?"

"I'd..." He cut off then blew a breath toward the ceiling, unable to finish.

"What could you possibly be afraid to say after what we just did?" She trailed her fingertips along his cheek.

Mike's sheepish grin sent shivers along her spine. "I'd like to make love, sweet and slow. Then build something lasting. In this house...with you."

"That's a dream I share. Make it come true. For us both."

He lowered her to the bed then covered her eyelids with tender kisses. She welcomed him home with open arms.

MORGAN'S SURPRISE
POWERTOOLS
JAYNE RYLON
NEW YORK TIMES BESTSELLING AUTHOR

1

Morgan aimed a puff of breath at the flame dancing on top of the candle.

"Wait! Too fast! Didn't you make a wish first?" Kate jerked the plate holding Morgan's cupcake out of the trajectory of the warm air. The orange glow dimmed but didn't extinguish. "There must be something you want."

Carnal visions burned hotter than the fire melting the sprinkle-coated frosting of her gourmet confection into a golden pool. The color reminded Morgan of the burnished skin of her crush. It should be illegal for Joe to gallivant without a shirt on as often as he did. Spectacular memories of his displays sparked her fantasies at the most inopportune moments of the day and wreaked havoc on her sleep patterns.

Kate was polite enough not to hound her while she let her gaze wander, devouring the glistening expanse of Joe's perfect shoulders. Morgan sighed when she thought about the painted wooden sign he'd crafted—and now hung—outside the plate-glass window of her fledgling bakery. It bore the name he'd helped her brainstorm. Sweet Treats.

So thoughtful. And sexy as hell.

It kind of surprised her not to see steam rolling off his bunched muscles. How could he be comfortable working half-naked in the brisk autumn air? She shook her head. The motion didn't erase all the naughty ideas sabotaging her rationality. The dirty thoughts tempted her with a variety of ways to warm the handyman up when he finished his task and rejoined them inside.

Morgan sighed when a snap of fingers returned her attention to the interior of her admittedly cute shop. It'd taken six months to decorate everything just so.

"You going to pick something...maybe someone? Or are you planning to wait until wax drips all over your birthday cupcake?" Kate chuckled.

Morgan decided denying her infatuation with Joe would be futile. Kate had been her best friend since grade school. The lucky bitch had referred the hunky craftsman and his crew of skilled friends in the peak of the summer heat—after she'd scored the crew's foreman for herself.

No way could Kate miss Morgan's similar craving.

The crew had taken on odd jobs, fixing up the crummy space in the strip mall that housed Morgan's boutique in exchange for loads of the decadent goodies she whipped up. Damn, those guys could eat. She wondered if manual labor accounted for all of the voracious appetite they possessed. It had to take more than swinging a hammer to burn off those calories. Lord knew they found some way to stay fit and trim.

She'd baked Joe's favorite today—a caramel apple tart. He deserved that and more for his considerate gesture. Two customers had already stopped in to say the colorful sign had caught their eye. Thanks to him, she'd sold out of brownies and cheesecake long before the after-work rush. Too bad she couldn't generate the nerve to offer him something a little more sinful than her luscious dessert as a reward.

She'd considered it once or twice before, but she couldn't stop drooling long enough to try. Always quick to flash his toned abs and rock solid biceps, Joe kept her off balance and lost in a haze of unvented desire. He'd become her favorite treat weeks ago. An instant addiction. Thoughts of him left her craving a taste—or more—of him in the dead of night.

She bit her lip when he reached for something along the roofline. From his perch on the ladder, his body rippled with strength.

"Damn, Kate. I don't think the birthday fairy would sanction what I have in mind." Morgan grimaced at the dopey grin on her friend's face. Three months of blissful dating and wild nights with her boyfriend, Mike, had turned the woman into a ridiculous ball of giggles with a perma-smile. Worse were the googly eyes that emerged when the love of her life entered the room. Kate and Mike's soul-deep bond was hell to be around.

Jealousy didn't exactly flatter a girl.

"The big 3-0's not until the weekend anyway." Morgan pried her stare from Joe.

"I know but Mike and I will be out of town then, so it counts today. Besides, you'll never know if you don't try." Kate squeezed Morgan's hand. "Sometimes dreams come true. Believe me."

Yep. There went that grin again. "Your face is going to stick like that if you're not careful."

Kate kept right on beaming.

Morgan swallowed hard then scrunched her eyes closed. She was tired of hoping Joe would ask her out. So she tried a new tactic instead.

I wish I had the courage to ask him on a date. It's time to move on. Time to try again. I wish I could take a risk—be wild for once in my life.

When she blinked into the amber autumn light streaming through the window, Joe had vanished. A cosmic sign? Or had he needed some extra tool off his pickup?

"So... Was Joe the only guy involved in that wish or did some of the other hot construction workers we know feature in it too?"

Morgan's mouth gaped open. More than Joe?

She never would have confessed to greed that titanic on her own, but Kate knew her better than anyone. Morgan had thought about it. A lot. The way the guys worked seamlessly together on projects made their bond impossible to ignore. When they'd crowded upstairs—in her tiny apartment over the bakery—for beer and cookies, they'd overflowed the cramped space with testosterone and something a bit more elusive.

Their camaraderie transcended their partnership. At least she thought it did. But she could have imagined the inside jokes, meaningful looks and secret smiles more common between lovers than friends.

The men's intimacy could have been a figment of her overactive imagination but there was no mistaking their open arms. They'd accepted her right away, making her more than just a friend of a friend. Every time Morgan witnessed the interplay between the partners, her mind had spun with possibilities. That didn't mean she had to say so. "Isn't it one of the cardinal rules of wishing—if you tell, it won't come true?"

"Come on, you don't believe that nonsense do you?" Kate joked but persisted with a wiggle of her brows. "Fess up. You've wondered what it would be like to have them in your bed. At the very minimum, you're burning up the sheets with Joe in your dreams."

"Okay, fine. How could any woman resist? They're buff, hardworking, playful, sexy as sin and sweet. I've got it bad for Joe. So damn bad. Like, worse than our Bon Jovi lust in high school bad. He's strong but gentle. I could talk to him for days. He's always surprising me with little things that make my day. And the way he fills out those ripped jeans has me thinking I'm going into cardiac arrest every time he bends over. But the rest of the crew isn't far behind. Hell I'm so distracted, I've burnt more cookies since they've come around than in all the rest of my life."

"About time you admitted it."

Morgan's heart froze at the deep rumble over her shoulder. It kicked in triple time when a broad hand settled on the side of her neck. She jerked from the retro-dinette chair she and Joe had salvaged and restored last weekend.

The sneaky bastard caught the vinyl-covered seat, saving it from crashing to the floor. Would he do the same for her if her jellied knees gave out?

"You set me up." She gaped at Kate, betrayal and humiliation burning her cheeks.

"No, I'm sorry." Her best friend stood, reaching out, but Morgan scooted further into the corner to avoid her seeking grasp. "I didn't know he was there. I swear."

"I came through the kitchen. Left my boots out back so I wouldn't track mud all over the place." Joe waved toward his socks. His grin turned feral. "But I won't pretend to be sorry about what I heard. You want me. Bad."

"Jerk!"

"Maybe. But only because I've let this shit go on too long." He scrubbed his hands over his eyes. "You're so skittish. I planned to take things slow. I thought if I didn't pressure you, you'd get comfortable with me. With the guys. I didn't want to chance things. Didn't want you to run."

"Tell him why, Morgan." Kate's soft advice rankled. "Tell him about—"

"Hell, no. Not now. Not after this." Morgan's hands flailed in the air. Her glare whipped between her best friend and the stud she'd made a fool of herself over.

"Kate, maybe it'd be best if you did a little sharing of your own."

Joe had never used that stern tone in Morgan's presence before. She hated how it dampened her panties when she wanted nothing more than to escape. It wasn't as if she could take back her declaration. Upstairs, she could lick her wounds. Maybe in a year or five she could show her face around her friends again.

"I..." The other woman attempted to speak but had to clear her throat and start over. Twice.

Her hesitation glued Morgan's sneakers to the floor.

"You have nothing to be ashamed of, Kate. Neither of you do." Joe stroked her friend's hair.

Morgan had to swallow the acrid burn of envy.

Kate nodded. "When Mike and I first started dating, I told him about a fantasy of mine. I wondered what it would be like to have more than one man as a lover. At the same time. The crew granted my wish. They shared themselves with me. And Mike."

Holy crap. Had Morgan heard that right? "You mean..."

"Yeah, cupcake. The six of us had a smoking affair. One hell of a pool party." Joe's gorgeous green eyes went glassy as he remembered. "I'm not going to lie, the crew has messed around before. With other ladies...and sometimes by ourselves."

The proud set of his jaw, as if he prepared for a blow, ticked her off. Couldn't he tell how much the revelation turned her on? She'd swear her nipples were about to poke through her shirt, and her thighs trembled. This time the reaction had nothing to do with fear.

"You expect me to run screaming? Rant at you?" How many women had rejected him after finding out about his sexual proclivities?

"Maybe." He shrugged then leaned against the counter, his shoulders relaxing.

"It's not something you learn about your friends every day." Kate winced when Morgan turned her attention toward her.

"How can you think I'd judge you? You've always been there for me." Morgan tilted her head as she studied her friend. "If anything, I'm upgrading your status from lucky bitch to queen of all lucky bitches. Damn you for not spilling the details right away. What's the use in having a best friend if she doesn't come running to gloat about five of the sexiest men on the planet ravishing her?"

Kate beamed as she lunged across the gap between them and threw her arms around Morgan.

"But...one question." She sensed both Joe and Kate holding their breath as she tried to rein in her disappointment enough to keep it from coloring her tone. "Why twist my arm about how much I want Joe—"

A growl startled her into meeting his forest green eyes.

"—if you already have dibs? Shit, I didn't mean to step on any toes." Her stomach lurched at the thought of damaging her dearest friendship.

"I think you should field this one." Kate held her palms out toward Joe.

He paused for several seconds before speaking. "It's not like that between us. I mean, we all knew Mike was serious about Kate. Never seen him mope around like a lost puppy before. I laughed when she had him chasing his tail for months. Maybe that's why I'm gettin' some of my own damn medicine lately."

Kate giggled. "Mike's enjoyed the payback for sure."

"When things started heating up between them, he came to the crew. Told us about her request. I can't explain what it's like with the guys. I'm not great with words. But I can say we're closer than brothers. Comfortable with each other—with what each of us needs and what our limits are. That doesn't mean we're in some kind of relationship though. Except for James and Neil. They *are* pretty much a pair for life. Man, this is clear as mud, I'm sure."

Morgan didn't realize she'd moved until her fingers rested on his tensed forearm. Explaining didn't come easy. The corner of his mouth tipped up at the contact.

"I guess the bottom line is we respect each other. Kate's one of us now. It doesn't mean anything beyond that, though. We're all adults. I may not be the sharpest tool in the shed, but I see her and Mike are in this for the long haul. If they want to share some of their joy with the rest of us then we'd be glad to join in. If not, we get that too."

"The guys in the crew see other people all the time." Kate shot her a poignant stare.

It was now or never. Morgan drew a deep breath then prayed birthday magic could work in her favor. Just this once. "So... If I asked you to check out the autumn festival with me tomorrow night—"

"I'd do this." Joe wrapped her in the heat of his muscles and squeezed her tight. He dropped a kiss on the tip of her nose before teasing the seam of her lips. She parted for him, but he didn't delve inside. Not now. Not with Kate staring at them, her hands clasped in front of her, standing on tiptoes, her eyes wide.

But the lingering tingle Joe's lips had inspired promised much, much more to come.

Morgan groaned then licked the spot he'd singed with his caress. Mmm... "You've been stealing cookies off the cooling racks again."

Somehow the Belgian chocolate she'd used in them tasted better after mixing with Joe.

"I'll make it up to you." The power of his grin caused her stomach to do flip-flops. "Tomorrow night. I'll pick you up at the bakery's booth around seven."

"Who'll take care of—?"

"Let me worry about the details. You like my surprises, remember? I guarantee you'll have a good time."

Morgan tried to convince herself she'd be satisfied with some mulled cider and a run through the infamous corn maze with this gorgeous man by her side. But when he patted her ass on the way out, she swore she wouldn't settle for less than a very naughty hayride.

2

—————

"You kids have a good time. And don't do anything we wouldn't do." Mike and Kate shooed them from the bakery stand with a wink and a nod.

"I understand if you don't want to leave." Joe turned to Morgan after measuring the line of customers. It stretched out the entrance of the old barn that housed vendors at the annual festival. He didn't blame the hungry crowd. The assortment of sweet creations looked almost as tasty as his date. Almost.

"No. Let's get out of here while we can. The store will sell out soon. The last of the stock I brought is on display now."

"Congratulations. I knew it wouldn't be long before the rest of the town caught on."

"Thanks." Her megawatt smile flanked by killer dimples stole his breath. The rare glimpse made him feel like a photographer on safari who captured never-before-seen wildlife behavior. Maybe now that things were looking up with her business, Morgan could learn to smile more. "Besides, Kate owes me for yesterday."

"I'm pretty sure *I* owe *her*."

Morgan cleared her throat and adjusted the hem of her light brown sweater over the seam of her faded jeans. He wondered if the fuzzy fabric was as ultra-soft as it looked. With any luck, he'd find out for himself before the night ended.

A rambunctious toddler veered into their path when she escaped from her harried mother. Joe cupped his hand around Morgan's elbow and steered her out of the chaos. Yep. The sweater caressed his palm, tempting him to burrow beneath it to the warm flesh inside.

Damn, he was screwed. He'd planned to take things slow, but weeks of keeping his distance threatened his restraint. He forced his grip to relax, afraid of spooking her again.

"Everything okay?" Morgan's cherry-scented breath tickled the side of his neck as she leaned closer to speak over the din of the throng and the music belting out of the local radio station's amplifiers.

"Uh...yeah." He stifled a groan. "Hoping you like what I have planned."

"Planned?" She tilted her head then peeked up at him from beneath the long, dark lashes that emphasized her gorgeous, dove-grey eyes. "I thought we were going to hang out at the festival?"

"Something like that." Joe grinned at the anticipation in her glance. He loved delighting her with little things and hoped she'd react as well to what he had in store for their evening. The way she lit up shifted something in his gut. And made him wonder about the man she'd nearly married last year. What kind of damage had that asshole inflicted?

Kate had refused to give him details no matter how hard he'd pressed, but it was clear the prick had hurt Morgan. Deeply. He intended to try his best to erase the sadness he'd sensed lingering inside her—hoped she'd let him be more than a rebound guy. But he'd settle for healing if he had to. If he could. It infuriated him to see such an amazing woman hiding from the world and herself.

One step at a time, buddy.

"How about we start with a hay ride?"

OH CRAP! Morgan blushed at the suggestion. Had Joe plucked the dirty thought from her mind yesterday? If she were so transparent, why would he pursue her instead of shoving her away like Craig had when he'd finally realized all she desired?

"Are you allergic to hay or something?"

She hadn't realized she'd stopped dead in her tracks until the pressure of his warm fingers singed the back of her arm.

"Uh, no. Sorry." Morgan studied the tiny scuff on the toe of her black leather boots. She hadn't worn them in quite a while, but the extra height afforded by the stiletto heels eliminated some of the disparity between her and Joe. In the commotion of preparation for the festival, she hadn't had time to search for polish.

"Why do I make you so uncomfortable?" His tense tone drew her gaze to his handsome, if rugged, face. The corners of his plump lips pinched together as though he hadn't meant to speak aloud. "I would never do anything you don't want. But, if you're more comfortable staying around here that's fine too."

Morgan couldn't stop herself from turning into the solid bulk of his chest and giving him a quick, one-armed hug. "Thanks for offering, but that's not necessary. I trust you."

Crazy but true.

She'd spent most of the summer with this man, alone as they worked on her store or surrounded by his equally burly friends. Funny how they'd never once intimidated her in the cramped space. Around them, she felt safe.

His smile answered for him as he dropped a kiss on her forehead. They resumed their leisurely pace toward the edge of the gravel lot where several tractors towing platforms, ringed with hay, waited for a full load of passengers. His knuckles stroked the sensitive space between her fingers as he held them in a loose grip.

A mix of children hopped up on candy, parents enjoying the brisk but not too chilly evening and young couples out for an evening of local entertainment piled into the wagon. Joe paused to boost a straggling kid onto the loose bales before leaping up himself. He turned and offered his hand. She gladly accepted. He tugged her into his arms as a few women nudged over to make room for his wide shoulders. When it looked like they'd run out of space, Morgan peeked toward the next wagon.

Instead of making a move in that direction, Joe settled in the gap remaining then scooped her into his lap before she could object. Not that she would have. The leather of his jacket smelled divine and quickly warmed with the heat of her cheek, pressed to the supple material. The woman to their right shot Morgan an envious grin before resuming her conversation with her friends.

The cramped space forced Morgan's hands to land against the taut muscles of Joe's chest beneath his thin T-shirt. Defined lines tempted her to trace them downward to the ridges of his abdomen, but she resisted. Barely.

"Comfortable?" He nuzzled her temple while his hands ran along the length of her spine. One settled on her knee, and the other on her waist, for several seconds before she remembered to respond with words instead of a simple purr.

"Very." Holy shit. Had that husky sigh come from her? Thank God for their chaperones or she might have been tempted to throw decorum out the window and beg Joe to touch her more intimately right here and now.

"Blanket?"

Morgan blinked up at the attendant waving a quilt in their direction.

"Sure." Joe winked when her mouth gaped into a giant O. "Wouldn't want you to catch a chill."

Between the helpful older man and her date, they bundled her under the well-worn cover in a matter of moments—right along with Joe's wandering fingers. She laughed when he traced the dip of her side beneath the hem of her sweater. Amid the banter of the other passengers, no one seemed to notice.

Her brows rose when Joe's palm cupped her ribcage, the side of his hand brushing the underside of her breast. No way could his touch be accidental. The warm hold soothed her. She relaxed further into the cushion of his thighs, chest and arms.

Joe flashed a terrible imitation of an innocent grin then proceeded to ask her questions about the new assortment she'd planned in order to capitalize on the change of seasons. They talked about the successes and failures of her recent product testing as the tractor began to pull them along the bumpy farm grounds toward the pumpkin patch.

To avoid embarrassing herself, she thought of things she had to do this week. That way she might be able to ignore the contact of their bodies shifting against each other and the hard length of Joe's denim-clad erection at her hip.

Before she left tonight, she'd snag a basketful of local produce to use in the tarts she'd unveil this week. "Do you like pumpkins? I have some new recipes I'd like to try if you don't mind being my guinea pig."

Her question came out more like a squeak.

"I'll eat anything of yours. After tonight, I have a feeling pumpkins may be my new favorite vegetable."

The children at the front of the wagon sang off-key loud enough she couldn't swear she'd heard him right. Before she could clarify, the cart lurched to a halt.

"I think this is our stop."

"Huh?"

"We're getting out. Come on, you'll see." Joe set her on her feet as the attendant collected their cover.

"Don't forget, the last ride comes by at midnight. After that you're on your own to make it back to your cars. If they haven't turned into pumpkins by then." The man laughed at his own joke.

Joe planted one hand on the rail then leapt to the ground with a hell of a lot more grace than she could muster. He wrapped his hands around her waist then lifted her from the wagon as though she weighed about as much as a bag of confectioner's sugar.

Her body slid along every hard inch of his on the way down.

Oh my.

The man in the wagon tossed Joe a flashlight then trundled off into the dark toward the main barns they'd started at. In the wake of the raucous gathering and the sputtering diesel engine, the still night rang in her ears. Vines curled across the ground, their leaves rustling in the soft breeze.

They stood in the middle of the farm's pumpkin patch listening to each other breathe for several heartbeats.

"Okay?" Joe spoke softly but his gentle question might as well have been gunfire. It sliced through the quiet. "Your phone works out here if you want to call the cops on me for abducting you or have Mike kick my ass."

"Not necessary." She shivered a little, but it had nothing to do with fear and everything to do with the excitement of being truly alone with the man she'd been dreaming of for weeks. Her curiosity grew by the second. "What are we doing out here?"

"Right this way, you'll see." Again he took her hand, entwining their fingers. Suddenly it was enough to be here, with him, walking side by side along a slightly wider row in the field.

A beam of light swept from edge to edge, guiding Morgan out of danger of twisting an ankle in her ridiculous boots as long as she kept to her toes. The heels made her calves look fantastic, but had no place in the tilled dirt.

The row narrowed, forcing her behind Joe. She hummed when he tucked her fingers into the waistband of his jeans. So warm. But even that distance made the walk treacherous in the moonlight.

Rocks and divots in the earth waited to trip her. She stumbled a bit before her eyes adjusted after the bright white of the flashlight. Joe stopped in front of her. She plastered herself along his backside before she could reverse her momentum. Pure male strength greeted every inch of her from the hard tips of her breasts to the soft curve of her belly, which met his firm ass.

Morgan took a step away, thanking all the powers of the universe he couldn't spot her face flaming in the shadows or smell the scent of her instant arousal. Instead of continuing on, Joe crouched, holding his arms out from his sides.

"Hop on. It's not far from here but I don't want to spoil the fun before it's begun."

When she simply stood and gawked, he glanced over his shoulder.

"What, you don't like the idea of riding me?"

Jesus. It was either admit she enjoyed the thought all too much or pretend her panties hadn't drenched at their collision and his naughty implication. Without another objection, she climbed onboard.

The powerful shift of his torso between her thighs had her groaning before she could prevent the sound from escaping. His fingers stroked the back of her knees. The motion, designed to soothe, instigated a hormonal riot of massive proportions.

"Too fast?" Joe slowed to a pace that jostled her less but caressed her core with each tread of his long stride.

She didn't attempt to answer. Clinging tighter to his sculpted chest, laying her head on his solid shoulder and surrendering to her hunger before it raged out of control seemed wiser. Her lips brushed his neck with each step, but sensory overload prevented her from fidgeting. If she moved her head, her rock-hard nipples would stroke his shoulder blades. If she adjusted her hips, her steaming pussy would graze his lower back.

Why was that a bad idea again?

Her tongue nipped out to taste Joe's nape. Salty spice and oak. He cleared his throat. Could she make it hard for him to speak too?

God she hoped so.

"We're here." He released her thighs slow enough she had time to ensure her footing despite her wobbly legs. She relinquished her hold on him one finger at a time. Too bad their destination hadn't been another five miles, or five hundred, away.

Joe turned to face her, blocking the view behind him. He took her hands in his, his thumbs brushing the sensitive centers of her palms. Then he lifted them over her eyes. "Don't peek. Give me a minute, okay?"

"Would now be a good time to tell you the dark isn't my favorite thing?"

"I'll be right here." The deep timbre of his voice continued to croon to her as he moved to the left then the right, a little further away then close again, so she never felt alone.

A whoosh carried to her ears a moment before heat and orange light washed over her cheeks.

"Can I look now?"

"Sure." His breath teased her face as he took his place behind her, wrapping an arm around her waist and drawing her back against his chest.

Morgan peeked between her fingers. "Holy crap!"

The digits slammed closed once more. That couldn't have been what it looked like. She must be dreaming again. But when she opened her eyes, his surprise hadn't vanished. Her jaw hung open far enough to swallow a handful of bugs. Fortunately, the brisk air kept them away.

"Is that a good holy crap or a bad holy crap?"

She couldn't answer immediately. A knot as big as a squash grew in her throat as she scanned the small pavilion sheltering them from the chill. A fire pit blazed in the center of the space, perfuming the air with the scent of applewood from the neighboring orchard.

Carved pumpkin lanterns of every size and shape ringed the perimeter of the cement-slab floor, hung from wires over the rafters and perched on sporadic wooden pillars. A few more made an elaborate centerpiece for the picnic table, laden with Indian corn, gourds, cider and other autumn treats. Geometric shapes glowed and bobbed with the radiance of the tea lights within. Warmth and welcome washed the entire space.

"You did all this for me?" She studied one of the beautiful designs so he couldn't see the sheen of moisture in her eyes.

"I did it for us," he whispered into her ear a moment before he cupped her chin in his fingers then angled her jaw until she couldn't avoid the sincerity in his gaze. "I wanted our first time together to be special. As special for you as I know it will be for me."

3

"First time?" Morgan didn't object, really. She'd lusted after the man for weeks, but she hadn't expected him to put it all on the line like that. Or to make the molten desire flowing between them so personal. Why couldn't she be more like him?

"Shit. I didn't mean that like it sounded, cupcake. I meant our first date, our first intimate conversation, our first dinner. Maybe our first real kiss." When she still didn't say anything, he sputtered. "Unless... I mean, I want you Morgan. Whatever you'll take from me is yours. I hoped, but never think I assumed."

"God, how do you do that?"

"Put my foot in my mouth? It's pretty easy." He laughed. "I have a lot of practice."

"No. You distill complicated issues to their essence. I would have worried for three days about how to say what you just did—and probably would have bungled it anyway or lost my nerve—but you follow your instincts and they never lead you wrong. I really admire that about you, Joe."

"I'm a simple man." He scrubbed his hands over his cheeks. Were they red from the fire, or from her praise?

"You're exactly the kind of man I like. Direct. Honest without being harsh. Strong and generous. They're all great qualities." She smiled. "I never have to guess with you."

"Again, is that a good thing?"

She crossed the gap between them and kissed his cheek before she started bawling. "It's a really good thing. Thank you. For everything. This has already been one of the most amazing nights of my life."

"And what firsts would you like to try to make it even better?"

"Can we see where things go?"

"Yeah. Of course." His smile returned, bigger than before. "How about we start with dinner?"

Her stomach growled in response. "Sounds good to me."

They both laughed as they tucked into the fixed bench of the picnic table, draped in black linen. Joe straddled the plank, seating himself on her right so that he faced her. His left hand stroked her hair and he stole a peck on her cheek before admitting, "Kate and the rest of the crew helped me organize everything. The guys know you're like a sister to Kate, and they're all happy we're finally doing something about—"

He gestured between himself and her.

"They said that?" She watched as he dipped mulled cider from the warmer into her mug. Cinnamon and cloves mixed with the leather of Joe's jacket, nearly making her high from the delicious scents surrounding her.

"They didn't have to." Joe tucked a strand of hair

behind her ear. "I can tell by the way they act around you and how much they've ripped on me for waiting to ask you out."

"What if they didn't approve of me?"

Joe waited until he'd finished plating several slices of fresh apples drizzled with caramel, a mixture of nuts and something that looked like herbed chicken with eggplant and other seasonal vegetables from the insulated bag on the table.

"Look, Morgan. I realize what Kate told you the other day could be confusing. I'm not sure I understand it myself. There aren't any hard and fast laws when it comes to the crew and the women we've entertained." Joe trailed one finger across the corner of her mouth, where a stray bit of foam from their drinks had landed. He brought the digit to his lips and licked it clean. "Let's make one thing clear, though. If the crew had been crazy enough not to care about you like I do, I still wouldn't have walked away. I couldn't have."

Her stomach clenched at his assertion. Almost as hard as when he sucked her taste from his fingertip. Desire coursed through her as she imagined his tongue lapping at her juices with such gusto. And what if it were more than just Joe devouring her? Could she handle three other men as potent and masculine as him? Would he still want her if she couldn't?

"What happens between us is between us. Anything else we decide to do or not do can come later. But, I am curious. You didn't say much yesterday. How do you feel about what Kate told you?"

"It's hot!" She clapped her hand over her mouth in horror. She had *not* blurted that in the middle of their heart to heart.

Joe laughed, then forked up a piece of chicken. He cupped his hand beneath the chunk of steaming meat and guided it to her mouth. She gathered her thoughts as she chewed. The savory dish delighted her taste buds.

"Mmm. This is great."

"Do you know how rough it is to cook for a chef? I got my balls in a bunch trying to pick the perfect thing."

"I'd say you did fine. Better than." She swallowed another draught of cider then bit the bullet. She could be as brave as her date. "And, yes, I'm completely turned on by the idea of the crew but it scares me too. I don't want you to think I'm a slut. I, um, care too much about you to ruin this for one night of fun."

"Morgan." He set his mug on the table hard enough to make the candles shimmer. "That's bullshit. Is that what you think? That enjoying a ménage with people who know you and respect you is the same as sleeping with any man who needs to get off? If it is, then this isn't for you."

"Damn, now I offended you." She bit her lip. "I only meant that sometimes men don't know what they want. A fantasy that sounds hot in theory can change the way someone looks at you afterward. It can kill a good thing. I don't want to take that risk."

Her lip trembled.

"Hey, hey. Sorry. I didn't mean to upset you." Joe petted her arm. His gorgeous green eyes closed to a slit. "Is that what happened with your ex? Did that douche offer to make your dreams come true then punish you for them once he'd gotten his rocks off?"

She focused on savoring the delicious meal Joe had slaved over. Anything was better than letting it go to waste. Because if she thought about Craig, everything would taste like cardboard.

"He did." Joe scooted closer until the heat of his thighs bracketed her. "That bastard."

Morgan set her silverware on her plate when he enfolded her in his embrace. He covered her face with butterfly kisses though his legs quivered with pent-up fury.

"Yeah, he sort of planted an idea in my head. He wanted me to try a threesome with another woman. I went along with it. No, that sounds like I didn't want to experiment. I was curious, and I liked it. She was soft and lush. So different from a man. It just wasn't what I want all the time."

"Holy shit, that's hot."

"Yeah, but he'd promised to try a threesome with another man if I did it with another woman. Only he never came through. He told me it was wrong to want to be with someone else if we were in love. He dumped me and asked me to return his ring."

"What a selfish asshole."

"Something like that. Actually, he decided he liked her better. They're together now. I saw them in the grocery store not long after. She was wearing my diamond. Some of my old friends told me they're living with another woman. I was lucky, really. Everything fell apart before we actually got married, had a house or kids. Before I was too invested."

"That would never happen with me, Morgan." Joe cradled her against his heaving chest. "I'd love every minute of making your dreams come true. And I sure as hell wouldn't change my mind in the light of day. I would expect the same acceptance from my partner. God knows I've done things a lot of women wouldn't condone."

"You mean fooling around with the rest of the crew?"

"Yeah." He looked straight into her eyes. "I've enjoyed sex with them. I've touched them, been touched, even tried fucking James once but it wasn't really my thing. Don't get me wrong. It was hot. And I don't respect his lifestyle any less. Like you said, just not what I want most times."

She swallowed hard as she imagined the two men together. The raw power and grace they both possessed would have been amazing to see unleashed. She moaned.

Joe laughed. "Glad to know that doesn't repulse you."

"Exactly the opposite. So what *do* you want most times?"

"A woman who's honest and open with her needs. Someone who makes me laugh, who gets me. I'm not rich or a genius, but I'll never let you down. I want someone who'll be there for me like that. Someone I can work through the tough times with. No matter what else we do or don't do together."

Morgan couldn't wait one more second. It was as though he'd stolen the words straight from her soul. She leaned into his hold, wrapped her hand around the nape of his neck and dragged him to her for a scorching kiss. Their lips sealed like pieces in a matched set. She tasted the spice and sweetness of their meal as it mingled with his unique flavor.

If she could extract his scrumptiousness and bottle it for her recipes, she'd be set for life.

Joe shifted and, for a moment, she thought he intended to pull away.

"No, stay."

"Not going anywhere without you. We'll be more comfortable over there." He jerked his head toward the opposite side of the fire pit. Black canvas had been strung up on three sides, affording some privacy—though the deserted field posed no threat except maybe from a curious deer—while still allowing the light and heat from the fire pit to stream through.

"But you worked so hard on this dinner." The idea of squandering his thoughtfulness warred with her ravenous appetite for his touch.

"Sometimes I like to eat dessert before the main course." He bit her lip then plucked her from the bench. "You know I have a huge sweet tooth."

"Is that what you're calling it these days?" She laughed at the temporary surprise in his eyes. Hell, she shocked herself with the liberation he inspired. Almost like her old self.

"Oh yeah, let me show you."

---

organ wrapped her legs around Joe's waist, this time indulging in his hard length tucked against her core. He walked them backward while she devoured his mouth and speared her fingers into the thick mess of his hair, which he kept long enough to dust his shoulders.

When he entered the screened area and tipped forward, she expected her ass to meet the cool, firm floor or maybe hard-packed dirt. Instead, she sank into a decadent pile of blankets topping a plush feather mattress. More pumpkin lanterns ringed the warm nest, each bearing heart carvings she took a moment to admire despite the flames licking her insides.

Joe stripped his jacket from his shoulders then kicked off his boots. She followed his example, or would have, but he stopped her from yanking her sweater over her head with a light touch.

"Let me, sweetheart. Please." His lusty gaze raked her from head to toe. "I've thought about this moment a million times."

How could she resist? Her hands fell to her sides as she submitted to his whims, melting a little more each instant he lingered over her.

"Yes, like that. I'll take care of you." Joe unzipped her boots then slipped them from her feet before tossing them to the side to join his discarded coat. The sure massage of his fingers on her sore arches had her writhing before long.

He tugged back a corner of the plush duvet then urged her to burrow underneath. "Should be nice and toasty in there. Dave helped me rig a heated mattress pad to an old car battery. He's good at wiring shit like that. I'm pretty sure it won't electrocute us."

She laughed. "That'd be my luck. Oh well, at least whoever found us would know we went happy."

"You have no idea." Joe beamed as he tucked her under the downy covers. He traced her cheekbone then twirled her hair around his fingers.

Morgan held her breath as he stripped off his T-shirt. Air escaped with a rush when he unbuttoned his jeans. Her wide-eyed stare flicked between his hardening nipples and the smoky trail leading from the base of his washboard abs straight into the gaping vee of his fly. He toed off his socks, revealing his sexy feet, then he met her eager gaze.

"You ready for this? It's not too late to stop."

"Don't you dare. I want you to hold me—skin on skin."

"Shit, yes." He stood to peel the denim from his toned ass and bunched thighs with one swipe of his massive hands.

She gulped.

He gave ideal male forms like David a run for their

money. Tan, tan skin made her itch to lick him, to discover if he tasted like salty caramel. No puny fig leaf would do the job in covering him up either. Morgan wet her lips when his cock bobbed, thick and heavy, against his inner thigh.

"Let me in, cupcake, or there won't be much to look at. It's freaking frosty out here."

"You, cold? Impossible." She laughed then invited him to lay beside her with a sweep of her arm. "It's nice and cozy in here. I think I'm actually starting to sweat a bit."

"What can I say, seeing me naked has that affect on girls."

"And some guys," Morgan added as he collapsed beside her, tickling her as punishment.

They giggled together like children telling naughty jokes, rolling beneath the heated blankets, mussing the perfect setting. Christ, had she ever enjoyed a man in her bed this much? When their chuckles died down, Joe swallowed the dregs of her laughter in another all-consuming kiss.

There was nothing funny about the way he made out.

His tongue swept past her parted lips to explore the ridges of her gums. First soft then firm as he tensed and relaxed—thrust and retreat—the moist tip flicking over hers. Teasing. Tasting. Morgan stared into the green depths of his eyes, noticing how much darker they looked when he got turned on. Before she could get her fill, he lifted up onto his arms. "Now, about that dessert."

Joe dove beneath the covers, settling between her legs. He shouldered her thighs apart then tortured her by laying his chin on her mound while he played with her abdomen. Muscles quivered beneath his exploratory strokes. He traced the swells and dips of her midriff beneath the sweater, inching the cashmere higher and higher to make room for his lips and tongue.

By the time he'd gathered the fabric below her bra, she struggled to catch a breath. His moist lips dragged across the sensitive ridges of her ribs, exacerbating her respiratory issues. If he hesitated any longer, she would take things into her own hands and speed up the process.

Morgan's hands snuck below the covers, prepared to clutch the hem and pry her sweater free when a whisper halted her motion.

"Ever want something so bad, for so long, that when you finally get it, you're not sure what to play with first?"

"Yes!" She hadn't meant to shout but she craved him everywhere, all at once. The anticipation had her on edge. "Start by stripping me faster."

His laughter held a strangled note.

Compliance had never seemed like one of Joe's strengths, but a wash of cool air snuck through the gap in the covers, replacing his scorching touch below her breasts. He skipped along her belly, avoiding her pussy entirely even when she arched toward his skimming fingers. The infuriating man caressed her legs until he reached her feet. He slid her socks off, massaged her ankles and calves then surprised the hell out of her when he fisted his hands in the fabric behind her knees. A solid yank divested her of her pants.

Thank God she hadn't opted for her skinny jeans.

A series of nips and licks along her knees to her inner thighs marked Joe's return journey to her core. He didn't screw around when he reached her soaked thong. His fingers tucked beneath the narrow ribbons forming the sides of the delicate covering then guided the scrap of underwear off her. Molten lust bubbled inside her, flowed in her veins and from her steaming pussy.

Joe emerged from their cocoon with the silky material between his teeth. He flung it to the side with a shake of his head that ruffled his hair and made her itch to feel it between her fingers again. The sight, which should have either horrified or amused her, somehow excited her more. He could recite the phonebook and it would make her hot.

Before disappearing out of sight beneath the blanket, he paused as though he couldn't resist tasting her swollen lips again. Morgan had never really enjoyed tonsil hockey before. Something about it had always seemed too invasive, too personal, too intimate. Kissing Joe brought new meaning to lip lock.

He fit her as if they were molded for each other, tasted like all her favorite dishes in one and somehow knew exactly where to focus his efforts to drive her past reason. He licked the inside edge of her lips, tracing her gum line. A shock of pure arousal zinged straight to her pussy.

In response, she flung out her arms, clasping him to her to encourage him to do it again. He groaned, sank closer and complied. The maneuver thrilled them both as their bare legs and abdomens pressed together for the first time. His broad shoulders overflowed her clenching hands, which marked him with tiny crescents from her nails.

"Jesus!" Joe drowned out her whimper. "You feel perfect against me. Silky, soft, curvy and warm."

His hands traveled up her sides as though on rails bolted to either edge of her torso. He gathered the sweater. "Lift up."

Obedient, she raised her arms and sat forward enough

for him to guide the material beneath her then over her head. The moment he revealed her cleavage, he descended to sample her abundant breasts. Her super-structured bra helped shape her, but she'd always thought her chest one of her best features.

"I'm sorry," Joe mumbled before burying his face between the pale mounds. He sucked a patch of skin above the lacy line of her bra into his mouth. The pressure of his hold stung a bit, but also beaded her nipples beneath the confines of the padded garment.

"Why apologize? So good," she panted. "More."

He angled his face to speak against the curve of her breast. "Some women don't like to be marked."

"I'm not some women." Proof of his possession, even a temporary claim, felt like a badge of honor.

"Definitely not." He licked the pretty purple spot while his talented fingers unhooked her bra with a deft flick.

"And I don't mind being marked by you." Morgan swore he held his breath as he unwrapped her chest as if it were an elegant gift. The chilly night fluttered across her nipples, crinkling them into compact nubs. Waves of contrasting heat radiated from the man above her when he swooped in, capturing the tip of one breast between his teeth, covering the other with his calloused palm.

Shocks of arousal coursed along her nerve endings, jolting them both with her reaction. She moaned long and loud when the blazing tip of his cock left a moist trail of pre-come on her thigh. Joe thrust against her as he continued to lave her breasts, suckling in time to the arc of his hips. The motion inspired her to spread her knees wider to welcome him closer to his goal.

When she snaked one leg around his hip, the blunt

head of his cock traced the wet furrow of her pussy. She had to have him inside. Now.

An outraged cry escaped her throat when he eluded the shift of her hips that would have buried him to the hilt in her clenching channel.

"Wait. Gotta grab a condom."

"No." She gripped the hair at his temples to keep him in place while she gathered her scattered thoughts long enough to convince her soon-to-be lover to stay. "I'm on the pill. Don't want any barriers between us."

"Always have safe sex." Joe shook his head as much as he could in her hold. "We never do it without a rubber."

"Then you're clean." She flashed him a grateful smile. "Like me."

"Really?" His chest crushed hers when he took great heaving breaths. "Bare. Inside you?"

"Yes." She squirmed beneath the heated pressure of his weight in an attempt to wedge her arm between them and force his cock inside. "Now. Please!"

Joe's hips rocked, notching the plump, dripping tip of his erection at her entrance. The initial contact caused her to cry out. Pleasure resonated between them at the simple connection. He cupped her cheeks in his palms then bestowed a tender kiss a moment before he began to work inside.

Morgan's breath caught in her lungs then rushed out in ragged pants.

Holy shit, he feels even bigger than he looks—and that's saying something.

Another tiny hitch out then he ground forward, stretching the clamped walls of her pussy as he spread her wetness along the swollen tissue.

"Sorry." She winced when he lodged, no more than a few inches, inside her. "It's been a while and Craig—no guy I've slept with—had nothing on you."

"You're soaked, but so tight." He withdrew, inciting panic in her fevered mind. "Don't want to hurt you."

She had to have him. "Not!"

Joe evaded her seeking lips as she tried to freeze him with a kiss.

"You're not hurting me."

"I am." At least he didn't abandon their pallet. Candlelight glinted off his skin, slick with light perspiration. "But I'll fix it. Relax."

This time the cold didn't disturb her when the blankets shifted to her waist. Nothing could have penetrated the bubble of energy surrounding them. Together, they generated enough electricity to light all the stars twinkling in the sky above them.

The man of her dreams licked his way along her belly, which rose and fell as her pussy flexed—attempting to grip the thick cock that no longer tunneled inside her. His pounding heartbeat echoed in the stiff length of flesh, making it bob and bounce near her shin.

One of his hands burrowed beneath her ass, holding a whole cheek in his palm, while two fingers of the other pressed to her dripping slit. Before she could register his intent, Joe's tongue darted out and stole a taste of the juices slicking her labia. He followed the crease of her pussy to her clit, placed a gentle kiss on the hard bundle of nerves then slipped one finger in her to the second knuckle.

"Oh, yes! Yes!" Even such minimal penetration provided some relief from the pressure building within.

But she had to have more.

Much, much more.

Morgan wrapped her hand around the back of Joe's head then drew him close while she thrust her hips, fucking his face with an abandon she'd never before possessed. He devoured her in return. His primal grunts and moans of approval rocked her, forcing his finger to plumb her depths. When it glided in and out with ease, he added a second, stretching her further. The sinful ache overwhelmed her, especially combined with the figure eight he made with his tongue around her clit.

His mouth was so talented, she didn't give a fuck how many women—or men—he'd practiced his moves on before her.

"Fuck me," she screamed as his expert manipulation drove her toward the brink. "So close."

He lifted his head long enough to grin and taunt, "I bet I can make you come in the next five seconds. I want to taste your orgasm. Hear you shatter. Feel you surrender. Finally."

Joe punctuated each desire with a lick, a thrust and a nibble. He spread his fingers where they speared inside her.

"No." She didn't mean to scratch his back like a wildcat, but she couldn't restrain herself from raking her nails over his bunched shoulders. "Want you. Want your cock. Buried deep."

"Soon." He added a devious suckling on her clit.

"No!" Her head thrashed on the pillow. She could no longer hold her neck up enough to watch him at work— her bones had liquefied. "Want to come with you."

"You will," he growled around her pulsing clit. "I promise."

She didn't believe him, but her disappointment

couldn't prevent the tide rushing toward her now. It had caught her in its force and dragged her out to sea, no matter how she struggled against its hold.

"Oh! Joe!"

5

Every muscle in her body tensed into a knot of pure ecstasy a moment before her orgasm ripped her apart. Inhibitions evaporated. Undiluted instinct took control. She writhed on the mattress, wringing pleasure from her climax until not one single drop remained untapped.

Her pussy clenched hard enough she feared she might break Joe's fingers.

Morgan trembled in the aftermath of the storm, but her lover refused to let her off so easy. He slithered up her torso until he could alternate sipping from her lips and whispering naughty reassurance. His hands roamed across the landscape of her curves—soothing, calming, comforting.

"You're unbelievable. Fucking beautiful." Another nibble on her bottom lip, this one hard enough to sting.

She moaned.

"I love that you nearly drowned me." His glistening chin slid across her jaw as he deepened their kisses, allowing her to ingest the mingled flavors of their desire. "Perfect. Gorgeous."

Morgan gasped when his cock brushed her ultra-sensitive mound.

Instead of retreating, he lifted onto a straight-locked arm and closed his hand around her wrist. While staring into her eyes, he guided her grip to his straining, flushed cock. It wedged between them, hot, satiny and ready. The protruding veins along his shaft would feel divine rubbing her from within.

Though she hadn't finished quivering from the mind-blowing rapture he'd built in her, she couldn't help fusing their bodies. After all, he deserved his reward for giving her the best orgasm of her life.

"That's right, Morgan." He aided her as she fit him to her opening. "Put me inside you. Feel how much thicker my dick is than my fingers. How much longer. Can you tell how much I want you?"

"God, yes." She jerked in response to his dirty talk. A fission of arousal sparkled along her spine when the motion embedded him further. "Fuck me, Joe."

"Have to." He grunted then drilled forward, impaling her on his shaft with ease this time. "Fuck. Gripping me tight. So sexy."

He began to move inside her, thrilling her with the novelty of being joined to a large, powerful yet gentle man. Her nails sank into his ass. She relished the flex and release of his cheeks almost as much as the resulting pistoning of his tool inside her.

Joe leaned forward to nip her neck. The love bite drove her insane. Embers of her climax rekindled, surprising the hell out of her. She'd never come more than once in an evening. Never mind back to back, following the most intense release of her life.

"You like that?" He released an evil chuckle against her jaw that proved he knew just how devastating he could be to her restraint. "Yeah, that's it. Squeeze me. You want my cock don't you, cupcake?"

"Yes." She moaned as he lifted his head to stare into her eyes.

"Tell me how much you love my cock."

"Love it!" she hollered into the night. "Fuck me."

"Like this?" He introduced his length in a slow, languid glide. His control tortured her.

"No." Morgan shook her head. "Harder."

Joe pinched her nipple, creating lightning strikes from her breast straight to her pussy. "Say it. Tell me you want me to fuck you. Rough. Deep. Fast."

He drove his hips into hers hard enough to rattle her teeth between each command. Where she'd tolerated such treatment from Craig, Joe had riled her need until it boiled her blood. Each forceful thrust escalated the rapture to a new level. Her breasts jiggled against his chest. The motion stoked the flames growing inside her, setting her ablaze. The promise of fulfillment lay within her grasp. If only he would give her more.

"Yes! Fuck me. Ride me." She moaned when he began to comply. "Take me."

She strained toward completion but he yanked his cock from her pussy. She almost broke down and cried at his abandonment. His hand strangled the base of his cock as though to keep from spewing come all over her dewy skin. The length of his shaft glistened with a mix of her cream and the pearly fluid leaking from the slit in the tip.

"Turn over." He nudged her with his free hand until she rotated. "Ass in the air. Now."

Morgan had never had sex like this before. Despite his gruff tone, his affection permeated each touch. She braced for his entry but still tipped forward beneath the driving force of the lunge that buried him to the hilt. Her hands skid beneath the pillows, providing some leverage to allow her to rock her ass toward his invading shaft.

Over and over, Joe hammered inside her. His palm settled low on her belly, the heel below her navel and his fingers curling over her clit. He tapped the hard bump with each skewering stroke until all her attention focused on the center of her arousal.

Morgan's pussy contracted further, making him work to drill to the bottom of her channel. The head of his cock tunneled to the far reaches of her body despite the increasing pressure. His flexed abs smacked her ass faster and faster.

The amplitude of his strokes increased until he exited completely then slammed back inside, reopening the ring of muscle at her entrance with each pass. Finally, she could take no more. "Joe!"

"Fuck. Yeah." He grunted as the first shimmering waves of orgasm fluttered her swollen tissue around his erection. "Hurry. Going to—"

He never finished his sentence or, if he did, she sure as hell didn't hear it. They exploded together. Morgan gripped his pulsing shaft, reveling in the splatter of his semen on her sensitized tissue. Five...no, six, spurts filled her to overflowing, each one triggering an answering convulsion in her pussy.

He jerked, roared, and then—finally—went still, blanketing her back. They collapsed onto the feather bed, too destroyed by what they'd shared to move a single muscle. Harsh breaths echoed through the night for long, contented minutes.

Morgan didn't realize she'd nearly drifted off until Joe cursed under his breath, departed her pussy then shifted onto his side next to her. She moaned softly.

"Didn't mean to crush you, cupcake. Or use you so rough."

"Felt good." She turned her head to meet his concerned gaze. "Amazing. The best of my life. All of it, the whole night."

"Mine too." When she dismissed his whisper, he gripped her chin. "That's no lie, Morgan. Something about you is different. Special."

She didn't argue when he sheltered her beneath one arm, tucked her trembling body tight to his chest, and kissed her with a tenderness that melted her heart.

Joe had lost track of how long they'd spent, eating dinner in bed, sharing stories and roasting marshmallows over the fire—something he'd never done in the nude before. But Morgan had just finished licking the gooey white confection from his thumb as they perched cross-legged and side by side when a quick double vibration from the general direction of his abandoned pants caught his attention.

"Son of a bitch."

"What's wrong?" He hated the alarm on Morgan's gorgeous face. For a few hours she'd lost the worry lines that usually bracketed her reddened lips and smoky, bedroom eyes.

"It's late. We missed the last ride back." Joe extracted

his phone from his pocket and unlocked the screen. Sure enough, the crew had sent him a text. "The guys are waiting to take us home when you're ready."

"We're going back tonight?"

The disappointment in her roughened voice both thrilled him and made him feel like crap. He wished he could give her everything she'd ever wanted but they couldn't stay out here until dawn.

"Yeah. The fire is burning out, and the temperature is dropping by the minute. We're not going to last all night. I don't want you to catch a chill." He stroked her hair into some semblance of order, though he preferred the messy just-been-fucked look on her.

"I don't think I could ever be cold when you're near me." Morgan's genuine sweetness went straight to his chest, cramping the spot over his heart.

Joe gathered their clothes. He tugged his on with brisk efficiency then helped her dress, cursing himself for every gorgeous inch of skin he covered. The potent combination of adrenaline and bright, shiny attraction they'd maintained most of the evening began to fade, leaving her sleepy and malleable. He bundled her in the duvet, and she snuggled up to his chest, molding to his lap as he sat on their makeshift bed.

With one hand, he texted the crew. The other stroked her back. He couldn't stop touching her. She dozed by the time the guys made it to their oasis although it took less than five minutes for them to arrive.

It seemed impossible. The evening's exchange had transported him. Joe felt like he'd traveled to the other side of the world instead of the middle of a pumpkin patch. The experience had changed him as surely as if he'd gone on a voyage to some faraway place and he knew he'd never be the same.

But the moment he saw the crew, it was as if he'd never left them either. They were his home, his brothers. Dave, Neil and James approached, shoulder to shoulder, with shit-eating grins stretched across their familiar faces.

"Looks like tonight was worth the trouble." Dave pitched his voice low enough to prevent waking Morgan.

"You have no idea." Joe raised her away from his chest with a grimace. Dave stepped forward to accept her from him. A few inches shorter than Joe, Dave had always been more muscular. He held Morgan as though she were light as a feather. She mumbled something under her breath then cuddled close to his friend, seeking the heat of the other man's hold.

"Christ, I'm starting to understand." Dave's gaze held a new appreciation when he experienced the full-impact of Morgan's unqualified trust and got his first taste of the lush softness of her perfect body.

"Let me put out the fire, then we can go."

As usual, the crew worked together without much instruction necessary. They assessed what had to be done and what they could each contribute to making it happen. Joe, Neil and James doused the flames in the pit and snuffed out the candles in the lanterns. They packed the leftovers into the cooler, tossed the bag of garbage on the back of their truck then hefted the mattress, blankets and other equipment in as well. In less than five minutes, they were ready to head home.

Joe damned their efficiency.

After one last look over his shoulder, he knelt and plucked a pebble from the dirt. He dropped it into his pocket before following his friends to their truck. James climbed in the driver's seat while Neil angled toward the front passenger-side door. Joe caught a glimpse of Dave rocking Morgan in the back row of the extended cab so he joined them on the bench seat.

The dome light stirred Morgan enough that she hummed and stretched, her lips brushing Dave's neck. The sight of the two of them together pumped Joe's cock hard again in an instant. She hummed at the first taste then lifted her face for a kiss, which his friend provided obligingly.

But the moment they separated, her eyes opened. "You're not Joe. You don't taste like him. Or kiss like him."

"Neither do you." Dave beamed down into her sultry eyes. "But I liked it anyway. Thanks."

Morgan patted his cheek then held her arms out to Joe. He scooted over to claim her—thrilled she needed him the way he needed her—but sat close enough to acclimate her to having a man flanking her on both sides. He could practically feel the vibrations rolling off the three other men in the truck as they observed the pivotal exchange.

They might have doubted her, but Joe didn't.

Morgan wouldn't be intimidated by their hunger.

She would blossom under their attention, exactly as she had with him.

"Where are Kate and Mike?" she wondered aloud as she settled against his side. Her right hand lingered on Dave's thigh. Joe had always been closest to Dave. It pleased him to know Morgan felt so at ease with his friend. He met the other man's stare over Morgan's head and grinned at the latent passion lingering there.

"They left from the festival for their weekend away,"

James answered from the front with a waggle of his eyebrows Joe spotted in the rearview mirror.

"I think he has something special planned." Neil cleared his throat.

James slugged his partner in the shoulder. "Shut up. Don't spoil his secret."

"You would torture me like that all weekend? Come on, tell me." Morgan came awake further as her curiosity got the best of her.

"Oh, we'd torture you all kinds of ways this weekend, if you'd let us." The corner of Dave's mouth tipped up in a feral grin that had Joe's cock throbbing in his jeans.

Of course, his girl noticed.

"I see you like the idea." She rubbed the bulge behind Joe's zipper without a hint of subtlety. Neil didn't bother to hide his interest. He spun in his seat for a direct view.

"Almost as much as you do, I bet." Joe couldn't help but consume the smirk that appeared on her fallen-angel lips. When they broke apart, still panting, he asked, "Why don't you let Dave see how bad you want him?"

6

———

Morgan shivered beneath the weight of Joe's dare. The consequences could be far reaching. But she believed what he'd promised earlier in the evening. He would never tempt her with fantasies then resent her for taking what she dreamed of later.

He was no hypocritical bastard. He was no Craig.

Joe gave her a tiny nod.

She wormed her shoulders into the crook of his arm—braced against his chest—then spread her legs, draping one thigh over Dave's knee. She peeked up at him, then back to Joe.

Joe bent forward to kiss her again, long and thorough.

With his tongue lulling her into a dazed state of arousal, she didn't notice the fingers tracing her pussy through her jeans couldn't be his until they'd made several full passes along the length of the seam at her crotch. From their positioning, the romancing hands had to belong to Dave. The realization had her squirming. The top of her thighs glided across the denim encasing them, and her breasts ached in the confines of her bra.

"Shit, I can feel how wet she is through her clothes." Dave groaned. "Soaked."

Her eyelids fluttered open, and she turned to meet his heated stare head-on. No point in denying it now. God, how could she be so greedy? She'd already had the best night of her life.

Morgan rocked from side to side in the men's hold when they turned from the gravel farm road onto the paved highway. Occasional lights from vehicles passing the other direction whizzed past them in the darkness. Who was out this late at night?

They couldn't see inside the tinted windows, could they?

"Her nipples are hard too." Neil's usually smooth tone had gone rough. "Someone rub them. She needs you to touch her."

Dave's hand meandered beneath her sweater to cup her breast. True, the satin of her bra still separated them, but he applied pressure to the aching peaks. Morgan inclined her head until she could flash Neil a grateful smile. The testosterone whipping through the air around her made it impossible to speak.

Impossible to move.

Almost impossible to breathe.

"Holy shit." The truck swerved a little when James caught an eyeful in the rearview mirror. "That's hot."

"Show us your tits." The frank speech whipped her stare to Neil, her eyebrows climbing. She hadn't expected it from him. That'd teach her to underestimate the laid-back man.

"It's been a while since we've played with a woman." Though unnecessary, James offered an apology for his mate.

She swore the four men all held their breath. Having that much power over the experienced studs went straight to her head.

Before Morgan could balk, she shoved her sweater to her neck and shimmied her arms from the sleeves. She peeled the bra straps from her shoulders and wiggled the cups until her breasts popped free. They rested on the material—plumped, straining and utterly exposed.

Neil jammed his hand beneath the waistband of his well-worn jeans to cup his hard-on, a ragged groan testament to his approval. "I wish I could suck your nipples right now."

"I wish I could suck your cock right now." James moaned from beside his lover.

"Don't worry, you're going to have all you can handle when we make it home." His gentle caress on James's knee belied the strong statement.

The interplay between the men set Morgan on edge before they'd really started to explore. They had to be most of the way to her nearby apartment by now, didn't they? Shit, yes, they slowed for the four way stop a couple miles from the shop. What would happen when they reached it?

She had to come before the guys scattered for the night. Had to steal one taste of the forbidden if that were all she had the opportunity to try.

"Go ahead, cupcake," Joe whispered near her temple. "Ask for what you want. We'll grant you anything you need."

"I need to come. Please, Dave. Joe." Her head rocked on her lover's chest as his breath sawed in and out. "Make me come."

Dave ripped open her fly then shoved her pants to her knees. With little finesse, he sank his fingers inside her as far as he could reach. Exactly as she needed. Joe scooted to the front edge of their seat then focused on her chest. He pinched her nipples, squeezing them with rhythmic pulls that matched the tempo Dave set in her pussy.

A strangled moan from Neil's direction pushed her closer to the razor's edge of desire. How must she look?

Wanton.

Hedonistic.

Truly alive.

She closed her eyes and surrendered to the physical sensations the men inspired but none of them had the impact of the emotional mind-fuck their infatuation delivered. Thinking of the four sets of eyes on her shoved her to the brink.

The lap of Dave's tongue on her engorged clit sent her flying.

Morgan's scream of fulfillment cut short when Joe covered her parted lips, showing her with his wild kiss how much she'd affected him. She reached her hands out to either side, seeking blindly in her rapture, and latched onto the bulge in his pants. He thrust hard against her palm then stiffened.

"Fuck, yes," he growled. "Coming."

Dave didn't speak but his short series of grunts made it clear he'd achieved his own satisfaction. Every carnal sound sent another wave of pleasure zooming through her body until she would have begged for mercy or swore her heart would explode in the next second.

After what could have been seconds or minutes, she began to return to reality.

"Get your mouth on me. Quick." Neil's command cut through her desire. She watched as he buried his fingers in James's sandy hair and tugged his boyfriend's mouth over the cock jutting from the open fly of his jeans.

Morgan hadn't realized they had parked at the foot of the wooden stairs leading up to the apartment above her bakery. How long had they been outside?

James's lips stretched to accommodate the proud length of his lover's cock. Thinner than Joe's hard-on, it had him in length by an inch or so. Impressive—and so fucking hot—James could take the whole thing down his throat. The instant his lips ringed the base of Neil's shaft, Neil fisted his hands at his side and groaned.

Morgan watched his balls tighten beneath his lover's chin. James's throat worked to swallow all of Neil's come but an opaque bead escaped the corner of his mouth and trickled onto the other man's trimmed pubic hair.

An echo of her orgasm contracted her pussy in an aftershock that squeezed more arousal from her slit. Dave responded by licking it from her in a never-ending spiral of lust and fulfillment. Part of something so intimate—by sharing that kind of elemental energy with these men—she felt larger than one person, more than one super-lucky woman who'd stumbled into a sexual exchange of colossal proportions.

Morgan felt connected.

She felt grounded.

Happy, for the first time in a long time.

"Better?" Joe caressed her face as he peered into her eyes in the wake of the destruction of all her preconceived truths.

"Phenomenal." She closed her eyes, completely exhausted, thoroughly relaxed, and remembered nothing until the next morning.

MORGAN BLINKED, afraid of what she'd find when she opened her eyes.

She shouldn't have worried.

Joe lay on his side. He propped his head on one hand as he studied her with a grin, which bordered on silly, stretched across his handsome face. "Good morning, cupcake."

"Mmm...morning." She debated saying more, but didn't know where to start. He beat her to it.

"Morgan, I want you to know I didn't mean for the guys to come for us last night. I lost track of time. I didn't plan for any of that to happen in the truck. Not so soon, with things so new between us." His forehead dropped to hers until the bare honesty in his eyes consumed her field of vision. "But goddamn I loved every second of it. The way the crew looked at you, the sounds you made when Dave touched you, how fast you came on his hand and tongue, how much pleasure we gave you together. How much you returned. All of it."

"Oh God, me too." Slick juices wet her thighs at the memory. And they'd barely scratched the surface of the possibilities. "Joe?"

"Yeah, cupcake." He rose above her, the thick length of his shaft dropping onto her belly with a thud.

"It's my birthday." She gave him a slow, devious smile then shifted until her pussy kissed the head of his cock.

"And I think I have the perfect gift." His tongue dueled

with hers as he plunged into her steaming core and drove all thoughts of anything more than this bond, this ecstasy, from her mind.

7

Morgan stepped from the shower into Joe's arms. He toweled her dry, paying special attention to her pussy and breasts until she laughed, grabbing the terry cloth from his rough hands. It still amazed her that he could touch her so gently with them.

He ducked into her closet while she wrapped her hair to dry. Alone with her reflection, she studied the various love bites he'd left last night and the more vivid ones from his ardent necking earlier this morning.

They'd spent the day together, exchanging stories about their past, things they hadn't discussed in the last several months—the things that had shaped them into the people they were today. People who seemed dangerously close to falling into something deeper than lust with each other. The more she learned, the more she cared and it seemed to work the same for him.

At least she hoped it did.

Joe broke her reverie when he dropped a kiss on her shoulder. His arm wrapped around her middle from behind. The band of dark, strong sinew against her pale belly in the mirror thrilled her. "You're so gorgeous like this. It's a crime to cover you up."

"I could say the same for you." She turned in his hold. "You have the most extraordinary body I've ever seen outside a movie. But you'll never be able to hide how attractive you are to me. Even with a parka and snow pants I'd still be able to see the man beneath. The man who turns me on with one look. The man I can talk to for hours..."

Could he actually blush?

Morgan could have sworn he planned to kiss her, maybe molest her on the bathroom floor, considering the careful distance they'd kept all afternoon. The brief abstinence had her strung tight, nearing her limit. Soon she would beg him to fuck her again.

She moaned then pressed closer.

Joe smacked her ass hard enough to sting before stepping back. He held up a simple yet sexy black dress she'd bought but never worn because it seemed so much more revealing in her apartment than it had in the store. "Put this on then meet me in the living room."

"Are we going somewhere?" She tried to hide her disappointment.

"It's a surprise. Get dressed, okay?"

"Yes, sir." Morgan chuckled when his pupils dilated.

"We'll have more time for those games later, cupcake. Then we'll see if you're still laughing...or begging for mercy."

She shivered then did as he requested, taking five minutes to blow dry her hair and apply a hint of makeup. The front door closed kind of hard, making more noise than usual since they'd left one of the windows open this afternoon.

With Joe nearby the autumn afternoon had seemed downright steamy.

Had he left?

"Joe?" Morgan traipsed into the kitchen, barefoot, to investigate.

Joe, Dave, Neil and James circled the countertop while Joe flicked a lighter, finally getting it to catch. She must have made a small sound when she realized they were putting candles on a birthday cake.

"Oops, I think our secret is out." James noticed her first.

"Surprise!" The guys pitched into an off-key rendition of the birthday song while Joe finished igniting the colorful wax sticks. Dave held out his hand as Joe tipped the cake toward her.

"Make a wish."

"I did, remember?" She grinned at the four men huddled around her. Neil rested his arm on her waist and Dave teased the locks of hair at her nape but she stared straight into the emerald depths of Joe's eyes. "And it already came true."

Morgan smiled at each of them as her gaze roamed among the four hot friends before she bent to extinguish the flames. "This cake looks familiar."

"I snagged it from the case downstairs." Joe looked sheepish for a minute. "Only the best for my girl."

Her heart stuttered and the other guys receded from her awareness for a moment. "Am I?"

"The best? Absolutely. My girl?" Joe grinned when she nodded. "God, I hope so."

Without thinking, she launched toward him, crashing into his side and knocking the cake off balance in his hand. Dave tried to avert disaster but the triple-layer, chocolate cake—complete with strawberry filling that would be a bitch to get up without staining the tiles—skid sideways on the doily-covered cardboard round. It smooshed into the palm he'd thrust in the path of doomed dessert.

The motion kept it from crashing to the floor but it tore into pieces, glued together loosely with globs of icing. Jellied fruit oozed up from the center as though the cake were bleeding to death. "Oh crap, sorry!"

The guys only laughed.

"You baked the thing, you're entitled to ruin it," James supplied.

"Plus, who cares what it looks like. It'll still taste fucking great." Dave's gaze heated. "Just like everything else you make."

He shuffled toward the sink to rinse his hand but Joe stopped his friend with a light touch on the other man's elbow. "Wait, I have a better idea."

The wicked glint in his eyes had her taking a couple giant steps backward. "Oh, no. No. Joe! This is a brand new dress."

"Then let's take it off so it doesn't get ruined. Cause, I promise, we're about to take the term feeding frenzy to a whole new level."

"I like the way you think." James sidled up behind her, trapping her between their work-hardened bodies. "Let me help."

When she pivoted her head to stare at him with bug eyes, he nodded reassurance then kissed her cheek. His fingertips teased the skin of her thighs at hem of her dress. He whispered, "I can stop if you're not ready."

Morgan didn't move.

She kept her stare locked on Joe while James stripped her slowly, revealing her by tiny degrees to his partners.

"Son of a bitch. I'm hungry." Neil shot his lover a dirty look. "Hurry, you tease."

James laughed but continued at his painfully slow pace. Joe still held the remnants of the cake, and Dave's hands were slathered in icing. Neil couldn't resist. He sank to his knees at her feet, running his palms up her calves, then her thighs.

"I wanted to touch you so bad last night." He nuzzled her mound when James revealed the lilac lace creating a flimsy barrier between them. "You're smoking hot."

It felt both odd and amazing to have someone other than Joe making contact with her skin. Another man's breath on her pussy. But the intensity of Joe's stare made it clear he enjoyed every moment, almost as much as she did. Knowing he watched heightened the arousal beginning to fire her blood. These four guys turned her on in ten seconds flat.

"I can smell how much you want us."

Morgan yelped when Neil licked the wet spot growing on her panties. "Screw the cake, I want to eat you."

"Soon," Joe interjected. "Finish getting her naked, then come help us. My zipper is about to leave permanent marks on my cock."

"You heard your guy." James nudged her arms until she raised them above her head. "Enough teasing."

He stripped her dress off then flicked open her bra with one smooth movement. Neil groaned, his lips drifting to her flat abdomen, his hands cupping her ass. When James revealed her breasts to his lover, Neil latched on to one of the mounds. His moan sent vibrations through the hardening nipple straight to her pussy.

"Nice," Dave moaned.

"Get rid of those panties," Joe barked at James.

James dropped to his knees beside Neil, who supported her with his big hands, which spanned her waist. James took the tip of her other breast into his mouth as he slipped his fingers beneath the elastic of her panties. Having two men sucking on her, together, had her crying out. She tangled her fingers in their hair, holding them tight to her.

When her panties fell to her ankles, she stepped out of them. The two men at her breasts molded the masses close together then rotated their heads. Their tongues slid all over her cleavage, her nipples and each other's lips. The lust they shared radiated out from where the men touched, catching her in the blast radius. Their ardor expanded within her, amplifying the desire already melting her inhibitions.

Morgan looked to Joe for help. She needed more.

"Bring her to the kitchen table." Joe broke through to the men feasting at her chest. Neil scooped her into his arms as he levered to his feet. She clung to his neck until he delivered her to the narrow, rectangular table in the center of her small breakfast nook. "Yes, lay her down."

Neil did as Joe directed.

The clear plastic covering over the antique surface made her gasp. The cool material contrasted with the intense heat of her primed body, which only rose in temperature when she realized James now knelt at Dave's feet. She didn't blink once as he used his teeth to rip open the button fly of Dave's jeans then reached inside to withdraw the other man's cock.

Neil kissed her cheek then moaned when Joe asked, "You like watching them together?"

"God, yes." Morgan's hand slid down her body, cupping her aching breast. "So sexy."

"Neil." Without another word, the man at her side spun toward Joe's call.

Her fingers slipped from her breast toward her pussy when the strong man obeyed her boyfriend. Neil sank to the ground in front of Joe. She couldn't help but run one finger beside her clit when masculine hands reached for Joe's zipper. Joe groaned as Neil relieved the pressure on his straining cock, freeing it from the confines of his jeans.

They made smoldering bookends. Joe and Dave stood, their messy hands outstretched, while Neil and James removed their pants and socks. Something about the exchange had Morgan's legs spreading farther apart. She inserted her index finger into her sopping pussy, amazed to feel how hot she was to the touch.

Nothing had turned her on like this before.

James and Neil cupped their friends' cocks and balls in their palms then stroked the rock-hard shafts from root to tip several times. The wet, fleshy sounds they made drew a moan from her. Joe looked up from where he and Neil intersected. His hips arched when he saw Morgan touching herself. The motion caused his cock to glide across Neil's cheek, leaving a glistening smudge of precome behind. Neil swiped at it then brought his thumb to his mouth.

"Son of a bitch!"

Morgan wasn't sure who'd said it but she totally agreed.

When James took the head of Dave's cock into his mouth for a quick kiss she nearly came on the spot. Both men shared a look of rapture that she felt privileged to share.

"Hurry." Joe spurred the men to strip off his and Dave's shirts. "I have to be inside her. Soon."

The guys did the best they could with the icing, cake and jelly but some of those fingerprints would never come out. Morgan would buy them new clothes. It'd be well worth the price for the sight before her now.

Joe and Dave closed in on her, gloriously naked, while James and Neil stripped themselves faster than she would have imagined possible before joining them around the table. Joe set the ruined cake near her hip and smirked. He plastered his sloppy hands over her breasts then dragged them along her torso. Dave daubed her lips with the tip of one finger. She opened for him, sucking the chocolate from his knuckle until it was mostly clean. He followed Joe's lead, cupping her mound then smearing his palm upward until he'd transferred most of the sugary wreckage to her skin.

The crew descended on her like starving men. They devoured the gourmet confection from her nipples, navel and abdomen. Their tongues stimulated every nerve ending on her front side as they licked, sucked and nipped.

Morgan cried out with the intense pleasure of their attention. She folded her arms beneath her head for a better view, thrusting her breasts more firmly into their hold. When two of the men cleaned a spot near each other, they'd sometimes pause to enjoy a taste of their friend. Joe flicked his gaze to hers as he claimed James's mouth.

Something about the two men kissing drove her wild.

She squirmed beneath them, begging for someone to

soothe the riot of ecstasy overtaking her pussy. As they removed the last of the icing from her breasts, they tracked lower and lower. Neil grabbed her hips and yanked so her ass perched on the very edge of the table. He kicked out the chair there and sat.

Joe and Dave each took hold of one of her thighs and spread her wide open. She glanced down her center until she met the dark blue of Neil's penetrating stare.

"Please," she begged.

He growled as he covered her pussy with his open mouth. He lapped at her cream, which mingled with the chocolate coating her. Her entire body tensed, poised on the edge of climax after less than a dozen bold swipes of his clever tongue.

The four men overwhelmed her senses.

Morgan reached for Joe, unable to put into words the rapture shooting like fireworks in her brain. Her hand closed around his cock and squeezed, drawing his attention to her plight.

"Oh shit, she's close already."

Neil groaned then redoubled his efforts. He ate her as though she were the sweetest treat on earth.

The bulging cock in her hand felt so good, she reached for Dave on her other side. Both men pumped into her fists, grunting and cursing beneath their breath as they witnessed their friend devouring her. The table shook a little, and she looked up to see James kneeling by her head.

"Doesn't seem right for the birthday girl to go without cake." His grin looked more like a grimace as need twisted it into something feral.

"Feed me," she moaned her permission.

James dug into the remaining cake and slathered his

cock with delectable goo. She opened wide as he guided his erection to her eager mouth. Neil zeroed in on a particularly sensitive spot on her pussy, making her moan around his lover's cock.

"Oh shit, yeah. Right there, Neil," James panted as he drove between her lips. "Don't stop."

Whether he spoke to her or Neil she couldn't say but she didn't plan on letting James go anytime soon, and she prayed Neil had similar inclinations. Joe shouted when her fingers wrapped tighter around him. He and Dave continued to fuck her fists as they played with her chest and kept her open for Neil. When the men's gazes clashed they leaned forward and shared a ferocious kiss.

Morgan shifted her attention when James groaned, though the image of that moment would be etched in her memory forever. She worked her way lower on James's shaft, cleaning him as she went. Though still impressive, he was smaller than the other guys. She appreciated that fact as she took him to the root, swallowing around him.

"Oh God." He went still above her.

"You see that, Neil?" Joe taunted them all. "Your guy is about to blow in record time. He's going to shoot down Morgan's throat."

She knew it was a warning but she didn't care. Instead, she sucked James harder, rubbing her tongue across the sensitive underside of his hard-on. The moment the first jet of come landed on her palette Neil embedded several fingers in her pussy. The combination of his expert manipulations had her joining James in climax.

Morgan strangled the digits inside her as she gulped around James's cock, swallowing every last drop of his release. She didn't realize he'd finished coming until the world returned to focus, and he withdrew his softening member from between her lips.

"Magnificent," he whispered against her mouth then kissed her, slow and gentle. In the aftermath of her orgasm, the soft touch brought her alive again. How long they made out for, she couldn't say. But, soon, she sought the cocks that had so recently filled her grip. The men had stepped back to watch, stroking their own solid hard-ons.

James stumbled away. He dragged the chair Neil had abandoned to the side of their makeshift stage for an optimal view then collapsed into it. Neil stood between her legs now, his erection full and ruddy. "Please, let me fuck you."

The raw longing in his voice fanned her arousal. Joe looked to her for confirmation. She nodded. He tossed a condom from a pile on the counter, which she hadn't noticed before, in Neil's direction.

He ripped it open and sheathed himself in record time.

Joe advanced, to stand beside her. He halted a hairsbreadth away then whispered, "I love seeing you like this. Open. Needy. Honest. Unbelievably fucking sexy."

She moaned into his mouth when he kissed her. Unlike James, he kissed her hard. His tongue delved into the recesses of her mouth. She wondered if he could taste the cake there, or his friend's semen. The possibility had her shivering with anticipation.

The tip of Neil's covered cock nudged her pussy. Her hips rocked instinctively.

Joe separated from her just enough for her to watch as his friend penetrated her for the first time.

"Oh Christ!" Neil scrunched his eyes closed. "There's no way I'm going to last."

He moved inside her, slow for the first couple of passes but quickly gaining steam. He fucked her with strong strokes that jiggled her breasts every time he filled her. Joe stayed close, whispering dirty talk. Telling her over and over how much he loved watching her secure pleasure from his friends.

Morgan's desire rebuilt, though not as rapidly as Neil's. He rode her hard now, fucking with intense motions of his hips that even her recently sated pussy couldn't ignore. Dave groaned then reached for the top of her slit. His fingers honed in on her clit as though he'd touched her a million times before. Neil's pelvis tapped Dave's hand with every circuit, causing his fingers to bounce and grind on her engorged clit.

"Yes!" She forced her eyes to stay open and drink in the sight of the men arousing themselves, each other and her.

When Neil's cock bulged inside her and his strokes grew jerky, James rose from his seat. He stood behind his lover, kissing Neil's shoulders and neck while his hand caressed the defined muscles of Neil's sweaty chest on the way to playing with his nipples.

Neil didn't seem to be able to resist the dual assault. His head dropped onto James's shoulder, and he shuddered as he emptied himself into the condom he wore. The sight of his surrender ratcheted her arousal higher. The moment Neil began to go soft in her and withdrew, she writhed on the table. Her sweltering gaze met Joe's.

"You." She couldn't quite catch her breath. "I need you. Buried deep. Now."

Joe groaned then glanced toward Dave. She squinted at her boyfriend's best friend and saw what Joe did. The tendons in Dave's neck stood out as he practically strangled his cock in his white-knuckled grip. He wasn't going to endure much longer.

"We could fuck her together." Dave's gruff suggestion hung in the air.

"Have you ever been fucked in the ass?" Joe petted the stray wisps of hair from her face.

"No." She grimaced.

"And you're not really into the idea." Even Dave could see through her brave face. "No worries, love. Each of us has our limits."

"You can fuck me." James turned in Neil's arms to face Dave. "It's been a while."

"Can we try something else first?" Morgan couldn't believe she'd spoken up. Her face flamed.

All four men seemed to take a step closer, eager to hear her suggestion. "Can't I take you both..."

She still had *some* shyness. She looked away.

But the crew knew what she meant.

"Fuck, yes." Joe plucked her from the table, enfolding her in his arms. He kissed her while Dave grabbed a condom from the counter and rolled it on.

James gathered the remaining crumbles of cake and transferred them to the sink as best he could. Dave hopped onto the table, reclining on his back. His cock pulsed, bobbing from where it lay on his abdomen. He collared the base with his fingers until it stood out perpendicular from his torso.

Joe deposited her on the table, placing her on her knees facing Dave's feet. With one hand, he guided his best friend's cock to her pussy. When it aligned with her opening, she sank onto her haunches, swallowing Dave to the root.

An unintelligible moan sounded below her. Dave's fists pounded the table as she bowed, working him inside her fully. His toes curled at the end of the table.

Joe leaned on the furniture, testing his weight, but the solid oak didn't even tremble. He crawled between her and Dave's spread legs, pressing her to her back in the process. The full-body contact with Dave's hard muscles and heated skin scorched her. He reached around to cup her breasts, teasing the nipples with light flicks while Joe got situated.

"Tell me if this hurts." He stared into her eyes without moving until she bestowed her promise.

Then he traced the thick vein on the underside of Dave's cock with his flared head until it led him straight to the heart of her pussy. He held his shaft down with two fingers, squeezing in beside his friend.

"Oh my God," she screamed at the ultra-fullness pervading her pussy. The swollen tissue stretched. The oversensitive walls simultaneously rebelled and craved more. Joe inched in further, fucking both her and Dave with tiny hitches of his hips. More than half of his length embedded in her.

"I think that's as far as I can go." His forehead rested on hers as he ravished her lips. "So fucking tight."

Dave groaned below them. "Fuck. Need you to move. Fuck her. Fuck us."

Joe needed it too. Morgan could see his fervor in the set of his jaw and the tension in his shoulders. Trapped between two infernos, she couldn't help but catch on fire.

Joe locked his elbows, hovering over her in an obscene version of a push up. He began to rock inside her, tentative at first. Every time he shifted, all three of them moaned.

James and Neil observed from between their legs at

the foot of the table. James groaned at the sight. "It's like you're stroking Dave's balls with your cock, Joe."

"I bet that feels un-fucking-believable," Neil muttered with envy.

"Does." Dave shuddered beneath her. "Harder, Joe."

He looked to Morgan for confirmation.

"Do it." She cried out when he thrust in deep. "I can't take much more."

"She's stretched so tight around you." Neil and James kept a running commentary, making all three of them suffer as they strained toward the promise of pleasure greater than any they'd known before.

The table rocked when Joe began to really pump inside her. Dave grabbed her hips and thrust from below. The two cocks inside her rubbed and slipped against each other. Morgan stopped thinking and lost herself in a universe comprised only of senses—the feel of them fucking her into oblivion, the sound of their grunts and moans, the smell of their arousal mixed with the lingering flavor of the chocolate cake.

All of it combined to detonate a violent reaction. Before she could say anything, before she could even prepare herself, her orgasm crashed through her. She convulsed around the men fucking her, dragging them with her in a shared release of epic proportions. Dave stiffened first, filling the condom inside her with pulse after pulse of come.

Her climax continued to drown her with waves of pure pleasure. Joe breathed a lungful of air into her constricted chest as he blew out a massive sigh, ending on a strangled groan. Hot jets of semen burst from his cock, splattering into the depths of her pussy and coating the latex barrier between them and Dave.

His orgasm seemed to drag on for hours, just as hers did.

And then the world faded to black.

WHEN SHE RECOVERED, Morgan was cradled in Joe's arms on the floor of her shower. Warm water began to cascade over them but neither had the energy to make a move for the soap.

"Welcome back, cupcake."

"Hi." She kissed his neck.

"How do you feel?" Joe's question sounded scratchy from the strain of his earlier shouts.

"Never better." She lay boneless in his grip. "You?"

She held her breath. It was the moment of truth. How would he feel now that they'd acted out the fantasy?

How weird would things be?

"Sublime. But I think we've only just begun, Morgan." He smiled against her damp hair. "Happy birthday."

Grateful for the droplets of water beading on his chest, she let the moisture seep from the corners of her eyes. The happiest tears she'd ever shed.

EPILOGUE

Sunday evening had arrived far too fast. The best weekend of Morgan's life was now history, though she would bet there were plenty more coming to rank high on her list. She ran past the crew, as they lounged on her couch, studying the sports highlights on TV, to answer a familiar knock at her door.

"You're back." She squashed Kate in a fierce hug. If it hadn't been for her best friend, none of this would have happened. But, before she could drag the woman somewhere private to dish, she caught the look on Kate's face. "Wow, even happier than when you left. I didn't think that was possible."

Kate wiggled the fingers of her left hand in front of Morgan's nose. A high-pitched double-squee turned four heads from the living room. Mike covered his ears then squeezed past the women as they bounced and giggled some more. The glow of Kate's smile nearly matched the glint from her gorgeous diamond ring.

"I'm so happy for you. Truly." Morgan hugged her best friend until she squeaked. "But..."

"What?" Kate angled her head.

Morgan grimaced at the shadow dimming her friend's enthusiasm. "Nothing. Sorry—"

"No, please. Don't do that. Tell me what you're really thinking."

"It's just..." Morgan lowered her voice then peeked over Kate's shoulder to where Joe leaned his hip against the counter. The crew took turns slapping Mike on the back and offering their congratulations. "Isn't this all sort of quick? You've only known him a few months. How do you know it'll last?"

As though he could sense her stare, Joe turned. Their eyes met, and his gaze intensified. A corresponding thrill ran through her veins. Could this be the real thing? A forever-after kind of love?

How could it not be?

"You knew Craig all your life. But deep down, you understood it would never last," Kate whispered. "It's kind of like that, but opposite. When he's the one, you know. Time doesn't matter."

Joe winked then held out his hand as though their thirty seconds apart had seemed as long to him as it did to her. She ached to feel his fingers surrounding hers, sheltering her with their calloused strength.

Without him, she felt incomplete.

"You're right." Morgan hugged Kate one more time. "Congratulations."

"Right back at you. Looks like you had a busy weekend."

The women laughed as they rejoined the crew in the other room. Joe's arm came around Morgan's shoulder, welcoming her into the heat and laughter they all shared.

It felt perfect.
And she knew.

KAYLA'S GIFT
POWERTOOLS
JAYNE RYLON
NEW YORK TIMES BESTSELLING AUTHOR

‎

1

———

"**O**h God, that's good."

"Harder?" Kayla intensified her motion when the man beneath her groaned.

"Yeah. Right there. Don't stop, baby."

"No worries, I'll take care of you."

"Always do." Dave sighed. "I look forward to coming inside all damn day. It's tough to concentrate when your gifted hands are waiting for me."

"But if you weren't aggravating this strained muscle by building my spa, you wouldn't need my fabulous massages."

"Is it any wonder I love my job?"

Kayla's fingers drifted from Dave's sculpted shoulders to tug the silky hair feathering over the nape of his neck. As if she minded his near-constant teasing.

Her work rocked pretty solid too—at least when it involved touching prime specimens of masculinity like Dave. While she lingered, she rubbed along his spine, eliciting another deep purr. The rumble curled her bare toes in the plush area rug.

"And here I thought the highlight of your career was your kick-ass partners." A gruff rebuke from the general direction of the entrance startled Kayla.

Dave's gorgeous body had consumed her focus. Bold ridges of sinew tempted her fingers to explore beyond the requirements of his treatment. She'd never seen anatomy so fine outside of her textbooks. Lying on his toned abdomen, the bull of a man threatened to destroy her portable table with his defined bulk.

She couldn't wait for the permanent equipment she'd ordered to arrive. Furnishing her new facility would be the final step in bringing her vision to life.

"You guys aren't bad, either." Dave angled his head to face Mike, the construction crew's foreman, who leaned his hip on the doorjamb. Her patient didn't scramble for a towel to cover his smoking-hot ass or flinch in the slightest. The muscles she'd worked so hard to relax stayed pliant. "What's up, boss?"

"There's a hell of a storm brewing outside. The snow's started, and the sky is black as shit. Joe and I are heading back to town. Our girls are worried. Kate's called twice. Morgan texted enough times to overflow the screen of Joe's phone. Neither one of them are naggers by nature. The unpaved section of the road turns into a skating rink when all those puddles freeze over. Too much longer and we'll all be stuck."

"They're forecasting what, a foot and a half, now?"

Kayla attacked the tension invading Dave.

"Nah, they upped the projection again. More like two to three." Mike shook his head. "Plus, the wind is kicking in. Froze my balls off on the roof, but we finished shingling in time."

She raised an eyebrow in his direction without faltering in her caresses.

"Crap, sorry. Anyway, James and Neil are making one last round, lashing tarps over our supplies and Kayla's firewood while you pamper that knot in your shoulder. Pussy."

"Yeah, yeah." Dave's broad back flexed beneath her fingers. "Jealous?"

"Hardly. No offense, Kayla."

"None taken."

"My Kate is the only woman who can heal me with her touch."

Kayla sighed. "Someday I'll meet a man who adores *me*, right?"

"Hell-ooo. Last time I checked, I was a dude." Dave squinted at her. "Didn't I tell you how much I love you less than two minutes ago?"

He had. Damn if the lame joke hadn't wreaked havoc on her hormones too. She knew better than to imagine his constant flirtations were more than habit. The guys in the crew had "player" stamped all over their hard bodies in between their bold tattoos. She traced an organic swirl of red ink around Dave's shoulder.

"Okay, kids. Before you become bicker buddies again, I'm heading out." Mike's grin slipped a fraction of an inch. "Are you sure you have everything you need, Kayla? It could be a while before we can make it back. I don't like the thought of you up here. Alone. My offer stands. Stay with Kate and me. You'd be friends inside a minute, I bet. The two of you could stir up a world of trouble together. Throw Morgan in the mix and..."

"God help us." Dave grunted when she pressed her elbow into the base of his spine.

"Thanks, but no thanks. Kate and Morgan sound like a riot though." Their respective fiancé and boyfriend talked about the women pretty near constantly.

"Come home with us and hang out." Dave tried again. "It'll be fun, not to mention safe."

"No different than here. James and Neil brought a mountain of groceries this morning. You checked the generator at least a thousand times." Kayla's lips curved as she contemplated the high potential for peaceful solitude. Her and a world blanketed in white. An occasional deer for company. "Really. I'm fine. Thank you."

"All righty then." Mike crossed to her and dropped a kiss on the top of her head.

She took advantage of the distraction to adjust her sweater away from her beading nipples, hoping the men couldn't detect the small hoops in them. An irregular beat of her heart fluttered her chest.

When any member of the crew stood so near, denying their potent charm became impossible. Wedged between two of the studs, she could hardly breathe. Every one of the guys rocketed straight off her hotness chart, each with his unique twist. Mike's fraternal care warmed her despite the chill creeping through the giant plate-glass window, which overlooked the mountainside and the lake in the distance. The flash of heat he inspired, though brilliant, was like a match compared to the bonfire Dave's searing sexuality lit inside her.

"Stay safe. I'm gone. Dave, you and the dynamic duo better hit the road as soon as they're finished." Mike slapped her patient on the ass and called over his retreating shoulder, "Five minutes or less. Start packing this away."

Kayla wondered at the easy confidence the crew possessed around each other.

"Hey, can I ask you something?" She grimaced when the thought flew off her lips. Great, now she'd introduce awkwardness to their light friendship.

"Anything."

She continued to work on Dave, gathering her courage while she kneaded the flushed red handprint Mike had left on Dave's right cheek. Her fingers trailed to the backs of his powerful thighs before she continued. "Most of my clients freak at the idea of someone spying their naughty bits, especially if my treatment... arouses them."

Neither she nor Dave could deny the solid erection he sported every time she touched him. Hiding his impressive equipment would have been near impossible even if he'd bothered to try. The guys who'd helped her bring her dream to life—by constructing a quaint log cabin to house her future lakeside retreat—never once hesitated to drop trou or practiced the floor-tile-meet-laser-beam-stare, which she'd witnessed from others, when she offered to rub them down in the presence of their crewmates.

"So?"

"You guys don't worry about stuff like that. If things get too intimate for one of you, you simply roll over, gather your clothes and put your—"

"Cock."

"Yeah." They'd tuck their junk into their ripped, paint-stained jeans. She shivered. "You zip up with no apologies. No false denials. No shame. More like a polite kiss on the cheek and a thank you."

"Why should we be ashamed? You're sexy as sin and

fan-fucking-tastic with your hands." He grinned up at her. "Does it bother you to know you turn us on?"

"Hell no! When people act like a natural reaction is some giant secret, they sometimes make me feel like I've done something dirty." The crew's lack of inhibitions refreshed her, gave her hope her crazy venture could work. "Your honesty is nice. Uncommon."

"You could say a lot of our relationship is unique. Me and the rest of the guys in the crew are close. We don't hide stuff from each other. We share everything without assuming attraction has to lead to action. I'm not gonna lie, though. It's great when it does."

If she hadn't been so lost in thought, she might have probed for more info.

They had no idea she planned more than an ordinary sanctuary surrounded by the wilderness outside. Not yet, anyway. She'd considered sharing her dream once she discovered how open-minded they were, but the opportunity hadn't arisen during the lunch breaks she shared with them or the massage sessions she supplied to discount her bill. They were usually too busy—pulling pranks, telling her wild stories or raising hell—to sit and chat.

She loved every minute of their company. Still, she'd fork over her autographed copy of Walt Whitman's *A Sun-Bath—Nakedness*, or at least grant a peek at the rare document, for a sounding board.

Kayla intended to open a nudist getaway. A spa where people could roam free of clothes and recriminating glares. Naked was her style. After her impulsive purchase of the acreage surrounding them, she'd spent loads of time on the mountain by herself. She'd indulged in both the luxury and the wildness of shucking her trappings plenty before hiring the five sexy men who comprised the crew to bring her vision to reality.

Her family and friends had called the venture everything from ridiculous to a poor manifestation of her free spirit. The team of professionals—two lawyers, a doctor and an accountant—her parents had bred couldn't comprehend the whims of their odd little sister.

"Hey, you okay?"

She blinked. When had Dave moved? He dragged faded denim over his lean hips. Damn it. She licked her lips as he tugged on a thin gray T-shirt, which obscured his firm pecs, then his six-pack and finally the ridge caused by his inguinal ligament—her absolute favorite spot on a man's body. She could lick the crest it created from his hip straight to his...

"Kayla?" Dave rested his broad hand on her elbow, shaking her from the daydream.

Shit! For a woman considering founding a naturist haven, she certainly had a hard time separating this man's form from his radiant attractiveness. A problem she'd never had before.

"Change your mind about staying? You can bunk with me if you're not interested in plugging your ears to block out the soundtrack accompanying all the sex rocking Mike and Kate's apartment."

She laughed. "Nah, I'm good. Ready for a couple quiet days, that's all."

"You're not sleeping enough."

No kidding. If she didn't order supplies, build a website, draft design concepts and secure the funding remaining to fill the gap after her sibling's generous contributions, who would?

"Yes, Dad."

"Fuck. Sorry. It's none of my business—"

"If her *friends* can't tell it like it is, who can?" Another heckler waltzed in on their conversation.

"James." She hugged Dave in a quick, silent apology as the slighter man neared. "You're right. Both of you. I promise to take a little time off to enjoy the season. You know, frolic in the snow and crap."

"Damn straight you will." Neil joined them in the suddenly cramped area. How had it seemed spacious to her before? "Not much else you'll be able to accomplish anyway. It's turning nasty."

Kayla ushered them out of her living room and onto the front porch, crossing her arms over her chest to ward off the intense chill. It could be a hundred below yet she'd rather endure the sting of the wind for a couple seconds than add another layer of clothing to her frame.

The more she went nude, the more it stifled her to be dressed. The holidays she'd spent with her family had driven her insane with discomfort. A few moments longer and she could retreat to the bliss of her fireplace.

Dave tugged on his leather jacket while the other two men piled into their beast of a truck.

"Drive safe."

Now that the guys prepared to pull out of her yard, a rebellious fraction of her mind wished she'd accepted Dave's offer. Several days without their easy company seemed like an awfully long time. How could that be when she'd only met them six weeks earlier?

"We will." He buttoned the flattering coat, inspiring a gulp.

She'd never seen him wear the thing before, never mind fasten it to the neck. Sporting something so constricting would suffocate her. Still, she wouldn't complain about the extra time his actions granted them.

"Call if you need anything, baby."

Like a hot construction worker to keep me toasty? Hopping from foot to foot to prevent her toes from numbing—still preferable than stuffing them into the prison of heavy shoes—she indulged her stubborn streak, which refused to abandon the porch until he'd vanished from sight. She chaffed her arms. Snowflakes swirled around them, drifting onto her hair. When one landed on her bottom lip, she licked the miniature puddle it left behind.

Dave's eyes slitted a moment before he growled, "Fuck this."

Kayla gasped between his parted lips when he swooped in to taste the moisture for himself. The kiss caught her completely off guard. He hadn't telegraphed a single hint he'd noticed the electricity arcing between them. Not once had he taken their flirtation beyond harmless.

Until now.

She sank into his loose hold.

His tongue stole its first taste of her mouth. The gust of passion he inspired knocked her off balance. She wrapped her arms around his neck to keep from losing her footing. When she thought she might try to crawl up him right there at the top of her stairs, in plain sight of his best friends, he retreated with a sigh.

Dave stroked wisps of hair from her cheek. "You'd better head in before you catch a chill."

"As though I could have a cool molecule left on my body." She touched her lips with her fingertips. "What *was* that?"

"I think it's called a kiss." He laughed.

"Jesus. Not hardly. I've kissed plenty of guys before." Dave frowned.

"None of them fired me up like that. Amazing."

"How about we work on it some more after the storm?"

She couldn't speak so she nodded instead.

"Call me, Kayla. Let's talk."

"Promise."

Dave pivoted and leapt down the stairs, grinning at her over his shoulder as he loped to the truck. If Neil had pressed his face any closer to the driver's side window for a peep at the exchange, he'd have left a nose print on the glass. The instant he spotted his friend approaching, he turned the key in his truck's ignition.

The powerful engine roared.

Then it sputtered.

Right before it died.

2

"How could you have checked the spark plugs so fast?"

"For the fourth time, they're fine." Neil knocked Dave away then dropped the hood with a resounding *clunk*. Six inches reduced visibility to shit considering the giant snowflakes buffeting them all.

Kayla caught the tail end of the closest thing to a brawl she'd witnessed from the men as she returned to the gathering. She'd scooted inside long enough to slip on her boots and a hoodie when she realized something had gone way wrong.

"It's probably the battery." Neil paced beside his friends. "This frigid weather could have sapped it if it were on the edge. By the time we haul Kayla's car over and jump it, plus run the engine long enough to guarantee we don't end up stranded in a snow bank halfway down the mountain, it'll be too late. This storm is nuts."

"Hell, I'm not sure leaving now would be a great idea." James scratched his chin. "This could be a blessing in disguise. It's coming harder than we expected. Driving in this would be unwise."

The three men faced her as one.

So much for a peaceful, *naked* vacation. "Come inside. You're welcome to stay."

"Are you sure..."

"Yes." Kayla grabbed Dave's hand to tug him toward the house. Neil and James shrugged then followed. She shivered despite her recent additions.

The guys shucked their boots and jackets as she headed for the kitchen. After working nearly twelve hours straight, they had to be starving in addition to cold. "What would you like for dinner? I'm guessing salted-caramel hot chocolate and Morgan's day-old spice cookies aren't going to cut it tonight."

The crew had fallen in love with her specialty beverage, spurring her to consider making it a staple at the spa. She'd brewed it for them every day at quitting time. Except today, since they'd tried to beat the storm. Tried and failed.

"You don't have to wait on us. I know you were hoping for some down time. Why don't you relax by the fire, read or do whatever it is you do in the evenings? We can fend for ourselves. Stay out of your hair." Dave approached behind her, inciting another chill.

When she trembled, he wrapped her in his heat. His strong arms banded around her, tucking her close to the furnace of his chest. She wished their offensive sweaters didn't create barriers between them. Long, thorough strokes of his broad palms infused her with warmth and dampened her pussy.

"Don't be ridiculous. This isn't exactly a mansion." She glanced around the log cabin. Open floor plans didn't allow for much privacy. A low bar separated the kitchen space from the main living area and a steep, narrow staircase led to her loft bedroom. The laundry room and extended pantry sat on the far side of her bathroom, the only truly walled-off space.

"We'll have to figure out the sleeping arrangements. You're the biggest. You should take my bed." She grimaced when she realized she couldn't accommodate them all comfortably. If she were petite, she could bunk on the chaise. At close to six feet, no one would call her dainty. Hell, James was shorter than her by a few inches and Neil only had her by a little bit. "I can fit on one couch, and I think James can manage on the loveseat but Neil—"

"Neil and James sleep together. They can have the bed." Dave didn't make a big deal of his revelation. Neither of his friends seemed to mind the sharing.

She stepped from the shelter of his hold in time to catch a glance James and Neil exchanged. They smiled at each other with a perfect combination smoky sweetness. How hadn't she guessed at their relationship before? She supposed the seamless interaction of all the guys had disguised the couple's intimacy. Could more than lifelong friendship be at play in the crew at large?

"I'll be good on the rug by the fire. That thing must be a foot deep. Don't stress." Dave grinned. "In fact, why don't you let *me* cook for *you*? This could be fun."

"Oh crap, you'd better supervise." James nudged Neil toward the kitchen. "Last time he said that he made chili so spicy I couldn't sit for a week."

Neil chuckled. He landed a playful smack on his boyfriend's ass before he joined Dave.

"Yeah, you weren't laughing then." James flung the

rebuttal at his lover's back before asking her, "Are you okay with this?"

James didn't look away or fidget.

"With the three of you crashing my alone time or your love for another man?" She sensed, more than heard, the two guys in the kitchen focused on their discussion.

"Both, I suppose."

"Don't insult me. You really think I'm some kind of ass cookie?" Kayla smothered James in a bear hug. She may have been taller but his lean, muscled arms embraced her with impressive strength. She rested her cheek on his forehead, encouraging him to snuggle into her chest. "You're always welcome in my home. If anything, I'm jealous. Your boyfriend is smoking hot."

"Better watch out, James." Neil's usual teasing floated over the bar. "I think you're riling Dave. No telling what he'll put in your food if you don't take your stare off her breasts."

They both laughed as they broke apart, any trace of discomfort banished.

PLATES PILED with spaghetti and meat sauce along with a basket of garlic bread perfumed Kayla's house with savory steam. Her stomach rumbled, blocking out the sound of ice pinging off the windowpane for a moment. Snow drifted higher than her shins on the porch. Steady streams of precipitation streaked past the light post, showing no sign of stopping anytime soon.

She tugged at the waistband of her jeans when her fingers encountered the denim. Though loose, it still irritated her abdomen. James set one more bundle of wood on the floor of the laundry room before shucking his coat, unwrapping his scarf and peeling off his gloves. She wished she could undress.

He joined them at the dinner table, stomping his feet to regain circulation. "Shit, it's colder than a well digger's left ass cheek out there."

"Want me to warm you up?" Neil's crooked grin inspired a moan to slip from her parted lips.

"What's that, Kay?" Dave teased.

"I said, 'Let's eat.'"

The guys grinned, but didn't hesitate. They dug into the meal. For several minutes, silence reigned, dotted with the occasional clinks of artistic handmade silverware against heavy earthenware plates, mugs settling on the rustic table and the obnoxious beep of Dave's cell phone.

"Shit! I forgot. I had...plans." He stalked from their gathering, already hauling the device from his pocket. Urgent whispers drifted from the far side of the cabin, where he huddled in the corner, facing away from their gathering.

Kayla dropped her fork. It clattered off her plate and skidded onto the floor. Did he have a date? Had his kiss been impulsive? Did he regret the brief collision still burning her lips? Was some other woman waiting for him —dressing up and putting on makeup in hopes of luring him into her bed after dinner and a movie?

Neil reached behind him in the cozy space to withdraw a clean utensil from the drawer on the bar. "Oops, here."

When she didn't accept his offering immediately, James patted her shoulder. "Hey, don't go there."

"Hmm?" She tried not to focus on the wisps of raspy conversation floating into the kitchen.

"It's not what you think. That didn't look good, but I'm

sure there's some other explanation." James sent her a soft smile. "Dave's been knotted up over you since the moment we spied you on the porch as we pulled up for our consultation. He hasn't seen anyone...any women, since then."

Kayla swore a blush dusted James's cheeks. Could he mean...? And why was the idea so appealing to her when she wanted Dave for herself? In a matter of hours things had spiraled out of control. The howling wind couldn't counteract the heat blazing through her kitchen, igniting insanity.

"So, what do you two plan to occupy yourself with over the next few days? Sorry to say I don't even have a TV," she rambled to avoid eavesdropping on Dave.

"I think we're capable of entertaining ourselves." James winked at Neil.

"That should be interesting." Dave ambled to his place at the table, straddled the chair and resumed devouring his dinner. "I don't mind hearing, seeing...whatever. But Kayla didn't sign up for the live edition of Skinemax."

Her spine steeled. She stretched the neckband of her soft shirt, trying to ease the constriction on her throat. So now he thought her sheltered because she didn't have a Friday-night hookup to blow off? "How the hell would you know what I'm interested in? Forget voyeurism. Maybe I have guys over for foursomes all the time. Women too. Maybe I'm a freak who enjoys roaming the mountainside in the buff and hooking up with anyone who flips my switch."

"Whoa. What the hell just happened?" Dave shot glances to each of his friends as though begging for a lifeline.

"I think you pissed her off." Neil attempted to hide his

smirk behind his napkin. Too bad no sauce had stained his curved lips. "Moron."

"Tell her who called." James earned a glare for his intervention. He shrugged then blew her a kiss.

"It was Joe."

"Why?" Neil tilted his head. "Did he and Mike run into trouble?"

"Nah." Dave adjusted his woven-cedar placemat. "It took longer than they hoped, but they made it home fine."

"Man, maybe you're dumber than I thought." Neil refused to drop the subject no matter how hard she concentrated on transmitting her thoughts to him.

Shut up. Shut up. Shut up.

If they guilted Dave into admitting something she couldn't erase from her memory, it'd be one hell of a long sentence for them all, confined in such close quarters until the road re-opened.

"Jesus. You'd think I kicked a puppy. Screw this." Dave shoved a couple inches from the table. "It was supposed to be a fucking secret, but it's not like you can spill the beans up here."

"About?" Neil and James leaned forward.

Kayla got the feeling they didn't often keep each other in the dark.

"Joe asked me to shop with him tonight. For a ring. An engagement ring." Dave's smile nearly blinded her. "He's planning to pop the question to Morgan next month, on Valentine's Day."

"No shit." James scrubbed his hands over his face. "Like it wasn't coming sooner or later. He might as well have asked her to marry him on Halloween. He was playing for keeps even then."

"I know." Dave shrugged. "He's still nervous for some reason."

"There's not a chance in holy hell she'll say no." Neil beamed. "Morgan's too smart to turn down her destiny. You can feel the electricity between them any time you're near. And I don't even mean the times we've..."

"What?" Kayla could have kicked herself for cutting in when their revelations stalled.

Dave scanned around the table. James and Neil nodded so subtly, she might have missed it if she hadn't stared at them with wide eyes.

"It's no secret we're great friends." Dave set his utensils on his plate and gave her his full attention. "The crew is tight. Closer than brothers. We share everything. Including sex. With women we've cared for through the years, and—"

"With each other," she finished for him. It made perfect sense.

"Yeah." Neil confirmed her suspicions.

Yum-o-licious. She squirmed in her seat. A pulse of arousal dampened her panties. "Nice. How does that work?"

"Figures." Dave laughed before reaching over to clasp her hand. She squeezed his fingers. "I debated telling you for weeks, and you're genuinely curious. No censure, no embarrassment, no disgust."

"What a high opinion you have of me." She rolled her eyes.

"It's hard to admit your kinks, no matter how sure you are someone's cool, that it's safe. It's still a giant leap of faith."

Kayla sighed as she recalled her own omission. Who was she to give him shit?

"You're right." She drew their joined hands to her lips and kissed his knuckles. "So if Morgan's aware of the crew's preferences, why is Joe worried about proposing?"

"It's dumb. He's afraid she might not accept his nature for the long haul. As if it's one thing to date and fool around, but another to marry someone, to bond with them forever, because their tastes are unconventional."

"Bullshit." Neil shook his head. "They're already fused. He couldn't pry them apart if he tried. They'd both shatter."

"Duh." Dave rocked onto the back legs of the pine chair. "I've been over this a million times with him. Part of him gets it, the rest is terrified he'll lose his soul mate. Morgan's been burned before. I think he's scared she'll bolt. Not that I agree."

Kayla peeked at him from beneath her lashes. He returned her stare as though waiting for her to weigh in. She barely resisted shoving her sleeves up her forearms. *Damn, it's hot in here.* "Sounds like Joe's freaked out over nothing. Tell me what it's like between you guys? How do things work now that Kate and Morgan are in the picture?"

"Why don't we clean up the kitchen then move this party by the fire so we can be more comfortable while we divulge our convoluted life story?" Neil suggested.

"We'll answer all of your questions." James nodded.

"Then maybe you can tell me if you're still interested in investigating the chemistry between us." Dave's murmur sent a shiver through her. "I'm dying to taste you again."

"You could be our dessert. Who needs TV?" Neil laughed when James smacked his rock-hard abs with the back of his hand. "What?"

"Behave."

"Make me."

The two men chased each other around the kitchen island, trading a few stinging spanks with a spatula and a wooden spoon before turning serious about their chores. Suds flew as Dave plunged his arms into the dishwater, scrubbing so fast a bit of the foamy liquid sloshed onto his socks.

3

The four of them snagged overstuffed husband cushions from the corner of the room and piled them on the area rug in front of the fire. They sank into the comfy cross between beanbags and pillows.

Kayla sighed, wishing she could feel the texture of the faux fur on her legs and the crinkled silk on her back. She yanked the hem of her sweater.

"What'd that thing do to you?" Dave winced then smoothed the pucker she'd made in the cornflower-blue fabric of her sweater. The caress of his hand on her trim belly made her hips jerk in his direction. If he noticed, he didn't call her out. "You're uncomfortable. Go ahead and change. We don't mind you hanging out in your pajamas. Hell, I'd sign on for dish duty for a week if it'd net me a pair of sweats right now."

"That won't help," she grumbled.

"Why not?" James narrowed his sexy blue eyes on her.

"Because." She debated explaining, but the truth stuck in her throat. Despite their earlier confessions and their permissive views on sexuality, Dave had been right.

Sharing her unusual preferences still frightened her. Too many others hadn't understood.

"You've been fidgeting with your clothes for hours." Dave stilled her fingers. They'd plucked at the seams of her jeans, which left skindentations on the sides of her thighs. "Actually, I've noticed you do it a bunch. Please tell me you're not worried about how you look. You're gorgeous."

"Thank you." She blushed. "No, it's nothing like that. I might have been self-conscious about my height, my size, when I was a teenager. Not now."

"Well, don't let us cramp your style." Neil waved at the three men. "We're fine with whatever you want to wear—holey sweats, ball gown or birthday suit. It doesn't matter to us."

"Be careful what you wish for."

"What's that supposed to mean, baby?" Dave scooted closer, taking her chin in his hand. He angled her face until she couldn't avoid his sultry eyes, which smoldered in the firelight.

She couldn't hide any longer without sacrificing her integrity. Besides, it would even their swap of secrets—seal their bond, sort of like blood brothers but hotter.

"I detest clothes," she blurted. "All clothes. I can't stand them."

Dave, James and Neil stared at her. None of them reacted.

Kayla poured out the truth she'd yearned to share for weeks. "My spa? It's not just for relaxing in the woods. I'm opening a clothing-optional facility. A place where naturists can come to indulge without worrying about others judging them. Someplace sheltered, beautiful and high-quality for like-minded individuals to enjoy a break from their daily routines."

She waited for the crew to laugh.

They didn't.

"That's a damn bit more interesting than a frou-frou spa." Dave smiled. "Sounds like a brochure when you pitch it. I can picture it. It's a great idea."

"With you in charge, it'll be a huge success." James rested a hand on her knee, where it tucked near his hip.

"So are you... What'd you call it?" Neil waggled his eyebrows. "A naturist?"

"Damn straight." She folded her arms across her chest.

"Then what the hell are we doing sitting around in our work clothes?" Dave unbuttoned his fly. "Do you have any idea how stiff and scratchy these are? I'm roasting with this freaking bonfire too."

"Wait!" Kayla covered his broad fingers with her smaller ones. Bad move. The bulge of his erection flexed beneath their joined hands. "Don't."

"Why not?" James raised an eyebrow at her.

"You're screwing me up. All three of you." She bounded to her feet, yanking on the roots of her waist-length copper hair. "You suck."

"Mmm." Neil moaned. "James and Dave do a respectable job. It's not really my thing, though."

"*Respectable*?" James flipped Neil off. "That's not what you said this morning."

"Guys." Dave shushed their squabbling before it escalated into a wrestling match. "Calm down a minute. What's wrong, Kay?"

She flinched when he brushed her hair aside to lay one palm on her shoulder. Her stomach did somersaults, begging her to pivot in his hold and steal another sample of his luscious mouth. How strong would the craving be if they were actually nude?

Undeniable.

"I've spent a large part of my life trying to explain my beliefs to others. Ignorant people will often confuse nudism with some kind of contagious, immoral hedonism. They assume because you're naked, you intend to fuck anything that moves—willing or not. As if you'll lure innocents to the dark side with bare skin. Sure... I'm open about my sexuality. I enjoy intimacy with the right man, woman or a combination thereof, but that doesn't mean I'm some kind of slut—"

"Stop right there." Dave cupped her other shoulder then pressed, gentle but insistent, until she pivoted. "You weren't really teasing at dinner, were you? Your belief in naturism does not make you some kind of dirty leper, driving you to roam around the mountain naked, fucking anything you encounter. We would never believe such bullshit. How could you imagine we would after what we told you about our relationship?"

"Because this time it's true." A tear slipped from the corner of her eye, horrifying her. She dashed it away before it'd traveled an inch across her cheek.

Dave reached out.

Kayla stepped back, evading his comforting embrace. "During sessions where I'm around you naked—any of you, all of you—sex eclipses everything else in my mind. The whole time I massage you, I wonder what it'd be like to have you buried inside me. I want to ride you. I'd give half this mountain to taste you. I'm *dying* for you to use me."

Dave groaned.

"When I need to be strong and sure in my purpose,

you've given me reason to doubt." She slumped. Holding her frame upright a moment longer seemed impossible. "Maybe I was kidding myself all along. Maybe it's impossible to separate nudity from sexuality."

"So, you're saying you're only attracted to me—to us—when we're undressed?" Dave crowded closer.

"Ah, no." She shook her head as she took stock of the ache between her legs and the heavy weight of her sensitive breasts. "But when you're bare, the magnetism's impossible to resist. It's not like that when you're covered up."

"Are you lying to us...or to yourself? Consider carefully or I'll prove you're a little fibber."

"How?" She gave herself a mental head slap. Why antagonize the man? *Because you're tired of wanting and not having. Tired of restraint.*

"Take off your clothes." Dave's command weakened her knees. "Do it quick, or I'll rip them to shreds so you never have to worry about wearing them again."

"Oh shit, now you did it." James shifted his gaze between her and Dave.

Kayla shrugged. No matter what happened, it would be a welcome relief. She shimmied her jeans off her hips without unfastening them then whipped her sweater over her head as she kicked the denim so hard it flopped over the armrest of the couch. She rolled her shoulders and stretched. Finally.

Though she forced herself to don the necessary garments, she never could torture herself with a bra or underwear. Naked, she propped one hand on her hip and stared down the three prime males fixated on her every move.

Dave breathed in and out several times, his fingers

clenched at his sides as he took in the smattering of bright, floral tattoos decorating her ribs and the modest silver hoops piercing her nipples. The metal tugged deliciously as her flesh reacted to his appraisal. "Lie on the rug between James and Neil."

Her body complied without conscious approval from her mind. Something about this man, these men, called to her on an instinctive level.

"I love it when he turns all bossy." Neil hummed his approval.

"Good 'cause you're about to assist." Dave doled out orders as she sank to floor.

Soft and fuzzy, the rug caressed her backside from her calves to her ass to her shoulders while allowing air to circulate over her skin. She squirmed, relishing the sensation while the fire cooked one side of her front and the cool air in the room regulated the other. Freedom sang through her blood with each pump of her racing heart.

Kayla surrendered to instinct, spreading her legs to tease the three men ringing her with the glistening fluid on her upper thighs. She painted the proof of her arousal over her waxed pussy with the tip of one finger, biting her lip when she skimmed her clit.

No one had ever dared to call her inhibited.

"Jesus." Neil untucked his shirt.

"No." Dave placed a restraining hand on the other man's tense forearm. "Leave your clothes on. Every stitch. We're going to make her scream. Blow her mind. Steal all her rational thought without showing a hint of skin."

"Fuck." James dropped to his knees beside her shoulder. She reached out to take his proffered hand, lacing their fingers.

"You win." Kayla could care less about her moral

dilemma at the moment. For now, it would be enough to erase the lust hazing her mind so she could think clearly about the issue in the aftermath of great sex. "I understand. No need for some great lesson. Just don't leave me like this."

"Oh, we're not about to abandon you." Dave situated himself on his haunches between her knees, opening them wider with one massive hand on each of her thighs. "This isn't at all how I planned to do this, but I'd be lying if I said the end result was much different. I want you. I want to share you, give you three times the pleasure I could myself."

"Mmm." She tried to generate an intelligent answer. Instead, her hips responded for her, rising to meet his roving fingers as they teased along her legs to stroke her smooth mound. Never one to sit passive and wait for her lover to take charge, she urged him closer.

"Keep her still." Dave barked the order to his friends, who didn't hesitate.

Neil joined them on the rug, grasping her wrist and pinning it to the floor beside her head. James followed suit.

The rustle of their jeans as they shifted sent butterflies racing through her abdomen. Something about the contrast seemed decadent. It amplified her joy at being nude. Rough grazes from the fabric shielding the men's legs had her breath wheezing double time.

Dave leaned forward, bracing himself on bulging forearms on either side of her head. He smiled as he observed her potent longing up close and personal before covering her lips with his. He explored with the tip of his tongue, teasing at the corner of her mouth until she relented and granted him entrance. They played—tickling, taunting, tempting—for long minutes, until neither had the breath to continue without passing out.

James squeezed her hand when she whimpered.

"You drive me crazy too, Kay," Dave whispered as he nipped her lip. "Just so you know."

Neil grunted. "No shit. How many trips down this mountain have we had to listen you ramble on and on about how smoking she is?"

"Am I wrong?" Dave lifted an eyebrow.

"Fuck no." Neil's lips quirked. "But you're still as annoying as an itchy nose when your hands are covered in drywall dust."

"I guess we know who's getting off last." James laughed. "Focus, boys. Kayla's on the edge."

"Not so easy. We can push her much further." Dave winked at James. "You were too busy fondling her to notice her reaction to your announcement earlier. I think she likes the idea of two guys together. Don't you, baby?"

"I support gay rights, yes." She salvaged the destruction of her rationality long enough to respond. "Everyone should live and love however makes them happy as far as I'm concerned."

"It was more than that, but I'll give it to you for now." Dave shifted his focus to James. He planted one hand on the back of his partner's neck and navigated their journey.

If the couple hadn't still restrained her, she would have touched herself while the guys shared a remarkably tender kiss.

"My turn." Neil cut in, devouring Dave's mouth for several seconds before reaching for his lover. The instant Neil and James meshed, Kayla could tell the difference. Friendship and shared sensual escapades had nothing on true love. The men stared into each other's eyes as they connected, letting their souls speak to one another.

She sighed.

"Pretty awesome, right?" Dave nodded at her.

The two men broke apart, panting. They faced to her together, both sporting wicked grins. They descended in unison, each laving the tip of one of her breasts. Her eyes rolled in their sockets when they tugged on the jewelry there before angling their heads for another taste of each other.

The alternating stimulation captivated her attention. Her eyes dried out from refusing to blink as the guys worshipped her chest, then each other, over and over. She almost forgot Dave, until he moved, settling deeper in the vee of her thighs. He lay on the floor between her legs, nibbling a trail from her knee toward her pussy.

She would have begged them to allow her to admire their fantastic bodies, touch them, if she could have found her voice. Neil bit lightly on her nipple, causing her to squirm. A trickle of arousal escaped her clenching pussy.

"Oh, what's this?" Dave mocked her. "I thought you only wanted us 'cause our hot naked bodies triggered some kind of naturism fetish?"

He swiped a finger through her engorged folds, collecting the damning evidence. He sucked the digit clean, groaning at her taste before swiping another sample to feed to James. The other man paused his attentions to her breast to savor the flavor of the ecstasy they inspired.

"She's delicious," he groaned before kissing Neil once more, sharing the mingled taste of all four of them.

Dave held her gaze as he replaced his finger at her opening. His hooded eyes turned glassy as he penetrated her tight rings of muscle with a slow, steady invasion. She cried out as her body hugged him, inciting a riot of pleasure that burned her from the inside out.

James whispered in her ear as Neil licked her belly with soothing strokes. The shirt covering his broad shoulders scraped her waist. "Your reaction to us has nothing to do with our clothing or lack thereof. Don't confuse the two."

She quaked as a precursor to orgasm rolled through her. The initial joining of their bodies thrilled her. James traced the dark outline of a delicate vine, which snaked up her side and across the underside of her breast, with his tongue. "So pretty."

"She likes that," Dave rasped when her tissue fluttered around his embedded finger. He lifted his chin toward Neil. "Feel for yourself."

Kayla expected Dave to withdraw, vacating the moist heat of her pussy to leave room for his friend. Instead, he paused the tiny nudges rocking his finger within her clinging sheath while Neil aligned his hand for the optimum approach.

Neil lifted his talented mouth from her breast to nibble her neck. She tensed when the heel of his palm settled on her mound and a broad finger tunneled beside Dave's, snaking beyond the initial resistance of her core.

The men stretched her boundaries and her body. Despite her earlier bravado, she'd never experienced something so intense, so wild or so decadent.

"Damn, she's hot." Neil claimed her lips less gently as her desire infected him. The weight of his full erection branded her hip.

He curled his finger inside her, caressing the ultra-sensitive front wall of her pussy with a circular motion that jostled him against Dave.

Wet smacks accompanied their joint explorations.

Kayla squeezed James's hand when he suspended his stroking on her side and breast, demanding his attention.

"Sorry, Kay." His harsh exhalation buffeted her damp nipple. "They distracted me. I wish I could feel how soft you are. How lush."

"Do it." Dave growled. "She'll surrender with all three of us inside her. Together."

The idea alone had rapture rippling the walls of her pussy. Neil adjusted his hand so a calloused pad jolted her clit, granting her a chance to regain control.

"Not yet," Dave insisted as he supervised. "Wait for James. I mean, I know you only want us when we're naked—"

"Shut up." She snarled as a blush crept up her chest.

He laughed and screwed his finger deeper, driving her insane. "Hurry, James."

The third man glanced at her and she couldn't stop the plea that burst from her chest. "Please. Join them."

James nuzzled their noses as he walked his fingers between her breasts and over her softly rounded abdomen. He layered his hand partially over Neil's. The other half rested on her skin, a thin sheen of perspiration adhering their bodies.

He traced his finger beside Neil's, trapping her clit gently between their hands. She groaned and tried to rub against them. No matter how she fidgeted, she couldn't generate enough friction to satisfy her longing.

Her mind blanked when James pushed into her soaked pussy. The wiggling of three independent intruders drove her insane.

"Help me."

James and Neil resumed their play at her breasts.

"Why? Do you want us? Even though we're fully dressed?" Dave spoke through gritted teeth.

"Yes!"

His smile looked more like a grimace. He dove between her legs, lapping at her clit and his friends' hands with sloppy passes of his soft tongue. Colors streamed through her vision. She focused on the sweet ache expanding in her pelvis. She tried to harness the power of the moment, ride it forever.

She didn't stand a chance.

Tremors built rapidly into irrepressible waves of desire. She threw her head back and shouted as she came around the three thrusting, massaging, spreading fingers that exported every last shred of rapture from the explosion. Dave hummed as he suckled her clit, extending the wash of contentment suffusing her being.

When the men exited her body, one by one, she peeled her eyelids open. James and Neil held their hands out toward each other. Neil inserted his long finger between his lover's parted lips. James licked, slurped and swallowed until Neil retracted the treat. James returned the favor.

She shivered with the aftershocks of delight.

The metallic rip of a zipper unknitting caught her attention. She flicked her gaze to Dave, who extracted his long, thick cock from the fly of his jeans. The flushed, veined shaft contrasted starkly with his otherwise clad form as he took it in hand. She licked her lips.

"Not this time, baby." He grunted as the ridge of his knuckles passed over the dripping head. "I think our guys here deserve a reward don't you?"

She reached out to place a hand on James and Neil's nearest thighs as they knelt on either side of her, finally realizing they'd freed her wrists. "Definitely."

"James loves to watch a guy shoot his come. Cleaning up the evidence never fails to set him off. Want to see?"

"God, yes." She cupped her breasts, pressing the tender mounds together as she imagined warm spray icing the tips. But why stop at one man? She reached to either side of her, fumbling in the general direction of James and Neil's veiled erections. They got the hint.

Within seconds, they'd made quick work of the fastenings on their jeans and arranged themselves so their cocks protruded, pointing toward her receptive torso. She couldn't help herself—her fingers sought their steely flesh. She moaned when she compared the weight and feel of them. James, so stiff it had to hurt. Neil, longer and thicker, though no more eager than his lover, who pounded into her fist when she didn't move fast enough to suit him.

Dave grinned down at her. "That's right, Kay. They can't take much more. Where do you want their come?"

She tipped their cocks, aiming them at her breasts.

"Shit, yeah." Neil pumped through the circle of her fingers, damp with the precome he'd coated them with. His pelvis knocked into the ring formed by the side of her palm with several quick, hard thrusts. The definition of the ridge at his tip increased, impressing her with the transformation. His shouted warning of impending release was completely unnecessary.

His balls drew tight to his body as though trying to force their way out of his cock. The first jets of silky fluid overshot their target, landing partially on her far breast.

The remainder decorated James's thigh. The man didn't seem to mind.

James groaned and joined his lover, painting her with his come. Splatters of hot fluid seared her skin, which looked more olive compared to the pearly white stands draping over her nipple rings and the colorful blossoms of her tattoos. Neil still twitched in her hold when James dropped lower to capture the last of Neil's orgasm on his tongue.

He ingested their mingled release before it had a chance to cool on her skin. The intoxicating sight couldn't monopolize her attention for long, though, when Dave leaned his hips forward, pressing his cock to her belly with one heavy hand. He thrust into the friction he created, making several long passes as James continued to shudder, intent on cleaning her torso.

The motion of Dave's cock rubbed his balls over her clit, inciting a flash of ecstasy to rejuvenate from the embers of her satisfaction. The dilation of his pupils sealed her fate. That much hunger would be impossible to deny. They rode the final wave of shared rapture together.

Her hips rocked, stroking him as his cock pulsed. The first blast of his semen landed on James's cheek. The man moaned then lunged, mouth open, tongue extended, to catch the remainder of Dave's gift. Kayla stared as her insides shivered, drowning her in wave after wave of pleasure.

Dave slumped, his shoulders heaving as he relaxed between her legs. James leaned closer to suck the last drop of fluid from the tip of Dave's cock before tucking the softening tool back into Dave's jeans and zipping him up. He patted the placket with a contented grin that elicited a moan from Dave.

Neil's reverent curse shifted her attention. He, too, towered over her, fully dressed once more. By the time she returned her wide-eyed stare to James, he'd also hidden himself from her view. Damn them.

"Ready to admit your attraction has nothing to do with naturism?" Dave's soft tone didn't rub her face in her earlier refusal to believe in the amazing opportunity she'd been given. In fact, his question sounded more like a plea.

"Yes." She reached out, taking his hand and using it to pull him over her until she could cover his face in light kisses. "It's all about you. Clothes or not."

"Ahem." Neil cleared his throat with a ridiculous, exaggerated noise.

"Okay, all of you." She giggled. "Thank you."

Neil ruffled her hair, then groaned as he regained his feet. He trundled off to the bathroom. James followed, granting her and Dave a moment alone.

"Things don't have to go any further—with them or without—if that's not what you have in mind." His throat flexed as she considered her response.

"And if I want things to go a hell of a lot further?"

"Thank God."

4

———

Kayla and Dave emerged from the shower together to find Neil and James cuddled on the floor, a stack of board games nearby. She smiled when they met her gaze—all four of them completely nude. Nothing seemed different than before, other than the lack of constriction she'd suffered beneath the weight of her clothes.

The three men took naturism to a new level. Their honed bodies paid homage to the human form. Comfortable and confident, they lounged in various levels of arousal. Dave wrapped his arms around her from behind, rooting his face in her damp hair. The erection he hadn't permitted her to soothe in the steamy mist of her bathroom nudged her lower back.

"Save it for later," he'd murmured when she rubbed against him like a cat beneath the relaxing spray that cleaned the last of their sticky pleasure from her chest and belly. He'd proven he had a hell of a lot more control than she did. *Yum.*

"Up for a game?" James disrupted her train of thought

before she could rotate in Dave's arms and steal what she needed. To hell with savoring the anticipation.

"I rule at Yahtzee." Neil grinned.

"What are you? Eighty?" James poked his lover in the ribs.

"I thought about recommending Twister, but...that's a little predictable, don't you think?"

They all laughed as Kayla and Dave settled opposite from the pair.

"How about Trivial Pursuit?" Dave suggested.

"It's my favorite." She sighed as she reclined against him. His arm encircled her torso, resting beneath her breasts. He didn't try to fondle her or take advantage of the placement. The easy contentment made her heart soar even as her pussy moistened.

"Done." He smiled at her. "We can be a team. As long as you're okay with the orange thinger. I'm always the orange one."

"Sounds good to me." She lifted her smile to his for a quick kiss before unpacking the pieces and setting up the board.

Hours flew by as they won, lost, rematched and laughed their asses off like kids discovering fun for the first time. At ease, she didn't realize she sat, cross-legged, bald pussy completely exposed, until Neil's stare lingered a little too long. She teased him by trailing her fingertips over the soft swell between her legs.

"You like my tattoo?" She traced the artistic squiggles of the abstract design where it flirted with her mons.

"Oh yeah, he's a real art connoisseur." James laughed then slapped Neil on the back of the head with a playful tap.

"More like a lover of all beauty." Neil bit James's lip.

His half-hard cock plumped where it rested on his thigh. "There's a lot of eye candy in this room."

"No kidding." Kayla didn't mind him looking. "A little skewed on the male side, though."

"Uh." Dave cleared his throat. "You said something about that before. Are you bi, Kay?"

"I'm not a big fan of labels. I do what feels right in the moment and don't worry about what outsiders would call it." She shrugged. "I've been with girls before, sure. Would I be again? Yep, if it was someone I felt a connection to. Is it something I have to have to be happy long term? Not if the person, or people, I'm with satisfy me."

"I couldn't have said that better myself." Neil beamed at her. "It's like we were meant to find you. This past year has sealed my belief in fate."

"How so?" She tilted her head as she studied him.

"I guess I always worried the crew's friendship had a life expectancy." He flicked an imaginary piece of lint from his leg before looking to Dave and James.

"What the fuck, Neil?" Dave glared at the other man. "You've never said anything about that. We won't lose each other. We're too much a part of one another."

"Yeah, but I also understand what it's like to love someone until you can't believe it's real." He locked his fingers with James's. "There's no walking away from that pull. I figured when it happened to you guys, you'd have to pick one or the other. The girl or the group."

James nodded. "I can see that. I wish you'd shared your worries with me."

"I knew, no matter what, I'd always have you." Neil sighed. "How could I tell you my fears without making it seem like that isn't enough? Like you're not everything?"

Kayla glanced away, feeling for the first time like an intruder.

"Shhh." James climbed into Neil's lap and soothed his lover with gentle kisses. "How many times have I told you I get it? You love me. When I watch you fuck a woman, or mess around with the crew, I can tell it's not the same as what you feel when you make love to me. You care for them. You respect them and please them. You take what you need from them, but you *love* me. I never doubt that."

Their connection acted as the biggest turn-on of her life. Kayla didn't realize she'd covered her aching breast with her fingers, tugging on the silver hoop in her nipple, until Dave blanketed her hand with his own and took up where she'd begun. He paused long enough to situate her in his lap, her back to his ripped chest so they could bask in the magic before them.

"The idea makes you hot, doesn't it? You're curious." His breath teased the edge of her ear.

"Mmm. Yes." She squirmed in Dave's hold, his hands sliding from her chest to her waist to keep her in place on his lap. They continued to descend until he cupped her mound in plain view of his friends, who'd focused on her and Dave once more. She didn't object. The weight of his hard-on pressed the small of her back, the tip painting a moist trail there.

"Would you like them to show you the bond between them?" He whispered, "They're fucking amazing together. They love each other so much it makes the sex ten times steamier."

Dave's open acceptance thrilled her. Finally a man who didn't seem threatened by indulging their shared needs, wherever the pursuit might lead. Nothing could have been more attractive.

"Yes. Please." Witnessing Neil and James's affection would rank as a high honor.

Neil smiled as he turned to his lover. He cupped James's face in his palms as though the slighter man were made of glass. They melded together, beginning with their lips. Soon their bodies pressed tight, chest-to-chest, thighs tangled, cock on cock.

Proud.

Vulnerable.

Gorgeous.

Neil directed their encounter, gifting his partner with as much rapture as he could. They traded nips, licks and glides of their lips. Intense focus didn't allow for anything else in the world to register on their passion. But Dave couldn't miss her escalating desire. She ground her ass against his shaft, stroking his hard-on where it nestled in the furrow between her cheeks.

In an instant, the world shifted around her.

Dave bore her to the floor in front of the fire, nestled on her side on the thick faux-fur rug. He snugged tight behind her, spooning her, pillowing her head on his bunched biceps to preserve her view. His other hand played across the exposed skin of her abdomen, as well as the curve of her hip and ass, driving her insane. She moaned loudly, drawing the attention of all three men.

Kayla arranged her legs, draping her top thigh over Dave's hip, granting him free access.

But it wasn't the man holding her who accepted the invitation.

James looked to Neil, who nodded.

"Can I taste you?" James separated from his lover and crawled to her, his gaze fixating on the shimmering arousal coating her pussy, beginning to trickle onto her thigh.

She tipped her head toward Dave.

"No, baby. It's not my choice. He's asking you." Dave reached between her legs to paint her juices across the softness of her inner thighs with the barest of touches. She needed more. "Whatever you like. No doubts. No jealousy. Take what you need. Give what you can. We all know where we stand here."

Did she know? What was she to them but an opportunistic fuck? Did she care at the moment? No. A chance to explore like this didn't come around every day.

Their intimacy was a gift.

She stretched until she could entwine her fingers in James's hair to guide him closer. He made quick work of cleaning Dave's fingers then groaned as he skimmed her mound. When his tongue peeked out to swipe through her slit, circling her clit before making another circuit, they both moaned.

Neil lay on his side behind his mate, holding the man eating her pussy with the same sheltering embrace Dave enfolded her in. All four of them lounged together now, Dave and her with their heads toward the fireplace, James and Neil toasting their toes, each couple facing inward toward the other.

The bundle of limbs and torsos grew denser as she thrust her pelvis toward James's talented mouth and he sidled closer, his abdomen nestled against the subtle swell made by her modest breasts. She undulated against him, enjoying the feel of skin on skin.

Behind her, Dave pursued. He tucked nearer the entire length of her, impressing her again with his extraordinary height. It wasn't often a man could make her seem diminutive.

"Damn, you have some sexy legs, Kay." Neil stroked along her thigh to her knee. "Long and thin, but toned. I'd love to have them wrapped around me while I sank into your softness."

Her pussy contracted, forcing a fresh wave of moisture onto her labia. James buried his face to reach all of the honey. The motion eliminated any remaining gap between them. His hips landed near her face, enticing her with his rock-hard erection, close enough to lick.

"Go ahead." Dave encouraged her impulse. "Suck him, baby. Show him what a good job he's doing between those pretty legs."

The wet smoothness of James's tongue slid farther back. When Dave cursed in her ear, she assumed the man holding her had received a reward for the suggestion. "Careful, James. I'm on the edge. Let me last."

Suspicion confirmed.

Ecstasy rioted in her mind. The close hold of three men, their skilled manipulation of her willing body and their open-minded quest for pleasure combined into a potent concoction. She was drunk on it after a few tiny sips.

Kayla opened her mouth, allowing James's cock—perfectly aligned—to slip inside. She laved the head in welcome as he pushed deeper within her grasp. His erection made a comfortable mouthful, astonishing her with its hardness and searing heat rather than its sheer size—unlike the ample shaft prodding her spine.

Spice melted over her taste buds. She peeked between James's legs as she sucked gently, in time to the swirl of his tongue over her sensitive opening and the swollen knot of her clit. Behind him, Neil's heavily veined cock throbbed insistently.

"You lucky bastard." Neil chuckled into his boyfriend's ear.

"Want to really blow their minds, baby?" Dave kissed her cheek. He ran his tongue around the edge of her lips, circling the base of his friend's cock with the tip.

"Hmm." Her assent caused James to jerk in her hold.

"Give him to me for a minute."

She blinked, not understanding.

"Release him."

James whimpered in protest when she pulled off his hard-on with a slurp, but he never paused in his devotion. Delirious with desire, she rocked until his mouth landed in the perfect position. The first signs of orgasm fizzled through her belly. She would have warned the men but, just then, Dave lunged forward to capture James's erection.

Neil cradled closer as his partner's hips jerked forward. The adjustment presented Neil's cock within reach of her mouth. She strained her neck until her lips wrapped around the head of his cock. Caught off guard, he bucked, driving several inches deeper. She choked.

Dave mumbled something unintelligible around James's cock. He stroked her flank, calming her. When she recovered, she stretched once more, reclaiming her tasty treat.

Catching on, Neil assisted by raising James's hips several inches in his strong grasp, aligning them all in the optimal position. She humped James's face as much as she could in the cramped arrangement. All that mattered was chasing the spears of sensation he launched into her center. Ragged gasps and unending moans surrounded her, setting her off. Her pussy tightened then exploded before she could fully enjoy the decadent tension invading her inner core.

"Yes, baby," Dave growled in her ear. "Come all over his face. Enjoy it. There's more where that came from. So much more."

Rekindled hope replaced her disappointment. The men paused, but only to shift slightly. James angled his head to kiss his partner, sharing the flavor of her climax. Neil's fingers pressed against her saturated folds, scooping generous portions of her come onto his digits. Before she could return to sanity long enough to wonder at his intentions, he slathered the fresh lubrication over James's exposed asshole. She watched from her front row seat as Neil primed his lover.

"I'd kill to fill you right now, Kayla," Dave groaned in her ear as the two lovers prepared to bond before her eyes. "No condoms, though. Damn it."

"I'm on the pill. Healthy." Hunger still clawed at her soul. She wanted to join these exceptional men. Had to be part of their joy. Coming alone hadn't fulfilled her craving. "Please."

"I'm clean too. I swear," Dave rasped. "Are you sure, baby?"

"Yes. Yes!" She shouted when he shifted a fraction of an inch and the blunt head of his cock notched in the entrance of her pussy. Her still-clenching muscles kissed his tip. Meanwhile, Neil fit himself to his lover's opening.

While each stared at the cock of the man opposite him, Neil and Dave thrust in time, tunneling a fraction of an inch into their partners. As if by tacit agreement, Kayla and James resumed their oral explorations simultaneously. Kayla forced herself to keep her lids open though they threatened to slam closed with every talented swipe of James's tongue and every nudge of Dave's thick cock stretching her channel.

Inside her. She finally had him inside her.

Oh shit. Sex had never felt so explosive, so natural or so right.

Effortless.

Her body climbed inexorably toward completion so fast she thought her heart might implode under the pressure of being fucked while another man licked her with exquisite tenderness. She couldn't say if it were her or James who whimpered when both men bottomed out at the limits of their reach within their gracious hosts.

Rings of muscle clenched around Dave, drawing a soft curse from his lips. He burrowed his face into the crook of her neck, licking, biting and kissing as he began to move within her. His cock stroked along the swollen tissue of her pussy, caressing where she needed contact most.

James's cock spilled precome onto her tongue steadily while Neil glided in and out of his lover's stretched hole. She followed her instincts, reaching up to tease Neil's balls, needing them all to shatter together. Experience together.

Dave and Neil synchronized the crescendoing tempo of their hips, which pounded into her and James in an undeniable rhythm. Each tap of Dave's pelvis on her ass jolted her body forward, driving James's cock deeper into her mouth. The mirrored thrust of Neil's hard-on pressed James's tongue to her clit.

Her toes curled as she attempted to resist the sparks that lit up all of her nerve endings. She whimpered in desperation when she realized no hope remained. She couldn't help but drown in the sensations these three men manufactured.

"Don't fight it, baby." Dave panted as he shuttled faster between her legs. His thick cock rubbed all the right places.

"We're here." Neil groaned as the smack of his tight abs on James's ass reverberated in her ears. "We're with you."

"Let go," Dave demanded as he bit her shoulder at the base of her neck.

The first jet of James's come may have graced the back of her throat a fraction of a second before she shattered. She couldn't say for sure.

Kayla drank the salty spray as she exploded around Dave's bulging cock.

He filled her with pulse after pulse of semen before her wild gyration tore him loose. The final spurts of his release flew from his broad tip outside of her body. The dismay ripping through her at the loss evaporated while she watched the base of Neil's shaft throb as it delivered his come from his tight, wrinkled sac into the depths of his lover's body.

Kayla lay gasping in Dave's hold, suffering the aftershocks of her orgasm for long, lingering minutes. When the men finally roused, James and Neil flipped over so they all lay the same direction, eye to eye.

Dave's weak chuckle bounced his chest against her shoulders. "Sorry 'bout that, guys."

Both Neil and James sported a partial mustache from the stray blasts of Dave's come. They looked at each other with matching, devilish smirks. Another round of contractions wrung her pussy when the men took turns licking the delicacy from each other. They shared the taste of Dave with gentle, though heated, kisses.

She angled her mouth toward Dave, who treated her to the same affectionate exchange. She couldn't say how long they made out before he nipped her bottom lip and nudged her jaw. She faced the sleepy stares of Neil and James.

Without thought, she closed the gap between them then kissed James. Soft, sweet and with no trace of awkwardness. Then she moved on to Neil, thanking him for the glorious gift they'd bestowed. The blended flavor of the three men rushed to her head.

She wilted in Dave's hold, utterly relaxed, and observed through half-closed eyes as he shared an equally intimate kiss with both men. The way their lips merged with practiced familiarity guaranteed they'd indulged in the extravagance before.

"I hope it snows forever," she mumbled before drifting off.

5

———

Sunlight stabbed through the giant windows, sparkling off the icy blanket of snow that covered the mountainside in a million dazzling lights—beautiful and impossible to sleep through. Kayla snuggled into the broad, muscular chest pillowing her cheek.

She grinned at Dave's soft snoring. Damn straight, she'd worn his ass out.

The orgasms she'd succumbed to last night had been the most powerful of her life. She couldn't wait to duplicate the pleasure. Would it be possible or had novelty driven the sensations?

Kayla squirmed as she imagined taking all three men, maybe more than one at a time. Each would come deep within her, proving she could please them too. Her rocking hips encountered the bulge of Dave's magnificent erection.

She blinked then grinned as she devised a plan.

"Good morning," Neil whispered to her from his place on the pile of cushions in front of the hearth. He and James wound together. The four of them, who'd slept together like a pile of puppies, generated enough heat to keep the chill at bay despite the ashes lying where the fire had blazed. Neil reached over James. His hand spanned her shoulders, spreading warmth down her spine as he stroked her back.

James shifted to smile up at her and Dave. "Go ahead. Make his day."

She hesitated. What if their liaison last night had been just another pastime to the man beneath her, an outlet for consenting adults to entertain themselves when board games lost their luster? For the first time in a long time, maybe ever, she craved more than mutual gratification.

James smoothed the corner of her grimace. "There's nothing to worry about, Kay. He'll love every minute. Nothing's changed between last night and now."

"I think *I* might have." She leaned into James and Neil's reassuring touches. "This is more than physical. It matters. I don't really do relationships. I'm pretty sure this isn't how you start one. What if I'm screwing everything up?"

"Don't you dare doubt yourself." Neil tugged a stray lock of her hair. "Take what you need. I think you'll find it's what he wants too."

"Should Neil and I go upstairs?" James ignored his lover's glare.

"No. Stay." She drew a deep breath when Neil's fingers clenched on her back.

James and Neil supported her with strong grips as she clambered to wobbly knees. James slid his hand into the gap between her and Dave to stroke the last of the necessary steel into Dave's morning wood. Neil trailed his fingertips down her spine, through the valley of her ass to her swollen pussy. She shivered, barely containing her moan when he pushed two fingers inside as James readied Dave.

Satisfied, James pointed Dave's cock toward her moist opening. Neil withdrew his fingers and painted the excess arousal over her tight ass. He left his hand in place, idle, while she fit the opening of her pussy over the plump head of Dave's hard-on, which James supported.

"He's huge." She gasped as she sank onto the intrusion. Each fraction of an inch lower stretched her pussy wider and wider until a delicious burn radiated from her core. Cradling him inside her while he slept seemed equally naughty and divine. His body responded to her on an instinctual level none of them could deny.

"No kidding." James ran one finger around Dave's cock, testing the fit.

The tip nudged into her channel, making her pant.

"When he fucks my ass, I swear it feels like a phone pole." James sighed. "He's always gentle though. Until I can relax. Once I accommodate him, he enjoys pounding me as much as I love taking it."

She moaned at the flicker of fantasy that played through her imagination. Her muscles tensed around Dave, hugging him tighter. Last night, too much had distracted her from admiring the way they locked together. He filled her to capacity. Exactly right.

"Have you ever had anal sex, Kay?" Neil resumed his tentative massage of her back passage. He paused every few seconds to gather more natural lubrication from the junction of her and Dave's bodies. The surplus fluid from her pussy cooled her sensitive skin even as Neil inflamed it.

"A couple times." She sighed as he teased her. Wonder

blossomed at the sensation, adding to the thrill of Dave's cock impaling her bit by bit. "It wasn't that good."

"I bet that had more to do with the guys you were with than the act itself." Neil's manipulation grew more insistent. The tip of his finger probed her ass. "Would you try it again?"

"With one of the crew? Yes." She panted when it became difficult to catch her breath. James captured her hips in his hands and situated her so Dave's cock tunneled farther along her channel. She smothered him as Neil drew circles on the inside edge of her anus.

His finger popped loose when Dave shifted beneath them. "Hmmm."

He groaned, but didn't regain full consciousness.

"Lean forward." Neil's free hand pressed between her shoulders.

James stared as she bent in half. She couldn't resist a taste of Dave's parted lips.

Kayla licked him, turning his sexy mouth glossy. When she nibbled the bottom of his jaw, tension infused his relaxed limbs. Her name spilled from his lips as his eyes opened. He squinted against the overpowering sunlight.

"Am I dead?" Dave whispered into the hushed intimacy of the room.

James laughed out loud. "She looks like an angel and fucks like the devil, but no, you're just fine. Dumbass."

She held her breath as she waited for his reaction. Had she gone too far?

"Jesus, I'm fucking you." He scrubbed his face as best he could with one hand. James plastered to his side, preventing the other one from budging.

"No, *she's* definitely fucking *you*." Neil kissed her

shoulder, then her neck, inspiring her to move without conscious thought.

Her pussy sucked and stroked Dave's shaft.

"Holy shit, she is." Dave's abdomen went rock hard beneath her. He lifted his hips to meet her pussy, which bussed his pelvis and the top of his scrotum. "Are you sure I'm not in heaven?"

This time she couldn't stop herself. She covered his mouth with hers, drawing on his tongue, which he thrust between her lips. Her hands landed over hard pecs, kneading the bulk there. When Neil's finger returned, covered in more of her slick juice, she nearly choked.

"What's going on back there?" Dave growled, more alert by the second. "James, is your guy getting fresh with my girl?"

"Sure is." James lifted his head to note Neil's progress. "I'm surprised you can't feel him yet."

"There he is." Dave and Kayla moaned together when Neil drove his finger into her tight ass. Dave's skull knocked on the rug-covered hardwood when he could no longer hold his head up. The slight discomfort dissolved in seconds. Dave kept talking. "He's rubbing my cock through her ass. Son of a bitch."

James glided his hand down his lithe torso, headed for his cock.

"No." Kayla flung out her wrist to stop him.

When both James and Dave stared at her like she was crazy, she laughed. "Gimme."

"Greedy, Kay." Dave thrust upward, fucking her so deep, so strong, the angle of their position rocked her world. "I like that. Tell him where you want him."

"In my mouth." She didn't hesitate for an instant. "Yours, too. It drove me insane when you sucked his cock."

Neil bit her right cheek then added a second finger to his act. "Fuck, yeah. I can't wait to see it as I introduce my cock to your ass."

"Either you should hurry or we should hold off a minute on the blow-jobbing." James surrendered a nervous chuckle. "Despite last night, I don't think I can take much more."

"I won't rush this." Neil spread his fingers in her ass, opening her passage a little wider. "I'm already afraid it might be too much without real lube. I'm not hung like Daveman, but damn she's tight. A rookie."

"Bathroom cabinet, over the sink." She gasped when Dave and Neil moved in tandem in response to her admission.

James lurched to his feet before she could explain. It didn't matter to the crew. They wouldn't blink twice at her previous experiences.

"Kay, you still have a good two inches left on Dave, can you take more? Do you want to?" Neil's fingers flittered across the taut tissue between her ass and pussy.

Dave's groan preceded a jerk of his hips that embedded him deeper in her swollen pussy. She shrieked. The invasion had lights dancing behind her scrunched eyelids.

"Sorry, baby." Dave apologized through gritted teeth. "Keep your hands off my balls, Neil. She feels great. Refuse to hurt her."

"I can take it." She gasped as she sat up. Gravity embedded more of his cock in her pussy. She slid down his tool until her clit tapped the pad of muscle above his shaft. Maybe she'd lied. His girth stole her breath.

"That's a good girl." Neil petted her ass until she stopped clenching.

The pressure eased, morphing from too much to just right. "Yes!"

Kayla rotated her hips in a tiny circle, desperate to build friction on the tight knot of her clit. The motion caused Dave's blunt head to nudge ultra-sensitive nerve endings deep in her pussy. They both groaned when she strangled the base of his cock with the ring of muscles at her entrance.

Dave gave the silver hoops in her nipples a few playful flicks with the calloused tip of his finger before cupping her shoulders and bringing her close to his chest once more. The pounding of his heart ricocheted through her right breast.

"You're so beautiful, so right, I wonder if I'm still dreaming," Dave whispered against her lips between soft, sweet kisses. "I had the most amazing dream of you last night. Do you want to hear it?"

"Yes." She stared into his eyes, deeper, darker now that arousal swamped him.

"Later, kids." James skid next to them like a baseball player stealing home in a world-championship game. "Look what I found."

He rattled the cardboard box containing the tube of unused lubricating jelly she'd gotten for free with one of the toy orders she'd placed online. She hadn't needed it with her neon-pink vibrator.

"Good work." Neil consumed his lover's mouth as he transferred his bounty. "Maybe if you're nice, I'll find some other uses for this later."

"Mmm." James shivered beside her.

Kayla broke from Dave's mouth with one last, lingering kiss. She grinned when he winked and nodded. They reached out together. Her hand landed high on

James's thigh. Between the pressure she added to the svelte muscles there and Dave's grip on James's waist, they positioned him where they preferred.

She bent toward her prize, engulfing his proud cock in one bold swoop. His balls dragged across Dave's parted lips. A small spurt of precome landed on her tongue when Dave opened wide to lave the bunched skin of James's tight sac with the flat of his tongue. He must have done a good job. More salty fluid oozed from James's cock.

Kayla savored the treat as pleasure eradicated what little inhibition she possessed.

"That's it," Neil coached her as autopilot took control of her body. She ground herself on Dave's cock, fucking him with tiny strokes that focused the ridges of his cock precisely where they did the most good. The walls of her pussy gripped his thick shaft.

"Are you going to come, baby?" Dave tilted his face to alert the men surrounding her to the early warning signs. "Come on my cock. Come on Neil's fingers. Come with James in your mouth."

Pressure built in her tummy. It rose like mercury in a thermometer on the hottest day of the year until she couldn't restrain the sensations overcoming her reason. She should wait—enjoy the anticipation. Wallow in rapture.

When Dave rolled his hips, increasing contact with her clit and Neil slipped a third finger in her ass, they defeated her. She screamed around James's erection, sucking him hard and fast in time to the contractions rippling her pussy around Dave.

Three strong partners held her up, grounded her, kept her from flying into space as her climax threatened to rip her apart. Pleasure smashed into her with reverberations that didn't seem to end. It slowed but kept pulsing in her core as Dave settled into a steady rhythm of thrusts from below that Neil matched in counterpoint.

"Hold on to it, Kay." James wove his fingers through her hair, positioning her where he pleased as he fucked her mouth. "Focus on the feeling. Grow it, keep it, tend it until it blossoms inside you again and again. You can do it. Ride the euphoria. Over and over. I've seen Morgan and Kate do it. Makes me wish I were a woman."

She didn't have a choice as their decadent stamina kept them hard and intent on satisfying her. They filled her with more desire than she could have imagined possible as recently as yesterday.

A particularly hard stroke from Dave sent her careening into another blast of bliss.

"Yes, yes," James chanted as he fed her his cock. "Just like that. Again, Kay."

The wet sounds of Dave tending to James's sac rushed to her brain, setting her off. A flood of come dripped from her soaked opening, saturating Dave's balls.

"There you go." Neil's fingers were forced from her ass by the rejuvenated convulsion of every fiber of her being. When he replaced them, they felt larger.

She whimpered around James's cock, inspiring a shudder from the man in her mouth.

"Keep going, Kayla." James rubbed her back, soothing even as he enflamed. Between the guys, six hands caressed her all over, driving her insane. "You'll come again when he penetrates you. Fills you."

She almost felt guilty for stealing James's fun. His reverent murmurs kept her from fearing the bite of pain she'd always experienced in the past. None of the crew would hurt her.

"You're ready." James moaned when the head of Neil's cock began to sink into her tense hole. "Push out now, keep breathing. Long and slow, sweetheart."

Kayla surrendered to their guidance. She let herself experience as her mind obeyed their commands without processing them. A swell of rapture carried her away when the mushroom head of Neil's cock breached the last of her resistance. He plunged inside, her ass swallowing him whole.

She shuddered in between Dave and Neil, packed, coming apart over and over just as James had promised. Her orgasms lingered and merged into one seamless expression of pure euphoria.

"Ah, yes." James crooned. "Like that. Just like that."

He slipped from her slack jaw, his expanded cock slapping Dave's chin. When she struggled to reclaim him, she ended up rubbing her lips over his shaft. The motion created a sandwich out of her and Dave's mouths, which slathered sloppy kisses on James's erection while he thrust between their eager lips and tongues.

Kayla stared into Dave's eyes as they delivered pleasure to his friend. She thought she read more than lust in the depths of his gaze but her ecstasy-hazed brain could have imagined it.

Neil pillaged her rear, invading deeper with every fluid glide while James fucked their faces, the tip of his cock poking into either her or Dave's mouth on occasion. When it did, they sucked hard, drawing grunts from the slighter man at their side.

Dave's eyes rolled when Neil picked up the pace of his shuttling cock. The motion caressed Dave through the thin membrane inside her, eliciting a series of curses, pleas and groans from them all. She couldn't survive much more of this perpetual bliss.

The three men jammed her full—pussy, ass, mouth, heart and soul. Their genuine caring and commitment to gifting each other, including her, with as much pleasure as possible caused yet another burst of desire to obliterate her reasoning.

She rocked backward, enhancing each of Dave's and Neil's thrusts while increasing the frequency of the flickers of her tongue, which brushed along the head of James's cock. Dave's hard-on swelled impossibly inside her. Neil choked her hips in a bruising grip.

They pounded inside her, racing for the finish line.

James watched them all through slitted eyes, his long eyelashes dragging on his flushed cheeks. "Now."

His shout shattered the spell like a sonic boom. He threw back his head and groaned.

"Fuck, yes." Neil's abdomen slapped her ass a few more times then froze, impaling himself deep within her. "Now."

Dave roared a moment before molten liquid flooded her pussy. He consumed the strands of semen erupting from James's cock as he gifted her with jet after jet of his own pearly come. Neil surrendered, depositing his release into her ass. The proof of their satisfaction singed her, triggering one last tsunami of passion.

She writhed between Dave and James, crying out her appreciation. Neil withdrew his softening cock from her body and collapsed on the floor behind his mate. She didn't realize she mewled, her body shuddering with the remnants of passion, until all three men began to soothe her. Dave rolled to his side, facing his friends, cradling her close to his bellowing chest.

"You're fine, Kay. Don't panic." He panted into her hair with rough breaths. "Overwhelmed, that's all. Let it fade. Relax. Float down slow. We have all day. You were amazing. Did great."

She tried to settle, but the lingering twinges of her ass and pussy sent sparks up her spine, jolting her back to the intensity of their encounter, time after time. James slithered down her torso, petting her, calming her. He tapped her hip, pressing until she rolled to her back.

The twisting motion dislodged Dave's cock—impressive even half-hard.

Come dribbled from her enlarged pussy, running into the seam of her cheeks. The rivulet of fluid triggered another arc of electricity to ping her over-sensitized clit.

"No more." She moaned and scrunched her eyes closed.

Dave cupped her cheek and placed tender kisses at the corner of her mouth until she turned, accepting his gentle distraction. He held her immobile when James descended, cleaning her, pacifying her with tender laps of the flat of his tongue.

Kayla squealed and tried to evade the initial intensity. Neil and Dave rubbed her arms, her chest and her belly until the overstimulation melted into something delicious.

She sighed as she went boneless in their grips.

James sipped the last of their fluids from her pussy and ran his tongue over the glazed portal of her ass, until all scraps of tension abandoned her body. He laid his cheek on her belly and surrendered, as though savoring his own colossal relief.

She might be sore for a week, but it had been worth it.

Kayla snatched her apron from the magnetic hook on her refrigerator and tied the string in the back before preparing her grandmother's famous chicken soup along with extra salty-caramel hot chocolate for dinner. The guys would probably appreciate the heat.

She glanced out the window over the sink and giggled as they chased each other around the driveway, which they'd spent the last few hours clearing, embroiled in a massive snowball fight. Damn, they looked more scrumptious than the meal she assembled as they ran, dodged, tackled and shouted. Their open coats and soaked jeans would chill quickly in the setting sun.

The storm had passed sometime during the night. A little more than two feet of fluffy white precipitation had added up. After a few hours lounging around, telling stories of the years they'd known each other and asking about her history, the three men had paced the cabin, stir crazy.

Accustomed to physical exertion, they didn't do well idle.

She'd hinted at a million naughty ways to pass the time. If they noticed her innuendo, they'd done a brilliant job of hiding it. By mid-afternoon they'd decided to shovel the deck and porch to relieve the weight from the structure. They hadn't stopped until tidy paths led from the house to the generator and to the wood shed. The entire driveway had been cleared too.

The soup pot began to bubble, demanding her attention.

Not long after she'd dropped in chunks of onion and carrots, the back door opened and a racket the likes of which her little house had never known pre-crew echoed through her laundry room. Boots clattered to the hardwood floor. Curses followed when clumps of snow landed on bare skin.

"Leave everything in there and I'll wash it," she shouted over the ruckus of three men in a tiny room.

"Thanks, Kay." Neil grinned as he emerged first, chaffing his arms. "I'm gonna grab a shower. Fucking freezing."

"If you're cold, please put some clothes on. You don't have to be naked all the time because I'm a naturist." She peeked over her shoulder at James and Dave, who followed shortly after their friend.

"Just don't check out my package for a few minutes, all right?" Dave cupped his palm over his crotch. He grinned as he strode to her bar and kicked out a stool.

James disappeared with Neil. The patter of the shower kicked on a few seconds later.

"Aprons don't count as clothes?" Dave gave a low whistle when she spun toward her meal in progress.

White canvas framed her ass, putting it on display for the man lounging at the counter.

"Safety first." She winked at him as she passed by, intending to retrieve a lid from the storage space beneath the bar.

He snagged her around the waist and drew her to his side. His broad hands surrounded her cheeks, his fingers massaging the back of her head as he kissed her with a double dose of sugar and a hint of spice.

"What was that for?" She sighed, her heart skipping a beat.

"Your apron says, 'Kiss the cook!'"

She glanced down at her chest and laughed. "I guess it does, doesn't it?"

Was it too much to hope the easy familiarity they'd enhanced over the past day would last? The guys hadn't touched her since their wake-up fun—which had led straight to a mid-morning nap—at least not with intent to set her non-existent panties on fire.

Were they showing her there was more to their friendship than sex, or had they already gotten all they wanted?

"Dinner should be ready in fifteen minutes or less. I'll get the laundry going as soon as I set this to simmer."

"You don't have to wait on us, baby." He smiled. "Though, I'll admit it's kind of nice."

"I don't mind." She didn't lie. Making a home for the men felt right. Someday, she hoped for a family of her own to pamper. Until then, she'd have the guests at the spa. Making people comfortable was a gift of hers.

"Probably not a bad idea either." Dave rubbed the back of his neck. "Mike called about an hour ago. Looks like they're making decent progress on clearing the roads.

He thinks they'll be able to break through sometime tomorrow. Maybe before breakfast."

"Wow. That's...fast." She hadn't expected their time to end so soon.

"I know."

"Who died in here?" James traipsed into the kitchen, scrubbing his hair with a towel. Neil snapped him on the ass with his own wet terrycloth. The two men engaged in a mock-battle, oblivious to the questions zinging around the room.

"Hurry up, Dave." Neil shoved his friend toward the bathroom. "I'm starving. Don't want to wait once dinner's ready."

Kayla slid a sheet of rolls into the oven, wringing a groan from one of the men when she bent to adjust the racks. By the time she straightened, Dave was nowhere in sight.

Did it bother him to leave not knowing where they stood? She wished she could talk to him alone. Maybe tonight they could whisper in the shadows when Neil and James slept. It might be fun to plot their course like two clandestine lovers.

She grinned as she stripped off her apron and headed for the laundry room, passing the bathroom on the way. Dave's off-key rendition of Bruno Mar's section of "Nothin' On You" cracked her up and gave her hope as she shoveled their soggy sweatshirts and sexy jeans into her washing machine.

When only a pile of their socks and boxer briefs occupied the corners of her laundry basket, she tipped it into the circular opening, wondering at the heft remaining in the plastic tote. A resounding clunk startled her into releasing a ridiculous squeak.

"You okay?" Dave must have heard it too.

"Yeah."

"What was that?" he shouted from the room next door as he closed the taps. A moment later he poked his head around the corner.

She rummaged in the machine for source of the racket. "No idea."

"Why don't I finish this up for you?" Neil burst into the space as her fingers landed on something cool and heavy in the sea of fabric. Make that a couple of somethings.

"What the hell?" She rescued the objects from the washer, holding them up so the guys—including Dave—could see. "Someone missing a pair of...doodads? What are these things anyway?"

"Oh shit." Neil's eyes bulged. James crashed into Neil's back when his lover stopped short. He knocked Neil the rest of the way into the room.

"Tell me I'm not seeing this." Dave turned an unhealthy shade of purple.

"Somebody better start talking." Kayla's throat burned with acid. The guys shifted from foot to foot without fulfilling her command. She dropped the basket and set the objects on top of her dryer very carefully before saying again, much softer this time, "What are those?"

Neil cleared his throat. "They're spark plugs."

"What—" *Spark plugs. Oh, no. Spark plugs.* "As in a pretty fucking integral part of a truck engine?"

"Son of a bitch." Dave propped one hand on the frame of the bathroom doorway and lowered his head. "I *knew* it didn't sound right. You little shit."

"You tricked me?" She tried not to panic, but her breathing grew erratic and her stomach plummeted to her toes. "Why?"

No one said a word.

"You planned *this*?" She couldn't seem to make her brain understand what her heart already grasped. They'd cooked up a scheme to corner her alone. To worm into her bed...or onto her floor, as it happened. Her laugh sounded twisted even to her own ears. "Joke's on you then. All you had to do was ask to fuck me. I wanted you bad enough I would have bent over for you before the storm and you could have been on your merry way, without having to sacrifice the whole weekend."

"Jesus," Neil snarled. "That's not what—"

"Shut up, asshole." Dave silenced Neil with a slice of his hand through the air. "You've done enough, don't you think?"

"Four pissed off people in a tiny cabin. Awkward. You should have considered that before you lied to get your jollies." She stormed past the three men staring at her.

Dave didn't try to stop her from running or attempt a lame excuse. He let her go. Maybe it was easier for them both to end things quick.

Painless.

Except it hurt like hell.

"I'll stay upstairs until you can leave in the morning. Let yourselves out."

KAYLA BROKE her promise not to look out the window. Minutes after the buzz of small engines shattered the ultimate stillness of the mountain, and her cabin, she stole a glance out of her bedroom. The crew, all of them, hadn't left. Three snowmobiles littered her frosted yard. Neil, James and Dave stood in a half circle, their hands jammed in their coat pockets. They faced Mike and Joe—

along with two women who could only be Kate and Morgan.

From inside, Kayla couldn't hear their conversation. Their faces spoke volumes. The men headed for the transportation. A sob cracked her resolve not to shed another tear over the studs who'd rocked her world then shattered her dreams.

The women stood their ground. When Mike waved, encouraging them to hop on the snowmobiles, the shorter one shook her head. Instead, she grabbed the other woman's hand and marched toward the cabin.

Maybe she needs to use the bathroom. Please, please, just have to pee.

No such luck.

"Hello?" A friendly greeting filled Kayla's sanctuary along with the whisper of snow jackets shedding onto her foyer floor. "Sorry to intrude, we know you're here and probably don't want to talk to us—"

"So what are we doing, Kate?" The other woman spoke softly, but her question carried. Unlike the hushed argument Dave, Neil and James had had the night before. Kayla's hitching sobs had obscured the sound carrying across the short distance in that case.

"We're coming up, Kayla."

"I'm naked." She hoped to scare them off.

"Nothing we haven't seen before," Morgan chimed in, supporting her friend's decision. Kayla hated the jealous pout overtaking her face for a moment.

The two women reached the top of the stairs and took in the tight quarters. "This place is super cute. I'm Kate."

"Hi." Kayla smiled despite herself at the woman's direct approach and her refusal to avoid looking at Kayla's nudity.

"Morgan." The other woman held out her hand, but didn't stop with a shake. She leaned in and hugged Kayla. "I'm sorry we had to meet like this. I've heard bunches about you."

"Are you okay?" Kate sat cross-legged on the end of her bed. "Dumb question, I know. It wasn't right to leave without coming to see how you're doing first. Can we do anything for you?"

"How about finding me a new construction crew so I don't have to be mortified every day when your guys come to work?" Kayla crashed into the pile of pillows on her bed then buried her face in her hands.

"If anything, Neil, Dave and James are the ones who should be ashamed." Morgan patted her knee.

"It was Neil who thought up this brilliant scheme." Kate rolled her eyes. "It's hard to believe now, but he meant well. He played matchmaker. Not like you four needed any help."

"Yeah, Dave didn't know anything about it," Morgan chimed in. "He's kicking himself because he heard the difference in the engine and still didn't force the issue. I think he was glad for the chance to stay. He's been dying to ask you out for weeks."

"It's true. It broke his heart to hear you crying up here last night, assuming you wouldn't welcome his comfort." Morgan put a hand on Kayla's shoulder. Though they'd just met, Kayla went with it, resting her head on Kate's thigh. "I know it doesn't fix what they did, but they're guys. Pretty awesome most of the time—"

"And dumb as shit the rest." Morgan rolled her eyes.

The door opened and shut once more. No one spoke up. Kayla swore she could smell Dave's unique scent, a combination of oak and cinnamon.

"Will you hear him out at least?" Kate vouched for one of her fiancé's best friends. "I'm sure he won't screw up again.

"I can't promise that." Dave's baritone lacked its usual luster. He climbed the stairs slowly, giving her the chance to throw him out. She didn't. "But I'll try my best to make you happy."

His nostrils flared when he spotted the three women sitting together.

The gaze scanning her form made her feel vulnerable in the nude for the first time in her life. Another thing he'd promised to understand then ruined.

"We'll wait outside." Kate and Morgan inched toward the stairs. "No matter what, we'd like to hear from you. Maybe we can have lunch sometime soon?"

"I'd like that." Kayla realized her polite response held more than a kernel of truth. "Thank you."

Dave waited until they shut the door behind them. "Kay, I'm so sorry."

"For what?" If he really had been in the dark about Neil's plotting, why hadn't he said so?

"For ignoring the facts. For letting myself go along with something I knew was wrong even if I didn't figure out all the details. For backing down without a fight. For leaving you to suffer last night. For hurting you." He deflated, sinking to the edge of her mattress. "Kate and Morgan informed me I fucked up at every turn."

Kayla couldn't help it. She laughed through the tears stinging her eyes.

"Truly, I'm so very sorry." He reached out and touched her hand. "If nothing else, for ruining the brief time we did have together. I'll never forget that."

Instant sparks arced from the point of contact

throughout her body. "I forgive you. And Neil. Thanks for coming in to straighten things out. At least now I won't feel so awkward when you come to work."

He stared at her so long she thought she might have misunderstood.

"Unless you don't plan to finish the job. If you give me recommendations—"

"We *always* finish the job." Dave leaned closer, treating her to the spice of his skin blended with her shower gel. "Don't you want anything more from me, Kay? Or did I ruin what I thought we had?"

"Me? You're the one who backed away. Even before the...incident. You didn't touch me at all after yesterday morning."

"I saw you wince when I pulled out." He closed his eyes and breathed deep for a minute. "You were tender. We didn't want to hurt you."

"I thought..."

"Oh, crap." He stared at her with dilated pupils. "You thought what? That I'd taken my fill? That I'd gotten what I came for?"

She bit her lip and nodded.

Dave shot to his feet and opened the window. He shouted out to his friends. "Go ahead without me. I'm staying."

A round of cheers, hoots and claps had a blush rising to her cheeks.

"Tell Kay I'm sorry." Neil's shout rose above the crew's celebration.

"See you tomorrow," Joe called up a moment before engines, with fully functional spark plugs, hummed once more.

"Baby." Dave took a deep breath as he climbed into

her bed and lay down beside her. "I haven't given you a reason to trust me yet. I'll prove myself to you however it takes. Yeah, you're sexy as sin and I love watching you come apart. I admire your adventurous side in and out of bed and hope to indulge it. Regularly. More than that, I adore your spirit, your laughter and your all-around brightness. I'd love to have you as part of my life. For the long run. Above all, I'm praying right now that your soul is as attracted to mine as mine is to yours. That you want to join my family, the crew, and make me the happiest guy in a two state radius. The king of this mountain."

"Only if I can be your queen."

"I never considered you a plaything." He nibbled her knuckles as if paying homage. "I'll kick Neil's scrawny ass for making you doubt my commitment for even an instant."

"Can we take things slow?" She admitted part of her reluctance stemmed from her own actions. She'd rushed into bed with him. The rash decision had eroded her confidence in their compatibility outside of the most magnificent sex of her life. The intensity of the chemistry they generated shocked her. Frightened her. Would it last? She hoped it could.

"Of course." He opened his arms. "Whatever it takes."

Kayla slid into his embrace and felt like she'd come home. She smiled against Dave's cotton-covered chest. "I'm so glad you came back."

"I'll never leave you again." He stroked her hair from her cheek, lulling her toward a nap after their restless night. "You're stuck with me."

She burrowed deeper into him, resting her hand above the steady beat of his heart.

"Sleep baby, I've got you. Maybe you'll have a dream as great as the one I had two nights ago."

"You never told me about it," she mumbled.

"It was crazy. Vivid. The most realistic one I've ever had. I saw you and I together, at Mike and Kate's wedding. You were gorgeous in a light green dress."

"I hate dresses."

He chuckled. "You'd wear one if it made Kate happy."

She couldn't argue.

He took a deep breath then whispered, "A diamond ring sparkled on your finger as we danced and twirled under the lights on the spring evening. I could smell the flowers. It was magical. Perfect. Only odd thing was you kept looking over your shoulder to a table where Neil and James sat."

"They wouldn't miss Mike's wedding for the world." She couldn't address the rest of his vision—her chest ached at the image and she swore she could picture it too. Crazy.

"No, but they weren't alone."

"What?" She tried to focus. Instead, she slipped away. The last of her anxiety fled, stealing her starch.

"Weird." He mumbled as he cradled her closer. "A woman sat between them, and she kept smiling at you. At us. Anyway, it was nice."

"Sounds like it."

He kissed her temple then whispered, "Sweet dreams."

They were sweet.

And *extra* naughty.

Through every one, Dave stayed by her side.

DEVON'S PAIR
POWERTOOLS
JAYNE RYLON
NEW YORK TIMES BESTSELLING AUTHOR

PROLOGUE

Neil swiped work-scuffed knuckles over his gaping lips to ensure no drool escaped. He couldn't help but stare. Painted toes peeped from strappy sandals. They led his bulging eyes to a delicate ankle then up the pretty, tanned calf that poked beneath the open door of a beastly black truck. The sexy shoe rested on the running board before its equally delicious owner hopped down to street-level right outside the crew's current fixer-upper.

Maybe the pick-up wasn't any bigger than the one he and James owned. It could have been the sultry yet petite driver who made it seem as enormous as the whale sharks he and his boyfriend had spotted while snorkeling in Mexico last year. There too, most anything would have seemed gargantuan beside the glorious plum smuggler that had hugged James's svelte hips as though he'd been shrink-wrapped into it.

Neil shook his head to clear the tropical memories of his lover. Between them and the chance run-in with this woman—one he'd love to lure inside and share with

James—he'd be sure to sport wood when he met their new employee.

The lecture James had delivered on their ride in this morning resounded in his mind. *"Try to tone it down until we get to know him, okay? The new guy might not be as accepting as the rest of the crew of our wild liaisons."*

Not many people were.

Wouldn't be good if their recently hired apprentice quit before lunch.

The dude hadn't showed yet, which meant Neil had to hang out here on the curb and wait for the schmuck. A mutual friend had highly recommended Devon Giles right when they'd decided they could use some temporary help. Most of the rest of the crew settled into new relationships and needed a little extra personal time compared to usual. After a bunch of debates, they'd agreed to try adding someone to their tight-knit group on a trial basis.

Running late on day one wouldn't earn the guy any brownie points.

Still, the sweet view made up for abandoning James, who'd already started tearing up the shitty old flooring by himself. Neil hated to let his partner shoulder more than his fair share. Generous and hardworking, his mate would push himself harder than he should. Neil swore he'd make it up to James with a killer back rub and slow, relaxed sex.

Maybe sooner rather than later if he ate his fill of such sweet eye candy.

The woman sauntered around to the other side of her truck and caused Neil to wonder if he was dreaming when she shucked her cornflower blue peasant blouse right there in the soft light of the spring morning. She left her racer-backed sports bra in place as she kicked off those sinful shoes and covered her cute pink pedicure with thick white socks before slipping her dainty feet into sturdy...construction boots?

What the—?

The petite-yet-toned woman's jacked arms flexed as she strapped a canvas tool belt around her miniscule waist. A hammer hung from one of the loops over her khaki cargo shorts. She flipped a pair of sunglasses onto her head. The eyewear, which had more in common with safety goggles than designer shades, pinned her cute bob of ash blonde hair off her striking face. The swell of her perfect ass stunned him as she reached into the truck. Next thing he knew, she had retrieved a large water bottle, locked up the vehicle and headed in his direction.

It was then he met her gaze. An uncommon shade of gorgeous jade-green eyes, which he'd only seen once before—on James—snared his attention. Her seamless mix of tomboy charm with pixie sass entranced him. When she noticed him and smiled, offering a small wave as she approached, he realized he was royally screwed.

The world popped into slow motion. His heart stuttered in its pounding beat and the ground lurched below his feet as he experienced the same supposedly once-in-a-lifetime sensation he'd had the day he'd met James, when their professor assigned partners in their trade school lab.

Love at first sight.

Oh, fuck.

Devon cringed when the hottie construction worker's smile morphed into a major grimace.

Not again. Damn it.

Her sister's roommate had rambled on and on about the *amazing* crew when she'd spotted the opening for an apprentice in an online job ad. Julie had promised Devon the all-guy team of five was forward-thinking, accepting and had a lot to teach her, though she refused to go into detail on how she'd learned of their reputation.

Give them a chance, Dev.

"Good morning. I'm..."

"Devon Giles. Of course." He scrubbed his hand through his messy hair before taking her fingers with a measured action more suitable for reaching for a viper than a trainee. "I was expecting someone—"

"With a dick?" She canted her head and planted her fist on her hip, daring him to deny it while hoping she'd misinterpreted his sour puss.

He barked out a laugh. "Well, yeah, I suppose."

"Look, if this is going to be an issue, I'd rather head out now than waste time—yours or mine. I'm a damned good worker and—"

"Hey." A man with a soft, kind voice interrupted her rant before the gorgeous, but assholish, guy could backpedal. "I thought I heard someone pull up."

Did she imagine the way the new arrival brushed against the first guy as though he were a cat winding around his owner's ankle?

"Ah..."

The taller guy grunted. "Yeah. *This* is Devon."

"Pleased to meet you." The smaller man's shake was firm, which she appreciated. She didn't need them to make any concessions for her. "I'm James."

"And I'm Neil." The original guy surprised her by pressing a kiss to her knuckles.

"Okay, Romeo." She had to nip this shit in the bud or it would spiral out of control. After the last job she'd had to leave—when the foreman deluded himself into believing she'd take orders to bend over as well as she did instructions on leveling framing jobs—she wouldn't risk giving anyone the wrong idea. "Enough of that nonsense. Would you have done that if I were the man you expected this morning?"

"Maybe. If he were as cute as you are." He laughed when James smacked him on the ass.

Holy shit. No mistaking the easy, familiar contact or the heat in the men's eyes when their gazes met and locked. Maybe she *had* found the perfect employers. If they were gay, they might leave her to work and develop her skills in peace.

The spring was looking brighter by the second.

1

———

"Dev, could you grab another tube of caulk off the back of my truck? This one isn't going to make it." Dave had squished his mammoth frame into the standard tub to run a bead around the base of the tile work she'd installed with his guidance. Of course, she'd added a little of her own flair to the design. As she surveyed it now, she had to say it'd come out better than she'd imagined.

Rewarding her for a job he approved of, Dave had done the grunt work and saved her back some strain. Pleasing the crew could be tough. The guys had lofty standards. In the past three weeks, she'd learned tons and had started surpassing their expectations. When she did, they made sure she knew it.

Dooming Dave to unfolding and refolding that stunning body would be torture. For both him and her, watching. "Devon?"

"Sorry." She cleared her throat. "Yeah, I've got it. Be right back."

She jogged down the hall. Plastic sheeting covered

new hardwood planks that made her light footfalls crunch in the long, empty space. Mike and Joe perked up as she trotted past the master bedroom where they were installing recessed lighting, which would add some flair to the space.

"Hey, Dev. You two almost ready for lunch? I'm starving." Mike looked pretty damn hungry when he glanced in her direction. Silly to wonder if that smoky look meant anything more than desire for the packed meal his adorable fiancée had shipped him off with this morning.

"Mmm. Yeah." Joe rubbed his flat belly. Dear God, did they have to work without shirts so much? It was enough to drive any red-blooded woman insane. "Morgan's testing out new cookies again. She sent a big box for us to share."

"And how many did you eat for breakfast?" She loved teasing the crew.

"As many as I could shove in my mouth on the drive in." He winked at her.

"Well, we all know your mouth is capable of some pretty amazing feats." Mike poked Joe in the ribs with the handle of his needle-nose pliers. "Hand me that housing so we can wrap up. Tell Neil and James they've got about fifteen minutes 'til break."

"Right-o, foreman." She saluted then jumped when Dave's yell reached her loud and clear.

"Dev! You coming or what? I'm going to be pulling a Taft soon."

"Definitely or what," Joe bellowed for her, somehow still managing to pout. "We're not that lucky. Give her a second. Mike distracted her. Besides, if you get stuck I know where to find some lube."

"Don't you usually grease up to try and get in, not out?" Mike's wicked grin sent shivers along her spine.

She pretended to dismiss his dirty implications with an eye roll and a little finger wave then continued her jog down the stairs. Thank God they couldn't tell how slick the tops of her thighs were. They were guys. Five of them, in all their sweaty and sexy glory. Holy testosterone overload. They couldn't help themselves and somehow their equal opportunity jokes didn't bother her. They aimed them at each other as often as they did at her. Being left out of the good-natured teasing probably would have made things awkward.

Luckily, she didn't know for sure. The crew had made her feel at home from the moment James had saved her from that uncomfortable start with Neil on the curb outside this house. The renovations had come a long way in the past three weeks. Within a month they'd be wrapping the place up with a big ass ribbon for the future owners. Moving on from the project she'd come to associate with her mentors would suck. Between the crew and their women, she'd instantly inherited eight new friends. Spending the spring with them would be no hardship.

It was leaving at the end of the internship that worried her. Maybe if she buckled down and absorbed as much as she could from them, they'd have a permanent spot for her as they headed into summer and the end of their three-month arrangement.

Lost in her thoughts, she didn't hear the rustle of denim on denim or the soft moans echoing in the vacant living room until it was too late. Devon burst onto the main level of the house, where Neil was making a late-morning snack out of James's parted lips.

She lurched to a dead stop.

Move. Look away. Keep going.

Devon couldn't force her legs to walk on past. Not when the fire between the two men burned hot enough to have tiny beads of sweat dotting her upper lip. She licked the salty sheen, wishing she could taste the partners' passion instead.

Pure devotion laced every tender sweep of James's fingers over Neil's bare shoulder, warring with the desperation of their mouths, as though they couldn't stand to be apart. Yet she could see the warm spring sunlight from the bay window behind them streaming between their torsos.

A golden beam cut through the dust in the air. It led her stare to the juncture of the men's bodies. They hadn't embraced closer because Neil fisted a double helping of beefy cock in his right hand, massaging their erections in time to the flicker of their tongues. He squeezed their shafts together. The tip of his cock tucked against James's balls though James's hard-on only reached most of the way back to Neil's groin. With a firm grip—much harder than Devon would have been comfortable administering—Neil made several circuits with his fist, drawing a sweet whimper from James.

The plea morphed into a groan as Neil's hand shuttled faster between them. James arched his hips, still wrapped in the ripped jeans he wore so well. The fly had been left open, allowing the V of denim to frame his cock. Devon wished she could see Neil's fine ass, but his pants remained mostly in place.

Would he guide the pair toward the inevitable conclusion of their escalating exchange? Or would he yank his hand free, bend James over the nearby sawhorse and ride...

"Devon!" Dave's holler broke through the steam fogging her brain.

She jumped several inches off the brand new hardwood planks, which the duo making out in the corner had laid this morning. Her boot knocked into a forgotten scrap board. It launched in the couple's direction, skittering across the unpolished surface with a scratchy racket they couldn't ignore.

James blinked.

He met her gaze, his eyes widening when he caught her spying on their break.

"Oh my God. I'm so sorry." Her cheeks blazed. She hadn't considered their privacy. Not that they should have expected any here. Still, she could have respected their relationship instead of ogling them as if they were stars in a seedy peep show.

Worse yet, when had her fingers strayed between her legs, pressing on the soaked crotch of her cut-off jean shorts? She stumbled backward.

"Dev, wait." Neil took a stride in her direction. His rock-solid cock bobbed and waved. He cursed as he tried to tuck it inside the unzipped flap of his jeans. As if that measly scrap of fabric had any chance of obscuring his impressive erection from view.

She bolted for Dave's truck, planted one palm on the open tailgate and boosted herself into the bed. In less than ten seconds, she'd snagged a tube of caulk at random and hustled up the driveway to the garage entrance. No way was she retracing her steps.

How could she face Neil and James after copping a self-feel at their display?

How could she have resisted the genuine love urging them to take the opportunity to bond? She'd never seen anything so beautiful in her whole life. Not even the gardens at Versailles that she'd studied endlessly in hopes of adding landscaping to her list of handywoman skills.

"WHAT THE HELL TOOK SO LONG?" Dave grunted. "My knees are turning into ground beef. Now I get why Kay hates blowing me in the shower. I'm never suggesting it again. Unless… Hmm. I could always hold her upside down, use the wall to—"

"Gah!" A strangled gurgle escaped her throat. Were they *trying* to give her a heart attack?

"Shit. Sorry, Dev. I forget you're not one of the guys sometimes." He winked. "Planning to give me that caulk or do you really think it's going to keep you safe from my wicked ways?"

She forced her fingers to uncurl one by one from the tube she hadn't realized she'd aimed in his direction like a gloppy version of a vampire hunter's stake.

"Seriously. Are you okay?" He tilted his head, his eyes narrowing. "I didn't mean to make you uncomfortable. Smack us upside the head if we get too wild for you."

"I don't think they'd have appreciated that," she mumbled below her breath.

"What?" Dave accepted the cylinder then frowned. "Devon, this is clear silicone. We were using white to blend with the grout, remember? Is that what took so long? If you're not sure of something just ask. It's okay. You're here to learn."

"For Pete's sake." She slapped her hands on the outside of her thighs hard enough to sting both the skin there and her palms. "I know the fucking difference between clear and opaque caulk."

"Whoa." Dave climbed to his feet with hardly a wince as he focused on her, his voice softening. "What's happening here?"

She hated the tremble in her quads. Surrendering to the weakness, she let it drop her to the closed lid of the horrid shell-pink toilet they planned to replace after they finished the shower. Her head felt like a fifty-pound bowling ball in her hands.

The big man, who'd just escaped the torture of the bathtub, crouched beside her, ignoring the pop and crackle of his poor joints. He rubbed one broad hand over her back in big circles. "Calm down, sweetheart."

"Don't fucking call me that." She may have objected, but she couldn't make herself brush off his platonic touch. "Would you use frilly nicknames for the rest of the crew?"

"Yeah, he probably would." Mike leaned against the jamb, nodding to Dave when the other man shot him a clear *mayday* look. "Devon got an eyeful of Neil and James trying to sneak a quickie. We warned them about trying shit like that these days."

"Damn it." Dave rubbed his temples.

"Does *these days* mean since I've been around?" Could she be cramping everyone's style? What rabbit hole had she tumbled down if that were true? This time *she* might be the one causing discomfort on the job site by forcing team members to repress their sexuality for fear of making things awkward.

Ah, crap. How was that for karma?

There was a difference between asking assholes at prior sites to keep their hands off her ass every time she bent over and forcing two men obviously in love to hide their affection.

Okay, so maybe there'd been too much for anyone's official workplace standards going on in the living room. If she'd forced them to keep a lid on it for weeks, it was no wonder they'd erupted in a spectacular display of passion. The two of them had the real deal. She refused to allow jealousy to turn her appreciation green.

"I think we'd better have a staff meeting. Come on you two. We'll eat our lunches and talk this through with the whole crew." Mike addressed them both though his warm eyes melted on her. "No slouching, newbie. You didn't screw up. They owe *you* an apology."

"No—"

Mike waved her off before she could explain. "Save it. We'll figure things out together."

She stood and accepted a hand from both men. Though their broad shoulders wouldn't permit them to walk side by side, they didn't let go as they formed a chain and headed downstairs together.

2

———

Devon grabbed her reusable lavender lunch pouch from the pile on the kitchen counter. The pretty bag stuck out like a sore thumb in the mix of dented aluminum boxes and crumpled paper sacks. She couldn't help humming a snippet of that old Sesame Street song, "One Of These Things (Is Not Like The Others)".

Neil had claimed the red plastic cooler, which was far too large for one man's sustenance even considering the astounding stomach capacity the guys in the crew possessed.

What other enormous appetites could they have?

Refusing to give in to the urge to huddle in the corner and let Mike navigate the tricky waters they'd found themselves in, Devon inserted herself between Neil and Joe, who leaned one hip against the crappy Formica they hadn't yet replaced with granite. His long, powerful legs were stretched out and crossed at the ankle.

"Could I get a boost?" She smiled when he nearly encircled her waist with his long fingers then lifted her as though she weighed less than a bag of cement. Tucking her legs under her in the front, she sat cross-legged, pleased to be somewhere near eye level with most of the crew.

"Sure thing, pipsqueak." Joe ignored her glare in favor of scooping up his prime sandwich for another colossal bite that demolished a fourth of the generous entrée in one fell swoop.

"Is that fresh-baked wheat?" Her mouth watered. Suddenly her PB&J on Wonder bread with a side of baby carrots and celery sticks didn't sound so appealing.

"Yeah, want a taste?" Joe ripped off a piece of the bread and held it out. "I think Morgan added some honey and oats or something. She's a goddess."

Devon didn't think anything of eating it from his fingers until she caught the strangled groan from Neil. Her knee brushed his ribs, which fluttered against her in time to his rapid respiration. Maybe he and James hadn't finished their session after her extra-rude interruption.

"Devon—" he began as she also spoke.

"I'm sorry. Didn't mean to ruin your fun." When James attempted to cut her off, she only talked louder. "Believe me, I understand what it's like to hide in plain sight. I would never wish that on anyone else. I hope that you won't let having me around change your behavior. If the rest of these guys can handle watching you two *work* together, then so can I."

"As enticing as that offer is, I'm not sure you know what you're asking for, Dev." Neil angled his torso toward her, his hand coming to rest on her stacked ankles. She tried not to thrust her pelvis at him when his knuckles brushed her pussy. Mistake or not, she didn't care. A persistent throb had taken up a slow, steady pulse in her core. He had the ability to soothe it. If only he weren't already in a relationship with a man he adored.

"Uh, the unintentional demonstration you gave was a pretty good indicator." She bared her teeth, hoping she looked like she was smiling instead of flashing a big-bad-wolf grin. All the better to eat them with. They'd been delicious together.

"That was nothing." James slinked toward her, coming to rest along Neil's side. A mysterious twinkle in his eye roused her curiosity. She tuned in to his teasing smirk. Did James bait her...or his boyfriend?

"Oh really?" She refused to be cowed. "Then why were you about to crawl inside him?"

"I think what James means to say is that we're used to doing a hell of a lot more together than jacking off. What you witnessed was only the tip of the iceberg." Mike corralled the crew, ensuring they didn't veer off course when so much remained unspoken.

More than *that*. She blinked.

"Really? And who's *we*? I've met your girlfriend, Dave." She waved her hand at Joe and Mike. "And your fiancées. Are you trying to say you're cheating on them? With each other?"

"Hold up a minute with the stink eye. We'd never lie to our girls." Mike corrected her. "They know everything. They've all played along at some point or another. More than once if you want the truth. And, well... We're still figuring things out. It's new. Different. We've sort of settled on an unofficial look-but-don't-touch policy. And we all reap the benefits of sharing those stories at home."

"Mmm." Joe's moan echoed three times louder than the one he'd surrendered at the taste of his lover's cookies. "Morgan *loves* hearing about what kind of trouble Neil and James get into. And when the four of us meet up, well, sometimes things evolve."

"Except *these days* I've been keeping you all apart?" She glanced from man to man.

Joe pushed potato chips around the paper plate he'd set his sandwich on. Dave studied the paint splatters on his jeans, and James reached for Neil's hand.

Mike swallowed hard then manned up. "Yeah. I'm sorry, Devon. We shouldn't have put you in the middle like this. We thought long and hard about bringing someone else into the crew. You're really a great addition. I'd swear we've known you a lot longer than a few weeks. You work hard, you learn fast and you never complain. You're fun to work with, and you've earned our respect. I think that's why these two felt comfortable enough to revert to our old tricks."

"Plus Neil is sporting a boner every time you're nearby." Dave winked at her. "That's got to make it hard to get work done."

"What?" she sputtered. She'd thought the pair was gay. Were they saying she worked with five sexy and sweet bisexual men? *Wow.*

Joe slapped Dave upside the head. "When will you learn to think before opening that big mouth?"

"You never complained about my mouth before." Dave parted his lips and wiggled his tongue in his friend's direction.

"Holy shit." She clutched her pounding heart and rocked herself like a trauma victim.

A hush descended over the usually boisterous men. She'd never heard them so quiet or seen them so still. It was almost as though someone had sculpted five perfect figures and replaced the guys with decoys.

"Does it bother you that much to think of us screwing around with each other?" James tipped his head.

"What?" The blood rushed from her face. "You think I'm grossed out?"

"Look at you." He reached toward her slowly, laying a gentle hand on her shoulder. He massaged her tense muscles with a steady, mild pressure.

"You're right. I'm upset." She bit her lip, trying to figure out how to explain.

Dave muttered a curse in the background.

"But not by the thought of you...sharing...each other and your girlfriends." Did they notice her fidgeting as she tried to contain the desire bubbling within her like an effervescent spring?

"Then what's wrong?" Neil laid his shaking fingers on her knee.

Devon swore a current flowed from his hand to James's, which lingered on the other side of her body. Electricity arced between the two points, lighting up every nerve ending between them. She shivered. "I thought I'd grown close to you all. Like a part of the team. And all along I've forced you to obscure who you really are. What you really feel. I've become everything I hated about the crews I worked with before. I've done to you exactly what they did to me—making me erase any traces of femininity so that I didn't upset their delicate sensibilities. I stole your freedom."

"To be fair, we didn't give you an option." Mike scrubbed his face. "I think this is my fault, not yours. I convinced the guys it'd be better this way. I should have known we can't change our nature. We've been spoiled. Indulged our cravings for close to a decade. Quitting cold turkey was never going to work."

Was he referring to her joining the team or to the changes they'd made after hooking up with Kate, Morgan and Kayla? She couldn't help them with the bigger picture, but she could solve her piece of the puzzle.

She plucked her unopened lunch bag from the counter. Her appetite might never return after she did what she should. Still, she scooted toward the edge of the counter. "I agree."

"You do?" Neil aimed a broad smile in her direction. The gorgeous expanse of his brilliant white teeth mesmerized her for a moment.

"Yes." She sighed. "So I'm sorry to say... I quit."

"What?" Dave whipped toward her so fast she flinched.

"Settle down." Mike put a restraining hand on his friend. "No one's going anywhere yet."

"I won't cramp your style." She shook her head.

"You're telling me you don't want to see the grand finale?" Mike crowded her, tucking in tight beside James, invading Joe's territory. The rest of the crew observed and she swore she didn't spot a single one of them blink. "Be honest, Devon. You liked what you saw. I can smell you. Hell, even upstairs I could tell."

She tried to cross her legs. No room to move. Suddenly there seemed to be hard bodies closing in from every side. Like a castaway floating in shark-infested waters, she suddenly imagined she could be dessert.

"I've known these guys a long time." Mike shifted his focus to Neil and James. He studied them for a while before continuing. "Unless I'm completely off the mark, there's potential here for something great. Something new. Dave might have been crude, but he wasn't wrong. Neil has it bad for you."

"What?" She whipped her head around to face the tall, lanky construction worker. "Of all the crew, you've been the least friendly. I thought I finally knew why. I'd be grumpy too if I were sexually frustrated all day."

Like she'd been for the past three weeks.

"No, honey." James saved his partner from explaining. "I think he was trying to keep his hands to himself. I was teasing him about it earlier. The way he watches you. I kept telling him to imagine what it'd be like if he asked you to play. If you said yes. That's what pushed him over the edge, made him take the risk. I'd give this man anything to make him happy. And he does want you. Something fierce."

She considered James's unasked question. Could she trade an afternoon of pleasure for potentially ruining an amazing job? Wouldn't it all be over anyway if she couldn't find a way to go forward?

Devon took a deep breath then pretended to be a hell of a lot more bold than she felt. She turned toward Neil and peered deep into his eyes. She read desire there. In response, she unleashed the matched answer from her center. It had infuriated her to find him so damn attractive. Especially when she'd thought he wished she was the normal guy he'd expected that first day. Now that she knew the truth, she couldn't resist.

His hair was soft between her fingers as she took hold of the unruly waves and tugged him to her for a scorching kiss. Initiative dissolved under his delayed assault. He came to life, as though his boundaries melted at the first contact of their lips. After what seemed like an eternity, she tilted her head before she suffocated. He'd stolen her breath.

A groan reminded her of their audience. Especially this man's lover. She cleared her throat.

"What about you, James? Is this what *you* want?" Power filled her when she focused her vision only to discover the naked longing in his gaze. "To watch your boyfriend with a woman?"

"Works for me. Especially if I can have a taste of you too." He leaned closer to nibble a path down her arm. When he reached her hand, he took her middle finger into his mouth and sucked. The tip of his tongue flicked against her sensitive pad in a swirling figure eight that left her gasping.

"No kidding." Neil rumbled a laugh behind her. "He's fucking amazing. The things he does with that mouth should be a crime."

"Show me." She panted. "Show *us.*"

"Hell yes." Joe abandoned the rest of his sandwich. He rushed into the other room and snagged a freshly laundered drop cloth. They'd planned to use it to protect the floor they'd just finished laying. The canvas rumpled as he shook it out over the open space where the breakfast nook would normally be.

A squeal escaped her when Neil growled and scooped her into his arms. She clung to him like a baby koala, wrapping her arms and legs around his fine body.

"That's right," he crooned. "I won't drop you."

His hands squeezed her ass before he tipped forward, depositing her on the makeshift bed Joe, Dave and Mike ringed. James knelt beside her, pillowing her head on his thigh.

Neil stared into her eyes and then those of his lover. "Gorgeous. Your eyes. They're exactly the same. A perfect match. My favorite color."

James wiggled his brows at Neil. "Now how about you

admire hers up close and personal. Kiss her again. Make love to her. I want to watch you let go."

"Wait!" The five men froze instantly at Devon's protest. "I won't steal this from James. I saw how bad he needed you before."

"There will be plenty of time for that later." James stroked her cheek. "He's dying for you. It's been growing over the past few weeks. Give him what he needs. Please?"

"Thank you." Neil looked back and forth between her and James. "Thank you for understanding. Thank you for sharing."

Devon sighed when the men kissed above her. She stared at them. Their mouths clashed and soothed over and over. Her hand snaked to her mound again, unable to ignore the ache there.

"*Ahem.*" Mike cleared his throat in a rather exaggerated chuckle. "Don't forget our guest so soon."

"And what about you?" It unnerved her to see so many faces hovering above her as she wobbled on the edge of surrender.

"Will it bother you if we jack off while we watch?" Mike didn't hem and haw, he cut straight to the chase. "God, it's been so long."

She bit her lip and shook her head. Is this what it felt like to be the star of a play, with so many watching on the fringes of the action? For the first time, she understood how that rush could be addictive. She had her own show as they unfastened their pants.

Holy crap. "Is this really happening?"

"Only if you're okay with it. Tell us if it's too much." Neil sank low over her. The pressure of his erection tucking against her swollen mound through their clothes inspired a wave of delight to break over her. Still, he didn't devour her. The hard shell he'd maintained for weeks cracked, revealing something tender and gentle beneath. "They're right, you know."

"About?" Her concentration fractured with so many distractions. Soft groans fell on them like gentle rain from the showers that had fed the blossoming flowers lately. Mike, Dave and Joe rubbed their chests and hard abs. They dipped long fingers into their pants as Neil and James seduced her.

"How much I want you." He nibbled a path from her ear to her jaw. "From the first moment I saw you. I needed this. You."

"You didn't know me." She rolled her eyes. "Don't be ridiculous."

"There's something about you. You're tough, compact and still so damn adorable." He rubbed their noses together. "I'm sorry I didn't make you feel welcome. There was no way I could without doing *this*."

His fingers inched up from her hip. They tucked beneath her black tank top with built-in bra. He caressed her ribs then fit his palm over her smallish breast. "A perfect handful."

"Here. Let us see what you're feeling." James reached between her and Neil. He snagged the hem of her shirt and walked it up her torso.

Devon helped by raising her arms, allowing him to peel off her top.

They worked as a team. Neil didn't bother to unbutton her cargo shorts when he shimmied them from her hips.

She wished she'd worn something flirty beneath, but she'd come to work, not frolic in the attention of her five spectacular bosses despite what they'd done in her dreams last night. Her lack of sexy lingerie didn't matter anyway. Neil dispatched her white bikini briefs with little ceremony. Completely bare, she held still as he stared at her, laid out before him.

"Jesus, she's pretty. You know how to pick 'em." James muttered, still supporting her shoulders so she lay at a slight incline.

"Damn straight." Neil grinned at his partner. "I claimed you, didn't I?"

The rest of the crew chuckled though the sound held an edge she didn't remember hearing in the past. Their corded necks and heavy breathing assured her she hadn't imagined it.

Neil ran his hands over her flat belly toward the soft, bare skin above her pussy. James took over where his boyfriend had left off, cupping the gentle swell of her breasts and brushing his thumbs over her beaded nipples. The dual approach had her struggling to keep her eyes open. No way was she about to miss out on the scrumptious scenery.

"No fair." She didn't worry that a whine carried her objection.

Neil's fingers brushed the top of her slit, dipping into the slickness coating her bare lips as her hips rose to meet him. He didn't seem very apologetic when he asked, "What's that, Dev?"

"I want to see you too. All of you." Whether she meant Neil naked or the entire crew bare, well, it didn't really matter. Both were honest desires.

Devon didn't have to ask twice. The distinctive *whoosh* of well-worn denim surrounded her as five men shucked their jeans. She would have liked to have the willpower to resist checking out their tools but who could deny themselves that kind of eye candy?

Her eyes widened as she realized just how much fun the men's lovers had gorged on. With bodies like those and the skill she knew they harnessed in using them... Well, it was a good thing only James and Neil were left unattached or her head would probably have exploded from passionate overload.

Dave chuckled. "Thanks. That look never gets old."

"I bet." She tried to ignore the spike of unwarranted possessiveness prickling her. Exactly how many women had they treated to the full-crew special? Why did it matter? She'd amuse herself and run. No muss, no fuss.

"You're cute when you're jealous." Neil pinched the side of her ass.

"I am not—"

He crushed his mouth over hers, aligning their bodies. Skin on skin. She couldn't have protested even if she wanted to. Oh God, he was so hot. A thin sheen of perspiration broke out across her chest, helping him to glide over her as he captured her lips in a scorching kiss.

Sometime after, stars danced in her vision.

"Let her breathe." James tapped Neil on the shoulder. "You're squishing all the air out of her."

She inhaled deeply when Neil slithered down her body. Open-mouthed kisses didn't help her regulate her respiration. Neither did his tongue, licking a path over her abdomen. "I can't get enough of the taste of her."

"Eat her pussy." Joe's usually calm voice reverberated with a gravelly growl she'd never heard before. "Make her come. Take the edge off. She's as jumpy as you have been all month."

"Is that true?" He lifted his head. The vulnerability in his dilated pupils shot a nail through her heart as surely as if she'd misfired the pneumatic gun they used.

"Yeah." She smiled when tension evaporated, making him more handsome without the stress lines around his eyes and mouth. "I need you too. You've been killing me. All of you. Strutting around with no shirts on all the time. Hot as hell. I've never felt this way about guys I worked with before. I wondered if I was losing it."

James petted her with slow strokes through her hair. He cradled her head on his lap and traced her lips with the tip of one finger. "I should have talked to you sooner. I'm sorry I waited. I'm sorry I let you doubt yourself."

She didn't question her instincts. Instead, she angled her face until she could lap at his erection, which stood proud against his abdomen. His cock wasn't heavy enough to weigh itself down so she opened her mouth and sucked lightly on his balls instead. With the tip of her tongue, she flicked the base of his erection.

"That's right." Mike encouraged her when James seemed to lose his voice. "Neil isn't big into blow jobs. Go ahead and treat James. It's been a while since he's had good head."

Usually she didn't care to go down on guys. After all, it was sort of like shooting herself in the foot if she wanted to be well fucked. But with two studs at her service, why not?

Devon opened her mouth and peered up at James.

"Yes." He hissed as he tipped his stiff erection toward her lips and tucked it inside. "So hot. Damn."

She got so into sucking his shaft—a comfortable mouthful—that she yelped when Neil settled deeper between her thighs and treated her pussy to similar attention. Her spine arched off the floor, giving him a perfect place to grip her waist. He capitalized on the leverage to tuck her tight to his skilled mouth.

James cupped her jaw, tracing her lips where they encircled his shaft. "Slow down, sweetheart. Or I'm not going to last."

She attempted to smile with her mouth full, but didn't change her pattern.

"Shit."

"Five bucks says James comes first." Joe drew her attention as he bet Dave.

"You're on. Neil saves all his oral skills for pussy." The bigger man's hand seemed to speed up as it drew on his beefy erection. "Kay says he's the best. Devon's gonna tip over in record time."

She hated to cost him the wager, but she'd never been a speed orgasmer. Most guys couldn't take her there at all without a little help from her hand. Impossible to facilitate with James clenching her fingers in his fists. She smiled as she tore her stare from the three men stroking themselves to monitor her prey.

James clenched his jaw so hard she worried about his dental bills. For about half a second anyway, until Neil distracted her with insistent pressure from his suckling lips over her clit. He took his time, exploring a variety of motions, until he did something amazing with his tongue that had her squealing around James's cock.

The shock of intense pleasure kept her from surrendering in the first instant of his treatment.

"Shit, I think you might have made a good call," Joe grumbled to Dave and pumped his cock faster.

Mike grinned. He slid closer for a better view. "I'm studying up. Kate loves it when I steal your tricks."

Neil hummed, only making Joe's demise a little more likely. She retaliated, concentrating on drawing the salty pre-com from James's pulsing erection. Mike reached out a steadying hand when his friend tilted off balance.

"Oh. Jesus. Yeah." James's fingers clenched in her hair. "Feels so good, Devon. More. Just like that."

She obliged eagerly. Every flick of Neil's tongue inspired her to reach out to the man in her mouth. Every press of Neil's lips and graze of his teeth had her mimicking his actions. The swell of passion that ballooned in her, causing tension to tighten her empty, aching pussy, inflated to astronomical proportions.

Her thighs quivered. She held stock still, afraid to move for fear of shattering.

"Damn. Damn. Can't hang on." James could have read the thoughts straight from her mind.

Either the creamy taste of his first jet of come or the insertion of one of Neil's long fingers in her pussy pushed her over the edge. She couldn't say which for sure. Perfectly timed, they triggered her orgasm together.

Devon swallowed greedily. The flex of her throat worked in time with the spasms gripping her channel around Neil's embedded hand.

She wished it had been his cock instead.

James collapsed beside them, laying his head on her breast. She rubbed his back with one hand as he soothed her belly with one of his own. Neil rose above them with a fierce shout. "Condom. Now."

Mike must have dug one from his wallet. He held it out and ready.

Neil's hands shook as he rolled it over his cock. When he fumbled for the third time, Dave reached over and finished sheathing his friend.

"Thanks."

"Don't mention it." Dave licked the glaze of pre-come

from his fingers before resuming his measured stroking over his stiff hard-on.

"Are you ready for me?" Neil sat on his heels between her thighs. "Or do you need some time to recover."

"Is he always this considerate?" Devon turned to James.

He kissed her gently then smiled. "I think he's afraid of breaking you. You're even littler than me. After fooling around with these hulks, you seem like a china doll."

"But you know better, right?" She could relate to James. It had to be hard being the smallest of the bunch. "Put him inside me. Don't make me wait."

"Yes, ma'am." James fisted Neil's sheathed erection and guided it to her slick entrance. "You heard her, Neil. She needs to be fucked. Don't think. Just do it."

Devon gasped when the blunt head of Neil's cock stretched her open. It'd been a while for her. The lingering spasms of her orgasm tensed the rings of muscle at her entrance.

"Let him in," Joe called out to her. "He's almost through. It'll get easier."

"Breathe, Dev," Mike added.

They didn't understand. It wasn't agony—no, it was ecstasy—that had her crying out. She opened her eyes and locked stares with James when Neil relented, backing off on the pressure driving his forward motion.

"No." James grabbed Neil's ass and forced him closer. "Keep going. Give her more. She needs more."

"Ah. Yes!" she screamed when Neil buried himself to the hilt.

He began to thrust inside her. Long, deep glides left no part of her untouched, unexplored. James lowered his head to take her nipple between his lips. He plied the hard tip with his tongue and sucked it against the roof of his mouth while his other hand roamed across her torso to make sure neither of her breasts were left out of the fun.

"So hot." Joe groaned from beside them.

Neil didn't respond. His focus stayed entirely on her. He pumped inside her again and again. Sweat trickled over his hard pecs and the defined ridges of his abs.

Why couldn't this last all day? This euphoric bliss caused by being the center of the crew's universe. At least temporarily.

Rhythmic grunts accompanied the shuttling of Neil's cock, loudest each time he bottomed out in her pussy. The three men surrounding the trio on the floor inched closer until their knees touched the entwined threesome.

James allowed his fingers to cruise down her center until they found her clit. He rubbed gently yet fast, in a maddening loop around her swollen nub. The combination of his fluttering touch and the pounding of Neil's pelvis had her curling her nails into her palms to keep from coming.

Not yet. Not yet.

"Let go, Dev," James whispered against her breast. "They're waiting for you to shatter. Look how badly they need to join you. Let go."

She forced her eyes to open. Each man around her met her gaze as she let them see everything they made her feel. When she returned to Neil, she had no choice. Her body betrayed her, clamping around his shaft, savoring the defined ridges of the veined tissue and the thick head of his cock.

Just as her spasms began to die down, a groan echoed in the empty kitchen. Warm fluid spurted onto her chest and belly in time to the jerks of Dave's cock. Joe and Mike joined in as though the sight of their friend's surrender tripped a switch inside them. They drizzled their pearly come onto her torso.

Neil yanked himself from the quivering tissue of her pussy and stripped his condom off in one motion. He aimed his cock at her and assisted his partners in decorating her tan skin. Several spots of his release dribbled onto her bare pussy. She swore the weight of the droplets caused another orgasm to roll through her.

As everyone soaked in their shared release, something warm and soft lapped against Devon's skin. She pried her heavy lids open to observe James cleaning every last bit of the mingled mess from her body. He hummed as he devoured the essence of his friends and lovers.

"That was the best staff meeting I've ever been to." She winked at Mike. "Impressive staffs for sure."

"I give you a ten for BJ skills. Seriously though, negative points for the jokes, Dev." Joe ruffled her hair.

She buried her face against Neil's chest and giggled. Thirty more seconds. Then she'd force herself to get dressed like the rest of the guys, whose clothes rustled somewhere farther away than the pounding of her heart, which gradually slowed.

"Thank you." Mike laid his hand on her knee and squeezed before climbing to his feet. Dave and Joe followed his lead, leaving the three of them to recover in relative privacy.

"You were amazing." James spoke when Neil seemed incapable of expressing himself. "You gave him everything he needed and more."

"And you?" She couldn't put her finger on when it had

happened but she'd developed a connection to James. A bond she hadn't expected.

"The same. Thank you." He kissed her forehead then stood to pull on his jeans.

"Break's over." Mike hollered from upstairs. The laugh in his tone had them chuckling along. The man was hardcore, but not a hardass. More like he provided an out from the potentially awkward situation. "Get back to work, kids."

"On it, foreman." She smiled as she rolled to her feet and tugged on her clothes.

Neil surprised her by catching her shoulders before she scooted off to finish the bathroom with Dave. He tucked her close, laid a long, sensual kiss on her parted lips, then spun her in the direction of the stairs and smacked her ass.

What did it say about her that she loved it?

She peeked over her shoulder for once last glimpse of him. Instead, she caught James sparing her and Neil a longing glance. At least she thought so. But when she squinted, he only smiled from his spot a few feet away.

"Great job today, guys. And girl." Mike clapped Joe on the shoulder. "We're ahead of schedule so I don't see any problem with taking the weekend off."

"Good thing." Dave perked up. "You know how much Kay has been looking forward to the barbeque on Sunday. The resort is almost ready to open, and she's dying for you all to share it this one time before guests start arriving."

Devon had heard oodles about the clothing-optional facility Dave's naturist girlfriend had built from the ground up, with the crew's help.

"And…" He cleared his throat, drawing interested glances from the rest of the gathering. "I was sort of thinking about asking her to marry me. This weekend I mean. Maybe at our bonfire."

"You've had the ring forever." James beamed. "Do it already. She's not the kind of woman who requires something elaborate. Just the place you share. Make it official. Ask her."

"I will. When the time is right." Dave sighed. "Maybe when you're all there."

"I think it's best if we each take tomorrow to think about our future." Mike spoke carefully. He'd obviously given the topic some consideration this afternoon. They'd worked twice as efficiently as before. Devon hadn't realized how much she'd been screwing them up. "Come prepared to talk. All of us, together. We need to make some big decisions about where we go from here. Ignoring things aren't going to make them any better. I'm not willing to fuck up the most important relationships in our lives. Not with our wives. Or each other."

Every crew member nodded. Except Devon. Where did she fit in?

"You'll be joining us too." Mike didn't phrase it as a question.

"I—"

"Please." Neil turned to her and enfolded her hand in one of his. With the other he reached for James, but his partner had taken a step back at some point. "Say you'll come."

She sucked in a huge breath and held it as she considered the plea in his eyes. Next she considered the open invitation in each of the other guys' answering nods. When she locked her gaze on James, she wavered. He stared at the juncture of her and Neil's fingers, not into her eyes.

"I don't think..."

James lifted his head and scrunched his brows. "You have to come. Neil needs you."

"What about you?"

"Let's take that time to think first." Mike stepped forward, breaking her connection with Neil. "Nobody say anything they'll regret."

They shuffled toward the door then dispersed as they angled for their vehicles. She hopped into her truck. The door hadn't shut yet when Joe, parked beside her, called softly, "See you Sunday."

"I don't know where I'm going." If that wasn't the statement of the century she couldn't have said what was.

"I'll email you directions. And if you need, Morgan and I will pick you up. We won't let you get lost, okay?" He smiled.

"Promise?" She wished she could hug him.

"Yeah. I promise. And so do they." He lifted his shoulder. She followed the invisible line he drew to where James, Neil, Mike and Dave watched their exchange with eagle eyes.

"All right then. I'll see you on Sunday." She backed out of the driveway, surprised by the unshed tears blurring her vision.

When had they come to matter so much?

Devon sat in the driveway, her truck parked behind the usual assortment of oversized construction vehicles. She tugged on the hem of her simple cotton dress, still wondering exactly what ensemble was appropriate for a clothing-optional facility. A solid hour and a half trying on everything in her modest closet—again and again—hadn't made her any more confident she would avoid a fashion faux pas.

At least Kate, Morgan and Kayla had seemed completely cool and relaxed the times she'd hung out with the whole group. They'd never make her feel out of place. Unless they disapproved of what had gone down at the job site on Friday.

A giant sigh ruffled the short bangs framing her face. She reached over and retrieved the simple veggie assortment she'd prepared as an offering. Not like she could whip up her mom's famous spice bread—her usual potluck contribution—when a professional baker would be in attendance.

Pitfalls loomed around every twist and turn in her

relationship with the crew. What the hell had she gotten herself into? Maybe she should bolt before they spotted her.

"Need some help with that?" Mike's greeting hammered the last nail in the coffin of her fledgling escape plans.

Damn it.

"Nah, I got it. Thanks." She tried to smile. Her muscles were too tense.

He ignored her and nabbed the tray from her hands. Good thing or she would have dropped it when she realized he strutted around the property in the buff. Muscles gleamed and flexed in the late afternoon sun.

The smell of grilling burgers wasn't responsible for her sudden drooling affliction.

By the time she'd recovered even a tiny fraction of her wits, they'd reached the front porch. Kayla ran out to greet her with an enormous hug. Devon didn't flinch from the warm skin that met her hands when she returned the embrace. In fact, the toned expanse of Kayla's back felt soft and warm. Comforting. Something about Devon's reaction must have clued Kayla in to her confusion. She retreated and narrowed her eyes.

"Sorry," Devon chuckled. "Not quite sure how this works."

"You're our guest." Kayla's smile seemed natural and light as she took the platter from Mike and shooed him off with a wave. The women headed inside together. "Do, or don't do, whatever makes you comfortable. It's a clothing-optional resort, not a clothing-prohibited one. It took Kate and Morgan a little while to loosen up enough to join in. No one will think poorly of you if you're not ready."

"Hey, I heard that." A clatter from the kitchen

announced the infamous cook was putting the finishing touches on their dinner. "Besides, I'm still not nude. I'm wearing an apron."

"Safety first." Kayla grinned as she turned toward the prep space in the open cabin.

Devon would have followed but the enormous floor to ceiling windows caught her attention. She wandered over for a better view of the gorgeous valley and the lake at the bottom. Instead of rustic charm, she caught sight of Neil and James chasing each other around the rear of the house.

Bare-ass naked.

Her breath rushed out.

"Like what you see?" Kayla asked.

"The view is amazing." Devon blushed as she realized how true her cover up statement turned out to be.

The other woman only chuckled. "Right you are. On both counts."

Kayla had a way of making Devon feel at home. What could have been awkward turned out to be organic. She was the only one making a big deal out of the bare skin deal.

When in Rome...do as the naturists do.

Devon gathered her skirt and pulled her light dress over her head. She glanced into the yard, the fabric dangling from her fingers, just in time to watch James smash into Neil. The taller man had stopped dead in his tracks. His gaze locked on her body, framed in the window. James shook his head like a dog emerging from the water then followed his partner's stare.

He laughed and tossed her a finger wave before smacking Neil on the ass, stealing the soccer ball she hadn't noticed before, and tearing off through the lush grass.

"Well, that's one way to make an entrance." Kate wandered from the kitchen with a dish in her hand. She looked even lovelier than she had in the little black dress she'd sported the last time they met up for dinner out. Somehow, she made naked seem like the new trend in designer eveningwear, complete with sedate pearl earrings. "So glad to see you again. I think the guys were worried you wouldn't come."

Devon didn't have the heart to admit they were right to be concerned.

"It's okay, hon. All of us were overwhelmed at first. Still are at times. It's a lot to get used to. No rush and no worries, okay? Want to bring your tray this way? I'll show you where we're setting everything out."

"Thanks." She swallowed past the lump in her throat. She should have known they'd make this easy for her. They were some of the coolest people she'd ever met. Reality was, it scared her to think of losing them so soon after becoming an honorary member of their bunch.

She'd spent her whole Saturday dreaming of what it could be like if her temporary position became something a hell of a lot more permanent.

"Dev!" Joe beamed at her from his place tending the grill. "Looking good."

Morgan swatted him half-heartedly with a hand towel as they arranged the last of the food. "Behave yourself."

He grinned then snagged his fiancée, dragging her close for a sweet kiss that had the potential to turn into something downright smoky. When they touched, so simply though completely, Devon understood the difference between a casual encounter and a soul-deep bond.

What they had was the real thing.

Kate coughed. Maybe the char wasn't all a product of the couple's searing kiss. "Hey now, Morgan. No distracting the chef. I don't like my burgers *that* well done."

"Fine, fine." Morgan removed her tongue from Joe's mouth and stuck it out at Kate. "I *am* getting pretty hungry."

"You know, I can round someone else up to do the honors here if you need me to feed you a little appetizer." Joe wiggled his brows. "Has that picnic table been christened yet, Kay?"

The tall, tattooed woman whistled a little ditty.

"Should have figured you two have nailed each other on every rock and up every tree on this mountain by now." He shook his head.

"Jealous?" Dave came around the corner with Mike, beers in hand. He tossed one to Joe then settled onto the stone wall they'd built a few weekends ago.

"Nah, but I do approve." With a grin, Joe began to plate the meat as James and Neil trotted up beside them. They panted, out of breath from their game.

James jogged until he was within arm's reach of Devon then slowed to a stop. "Hi."

She let her hands hang, awkward, at her sides since she had no pockets to stuff them in. "Hey."

"Oh, damn. We're not doing this weird first-time-we-see-you-after-having-sex thing are we?" Neil strode right up to her and wrapped her in a tight embrace. He planted a juicy kiss directly on her lips before retreating. "I'm no good at pretending. I missed you yesterday."

"No mistaking that." Kate dropped her gaze to his solid hard-on. "That thing stood up and waved hello from across the field."

The group cracked up as they selected brightly colored plates from a stack and dished out the food they'd made together. The last traces of Devon's reservations disappeared with dinner. Great conversations, a generous helping of ribbing and easy camaraderie made her forget all her concerns. She didn't realize she'd shifted in her seat, leaning against Neil with her legs in James's lap, until the rest of the crew piled their plates in the center of the table.

"Guys are on clean up duty since the girls cooked." Kate stood and stretched. She claimed a fresh pitcher of the sangria someone had mixed up.

"Hey, I grilled." Joe's pout earned him a kiss on the cheek from Morgan.

"Too bad. It's time for girl talk. Come play in a little while." She patted his chest then sauntered after Kate, plucking a pair of fresh glasses from the supplies.

"Who are we to argue?" Kayla entwined her fingers with Devon's and tugged. "Wait 'til you see what Dave designed back here."

Devon glanced over her shoulder, pleased to see James's and Neil's gazes locked on the sway of her hips. She blew them a kiss.

"Are you teasing them or are you serious?" Kayla slowed as they sauntered down the hillside. She kept hold of Devon's hand, using it to guide her along the soft, sandy path fringed with pretty river rocks and flower beds. Perfect for bare feet.

"Uh..." Putting her heart on the line didn't seem wise. Especially when she hadn't gotten to talk to the two men, whom she'd dreamed of every second since Friday afternoon, about what had happened. She shivered a little. The setting sun made her wonder if she should run back to grab her dress. Though late in the spring, the nights still got chilly.

"Don't worry, you'll be warm soon. Unless you're screwing around with our friends. Then you might find yourself getting the cold shoulder. Neil has feelings for you. It's obvious to Dave, and after seeing you together tonight, I agree with his assessment of the situation."

"What?" Devon faltered on the path. Good thing the padded walkway absorbed her stutter steps.

"He treats you different than us. He's protective, like he is with James. He cares for me, Kate and Morgan. Hell, he's even fucked us silly from time to time. But with you... He's softer. Careful. I know things are happening fast, but I'm asking you to respect him." Kayla squeezed Devon's fingers again and led her into the glade ahead.

"I will." Devon cleared her throat then spoke louder. "I do."

"Good." Kayla smiled. "Then let's get nice and comfy. They've been dying to try this doohickey out. I want tonight to be perfect for all of us."

"What thing?"

"You'll see." They followed a curve around thick foliage. On the other side, Kate and Morgan were lighting several gas fire pits placed artfully around a patio. Crew-made waterfalls edged the rockwork. They fed a tangle of streams that meandered through the space. Tiny bridges crossed the wandering flows, which emptied into an asymmetrical koi pond near the center.

An enormous woven rope lounger stretched above the gurgling water. Plenty big enough to hold a dozen people comfortably, the modified web impressed Devon with its scale and creative use of the materials. For naturists, the air swirling around their relaxing bodies would feel like heaven.

She visualized lying face down, peering at the fish swimming in lazy circles below. Unlike a hammock, the netting was bolted at the four corners, preventing it from swaying too much.

"We can try out the new pads I sewed this week." Kayla opened the top of a cedar storage bin off to the side and withdrew puffy strips that would prevent the rope from digging into sensitive skin. A pile of blankets and pillows overflowed the rest of the large trunk.

Kate snagged one of each and climbed onto the mesh. She reclined, crossing her legs at the ankles as she stared up at the gorgeous colors streaking the sky. "You're going to make oodles on this place, Kay. I'm sort of sad we won't have it to ourselves much longer."

Morgan heaped Devon's arms full of pillows then she grabbed some blankets. They acclimated themselves to the surprisingly comfortable seating, taking advantage of the pads while each of them downed a glass or two of sangria. Chatter came easy—about their guys, the books they'd been reading, deals they'd scored at the mall the day before and life in general. They collapsed onto the bedding to study the emerging stars like pampered members of an elaborate harem.

"It's still a little nippy out for this." Morgan chaffed her arms.

"We can head inside if you want." Kayla tried not to sound disappointed. She failed miserably.

"No way." Kate scooted her pad closer to them. "Let's snuggle up. The guys will be here soon to keep us warm."

Devon didn't hesitate when Kayla patted the spot beside her. Warmth from the fire pits paired with heat waves rolling off her new friends to keep her nice and toasty. She relaxed, not caring that her head rested on Kayla's shoulder. Stress and worry over what might or might not come to pass seeped away. Lids heavy, she closed her eyes.

"Now there's a Kodak moment if I ever saw one." Mike groaned. "Gorgeous women curled up like a pile of puppies."

Devon couldn't believe she'd just about drifted off. She started to sit up. A warm hand pressed her shoulder against the netting. *Neil.* With one touch, she knew it was him. Her body arched toward the contact while she searched with the other hand for James. He wouldn't be far behind his boyfriend.

At the same time, Dave reached for Kayla, settling her closer to where he'd climbed onto his masterpiece.

"Stay. Please." Neil crawled beside her, tucking her against the furnace of his chest.

"Mmm. Toasty." Devon didn't flinch when he rolled, presenting her to James. The other man sandwiched her between them, infusing her shoulders, ass and the back of her thighs with a twin blast of heat.

The ropes shifted as Mike and Joe joined the fray. A gorgeous tangle of limbs and sleek, toned bodies littered the expanse. They paired off and spread out a little—enough to be comfortable, but not so far that they added unnecessary space.

"Look, I don't say this enough..." Mike stole the opportunity to address them while they studied the deep royal blue of the twilight sky. "I can't imagine my life without you all. Without this connection we have. The wedding is coming up quick, and I believe I'm the luckiest bastard in the whole world. Honestly. I do."

Joe rumbled from beside them, where he cuddled Morgan against his chest. "Why do I sense and enormous *but*?"

"It's true." Mike sighed. "I'm worried, for the first time since we found each other, that if we're not honest now, we could lose this closeness. I refuse to let us drift apart."

Devon felt like an interloper. Hell, she'd barely gotten to know them and they were a decade into their friendship. "Should I go?"

"Shh." Neil put his hand over her mouth.

"Hell no, you shouldn't leave." Dave rounded on her. "He's talking to you too. You're part of us. Can't you sense it? This crazy bond? It's happened to us enough times now to recognize when we meet someone that belongs here. It doesn't take long to be sure. Unless you don't sense it?"

She bit her lip until Neil removed his fingers to let her speak. "There's a connection."

"That's good enough for me." Mike shifted, rising to his knees so they could see him better. "I'm telling you right now that I trust you. Each and every one. If something were to happen to me, I'm confident you would look after Kate."

She whimpered beside her soon-to-be-husband.

"Don't worry, babe. I'm not planning on checking out anytime soon. But why should it be any different when we're here? Now. Together. I love you, Kate. Same as Joe does Morgan and Dave with Kayla. Neil, James and Devon too. Being with the crew before we met you didn't impact that. Changing how we act around each other is stifling us. I'm afraid it will lead to fights. To discontent." He rubbed his temples. "I've been thinking about it a lot lately. I'm more sure now than ever that how we've gone about things is not the answer. Watching and staying apart sucks. We need to be together. It's how we're best. However feels natural. Right, Kayla?"

"It makes sense to me, yes." She roused from Dave's embrace. "If you want to express your affection physically, you should. Like the other day. I could tell when Dave walked through the door. His eyes were brighter and he hugged me twice as hard as usual. It's a vital part of you guys. Sharing like that. Whatever seems right and nothing else. But I expect you to tell me all about it, in detail, if I'm not there to enjoy it firsthand."

Murmurs from around the group ensured they were all in agreement.

Devon shivered. "If I had a vote, I would love to watch you do more than play voyeurs. As hot as things got the other day, I saw you struggling to stay detached and I wondered... God, you have no idea the dreams I've had the past two nights."

"You *do* have a say." Mike nodded at her. "Each of us does. I'm guessing we'd all be in favor of sharing that link with each other. With you."

A smattering of curses, moans and pleas—both masculine and feminine—filled the wild evening. Rice-paper lanterns with botanical prints cast a soft glow over the gathering. Radiance enveloped them as darkness gathered outside the boundaries of their intimate world. Nothing beyond the reach of their spell mattered.

James moaned and Neil caressed her shoulder. "Sort of like your first time all over again."

"Unless you count fantasies, group sex is definitely something new for me." She smiled up at him, accepting his light kiss.

"We'll be gentle. At least where you're concerned." Mike grinned. He didn't hesitate in resuming his usual role, foreman through and through. "James. Get on your hands and knees in the middle of us. Let's see how well Dave designed this contraption."

5

———————

The men surrounded the slightest member of their group, staying low and helping him stabilize while they caused ripples in the surface of the lounger. If the presence of four smoking hot men and their fantastic ladies messed with James's equilibrium as much as it did hers, Devon understood his need for their steadying touch.

The women followed their guys until one couple occupied each side of the square rope-work. It then resembled a dirty version of *Hungry, Hungry Hippos* with James in imminent danger of having his marbles devoured. *There* was a game that had taught major life lessons… Slam the handle—as hard and fast as possible— over and over and over until somebody wins. No wonder it had been her favorite.

The adult jungle gym turned out to be great for more than relaxing. They could indulge their creativity. James spread his legs. Pliable cords, set close enough that he didn't have to worry about sinking through, supported each of his knees.

What was the rope made out of? It was soft enough to be silk. She'd ask the crew later.

Much later.

James's knuckles went white as they wrapped around one of the strands that created perfect grips. Spaced at frequent intervals, they ensured no matter what height he was, there would have been a rung guaranteed to be comfortable.

"Simple and ingenious." She didn't realize she'd spoken aloud until Dave answered her.

"Thanks, Dev."

"The possibilities are endless," Kate murmured as though she contemplated a thousand or so positions she'd like to experiment with.

"We have all the time in the world to try whatever you can concoct," Joe chimed in, making James groan.

"Speak for yourself. If someone doesn't touch me soon I'm going to die." He attempted to rub his crotch, but tipped. Mike righted him, chuckling at James's plight.

"Diabolical." The smaller man shook his head. "I should have known."

"So, how are you going to convince Joe to stroke your cock for you?" Mike's inquiry turned squeaky at the end. It took Devon a second to notice Kate's arm had snaked around his hip from behind him to fondle *his* package. Devon couldn't help but stare as his cock thickened, overflowing his fiancée's palm.

"I'll blow him." James didn't sound like he minded. In fact, it kind of came out like begging.

"I'm sure he'd appreciate that. Fair trade, Joe?"

"Yeah. I want him to get me nice and hard for Morgan." He angled his head to steal a red-hot kiss from his lady.

"After watching James working your hard-on I might not need you to fuck me." She panted when he released her lips.

"I'll always need you, Morgan." The intensity of his stare seemed to melt his future wife.

Devon could relate. She didn't think before sidling closer to Neil. His abs scorched her hands when she rested her palms on the flexing muscles.

"Mmm."

"If you really want to rev him up, rub his chest." James tossed the hint over his shoulder in her direction.

"No fair, tag-teaming me like that." Neil groaned when Devon massaged his pecs, pausing to flick her thumbnails over his hard nipples. "Ah. Damn."

James's chuckle was short lived. Joe scooted tighter in front of James and fed the kneeling man his erection. Their lover obliged greedily, sucking the shaft down to the base in one fluid slurp.

"I have a plan," Mike announced. "We're going to play spin the construction worker. Whoever his mouth points to wins the BJ lottery. If you're on his right, you'll work his cock. I think the person in the rear can figure out something that suits you both."

"What about the guy on the left?" Dave, currently in that position, actually raised his hand, making Devon and several others laugh out loud.

"That lucky bastard will fuck his woman. When he makes her come, we'll turn James ninety degrees. Not one second sooner." Mike grinned, clearly pleased with himself when Joe slowed James's sucking with a light tap on his cheek. "And if James can hold out until each of our girls has come at least once, we'll make sure he gets a special prize. Whatever he requests. Sound like fun?"

"Hell, I'm halfway to orgasm thinking about it." Kayla shifted beside Dave. She rubbed her thighs together, drawing Devon's attention to the glimmer of arousal coating the tops of them.

James paused his sensual assault on Joe's cock. "I know what I want."

"Yeah? What?" Joe painted moisture over James's lips with the tip of his cock.

"I want all of the guys to fuck me, to come on me. It's been almost a year since…" He trailed off.

Kate petted his flank from her position at his side. "I'm sorry, James. You should have said something sooner. I wouldn't have kept Mike to myself if I had understood how you missed him. All of you."

Devon didn't realize she'd held her breath until Neil cupped her hand in his and whispered over his shoulder, "Are you ready for this? There won't be any stopping them soon."

"You could say that." From her position, crouched behind him, she ground her mound against his hip.

He growled and captured her mouth in a brief yet fierce kiss. When he relented, her eyes fluttered open once more. Mike had shifted closer, reaching beneath James to cup his balls and stiffening shaft. Kate hugged the foreman from behind, kissing his back and studying the motions of his roaming hand.

James moaned and spread his legs wider, arching his back. The motion presented his ass to her and Neil.

"Hang on a sec." Dave lunged for the edge of the net and jabbed his hand into the plants surrounding one of the supports. He retrieved something then tossed it to Neil, who caught it effortlessly in one palm.

"Dude, did you pluck this from the lube bush?" Neil laughed as he uncapped the small bottle.

"Always prepared, you know." Dave wiggled his eyebrows. "I stashed some supplies earlier, just in case."

"I'm not sure what merit badge you get for this, but nice work." Neil grimaced. "I don't suppose you have some condoms over there too, do you?"

Devon tapped Neil's elbow. When he glanced at her, she whispered, "I'm on the pill. You don't have to if…"

"We're clean. All of us." Neil groaned. "Are you sure?"

"Yeah." She bit her lip.

Neil groaned. He tried twice to open the bottle before he drizzled the gel over his fingers. Some dripped off, landing on James's exposed ass.

The kneeling man twitched, dislodging Joe's cock from his mouth long enough to beg, "Hurry, Neil. Mike's still fucking amazing at hand jobs."

"You always did like his technique. A little rougher than the rest of us, huh?" Neil painted the lubrication over James's ass, notching the tip of one finger at his clenched hole.

Devon inched closer for a better view. She allowed her hands to cruise over her body. They soothed the flames licking at her chest and pussy as she observed the guys— whom she'd come to respect on the job—transform into versions of themselves so much more primal and honest than the reserved shells they'd donned before.

"Amazing." She scanned the men and women ringing James. They were focused on his pleasure and their own. Nothing so powerful had ever graced her life. Privileged to be among them, she abandoned any reservations and soaked in the raw passion they created together.

"Yes, you are." Neil kissed her without slowing the

steady penetration of his finger into his lover's ass. With his free hand, he cupped her breast, rolling the pad of his thumb over her hardened peak.

A cry from her left drew her attention. She looked over in time to see Dave finish burying himself in Kayla. He blanketed her long, strong body, shuddering when she wrapped her arms and legs around him, drawing him closer to her center.

A spasm clenched Devon's pussy. She had to avert her eyes or risk coming right then. Except every place her greedy gaze landed, it feasted on another treat. Joe threw his head back, exposing the cords of his neck to Morgan's nibbles as he began to rock into James's mouth. Kate had lowered herself to her back to reward Mike for his dexterous hands by laving his cock and balls with slow laps of her tongue.

Devon couldn't stop herself. She reached down and took hold of Neil's erection, which strained against his six-pack abs. She fisted him despite his groan and his attempts to convince her to let go.

"I won't last if you do that." He bit her lower lip then soothed the sting with flicks of his tongue.

"You'd better." Mike gritted his teeth. "No disappointing your lady, unless you're hoping another crew member will pick up your slack."

The threat alone was enough to weaken Devon's legs. If she hadn't already been kneeling, she would have crashed to the netting.

"Fuck, no." Neil snapped. He pumped his finger deep into James's clenching hole, adding a second digit when the man in front of them rocked back, asking for more.

"Dave, you'd better not dally," Mike called out orders.

"I'm sure you can push Kayla over the edge faster than that."

The woman's response was unintelligible. However, the trails left by her neat nails as they scratched down her lover's back spoke volumes. Dave's hips ground against his girlfriend's, escalating her whimpers to full out cries in less than a minute.

"There you go, Kay." Neil encouraged her. "Open your eyes. Watch what you two are doing to us."

When the naturist peeked from beneath the shadow of her enthusiastic lover, she groaned. Her arm flailed out, grasping onto James's wrist where it supported him. She shivered violently as she inspected Joe's shaft tunneling between James's generous lips. Then she scanned to Mike's impressive manipulation. When she observed Neil preparing his lover for the rest of the crew, she lost it.

"Oh, Dave," she whimpered. "I want you to fuck him like you're fucking me. Hard. Relentless. Perfect."

"Shit." Dave's hips hitched in their fluid stride. "Don't talk like that, Kay, or I won't make it. You're so fucking hot. So tight. So wet. Jesus."

"Tell me." Kayla drew him to her for a kiss, eliminating the possibility of him responding for long seconds.

"Yeah. Fuck." He grunted. "I'm going to ride him for you, baby. You want to see it, don't you? Me feeding my cock into his tight ass?"

Poor Kayla. Devon shuddered as her new friend succumbed to the sexy verbal assault. Hell, when Neil pressed two fingers inside Devon's soaked pussy, she almost joined their host in her epic climax.

Dave roared, making Devon wonder if he hadn't spilled inside the sultry woman writhing beneath him. When Kayla quieted, he sat up, resting on his haunches, his fingers clamped around the base of his massive hard-on like a poor man's cock ring.

"Nice work." Mike's praise lowered an octave or two from his usual tone. "I didn't think you stood a chance there."

Dave grimaced, his cock still throbbing with every beat of his heart. He took several deep breaths then nuzzled Kayla, bringing her back to reality gently. She whispered to him, too quiet for the rest to hear then kissed him so tenderly Devon wasn't surprised to find tears prickling her eyes.

Kay patted her guy on the cheek. She relaxed into the netting. Dave tucked one of the blankets over her then smiled. "I love you."

"Love you too," she murmured. "Now run along and play. I think James is ready for you."

"Who cares about James?" Morgan drew chuckles with her false dismissal. "I need Joe to fuck me. Now. Enough teasing."

Neil squirted another generous dollop of lube onto James's ass, making sure to incorporate it before withdrawing his fingers. He smacked the cute bubble butt then nudged James's hip, encouraging him to turn. Devon loved how Neil supported James, helping him into his new position, rubbing his ankles and knees to keep the blood circulating.

While James concentrated on giving Joe's cock one final kiss goodbye then welcoming Mike into his mouth, Neil reached over to Dave. He wrapped his hand around his partner's cock and slicked the shaft, though it already bore the remnants of Kayla's pleasure. Neil wouldn't take any chances with his lovers' comfort. That much was clear.

"Go slow." Neil guided Dave to James. "You're a lot thicker than me, and it's been a while since he's had anyone else."

"You might have thought about that before Mike let me fuck Kayla. You know nothing turns me on more. Unless it's this. I can't believe we're doing this again. That she's watching. All of you are."

So much for restraint. Dave fisted his hands at his sides and pressed forward.

Mike withdrew his cock from James's mouth. "Watch your teeth, kid."

"Hard when he's splitting me open." James's back heaved as Dave attempted to seat himself.

Neil nuzzled James's shoulder, whispering in his ear. He rubbed his boyfriend's back.

Devon couldn't stop herself. If she could make this better for James, she would. She crept up next to Neil and placed her left hand over the base of James's spine. She soothed him as best she knew how, dropping light kisses to the concave dip above his ass.

"If you stroke him, it'll help him enjoy this." Neil advised her.

Devon ran her right hand from James's ribs over his flat belly, admiring the contours of his svelte muscles. She arrowed south until her fingers bumped into his semi-erect dick. Then she explored. Soft skin, heavy balls, his firming shaft—everything about him intrigued her.

"There you go, James," Dave crooned, wrapping his hands around James's trim hips. He held James in place as he applied steady, unrelenting pressure with the tip of his cock on the smaller man's stretching hole. "Almost have me. Think how amazing it'll be when I'm in you all the way."

"Ah. Yes." James's head hung between his shoulders. "Do it. Now."

Devon began a gentle tug on James's cock. It expanded in her fist, forcing her to loosen her grip and travel farther on every pass to stroke the entire length. When the head of Dave's erection poked through the last resistance of James's ass the guys moaned in unison.

James cried out. Pain, pleasure or both, she couldn't say for sure.

"That's so damn hot." Kayla cheered them on from where she curled on her side behind the action. If Devon guessed right, the other woman touched herself beneath the blanket.

"Let me see." Joe sat up far enough on the other side of James to get an eyeful. "Shit, yes. Fuck him good, Dave. Open him up for me. I want to ride him hard."

"Me first." Morgan settled herself in her fiancé's lap, reverse cowgirl style. She faced the group as she lowered herself onto the stiff flesh jutting from Joe's crotch. Devon increased the pace of her stroking. She imagined how good it would feel to be filled right now. Joe's cock disappeared inside Morgan until her pussy rested on his balls.

Dave must have enjoyed the abandon on Morgan's face as much as Devon did. He began to move with long, careful glides until he fused his abdomen to James's ass.

"Feel better?" Mike wrapped his fingers in James's hair and guided the smaller man's mouth back to his cock. "Yeah, damn. That's what I thought."

James devoured Mike.

The foreman wrapped one arm around his soon-to-be wife and tugged her close to his side. He bent down to suck on her breast as another man serviced him. Kate stared. She reached out, tracing one finger around the girth of Mike's cock, which was surrounded by James's supple lips. Her wandering hands ended up pillowing Mike's balls as they swung against James's chin.

Neil turned his attention to Devon, nodding to where she had pumped steel into James's flagging erection. "You have that covered?"

"I think so."

James moaned his agreement and fucked into her grasp.

"Good." Neil smiled. He surprised her by sliding to her rear. "I guess that means I'm free to play with you instead."

Her head lolled onto his shoulder when he bracketed her from behind. His long fingers skimmed down her front from her breasts to her abdomen. He paused over her mound, drawing lazy circles on the sensitive skin there. When she whimpered, James tensed. His whole-body flex wrung corresponding groans from Dave and Mike.

"Joe, you better be doing your best with Morgan over there." Neil laughed, buffeting strands of Devon's hair. "I can already tell these two are riding the edge."

Morgan shrieked, confirming his suspicions. Joe hammered into her from below, all of them focused on the guys who formed the centerpiece of their lascivious display.

"And how about you?" Neil sucked hard on Devon's neck. "I can't believe how wet you are."

She sought his teasing fingers with her pussy, painting his hand with her arousal.

"By the time it's your turn, you'll combust with one

stroke." Neil didn't do much to preserve her self-control. "Ever come from a man sliding inside you before?"

Hell, she wasn't going to make it that long if he kept this up.

"Joe!" Morgan cried out as she bounced on his lap. She made the motion look effortless and graceful as she swung her hips, tracing a sinuous glide path on every pass.

"Yes." Her mate molded his hands to her breasts, pinching the hard nipples. "Come for me. For us."

Dave yanked his cock from James's ass. As Morgan mewled and arched impossibly in Joe's hold, the first splash of Dave's come jetted onto James's back. The moment the warm line of sticky fluid branded James's skin, his cock pulsed in Devon's grip.

"Not yet." She removed her hand. "I want you to come with us."

He whimpered, already spinning so that his ass aimed toward Joe. Morgan untangled herself from her fiancé, collapsing onto one of the puffy pads Kayla had made and grabbing another blanket to settle in for the rest of the show.

Joe didn't waste any time. He sprang forward, causing a wave to roll through the rest of the net, impacting them all. They leaned on each other, finding support and mutual longing waiting.

Devon twisted to the side to make room for Neil to approach James's mouth with his cock, but the man behind her prevented her from moving. "You'd better take my turn, sweetheart. No way can I let him suck me now."

"Is that okay?" She looked instinctively to Mike.

"Whatever feels right, Dev."

She glanced down at James. His startlingly familiar

eyes seemed enormous in the low light. He reached for her. She went. "You're sure?"

"Mmm. Yes, please." He waved his fingers, motioning for Neil to position her closer. Neil wrapped her in his strong arms. She rested on his tight, muscular chest so she didn't have to sacrifice the view of Joe plunging into James's ass.

Over and over.

Harder and harder.

James nudged her thighs wide apart then buried his face in her moist lips. He flicked his tongue around her opening then up to her clit. Every thrust Joe made into James's ass shoved James's lips tight against her swollen pussy. And yet she needed more. Needed to be filled. Fucked. Joined together with one of these phenomenal men.

Like Kate, who lay on her side, facing the main attraction while Mike pumped into her from behind. He held her knee up high in one hand, opening her impossibly for his savage fucking. She slipped one hand down her torso. Her fingers flashed ultra-quick over her clit.

Devon whimpered as she considered how good that would feel. She fought the current lifting her toward orgasm, wanting to hold out for the ultimate merger. Just when she thought she wouldn't make it, Joe froze. He rammed inside James once, twice more before pulling out and spilling his seed all over the swell of James's ass.

"You were supposed to wait for Katiebug." Neil *tsked*.

There was no need to be worried. Kate screamed, bucking in Mike's strong grasp as Joe painted the last strands of his release over James's soft skin. Mike bit Kate's neck, slowing his frantic thrusts as she glided down the far side of ecstasy. Morgan handed Kate a pillow and a blanket. Then she lifted the edge of the nest she'd made to invite her lover into the warmth she'd generated for him.

Mike impressed Devon. He rose to his knees after one final sweet kiss on Kate's forehead. He was controlled yet powerful when he advanced inside James. Dave should have been up for occupying James's mouth next. However, he seemed loathe to leave the comfort of the spot where he snuggled with Kayla.

They redefined the rules to accommodate the needs of the remaining players.

"I have to fuck you, Dev," Neil growled as he pressed her back to the rope mesh. He smothered her body in welcoming heat. She strained her neck, attempting to connect with James and see how he responded to Mike's expert loving.

"Help him, Dave." Kayla nudged her boyfriend toward James while she angled herself closer to Devon and Neil. "Here, watch them."

Devon didn't flinch when Kayla used her body to prop up Devon. Her head was pillowed on the other woman's chest. Lush and inviting. Devon closed her eyes and lost herself in sensation, untroubled by false boundaries or the labels people would try to apply to what they shared here tonight. None of those stigmas mattered. She opened her heart and allowed the experience to take her where it would.

"You look so sexy together." Neil sighed as he stroked first Kayla's hair, then Devon's. He settled in the V of her thighs, rocking his erection over her saturated pussy. "I have to have you."

"She's trembling." Kayla chaffed Devon's arms as though it were cold making her system go haywire. Too bad there was no cure for sensual devastation. Then again, if this was what it felt like to be sick she never would hunt for a cure.

"Please." Devon couldn't muster anything more intelligent than that. She feared if he didn't possess her soon, she'd come with the next breeze over her clit.

"You're pretty when you beg." He flashed her a wolfish smile as he fit them together and pushed.

"No. No." She tried to shove him off when she realized that his invasion would mean surrender, but Kayla's hands kept her arms pinned by her side. "Not yet."

"I told you I'd make you come with one stroke, didn't I?" His arrogant grin stole her last shred of resistance.

Devon shattered around him as he advanced down her channel, battling the tight rings of muscle contracting in rhythmic cycles. Instead of slowing, he ramped up his attack. A quick, harsh explosion of rapture turned into something she'd never experienced before. The peak of her climax extended. It picked up again and again the moment she thought it might flag.

"That's right, Dev." Kayla combatted the fire in her skin with gentle caresses. "Let go. Let him push you further than you've ever gone before."

"Oh, shit." Mike grunted. "It's too much."

Devon saw arcs of his pearly come shoot from his cock to drape over James's ass and pool in his lower back. The proof of their leader's satisfaction seemed to be too much for James. He shouted a warning. Joe continued to milk James's cock.

"You earned it, James." Dave held the kneeling man as he surrendered. Neil's hips stuttered as he allowed his glance to stray to his lover.

"Give it to him, James. All of it. No holding back." The

animalistic command from Neil had Devon clamping down on him again... No, still.

James spilled his release over Joe's hand, which pumped him dry. Unlike the other guys, he didn't relax or cuddle with his spent crewmates. Instead, James crawled closer until he joined her and Neil where Neil still pummeled her.

The power of so many hot stares on her ratcheted Devon to new heights. A foreign pressure built low in her belly. From an endless orgasm, something new and bright developed. It glowed stronger, hotter, inside her when James knelt between Neil's spread legs. He put one hand on each cheek of Neil's ass and spread him wide.

If James hadn't just sprayed Joe's hand with enough force to sandblast Joe's skin, she might have thought he planned to fuck Neil while Neil fucked her. Oh God. Then he did something she didn't expect. His tongue slithered from between his lips and rimmed Neil's ass.

The cock buried inside her jerked as though someone had touched it with a live wire. Neil cursed, held perfectly still for half a second then went wild. He fucked her with an innate grace that complimented his complete surrender to base instinct. James dipped his tongue inside the clenching portal of his lover's ass, fucking it even as he wriggled the wet muscle all around.

The knot of tension drew tighter inside Devon until she feared falling from so great a height. Could she survive the drop?

Neil lifted his head, staring straight into her eyes. "Need. You. Now."

She whimpered because she couldn't give him what he craved. The power of their exchange frightened her away from the edge. He fucked harder, the ridges of his veined shaft stroking her in all the right places. James increased the frequency of his devious manipulation.

"We've got you, Devon." Kayla smiled down at her. "I won't let you fall."

The relief that suffused her made her reach without thinking. Devon wrapped her fingers around the back of Kayla's neck and tugged. She accepted the warmth her friend offered in a gentle, grounding kiss that rocked her foundation.

"Oh Jesus." Neil gasped. "So damn hot. I'm coming."

She didn't need his warning to know that. Liquid fire seared her insides as jet after jet of his come overflowed her pussy. James sank from his attentions on Neil's ass to lap at the excess. He nuzzled Neil's tight sac and feasted on the creamy result of their loving.

Between the silky press of Kayla's lips on her mouth, Neil's body and cock imprinting on her core and James's tongue lapping at the seam between them, Devon lost control. She came so hard she thought she might injure Neil. His agonized moan seemed ripped from his chest as she squeezed him again and again and again.

She exploded in an orgasm strong enough to trigger an out of body experience. She could see her toes curling around one of the silken strands of the net, watched herself getting lost in the arms of a man and woman she had met not long ago but could never again be separated from.

Devon reached for James, unable to find him in the sea of pleasure and light that consumed her. She searched as far down Neil's back as she could reach, longing to complete the circuit by linking her fingers with James.

He wasn't there.

As though dunked in ice water, she cooled rapidly.

Neil crashed to the woven lounger beside her, huffing as though he'd run a marathon. She stroked his still flexing ass as she scanned the area wildly for the other man who'd given her pleasure.

A mop of unruly brown hair disappeared behind the hedge.

Devon would have scrambled out of the netting, less than gracefully, still trying to coordinate her limbs. Except Neil clung to her, smiling against her breast as though he hadn't noticed James missing.

"We need to find—" Her warning cut short when Dave pitched his voice above the sighs and soft whispering of the other couples. They groaned when the beefcake jostled them all by rolling to the edge of the lounger where he plucked something from one of the pretty flowerbeds surrounding one of the corner supports.

No more lube needed, Davey.

He returned, tugging Kayla to his side.

"I realize this might be the most unorthodox time for this, but like you always say...it feels right." He cupped Kayla's cheek in fingers that looked far too large for how gently he touched her. "You and me. We're permanent. This. You. I need it forever. Please tell me you do too, Kay."

He cracked open a small velvet box and withdrew a ring featuring a rock large enough to glitter even in the diffuse lighting from the lanterns.

"Is that—?" She sat bolt upright.

"Yeah." He grinned at her slack jaw. "Will you marry me?"

Things kicked into slow motion right about then. Devon's heart expanded as Kayla's eyes filled with joyous tears. She smiled when Kay flung herself at her sturdy lover, squealing.

Dave reached for her at the same time.

Somewhere in the middle, their limbs collided and the ring pinched between Dave's banged-up thumb and forefinger popped into the air. It flipped end over end, sending a cascade of rainbows across the wide-eyed faces around the couple, before splashing into the pond below them with a distinct *plop*.

"Oh shit." Neil tried to muffle his laughter against Devon's shoulder.

Mike reacted first. "Don't freak. It's all right. This is a closed system, we'll wait until morning and then fish it out nice and easy."

"Morning?" Kayla framed her face with her palms. "Oh no. I'm so sorry—"

"My fault. I came so hard I almost blew the top of my fucking skull off. Then when you kissed Devon... Christ. My fingers aren't working quite right." Dave groaned. "It fell right through the ropes. I heard the splash."

"So did I." Neil already scanned the space below them. Aside from the occasional glint off a ripple on the surface, the rest was inky blackness.

Dave looked around at his friends. "This is going to be funny one day, right?"

"It's cracking me up right now." Neil smiled.

"I thought I was following my gut. Maybe I had gas from all those baked beans." Dave *thunked* his forehead with the heel of his hand. "She didn't say yes, did she?"

"Start over." Mike suggested. "We'll worry about the ring in a minute."

Dave took a huge breath. "Kayla. I think tonight proved everything I already knew. I've found the only place I want to be. The only people I want to share my life with. I wanted to ask you to accept the ring I dropped in the motherfucking koi pond as a symbol of our love. I wanted to know... Will you marry me?"

Kayla squealed again and tackled Dave.

They tumbled to the lounger in a knot of arms and long, tattooed legs.

Coming to rest on his back, Dave held Kayla's hips as she straddled him. "Is that a yes?"

"Yes!" Half the crew shouted the answer at the same time as Kayla.

Tears poured down Devon's face. It was the most beautiful moment she'd ever witnessed. Goof and all.

The guys kicked into action, making arrangements to pull lights off their trucks and haul a battery down to power them.

"I'm the smallest. I'll go in once you guys grab the gear. It shouldn't be hard to find if I can slip under the edge there. Dave and Kayla stay where you are so I have a reference point."

She shouldn't have bothered with that directive. The couple didn't appear to be moving anytime soon. They cuddled, lost in each other and the pure love they shared.

DEVON ROUNDED a bend in the path, planning to run up to the driveway and retrieve the waterproof flashlight she'd recalled she'd stashed in her glove compartment. She jogged up the hillside, grateful for the warmth her muscles and lingering adrenaline generated.

Harsh voices caught her off guard and she slowed.

"Why are you being such a dickhead?" Neil's frustration sliced through the night. She couldn't be sure, but she thought he might have shoved his lover, who appeared to be ignoring the aggravated man.

This time her tremor had nothing to do with the cold, unless it was the frost in Neil's tone.

Guess he'd found James. She started to turn around and leave them to their privacy.

"You made love to Devon." James sounded both admiring and wrecked if such a thing were possible.

The agony in his proclamation had her longing to wrap him in a hug though she was probably the last person he'd welcome comfort from. Torn, she couldn't walk away yet she didn't dare to intrude.

"I've fucked dozens of women while you watched. You never minded before. All of a sudden this is a problem?" Neil didn't cut him any slack. "You know what I need. Hell, you've gotten off on sharing plenty before."

"You've never looked at a woman the way you look at her. You've never fit with one of them like you were meant for each other." James's voice cracked.

Whoa. Devon couldn't justify hiding in the shadows a moment longer. She emerged into the open meadow, approaching them as carefully as if they were an improperly braced structure. "How exactly does Neil look at me?"

They turned toward her with matching frowns.

"Like he looks at *me*." James shook his head. "Looked at me. Like you're everything to him. I never cared about playing around before because I could tell his exchanges with women were purely physical. This is the first time he's really taken a lover. I guess I assumed it'd always be me he went home with at the end of the day."

"I'm not trying to change that." Devon's heart ached. Because somewhere deep down she could admit she was lying. She wanted Neil. Tonight. Every night. Forever. She should have known whatever unconventional role she'd been playing was too good to be true.

"It's too late. Has been since the very first day. When I found you on the curb, he'd already fallen. I could see it in his eyes." James shrugged. "You didn't do anything but be you. I want to be pissed, but I can't. He loves you. And I can see why. You're sweet, strong, funny, hardworking, sexy and kind. Just promise me you'll treat him well. I won't stand for him to be hurt."

Neil interrupted. "James, what are you saying?"

"I'm going to grant your wish. I've only ever wanted you to be happy." James bit his lip to still the quivering there.

"He wants you." Devon had never been surer of anything in her life.

"No, he wants *you*." James didn't scrub the tear that ran down his cheek.

She leaned closer, opening her arms.

James spun away.

Before she could follow, Mike and Joe crashed up the path, laughing and causing a ruckus. "What's taking so long? Dave's getting his panties in a bunch."

Devon shrugged and left the men alone. Maybe Neil could talk to his boyfriend if she gave them peace.

TWO HOURS LATER, Devon held the ring in her fist and pumped it over her head while doing a silly victory dance. Dave and Joe stared at her tits for a second or two before hauling her from the pond.

"I believe this belongs to you." She placed the gorgeous hunk of diamond and platinum in Dave's broad palm.

"No, ma'am. It belongs to her." He knelt at Kayla's feet and slid the ring onto her shaking third finger. "I love you, Kay."

"I love you too." She sniffled. "It's gorgeous, Dave. Truly."

"Not half as much as you." He climbed to his feet and kissed her temple before turning to Devon.

"Thank you." They both enveloped her in a hug despite the rivulets of pond water dripping off her. "Oh, no. You're freezing."

Mike and Kate swooped in with blankets to wrap her in, though even a blowtorch couldn't combat the ice solidifying her heart. She stood on the fringes of the gathering as the rest of the crew celebrated. Neil pulled James into a fierce hug. Sometime during the search, their tempers had dissipated.

Neil kissed the slighter man full on the mouth. Their lips slanted, interlocking. They got lost in each other. No way would she risk destroying that bond.

Devon backed slowly into the shadows, outside the glow bathing the rest of the crew.

When she was sure they hadn't noticed, she ran.

Toward her forgotten dress.

Toward the keys to her truck.

Toward her lonely reality—one that didn't involve a fantasy come to life in the form of two hot studs and an array of loyal, lifelong friends.

When she crested the hill, dragging the blankets through the grass behind her, Devon's shoulders slumped. Neil and James leaned against their truck as though they'd used their dynamic duo powers to leap up the hillside in a single bound.

"How—?"

"Not important." James crossed his arms over his chest.

"Where do you think you're going like that?" Neil surveyed her from her damp hair to her bare, painted toes.

"Home." She hated how her teeth chattered.

"Our home, sure." James relaxed his stance, opening his arms. "I'm sorry you overheard us arguing before. I didn't mean to scare you off."

"Does that mean your feelings have changed?" She allowed herself to lean on him, no matter how weak it made her. His arms came around her. He was so generous considering the depth of the despair she'd glimpsed in him earlier.

"Why don't we talk about that when we're not all exhausted and hypothermia is less of a possibility?" He evaded her questions, killing her with kindness.

"He's right, Dev." Neil opened the door to their truck and ushered them inside before rounding to the driver's side. He trapped her between them. "Let's figure things out in the morning."

James cranked up the heat and sang softly to her while he rocked them both. Before they'd made it out of the driveway, her lids were unbearably heavy.

6

From the doorway of the walk-in closet he shared with his boyfriend, James's peripheral vision treated him to a glimpse of Neil exiting the shower. He refused to stare though Neil ruffled his hair with a thick gray towel, and then slung it low around his waist. The dreamy smile he wore as he sank to the edge of their bed beside Devon looked even finer on him than the tux he'd rented for Mike and Kate's wedding. And that was saying something.

James couldn't bear to spend the night pretending not to notice such blatant gooeyness. He reached for the duffel he'd packed and stashed beneath the neat row of the few button up shirts he owned. After tugging on a fitted T-shirt, he slipped the strap of the bag crosswise over his chest.

He rehearsed his departure announcement several times before he shut the door behind him, determined to keep calm.

A deep breath didn't do him any good when he spun around and caught the pale, hollow cast to Neil's cheeks, devoid of the dimples he'd so recently sported. Air lodged in James's throat, choking him. Still, he managed to spit out his decision. "Gonna bunk over at Joe and Morgan's tonight."

"Are you leaving me?" Neil tried to stand. He lost his balance and plopped onto the mattress once more. The gap in his towel wrap widened.

For once, the flash of bronzed skin didn't entice James. He rubbed the ache in his chest. A heart attack couldn't hurt this much. "I'm giving you room to take what you need."

"I need *you*," Neil whispered.

"You need her too."

Even now, Neil's fingers rubbed the crook of her knee as though he could leech strength from their cute, tomboyish assistant.

"Too. As in *both*. Not one or the other." It sounded as though every syllable cost Neil a year of his life. The scratchy, desperate pleas were foreign territory for James's confident lover.

"Are you sure? Maybe you should spend time alone with her and see." It killed James to offer. But he wouldn't risk what they had by allowing Neil to develop a sliver of regret. It'd be better to sell out on an amazing high than tarnish their gleaming relationship by dragging it through the muck of a prolonged degradation.

"I'm positive." Neil glanced from where Devon had crashed on their bed. Tiny and angelic, she nestled in the chocolate and sky-blue, satin-covered pillows. "Look at her."

James did. He cleared his mind and opened his eyes.

Something in him stirred.

Was that because she was his boyfriend's girlfriend?

Or because a spark grew in his gut every time they shared her? Or even hung out with her at work or for fun? Could he remove Neil from the equation and still feel... something...for her?

Women weren't usually his thing. Still, her honest curiosity called to him. He toyed with the overnight bag, lifting it partially over his head before he realized what he was doing.

"And look at you." Neil rose and stepped closer. He framed James's face with gentle hands. "You're so generous. Ridiculously self-sacrificing. A man I wish I could be half as decent as. How can I not want you both? Please, James. Don't make me choose. You. Her. You're perfect. For me. And for each other."

"I—" Some of his doubts evaporated as he stared into the eyes of the only man he'd ever loved so ferociously. Could there be room for another person? Maybe. God knew they had plenty of passion to spare.

"Trust me?" Neil drew the duffle the rest of the way off and kicked it into the corner. He grabbed the hem of James's shirt and dispatched that too.

"I do." James gasped as Neil sank before him, unbuckling his belt then lowering the zipper on his well-worn jeans. "Neil?"

"Yeah?" He looked up from his position on the floor, his lips half an inch from James's cock.

"What are you doing?"

"What do you think?" He licked a trail from James's balls to the tip of his rapidly hardening shaft.

"Did you forget you *hate* giving blow jobs?" As if Neil needed to be reminded of his own dislike. "You don't do it. Not even on my birthday."

"I would do anything for you." Neil serviced James with a tenderness that speared straight to his soul.

James couldn't resist the sublime treat. Within minutes, his knees weakened. Neil braced them on his shoulders as he worshipped the solid hard-on James had for the man he adored. Safe, protected, cherished—James read a dozen promises in the tender ministrations his lover pampered him with.

He tried to prolong the pleasure. Keep it going forever, always knowing that was impossible. Which didn't mean they couldn't revive it again and again. A million times. In each other's arms. As long as he stayed around for Neil to lift him up next time.

With a tortured moan, he poured himself into Neil's hungry mouth.

After drinking every last drop of James's release, Neil led them to their bed. He lay in the center, drawing James with him. One sculpted arm curled around Devon and the other sheltered James. Neil held them both so they rode the ragged rise and fall of his chest.

James listened to the pounding of his mate's heart, so strong he almost missed the ghost of Neil's begging. "Please don't leave us. Please."

"I won't." He couldn't. He'd never be able to walk away without destroying himself in the process. Anything else he'd convinced himself of was a lame combination of bravado and delusion. "I promise. I'm yours."

"Both of ours?"

"We'll see. It's the best I can do." He rubbed the flexing abs he'd often admired until Neil seemed to calm and his respiration evened out.

James lifted his head to study his sleeping boyfriend. After sipping tears from Neil's eyes, he dropped his head to Neil's sturdy shoulder and tried to follow him into sweet dreams.

Despite the exhausting drain of the day and night, he couldn't relax. Restless, he shifted. Devon did too. Her hand covered his on Neil's belly. Delicate fingers wove through his. She sighed, squeezing a little even while unconscious. Rather than being uncomfortable with the gesture, James found the heat of their connection eased him into slumber.

Maybe this could work.

Devon's lids fluttered open. She stared across the chiseled expanse of Neil's abdomen, where her cheek rested, to the man occupying the far side of her lover's torso.

Mmm. James. Her other lover. How decadent?

Soft blue light flickered over the slight whisker burn rouging his cheeks. What had she missed by checking out early last night?

A moan rumbled from the chest of the man pillowing them both. Neil's fingers flexed on her ribs as she watched his other hand mirror the pressure on James, hugging them both tighter to him. Devon couldn't muster the energy required to lift her head and check out the television Neil stared at. She murmured, "Are you watching porn?"

James didn't move from his contented slouch. However, the corner of his lips kicked up. "Doubt it. He's not hard. I checked."

"You two know I can hear you, right?"

Her head bounced a little when Neil chuckled. The growl of his stomach almost startled her bolt upright.

With one ear pressed to his svelte torso, the rumble echoed louder than a jet engine.

"Oh, yeah. I'm sure now." James blinked then grinned at her. "He's watching the Food Network. Probably *Barbeque University* if I know our boy. I wouldn't be surprised if he came in his pants every time the host gets to the part of the show where he lays on the *crosshatch of grill marks*."

"I'm not wearing pants, smartass." Neil ruffled James's hair. "You know, I wouldn't be forced to drool over another dude's meat if you could cook worth a damn."

"You should be an expert by now. You watch this shit enough." James poked Neil in the stomach. His steely abs didn't dent in a single millimeter.

The pause hung in the air long enough all Devon could do was laugh. "If you're hoping I can channel Rachel Ray, you're out of luck. Sorry, guys. Although, I do have some pretty awesome delivery places programmed into my phone."

She sighed and wondered where they'd stashed her purse.

"No need." Neil snagged a cell off the nightstand and punched in a series of digits from memory. "Do you like chicken lo mein?"

"For breakfast?" Devon raised a brow.

"It's almost noon, sleepyheads." Neil caressed both of their shoulders.

"How long have you been sitting there?" James shifted uneasily.

"About four hours I guess." He shrugged. "The time went by fast. But I really could use something to eat."

"Okay then." Devon grinned. "I *love* chicken lo mein. *If* you order it from Mr. China."

"Wouldn't dare to try anything else." James smiled at her. "We're regulars. Too bad they're pick up only. Give me a minute and I'll get dressed."

"No, I woke you up." Neil untucked himself from their drowsy tangle of limbs. "I'll be back before you know it. Doze off again and I'll help you refuel with steamy, noodley goodness in no time. Or maybe you two could... ah...talk. Or something."

He glanced between them as though they might tear each other limb from limb if he weren't there to referee. Devon laughed. "We'll be fine without a chaperone."

"If only that was my concern." He scrubbed his hand over his sexy scruff.

"You're good?" He shot James a pointed glance.

"Yeah, dad." James and Devon laughed together.

"Fine, fine." Neil flipped them the bird as he hopped into a pair of maroon running shorts and snagged James's discarded T-shirt from the floor. The fitted style, a size smaller than he usually wore, snugged to his muscles. "Don't miss me too much."

They giggled some more until the barking of the neighbor's dog replaced the fading roar of Neil's truck engine, reminding Devon just how alone they really were. "So..."

"So." James covered his face with his palms. "This is horrible. Awkward. All my fault. I'm sorry for yesterday."

Devon hesitated for a moment before reaching out. She nudged his hand from his cheeks and laced their fingers. "That's not necessary. I can't imagine how hard this must be for you. I would be insanely jealous if my boyfriend suddenly had a perma-boner for someone else. Never mind if he introduced them to our relationship. I probably would have walked. After scratching his eyes out with a rusty screwdriver."

"Last night... I'm not proud of it, but I almost did. Walk. Not the gouging thing. That's such a girl move." James grinned as he rearranged the pillows. He rolled to his side so they were eye to eye.

"I realize I'm probably the last person on earth you'd choose to talk to about this. I promise to be open minded if you need to vent. And I meant what I said yesterday, I won't come between you two. What you have is too special. I could leave before he comes back—"

"Don't. You're part of us now." James surprised her by reaching out to prevent her from rising. He traced one of her brows with the tip of his finger. "I admit this is something new for me. Talking. I could get used to having someone to confide in. Neil isn't always the best at emotional frankness."

"Okay, then. I'd like to be totally honest if you'll lend me your ear." She closed her eyes, trying not to purr when he expanded his path above her eye to include her cheek and neck as well.

"I insist." His breath warmed her chin.

She opened her eyes, wondering when they'd drawn so close together.

"If it weren't for you, Neil probably would have scared me away in the beginning. Before I got to know him better. He's a little too...brash sometimes."

"Really?" James considered that for a minute. "I guess I can see that."

"For example, my first day. It was a cluster of an introduction until you came out. Like a translator, you made everything flow between us. You know when to pull him back or when he's skirting my comfort zone. I don't think you realize you temper him."

"Actually, I've always felt like I have to clean up after him when he chows down on those enormous feet of his. I didn't think anyone else noticed." James stared into her eyes, really looking deep for the first time.

Did he see some of himself in her?

"I've noticed a lot about you, James." She narrowed the chasm of remaining space between them, resting her forehead against his. He didn't flinch when she ran her hand up his side, loving the dip and curve of his ribs. "Like how you grit your teeth when someone makes short jokes about you. Or how you take the newspaper to the old lady who lives next door to our project so she doesn't have to struggle down her front stairs every morning. Or how you set aside some of your sandwich meat for that stray cat that's been coming around. Tell Neil you want to adopt it, would you? He can't say no to you. I wouldn't be able to either. It was you I had a crush on first."

"Really?" He seemed so surprised.

"Yes." She dredged courage from the far reaches of her psyche then leaned forward to brush her lips against his. When he opened his mouth, inviting her to take more, she retreated, needing to finish their conversation first. He had to understand. "You're pretty fantastic. And totally my type—loyal, sensitive and smoking hot without trying."

"I'm not usually attracted to women." He tugged a strand of her short hair. "You're not very girly though."

"Gee thanks." Devon barked out a laugh as though the barb hadn't hit a sore spot. "I take back the sensitive part."

"I *like* the way you are." His hand wandered from her face, around the shell of her ear, down her neck then ended up palming her breast. Not that she had much to speak of. Unlike Kate and Morgan. "You're so soft underneath your tough girl act. I'm afraid I'll hurt you."

So was she.

"I never have to worry about that with the crew. They can handle anything I can dish out and then some." His hand skimmed her skin again, this time landing on her ass. He yanked her tight to him, impressing her with the bulge of his cock.

Hallelujah.

"I think I can take you too." She cupped him, savoring the hiss of his intake. "Why don't you try me?"

He nodded almost imperceptibly before gliding his lips over hers with sips lighter than a feather. Something in her unfurled, like a sprouting flower. She knew it would be gorgeous when fully grown. All it needed was the sunshine of his attention and water to fuel the process, which Neil would be happy to supply as the gardener of their affection.

"Damn, Dev." He moaned before sealing their mouths more fully.

Their kiss lingered forever. Playful, intense, exploratory and genuinely affectionate—making out had never meant so much to her. Their flickering tongues communicated more than simple promises.

Her entire body flashed hot when he levered her thigh over his hip. The pressure of his erection riding her slit coupled with the glide of his smooth chest over her nipples as they moved together. Sighing. Smiling. Dancing in time to the synchronized heartbeats that amplified where their bodies converged.

"I want to make love to you, Devon." He groaned against her neck when he retreated to catch his breath. "Not because you're Neil's, but because I think you might be mine too. Will you let me inside you when he comes home?"

"Of course." She squirmed against him, drawing a tortured groan from his delectable throat. "But I don't think I can wait very long. I'm dying to have you."

"Lucky for you both, I'm right here." Neil spoke low enough not to startle them. "Have been for a little while. Couldn't bear to break you apart though."

Her senses went on high alert. She could detect the quickening of James's pulse at the juncture of their torsos. Especially when Neil stalked closer, sliding onto the mattress behind her so she was sandwiched between them both, all three on their sides. The slow, gentle rocking that followed made her pretty sure he stroked himself as he watched her and James continue to grind on one another.

"And for the record, I never expect you to wait. You should do what you like. Make each other happy. Nothing would please me more than to know you're taking care of one another when I'm not around." Neil dropped a kiss to her cheek then squeezed James shoulder. "Go ahead. Forget I'm here."

Devon and James laughed together. As if that were possible.

Still, the prodding of James's cock grew more insistent as he drove it in an arc against her moist folds. Devon didn't suppress the instinct that had her changing the angle of her hips. His blunt tip aligned with her opening.

"You're sure you're ready?" James whispered. "We're not easy men to love. Working together...and the crew..."

"There are a million excuses we could manufacture to quit right now." She silenced his objections with another scorching kiss. When he'd surrendered to the power of their lust, she continued. "I'm not taking the easy path and neither are you. Let's reach for something bigger. Together. All three of us."

"Nine of us," Neil whispered behind her.

"Mmm. Yes." She accepted his refinement.

"Yes." James proved his agreement in the basest method possible. He bored inside her, slow yet steady. His cock seated comfortably in her wet pussy. Being petite had never served her well during sex. Often it became painful. But James fit her just right. He filled her tight channel, gasping her name when he bottomed out.

Neil assisted his lovers by raising Devon's top leg higher, giving James more room to operate. "Go ahead, she's ready for you."

Ready? She might stroke out if he didn't diffuse her skyrocketing blood pressure.

James didn't need to be told twice. He trusted Neil to guide them. The escalating frequency and power of his thrusts inside her didn't mean he abandoned the sweet grind they'd fallen into. No, he combined the two into a rhythm all their own. His pelvis circled her clit at the peak of every driving stroke.

"She's getting tighter." James groaned, his eyes flicking to Neil. "She's going to come on me, isn't she?"

"Damn straight." Neil beamed as he ran his hands all over her shoulders, ass, legs and the breast he could reach. "You're doing good, James. Real good. Make her shatter and I'll take care of you. Show her how much you like being in that pretty pussy."

James stared straight into her eyes.

She knew. Without words. Without sex. He let her see exactly what occupied his soul. She understood because it was the same for her. She'd found her place in the universe. Right here with them. And their friends.

Devon surrendered to the bliss shimmering through her veins and along every nerve ending in her body. She clenched, trying to hold James as deep inside her as he could reside. He cursed as he continued to caress her from the inside, granting every one of her wishes when he kissed her as he pushed her over the edge.

Neil closed in, bracketing her between them, protecting her back from the world outside their group. His cock nudged beside James's. The waves of orgasm built higher as he poked the very tip inside her with his boyfriend's. The unrelenting convulsions of her pussy wouldn't allow him to penetrate completely. Even that little bit was enough to set her off again and again in an unending storm of pleasure filled with chain lighting strikes. Electricity arced between Neil and James, with her conducting the current.

"We'll work up to that, baby." Neil promised. "Someday soon you'll have us both."

James cried out. The desperate shout made her aware he hadn't come with her. Not yet.

"Help him," she begged Neil.

"I thought you'd never ask." He flashed a toothy grin.

When she started to pull away from James, Neil smacked her ass. "Don't you dare. We're going to do this together."

He reached to the nightstand. When the snick of a cap cut through the ringing in her ears, she grinned. "James, you want him to fuck you while you fuck me?"

He grunted, unable to form coherent speech. He followed her as she rolled to her back, spreading her legs wide so he could nestle deep in the V of her thighs. He continued to ride her, less frantically now, prolonging the life of the embers of desire still sparking inside her.

"Fast, Neil. Hard." James tried to tug his boyfriend closer when he approached. A single raised eyebrow from the taller man had James sighing as though turning to putty.

"I'm aiming for slow and gentle." Neil laid a trail of open-mouthed kisses down James's spine. His fingers must have probed James's back entrance. James tensed between her legs and fucked deep. The motion ignited a flare of ecstasy.

"Oh my God." Devon gasped. "I vote for James's idea. Two to one. Hurry, Neil, I think I'm going to come again."

"So responsive." James kissed her until all she could focus on was his taste. Then he grunted.

"Who am I to argue?" Neil fisted his cock in one hand, towering over them as he squatted behind James. With one smooth push, he introduced his hard-on to his lover's ass. "I'll always do my best to give you what you need. Both of you."

He set a demanding pace. Every lunge seated him to the hilt, driving James forward into Devon. The weight of both their lean bodies on her didn't suffocate her. It cocooned her in warmth and security.

"Oh God. Yes. Yes!" James buried his face in the crook of her neck.

Devon speared her fingers into his hair, massaging his scalp.

Neil smiled, slow and broad, as he observed them together. "Thank you. Both of you. I'm the luckiest bastard in the world."

He leaned down to kiss Devon, melting her with the tenderness he showed her lips while fucking them both into oblivion. Then James titled his face, joining the fray. The instant their tongues tangled, another climax struck.

She unraveled, drawing James with her. The flood of his hot come poured into her pussy. At the same time, Neil shouted and his movements became uneven.

"Ah yeah." James kept coming with spurt after spurt that overflowed her. Moisture trickled along the seam of her ass. She would bet James could say the same if the corded tendons and still pumping hips she saw on Neil were to be believed.

With one last fierce spasm, she hugged James tight. Then they collapsed together. Somehow the guys managed not to crush her as they tumbled to the mattress beside her. Snuggled between their sweaty, heaving chests, she allowed the world to fade away.

But not before she heard them declare their love for each other.

And for her.

EPILOGUE

Devon licked the last of the butter cream icing from her fork one tong at a time. She pretended not to notice the inappropriate stares of her two lovers though she promised herself she'd make up for teasing them later. First, she had a bouquet to catch. Hopefully.

"I can't believe how perfectly everything went off. Most weddings have at least one catastrophe." She scowled. "Then again, I'm wearing a fucking dress. That's pretty horrific."

"You look great. Kate picked something nice for her bridesmaids. Probably since she knows she'll be standing up for Morgan and Kay soon." Neil offered her a bite of his slice of Mike and Kate's wedding cake.

"You don't want it?" She shot him an are-you-crazy glance. "Morgan did an awesome job."

"It's delicious." He agreed. "But watching you devour it is even better."

"I'll give you a dollar if you smuggle us a few slices to eat in bed." James squeezed her knee under the lilac tablecloth. "No utensils needed. I've heard women make pretty great plates."

"Damn. I've always admired the way you think." Neil shot his partner a heated glance. "Although this is wedding cake, not birthday cake."

They laughed together.

Every instant was foreplay for the wedding night that wasn't theirs but might as well have been. Devon glanced up in time to catch Kayla watching them with her head canted as Dave swirled her around the dance floor.

Things had been insane lately as they rushed to wrap up their latest project before Mike left for his honeymoon. The crew hadn't gotten to spend as much time exploring as usual. Could that be why Kay seemed so...interested?

"Guys—?"

"Yeah, Dev?" Neil angled her face toward his to lick a dollop of chocolate from the corner of her mouth.

"Ah, never mind." She shook her head.

"Since when are we keeping secrets from each other?" Neil's intense focus stole her breath.

"Don't let him pressure you." James rubbed her arm. "You don't have to share your thoughts."

"It's more like I'm not sure now is the right time." She surrendered a small sigh. "It's just that I've been wondering lately... How do you know when to act on one of your fantasies with the crew and when you're having an idle daydream?"

"Uh, honey, we've pretty much done everything I ever imagined. Most everything that's possible and a few things I didn't think were." Neil barked out a laugh. "What's left?"

Devon reached for James. He gripped her hand. She

peeked up and found Kayla still staring. She met the other woman's gaze and smiled at her friend.

"Do you remember that first night with the whole group?" She looked between her two men, amazed she was so lucky and ashamed of being so greedy.

"You really think I could forget it?" Neil laughed.

"One of the best nights of my life." James bussed her knuckles.

"What about when Kay kissed me?" She couldn't believe heat tingled in her cheeks after all they'd been through.

"Holy shit, Dev." Neil knocked a napkin into his lap when someone passed close behind them. "Are you saying...?"

"Maybe." She shrugged. "I think I'd like to try it. Do you suppose she would—"

"Yes!" Both guys answered in unison.

"Kayla's bi, Devon." James stroked a wisp of hair from her face. "She mentioned it during that snow storm we told you about. The one that finally forced her and Dave to come together."

"Well, then." She cleared her throat. "Maybe next time, when we're all sharing, we could see what happens?"

"Damn, I love you." Neil nibbled a line down her neck while James kissed her sweetly.

"We'll be there with you. No pressure. You know how the crew works." James held her shaking hand. "It gets better every time we're together. And I've noticed lately that some of the girls have wandering hands. It might be time for another crew meeting. Have you ever wanted to touch the other guys? How would you feel about Kate or Morgan with me or James?"

"Oh." She blinked. "That would be…interesting."

"Interesting hot or interesting not?" Neil didn't pressure her. He seemed genuinely concerned.

"We better talk about this more upstairs. In bed. After someone takes the edge off. Or maybe we could slip under the table here for a minute." She practically panted. "Then I could probably think more clearly."

Both guys laughed.

"Yeah, I feel the same about it." Neil grinned.

"Me too," James echoed.

"Why exactly do you three look like you're up to no good?" Mike sauntered over, his chest puffed up to ridiculous dimensions with his lovely bride on his elbow.

Kate was radiant in her antique lace gown.

"I guess it's because every time I think we can't get luckier, I realize there's more to explore. More love to share." James stood to kiss Kate on the cheek. "I think today's the beginning of a new era. One I can't wait to spend with my best friends."

Morgan and Joe rejoined the head table, a pair of shit-eating grins on their faces. Neil stealthily retucked Joe's shirt while Devon plucked a leaf from Morgan's hair.

"The gardens are lovely, aren't they?" Kate winked.

"Spectacular." Joe nodded, trying to keep a straight face.

The pop song in the background faded into a familiar wedding standard. *What a Wonderful World* had never seemed as perfect to Devon as it did in that moment. The lyrics washed over her as Kayla and Dave took the last two seats at the table.

"Tired of dancing?" Joe poked Dave in the ribs.

"Maybe we missed you guys." Kayla rested her head

on Mike's shoulder. "It's going to be weird not having you around for a few weeks."

"Don't let things go to shit. Morgan, you're in charge. Keep these guys in line, would you?" Their foreman chuckled. "I'm going to be too busy to answer calls for bail money."

Kate scooted as close to her husband of three hours as her voluminous crinoline would allow. "You might be the one phoning a friend. I'm pretty sure some of the things I'll be doing to you are illegal in most countries."

"Then what the hell are we waiting for?" He stood up so fast he almost knocked his chair over.

"I wanted to say goodbye to everyone." She sniffled. "Thank you all for making today the best day of my life. I love you. Every one of you."

"Crap. Not again." Morgan dabbed her eyes with the corner of a napkin. "Go on. Take your ridiculously handsome husband and get out of here."

"All right, then I guess there's only one more thing left to do." Kate bustled from her chair with Mike at her elbow for support. She made it halfway across the dance floor before peeking over her shoulder and taking aim.

She tossed her bouquet in Devon's direction.

It would have been a direct hit if not for the ceiling fan over their table.

A *whmmmp* similar to a table saw cut through the sappy music and the din of conversation before a shower of petals rained onto the rest of the crew. Devon raised her hands, palms up, to catch as much of the floral confetti as possible.

Rainbow colored bits of fauna decorated them all evenly.

The photographer Mike had hired swooped in close

and took a candid picture of the disaster. Devon knew she would frame one of the standard portraits of the group they'd sat for earlier to hang in the living room of the apartment she shared with James and Neil.

But the snapshot he'd just captured would go in their bedroom.

It would live in the hearts and minds of the crew.

Forever.

NAILED TO THE WALL
POWERTOOLS
JAYNE RYLON
NEW YORK TIMES BESTSELLING AUTHOR

For Eleanor Lees, the undisputed queen of that's what he/she said jokes. I especially love it when you do it to yourself (that's what she said!). You crack me up.

1

————

"**M**y hands are full, stick it in my mouth." Devon wrapped her lips around the stem of the lavender rose Kate wagged in her direction.

Kayla sing-songed, "That's what *he* said."

Devon choked. She met her friend's gaze in the mirror, then burst out laughing. It was even funnier because her joke held a kernel of truth. When their husbands and the rest of the crew got together for one of their steamy sessions, the logistics of five guys going at it made for some interesting challenges.

Somehow she managed not to drop the pretty prop clasped between her teeth. The laces on the corset Morgan had been tightening around Devon's slim ribcage slipped in the aftermath of their raucous exhalations.

"Shit, sorry," she mumbled around the flower, hoping it had no thorns. Then she forced herself to calm down. An extended sigh deflated her torso. She yanked taut the panels of the garment she attempted to squeeze into, less certain than ever about this foray into femininity.

Being girly was not her strength.

Morgan seized the opportunity to cinch the black satin. Embedded with boning, it hugged Devon tight. A few flicks of Morgan's fingers left the long tails of a bow dancing over the swells of Devon's ass. She'd seen postage stamps bigger than the matching thong they'd bought to complete her ensemble. It didn't protect the skin bared between her skimpy undies and the top of her fishnets from the brush of the soft laces.

"Damn, you're smoking hot." Morgan surveyed her handiwork before nodding.

Devon angled her torso sideways to the mirror, cupped her breasts, then plucked the rose out of her mouth. "It's magic. It makes even me look stacked."

"Because it squishes your already tiny waist down to the size of my pinky." Kayla pouted. "I hate you."

Ever the practical one, Kate marched over. She slipped her hand around the edge of the bustier. "Are you sure you can breathe okay? How does it feel?"

Devon twisted from side to side, testing the bounds of her hindered flexibility. "A little uncomfortable, but nothing I can't handle. Sort of a nice pressure once you get used to it."

"That's what *he* said," Morgan chimed in this time.

Another round of giggles bled some of the nervousness from the gathering of scantily clad girlfriends who milled about in Kate's living-room-turned-studio.

Relief relaxed Devon enough that she blurted, "Okay, so, don't laugh. I know we've seen each other naked more often than with clothes on. We've gone wild and crazy during not one but *three* bachelorette parties scandalous enough to require a Vegas-esque pact of silence. And I can't count the number of nights we've spent watching each other or our guys get fucked senseless. But suddenly this seems a little... I don't know."

"Intimate?" Kate supplied.

"Yeah." Devon gnawed her lip. Sometimes it sucked being the youngest, least experienced, of the bunch. She was the newest too, though it'd been almost a year since they'd adopted her as the runt of their tightknit group. Their family-by-choice was comprised of a five-man construction crew and their four female lovers. "Am I the only one who's sweating?"

"No." Morgan plopped onto the padded bench Mike had painstakingly restored for Kate, who had fallen in love with the previously half-rotted carcass at a garage sale. Devon smiled, recalling how they'd struggled to jam the thing in Kate's tiny hybrid sedan. In the end, she'd had to ride to Kate and Mike's place on Kayla's lap while their treasure occupied the other half of the backseat. They'd laughed the whole way.

The furniture fit in the renovated house Kate had inherited as if it had been designed specifically for the nook by the stairs. Devon considered her niche in the crew and could relate.

Morgan's sudden drop to the tufted-fabric seat fluffed out the frilly edges of the microskirt on her naughty peek-a-boo nighty. She wafted cool air across her artfully painted face with a vintage hand fan. Sultry and sleek, she could have come straight out of a girly magazine or maybe the classiest of Amsterdam's famous red-lit windows.

"Let's jump right in and do this." Devon rolled her eyes when Kate opened her mouth to interject. "I know. That's what *he* said. Seriously though, if we don't get a move on, we'll be more nervous than a roofer in an electrical storm. Next thing we know, Kate will have chewed a hole in her lip and my hair will wilt like week-old lettuce. I can't believe you were able to fluff it so damn high to begin with. Anyway, that's not going to be a good look for our boudoir photos. Our pictures will suck and our husbands will leave us and we'll all die old and lonely."

"If they're hideous, we'll figure something else out," Kate shushed her.

"We're running out of time to come up with an alternate Valentine's Day present." Devon paced. "It has to be perfect for them."

"Stop before you hyperventilate, munchkin. This only feels weird because we let our guys maintain their illusion of control." Kayla hugged Devon. Warmth seeped into her from her friend's embrace. It settled her like a shot of steamed milk before bed or the afterglow of a really good orgasm. "With them gone, things are out of sorts. I miss them too, you know."

"Stupid ice-fishing trip." A lonely long weekend hadn't sounded so awful when the guys had first proposed it. The sparkle in their eyes at the thought of three whole days filled with beer, trash talk and freezing their nuts off had guaranteed that none of the women objected. "Why couldn't Joe's Uncle Tom have brought his gang to Kayla's resort instead of luring our crew to the middle of nowhere? What if they get attacked by a herd of psychotic moose? Or sucked into a vat of maple syrup? Neil has a massive sweet tooth. I could see him leaning over for a taste and tumbling right in."

"Um." Kay looked like she'd bitten into a lemon. "All those crazy cousins are more than my retreat can handle. They're so feral they make our husbands look tame by comparison. No thanks. Canada is barely far enough away. It's only one more night. We'll survive. And so will the crew. I'm pretty sure."

Devon sighed. "Do you know how many spooky noises our pipes make at two o'clock in the morning? I've never noticed that before. It got so bad last night I stayed up until dawn trying to fix some of the loose joints in our ductwork. Granted, HVAC isn't my specialty. That's more of Joe's thing. But I swear, I'm usually pretty terrific with my hands. Not today. I sucked big time."

"That's what *he* said." Kayla winked.

Devon smacked her forehead with the heel of her hand.

"There aren't any monsters under your bed or in your freaking H-whatever. You've just never listened hard enough before. Probably because you're moaning too loud to hear the creaks and pops or knocked unconscious by a zillion big Os in a row." Morgan wiggled her eyebrows.

"Good point. But that's not my fault. You know how it goes. Everyone has to have a turn. And then sometimes I have seconds. Or fifths. Or seventeeths. I mean, sex with James *and* Neil is the best-tasting, calorie-free dessert of all time." Devon pouted. Spoiled? For sure. She liked it that way. "How can I resist the temptation of *two* fine men in my bed? And once I'm snuggled between them, the rest of the world melts away."

"They make it easy to surrender. All of our guys do. They have a knack for affection—giving and getting. It's part of who they are. Maybe it's time to sprinkle a little girl power in the mix." Kate's lips angled up in a wry smile. She propped her hand on her hip. Manicured fingers splayed over the delicate ivory lace of her cat suit.

Skintight and translucent, it covered every inch of her yet left nothing to the imagination.

A pair of nude platform heels added to her stature. They made her legs seem longer than the fifteen-foot extension ladder the crew used for painting exteriors. The wife of the crew's foreman could have doubled for a pinup girl given the lustrous fall of her loose, wide curls.

"What did you have in mind?" Kayla slung her arm over Kate's shoulder and bumped her hip into their friend's. The flattering lines of Kay's ruched, purple merrywidow complimented the troublemaker glint in her eye and the assortment of body art escaping the limited cover-up provided by her lingerie. Wicked black leather boots rose above her knees, completing her alternative ensemble.

"Well, let's see how sexy we can make these pictures, shall we?" Kate winked. "I figure it won't take much to have the crew eating out of our hands. They'll be our extra-horny hostages. Then maybe we can draw up a list of our demands."

"Sounds like a plan to me." Devon stalked to the tripod standing in the center of Kate's living room, which they'd cleared of furniture other than a cameo-backed occasional chair and mounds of cushions they intended to use as props. They'd also strategically crumpled a creamy silk sheet before hanging it as their backdrop.

She aimed the digital SLR camera at the top of the mountain of pillows they'd arranged earlier. While she fiddled with the focus, her best friends entered the frame one by one. Lots of natural light from the late-afternoon sunshine flooded the space, making the women practically glow. Or maybe their flushes were a side-effect of envisioning what would happen when their guys got a hold of the final product of today's session.

The photography classes Devon had taken at the local community college would pay off a thousand times over.

"Okay, I have the settings where I want them. But if we'd like to review the images as we take them with the remote, we'll have to rely on my laptop. I tried to connect it before. The video cable wouldn't work although I swear it's the right one. I'll give it another shot. If that doesn't do the trick, we'll have to wing it. Where's Dave and his geeky tendencies when you need them?"

Before she'd finished mumbling, her friends began shouting out suggestions in the tried-and-true fashion of onlookers providing impromptu tech support. Devon ignored them. She fiddled with the connections while the bombshell peanut gallery peppered her with advice.

"Nothing's happening. Push the wire in deeper. Make sure the connection is tight." Morgan surrendered a mini-snicker.

"Maybe you're aiming for the wrong hole?" Kate asked with faux innocence.

"Take it out, then put it back in again." Kayla joined the fray. "Give it a tug and wiggle."

"Damn it. Let me concentrate." Devon bit her lip to avoid granting them satisfaction by cracking up. Had they forgotten she was supposed to be the juvenile one of the bunch?

She focused on the stubborn cable. The slightly misshapen prong looked like it might have been stepped on. Probably by someone wearing steel-toed construction boots if she had to guess. Crap, this had to work or they would be shooting blind. No way would they be able to arrange a second session without their guys getting suspicious.

She changed the angle of her laptop for better access, then shoved hard enough to void her warranty.

"Good idea. Sometimes it's easier to slide it in from the rear." Morgan hid her smile behind her hand.

The cable locked into place.

"I knew I could work it in if I was patient. Or barring that, if I rammed it in. Whatever works to open that bitch up." Devon laughed as deeply as she could, given the snug fit of her corset. "All right already, I surrender. That's what *he* said."

The other three women clapped. Morgan chortled until she snorted. Of course that set off another round of giggles. By the time they'd recovered, their cheeks were flushed and their eyes were bright.

Devon hustled to join the gathering. She tipped onto her side in the foreground, propping her cheek on one hand. With the other buried beneath a silk pillow, she depressed the remote shutter release. Several frames were captured in rapid succession.

Oohs and *aahs* rained around her as the women caught sight of themselves on the laptop screen. Their reactions led to some unusable shots dotted with awkward expressions.

They took the visual feedback and adjusted their poses, displaying themselves to the best advantage in their naughty lingerie. Kate leaned over the chair-back, thrusting her pert ass into the air. Morgan and Kayla stood back to back. Each bent one leg to display their shapely thighs. Devon tipped onto her tummy for a few cheeky shots, her stilettos kicking in the air as she touched one fingertip to her pursed lips. Then she curled up at the other women's feet, shifting the splay of her legs until she threatened to expose herself to her friends, their lovers and anyone else who went digging around on her memory card.

"Yeah, I think they'd like some raunchier ones too." Kate switched her stare to each of them in turn. "Don't you?"

"Yes." Kayla knelt on the cushion Devon had used to prop herself up. "Come here."

Devon obeyed automatically.

Kay wrapped her hand around Devon's nape, squeezed gently, then guided her close. Close enough to kiss if she'd wanted to. Instead, she paused a hairsbreadth away and let the camera immortalize the moment of anticipation.

Sweet strawberry lip gloss tempted Devon's tongue to peek out and steal a taste from Kayla's mouth. She held the urge in check. It wouldn't be the first time they'd kissed. But it didn't feel right to indulge without Neil, James and Dave there to enjoy the moment.

From what she could see of the next few shots—a couple of which involved Kate spanking Devon playfully while the others cheered her on—the guys would cherish their gift almost as much as they did their new wives.

In her case, their committed life partner.

Devon let her smirk linger for a few more frames before tipping forward and eliminating the chasm between her and Kayla. Too bad Morgan's excited cry startled them apart a few instants later.

"That's the one, right there." She did a little fist pump. "It's perfect. We all looked hot. I think that's a wrap. Agree?"

"Yeah, this thing is starting to itch and there's no Mike waiting upstairs to rip it off me." Kate frowned.

Devon didn't meet Kayla's gaze as she popped to her feet, practically racing to the camera and laptop stations. She disconnected the equipment, packing each component into a neat bundle before dropping it into her carrying case.

When she pivoted, she realized the other three ladies had wandered off to change and gather their belongings. Kayla returned just as Devon tucked the last of the supplies away.

"Dev—"

"I'd better try to wrestle this corset off before it gets too late. You know I'm not a fan of driving in the dark." Truth was, the frisson zipping up her spine had more to do with the questions in Kayla's gaze than her nightmares of hitting a deer or breaking down in an unfamiliar neighborhood.

Damn her guys for leaving her alone for three whole days. Her system had grown accustomed to regular relief. The lack of orgasms must have been turning her brain to mush and making her senses go haywire, as though she were in endorphin withdrawal. Hell, she probably was.

As Devon prepared to make her escape, a hand landed lightly on her forearm. She glanced over her shoulder. Directly into Kayla's eyes.

"If you'd rather not be alone, you're welcome to stay at my place tonight." She smiled with enough warmth to soothe the goose bumps rising on Devon's skin. "You're *always* welcome."

A reflexive refusal hovered on the tip of her tongue.

Kayla's fingers trembled where they touched.

Devon reconsidered in a flash. It hadn't been an easy

offer. They had too much at stake to fuck things up. Who was she to reject Kayla? Especially when Dev wanted to accept the invitation more than she craved the pink leather tool belt she'd spotted at Chicks Construct?

"Thank you." She smiled. "It's been a long time since I had a slumber party."

"Oh, damn. That's a great idea. Why didn't we think of it before?" Morgan rejoined them, Kate trailing a handful of steps behind. "We could rent a bunch of movies, do each other's hair, whip up a batch of skinny margaritas, compare notes on our guys..."

"This might be a private party." Kate tried to rein Morgan in.

Kayla looked to her three friends. She shrugged at Devon.

"Since when is anything between us a secret?" Devon grinned. "The more the merrier and all that jazz."

"Yes! I think we should watch *Dirty Dancing* first." Morgan started a list while Kate ran upstairs to pack an overnight bag. "Then *Breakfast Club*, and maybe a slasher flick."

"No, no." Devon shook her head vigorously. "I don't do scary shit."

"Don't worry, we'll be there to protect you." Kayla smiled.

"God only knows what kind of Bigfoot lives in your woods, or maybe a creepy lake monster. No point in tempting fate." Devon crossed her arms over her chest.

"I think it might be too late for that." Kayla met her stare. Then she grabbed for one of Devon's bags and slung it crossbody. "Almost ready?"

"I think so. Let me change first." A wicked grin escaped before she could think better of it. "Unless you'd like me to ride naked to your house. No sense in putting clothes on only to take them off again when we get there."

"Just because it's a naturist retreat doesn't mean you have to…"

"I know. But I've kind of gotten used to it." Devon shrugged. "It is pretty cold out today, though. I think I should at least wear my overcoat."

Kayla choked as Devon sauntered off, adding an extra swing to her step. She wished her men had been there to witness the exchange and maybe give her the push she needed to see what could evolve if they let it.

2

Devon popped another handful of caramel corn into her mouth, despite the fact that the credits of their third movie scrolled past on the muted TV. She smiled as she thought back to Dave and Kayla's first fight—a battle over the installment of the enormous flatscreen. Secretly, she was glad her friend had compromised and allowed the technology in her haven. The custom oak cabinet the crew had devised to hide any trace of ugly black plastic was a work of art.

Crispy, coated kernels surrendered to her chomping. She licked sticky sweetness from her fingers. When she looked up, she caught Kayla peeking at her from the corner of her eye.

Devon knocked her knee into her friend's. "Want some of this?"

"Yeah." Kayla made no move to grab a snack.

Morgan refilled their pretty, hand-blown margarita glasses. Colorful blobs encased in the clear material looked like confetti. They swirled and mixed in Devon's blurred vision. Last round for her. Being petite had been a curse she'd endured her entire life. Little to no tolerance for alcohol was a related inconvenience to suffer.

When Morgan finished serving them—all except Kate, who'd opted for fancy tea instead of booze—she plopped on the floor beside her best friend.

"So…" Kate leered at each of them in turn. "Truth or dare time."

"My favorite." Devon grinned.

"Good, then you first."

"Truth." She had no qualms about sharing herself with these women regardless of the silly game they played.

"Make it something juicy." Morgan poked Kate in the ribs. "You're evil at this. I should know. Remember when you forced me to admit my crush on your boyfriend in high school? Holy crap. I forgot his name. How can that be?"

"I think it was Tim. Or Ted maybe. Damn." Kate squinted. "It seemed like the end of the world at the time. Now that we have the crew, I can't help but think you saved me from potential disaster."

"Plus you got even in college with…" Morgan paused.

"Dan?"

"Uh, something like that. No, no, Doug. Definitely Doug." Morgan laughed. "I guess we've always had similar taste in guys."

"Great hormones think alike." Kate winked. "And now I *know* you've got it good with Joe."

"Lucky bitch." A slap on Kate's bared thigh accompanied the half-hearted curse.

"That's me. Anyhoo… It's been a while." Kate tapped her chin, then glanced at Kayla and Morgan. "I'm rusty. Help me. Both of you."

"Hell-oooo. You're the only sober one here." Kayla rolled her eyes. "You've got a pretty big advantage."

"Good point." Kate utilized their fit of giggles to consider. "Okay. But maybe we should change the rules. No singling anyone out. We'll all answer the question."

"Why the hell not?" Morgan shrugged. "We don't really believe in the whole solo thing around these parts. We're like the nine musketeers. Or is that three, three musketeers?"

"I can't do math after four margaritas!" Kayla rubbed her temples.

"You've had five," Kate corrected.

"You sort of proved her point." Devon nodded gingerly enough to avoid rattling her brains.

"Okay, okay." Kate held her hands up in surrender. "How about this? What's one thing you always hoped to try with our guys but haven't had the balls to go for yet?"

"Time to start planning our coup, huh?" Morgan *clinked* her glass against Kate's teacup.

"Yeah. I'll kick us off with some honesty of my own. Part of me is nervous. It's been a while now, coming up on two years, since I met the crew. I feel like we need to keep things fresh for Mike and the rest of them. They're used to adventure. I couldn't stand it if we didn't satisfy them as much as they've done for us." The rush with which the confession burst from Kate had them all sobering a tiny bit.

"You've thought about this a lot. Worried." Devon leaned forward to pat Kate's shoulder. "Mike adores you. You're all he really needs. You know that, right?"

"Yes." Kate swallowed hard enough for Devon to spot her throat flex. "I do. Deep down. That doesn't mean I don't want to give him the world. Better than only what he requires. Bare minimum isn't enough for the man of my dreams. We've also..."

"What, Katiebug?" Kayla defaulted to the nickname the guys had given their friend.

She released a dreamy sigh, then confessed, "Mike and I have toyed with starting a family."

"No wonder you're not drinking tonight." Kayla stared at the cup of tea clutched in Kate's white-knuckled grip.

"I've been dying to tell you all. I just..." She shook her head.

"You've been keeping too much inside." Morgan glared at Kate. "Don't you know we're here for you when you need us?"

"If we'd hidden something like this, you would have kicked our asses." Kayla leaned in closer. Morgan didn't harp, though. She glanced away, and her cheeks seemed to blush. Before Devon could dig deeper, Kate sighed.

"I know." At least she didn't attempt to deny it. "I'm sorry."

"So what's your main concern?" Devon tilted her head as she tried to decipher the issue.

"Once we have more responsibility, what if Mike is restless? As much as I can already feel a burning love for the baby we're praying for, I also know things will get harder. More stress. More obligation. More work. Our relationship could suffer. I'm terrified this brilliant magic we've created could fade into a perfectly comfortable, ordinary life. While he might be content, I can't imagine him happiest like that."

"Never forget we're a team." Morgan smirked. "With this many aunts and uncles to love a child, he or she won't be hard up for attention. And you'll never have to worry about a babysitter if you two need some time alone. Then, maybe someday, you could return the favor for Joe and me. Just think, our kids will grow up like brothers and sisters."

"That *is* nice to dream about." Kate brushed discreetly at the corner of her eye with a knuckle. "So I guess I'm going to answer my own stupid question. Tell me if I'm crazy."

"You are," Devon answered immediately.

"Brat." Kate's insult held no heat. Some of her seriousness dissolved. She took a deep breath, then admitted in a rush, "I'd like to watch one of you with Mike. I can't promise I won't get psycho jealous and try to rip you apart—gouge out your eyes or pull your hair or scratch you to shreds—but I'll do my best. I think he should have the option. And secretly, though he's never said anything, I think he's a touch jealous of the other guys. They got to be with some of you and he never did. Not that he wants to screw around or anything. But he's possessive. He considers all eight of us his in some way, you know?"

"You're both similar in that regard. Always taking care of the gang." Kayla grinned. "So how about a trade? Dave told me you were pretty damn hot that first time they shared you in the pool. I'm sure he'd be up for another taste. And he's plenty strong enough to keep your catfighting ninja moves in check should you make a break for me."

Devon noticed Morgan nodding in agreement. She thought about her relationship with the rest of the crew and how easy it would be to take the last step toward full-on intimacy. She loved each of the men for things they had in common as well as their individual strengths and quirks.

Morgan added softly, "I've grown so close to you all, and our guys. Most of us have been with some combination of them already...when we were first finding each other. One thing I've wondered about is making our sessions a free-for-all. The guys share each other. So why not us too? There are times, when we're all together, it would be so easy to reach out and touch Mike, Dave, Neil or James. They're gorgeous, and I love each of them. I'm sure I could improve their experience, same for them with me, but I'm afraid they're off limits. Why do we do that?"

Devon gnawed her lip. It was no secret Neil and James had played around with every one of her friends before she entered the picture. Truth be told, she imagined sometimes what it would have been like to be Kate. To have had all five men focused on her pleasure.

Greedy much? Hell, yeah.

She cleared the lump from her throat when no one spoke immediately. "Okay. I see your point. And I agree. None of us should be restricted. I trust you. You should do what comes naturally. If I'm being really honest, I'm envious of the time you had alone with the guys before I met you. Being the center of their attention had to rock. Sort of like Mike with you ladies, I've done the least playing with the crew."

"Holy shit." Kayla put her hand on Devon's knee and squeezed. "I never even considered you might feel like you missed out. Then again, you have two guys in your bed every night, so I don't have *too* much sympathy for you."

Another round of laughter broke out. Morgan nodded so vigorously she tipped off balance. Kate launched a potato chip in Devon's direction. Dev impressed herself by catching it in her mouth despite the alcohol dulling her reflexes. Useless skill #2184 learned in her years of working job sites filled with dudes, most of them a hell of a lot less evolved than the crew.

When they calmed down a little, Kayla continued, "Seriously, though, being with Dave, Neil and James is an experience I'll never forget. If you want that too, Dev, I'm fine with it. I think it would be hot to watch."

Devon's eyes grew wide when her friend—her worldly, open-minded, naturist friend—blushed bright red. "Um... and as for me, and the thing I'd like to try..."

Breath locked in Devon's lungs. She should have said something, done something, to encourage Kayla to continue. Instead, she froze.

"Uh oh. I think Morgan might be done." Kate poked their friend with her toe. She only mumbled and curled into a tighter ball on the floor. "Let's settle her on the couch before she's out cold. Otherwise, she'll regret it in the morning."

Together, the three of them managed to half-lift, half-coax Morgan onto the comfy, makeshift bed. Kate tucked a blanket around their sloshed friend, then fluffed a pillow to mitigate the awkward angle of her neck. Passing out like that all night would have guaranteed a strained muscle the next morning. Only once Morgan was set did Kate accept the quilt Kay furnished.

"I'll stay down here with her." She claimed her spot, reclining on the loveseat.

Disappointment rushed through Devon. Were they just going to abandon their discussion? Had things gone too far for her friends? They'd made some serious progress she would hate to erase. Maybe the other women had developed cold feet?

"It's okay, Dev." Kate reached out to pat her hip. "No one's going to change their mind between now and tomorrow. We'll finish our chat when everyone has a clear mind. Sleep well, girls."

"Thanks." Kayla smiled.

"Okay. You too, Kate." Devon wiggled her eyebrows. "Dirty dreams."

Morgan roused a bit when the lamp flicked off, leaving the glow from the dying fire as a soft nightlight. "Where they going? We're plog-ging."

"Plotting?"

"'S what I said. Blotting."

"Right. Well, we agree on the important stuff. Our plan of attack can wait until tomorrow," Kate reassured their friend. "Go to sleep."

As Devon followed Kayla toward the loft, she wondered if Kate realized what a great mom she'd make. She took a mental note to share her opinion when Kate couldn't blow off the compliment as an alcohol-induced warm fuzzy.

Not surprising, Morgan seemed to be on the same page. Devon caught a snippet of the best friends' whispered conversation while she and Kayla trekked up the steep, narrow loft stairs.

Morgan murmured to Kate, "Wow, a baby."

"I know. I'm freaked out and excited. Nervous to get my hopes up. We just started trying." She didn't pause to catch her breath as she rambled. "Maybe it won't happen for a while. Or ever. You know how much trouble my sister had…"

"Gonna be fine. Cutest kids ever, I bet." Their soft exchange drifted away as Devon entered Kayla's loft room. "Can't wait. Spoil 'em rotten…"

Kayla folded her thick down comforter to the foot of the bed and started to climb into the fluffy nest. Devon hopped onto the mattress and snuggled into the pile of pillows on Dave's side. When the other half didn't dip, she opened one eye and caught a shadow marking the spot where Kayla had paused.

"Kay?"

"Should I put pajamas on?" She sounded uncertain for the first time, maybe ever. "I can dig up one of Dave's T-shirts."

"If I can handle sitting in the stands while your husband fucks you—or my guys—senseless, I'm not about to turn squeamish about sleeping next to your bare tatas." She grunted. "Get your ass in here. These sheets are chilly."

Kayla didn't need to be asked twice. She slid beneath the covers but stayed so far away, Devon thought she'd tumble out the other side if she so much as sneezed. Stiff, awkward silence ballooned inside the loft, making it hard to catch her breath.

"What the hell is this crap?" Devon slapped a hand on Kayla's shoulder and tugged until her friend faced her.

"What?"

If Kayla intended to play dumb, Devon could do the same. Time to force them both to acknowledge the elephant in the room. Anything less would drive her batty before sunrise.

"You never did say what *you'd* like to try but haven't." Devon couldn't remember the last time she'd been coy in her life. Still, some tiny insecurity kept her from whispering her own desire into the night. The admission would have been so much easier if Neil and James were there to coach her and hold her hand.

"Okay, fine. I think you know what I'm after," Kayla

murmured. "When you're ready. *If* you ever are. All you have to do is say so. No pressure."

Devon grew warmer the instant she laid her hand on top of Kay's in the space between them. The other woman's pulse tripped against her own wrist before tapering to a more regular rhythm. Kayla sighed, and entwined their fingers. The bond they created transferred heat and reassurance that lulled them both to sleep in no time at all.

3

"Rise and shine, sleepyheads."

Devon groaned and burrowed closer to the warm body beside her without poking her head from beneath the jumble of covers. It wasn't until the racket caused by two people climbing the hardwood stairs roused her a little more that she realized the person snuggled up to her was soft in all the places her guys were hard. *Mmm, nice.*

"Kayla."

"Yeah, I'm awake." Her clear voice didn't seem to indicate she'd been jerked out of a wonderful dream about sexy, naked construction workers mere seconds earlier either. How long had she been lying there, thinking?

"Damn. What time is it?" Devon blinked in rapid succession. She squinted into the unusually refulgent morning sunlight as she attempted to shove onto a straight-locked arm while clutching the sheets to her bare chest. She blew rogue strands of hair from her face.

"Almost noon," Kate informed them. She set a tall

glass of orange juice on the nightstand, then towered over Devon and Kayla. "I couldn't let you miss out on the chance for one of Morgan's amazing breakfasts. She made waffles from scratch, the kind with fruit and her secret spices in them."

Devon sniffed the air. "Oh my God. Do I smell bacon too?"

"Could be." Morgan grinned. She set a tray of food carefully on the nightstand.

"Hold that thought. If I don't pee right now, I'm going to drown." Devon scampered from the bed. Less than a minute later she bounded to the loft once more.

Kayla, Morgan and Kate held congress in low tones from their perches on the rumpled duvet.

"No, nothing happened..." Kay bit her lip and hesitated when she caught sight of Devon returning.

"What's going on?" Dev asked.

"We're waiting for you to get your act together so we can savor our feast." Kate deflected genuine concern with sarcasm. "So hurry it up, punk."

"Oh yeah? I'll give you *punk*." Devon sprinted the last few feet. She leaped and tucked her knees to her chest, cannonballing into the pile of plush covers between her friends. The mattress bounced, jostling them all.

"Very funny." Kayla laughed as she whipped a pillow from the head of the bed. "But you left yourself unprotected."

Whap.

Something puffy smashed into her face. "You did not just hit me with..."

Whap. Whap.

Kate and Morgan joined in the battle. They took turns pummeling her with the light bundles. Devon's fit of giggles didn't do much for her coordination. She lunged for the fourth pillow while unsuccessfully attempting to evade the incoming barrage.

Battling to her knees on the mattress allowed her to launch a counterstrike. Her one-against-three odds improved when her friends' coalition deteriorated. They whacked each other as often as they did her. Every woman for herself.

They shrieked, chased, ducked, whooped, dove, tackled and smacked each other. Feathers flew through the air. They fell as thick as the flakes that had blanketed the mountain during the legendary blizzard that fused Dave and Kayla in an inseparable pair the previous winter. Busy daydreaming about what it would have been like to watch Dave, James and Neil ravaging Kay in front of the fireplace downstairs, Devon got caught off guard.

Whap.

She leaned into the force of the blow, but it was no use. Her arms windmilled. Gravity pitched her inevitably toward the floor. She braced herself for impact, heart racing as she completed a split-second assessment of the minimalist railing that kept the space open to the cabin below. It would probably hold.

Instead of a slat of wood to the ribs, strong arms—too thick to belong to one of her female friends—banded around her.

Neil. She would recognize his hold anywhere. A perfect blend of tender yet unbreakable.

"It's all fun and games until someone cracks their skull open." He rocked Devon against his chest. "Careful, baby. I have plans for today that don't involve a trip to the emergency room."

"Unless it's because you've fucked yourself into

complete exhaustion and dehydration, right?" Joe smacked Neil's back, rattling both him and Devon.

She hated that she nearly cried. Clawing at Neil's shoulders, she encouraged him to squeeze her tighter. "You're home early! Damn, I missed you."

"Same goes. Couldn't stay away any longer." He buried his nose in her hair and breathed deep.

"What the hell is going on in here?" Mike asked as the rest of the crew piled in close on Neil's heels.

The loft had never seemed cramped before. Hard bodies and testosterone overwhelmed Devon's senses. She couldn't speak so she indulged in the luxury of having them surround her.

"A pillow fight?" Dave groaned when he took in the four women, naked except for the feathers tangled in their hair and stuck to the light sheen of perspiration coating their flushed skin. They breathed hard where they'd collapsed onto the bed. "And here I thought you couldn't get any sexier."

"Why the hell did we need a vacation again? We're living the dream." Joe stared, licking his lips, while James sidled up beside Neil. He sandwiched Devon between their chests. Neil angled her so she faced their partner. Several inches shorter than Neil, he easily claimed her mouth in a scorching yet infinitely tender kiss. His fingertip traced the tattoo—similar to the one both he and Neil sported—on her ring finger.

"I missed you too," Devon whispered when they finally broke apart.

"But not as much as Kay missed me. Right, babe?" Dave strutted to the side of the bed near his wife.

Morgan surprised them all when she whacked him hard in the gut with her pillow. "Ha! She's got nothing on me. Without Joe, I almost died of loneliness. And horniness."

The women's ceasefire erupted into a second round of good-natured exchanges. Devon squirmed from Neil's arms to join the fray. The crew cheered on their girls, calling out helpful tips. When Kate swung wide, her pillow caught the edge of the tray on the nightstand.

Mike dove for the tipping platter. The guys roared when he rescued it. Sort of like he'd done for Kate that fateful afternoon two summers ago.

"Hey, now. Truce. That's not funny. Bacon almost became an innocent casualty. Wasting it would be a cardinal sin. Straight to hell, do not pass go." Joe snapped up a slice and devoured it in one bite. If he were a cartoon, they would have heard the *galoomp* of him swallowing it whole.

"Did you even chew that?" James shook his head, whether in awe or disgust it was hard to tell.

"There's nothing better than salty breakfast meat."

"That's what *he* said." Kayla had her friends rolling with her snide interjection.

As if they were universally wired, the guys scanned first the pile of steaming waffles, then the assortment of women. They made the circuit several times. Dave practically gave himself whiplash before growling, "We can reheat the food when we're finished working up our appetites."

"No bacon left behind," Mike agreed.

"I'm dying for a taste of you." Joe rushed Morgan. He triggered a stampede.

The crew invaded the girls' sanctuary, pairing—or trebling—up with their mates. Moans and sighs replaced battle cries as they held sensual reunions.

Devon gasped when Neil pressed her to the bed. A welter of limbs cascaded over her as nine people found a way to share the king-sized bed in some fashion or another. They writhed in the wake of equal pleasure.

"I have a better idea." James lifted his head from where he'd suckled Devon's nipple into a taut peak. "No reason we can't have our women and eat them too."

"I like the way you think." Dave groaned. "Hand me some of that whipped cream."

Neil's hand shook as he passed the gravy boat heaped with fresh-made topping. The cobalt glass slipped from his grip. Joe snagged the handle, keeping the vessel from bonking Kayla. The rapid deceleration launched the contents all over. Splatter dispersed across Kate, Mike, Kayla, Devon and anyone else in the path of the sweet cream.

"Shit." Neil's pupils dilated when a glob dripped off James's pec onto Devon's tummy.

Before she could register the chill accompanying the splash above her mound, the moist heat of Neil's tongue swiped across the same spot. All too soon, he'd licked her clean.

"Excuse me." James grinned as he slipped his hand past Dave, who'd crawled between his wife's legs for the best seat in the house at the unusual buffet.

Kayla arched. Each of the men scooped a portion of the treat from her skin.

"You like them petting you?" Dave murmured against the succulent flesh of her pussy.

"Yes. God, yes." She spread her legs wider, rocking her hips toward her husband's parted lips. "Eat me."

He did.

Devon observed the industrious man devouring her

friend. He made up in gusto anything he might have lacked in finesse. Long laps of his tongue gathered whipped cream mixed with the glistening arousal spreading across Kayla's inner thigh.

Neil groaned. Devon's fingers clenched on his shoulders, urging him closer. He obliged her unspoken command by lavishing similar attention on her.

James wormed into an available space between Devon and Morgan. The entire loft overflowed with passionate cries and hard-bodied males worshipping their women. He rolled onto his side, his cock prodding the curve of her hip as he settled his lips over hers for a series of sinful kisses. His mouth tasted faintly of vanilla.

He burrowed one arm beneath her neck, supporting her head. He held her at the angle he preferred for feasting on her lips. Their tongues flicked over one another. His detoured to trace the corners of her smile and tickle the roof of her mouth. They alternated ravenous sucks with dainty sips.

She shivered when Neil thrust his firm tongue into the opening of her pussy. Her hands glided upward, burying in the almost-too-long strands of Neil's thick hair.

"Dev, if *you're* touching him..." James angled his head to verify she hadn't shifted as he murmured to her. Before he could sort out the puzzle, his brains understandably addled by the outrageous level of pheromones battering their systems, Morgan came to his rescue.

"Hey there, cutie." Morgan winked before tugging on James's erection.

"Um." His stare flew between Devon, Neil, Joe and Mike to gauge their reactions. "Am I allowed to enjoy this?"

Mike shrugged. "Why do I get the feeling we should

have known better than to leave these vixens to find trouble without us?"

"It's okay with me." Devon grinned.

"Joe?" James stayed stock still.

"Shit, it's hot. If my wife wants to jerk you off, I vote for letting her. She passes inspection in my book when it comes to hand jobs."

The other crew members groaned.

"Alrighty then." James clamped his fingers around Morgan's, which were slick with whipped cream, encouraging her to stroke faster.

"Well, since we're playing like that..." Mike swiped a dollop of fluff from Kayla's chest, lingering longer than necessary to massage some of it into the swell of her breast. He walked his fingers up her neck and allowed her to suck his index finger clean.

"Yeah, that's right, sweetheart." His hand shook as Kate straddled him, grinding on his obvious hard-on. Only then did Devon realize the guys were naked. They must have shed their standard jeans and T-shirt uniforms on arrival at Kay's naturist retreat. She certainly didn't intend to complain about the display of cut muscles and sleek bodies.

"Neil." She whimpered his name several times before her plea registered.

"Dev?" He glanced up though he didn't stop teasing her for longer than it took to whisper her name.

"Will you fuck me? Please. Need you inside me."

"No." He shook his head, causing the nerves in her swollen folds to riot. "But I will make love to you. Here. With our friends surrounding us. Joining in."

Devon smiled when she thought about sharing the

positive energy they generated. She'd been hanging around Kayla and her New Age junk too much lately.

James reached for Neil's cock when their lover rose over her. The smaller man guided their mate's long erection to her opening. The slickness the men inspired ensured Neil glided through her rings of muscle despite the tight fit he still made with her body.

"You love watching them together." Morgan didn't ask James. She didn't have to with her fingers wrapped around his steely shaft. "I swear you just got twice as hard, and that's saying something."

"Yeah." He groaned.

"And you. You're soaked." Joe snuggled tight to Morgan's back. With her front pressed to James, she could have felt claustrophobic. Her guttural moan proved that wasn't the case. "You like being a dirty girl, don't you? What does it feel like to grope my friend while I'm fucking you?"

"Gah!"

Kate chuckled at Morgan's helplessness. Grunts and sighs fell from the couple. Joe draped Morgan's knee over James's hip to guarantee he'd penetrated her completely.

Devon tried to watch. Flat on her back, she missed some of the action.

"Here, shorty." Neil scooped one arm beneath her shoulders without a hitch in his stride. He rocked into her as he rearranged some of the pillows, inclining her shoulders until she could survey the entire lascivious landscape.

Despite only sixty-seven and a half hours apart, she could tell he worked harder to penetrate her than he had when he'd said goodbye. Luckily, the visuals turned her on even more. She appreciated the distraction from slight discomfort that quickly became something entirely pleasurable.

"We can't all be giants like you." She nipped Neil's bottom lip before he rose to optimize the angle of his stokes. With the view clear, she allowed her gaze to wander.

She lay on her back with Neil pumping into her, making her see more stars than the night sky held far out here on the top of the mountain. James lounged on his side facing her. Morgan's hand brushed the dip of her waist and the side of her ribs as she worked the gentle man who'd captured Devon's heart from her very first day as the crew's intern.

She paused to stare into his eyes, which looked so much like her own it startled her on occasion.

"I love you," he moaned before stretching his neck toward her for another taste. Neil swooped in to lick the seam of their mouths. Soon the three of them traded open-mouthed kisses.

When they came up for air, Devon continued to feed off the scene before her. Beyond James, Morgan took Joe's increasing strokes, writhing between the men bracketing her. The roving action of her hand on James's cock grew less regular. James facilitated the exchange by fucking into her hold. The ruddy tip of his hard-on poked Devon in the side at the apex of each thrust.

Beyond the three lovers on their sides, Mike reclined, stretched out like a sultan enjoying his harem. With his arms crossed behind his head, he held himself in a suspended crunch as though it were no effort at all. With ripped abs like his, maybe it wasn't.

"Like what you see?" He smirked when he caught her staring.

Kate must have read Devon's mind. She tweaked her husband's nipple. The cocky foreman jerked, rubbing the sting from his chest even as he laughed. Still, his raging erection never wilted.

"Behave yourself." Kate wagged her index finger at him. He rocked upward to catch it in his mouth, sucking until his wife melted a tiny bit.

"I could say the same for you." He dusted light kisses over her knuckles between every couple words. "But I'd much rather you be naughty. Quit teasing me. Three days is too long to be without you. Put my cock inside you. Now."

Devon shivered at the command inherent in his tone. Mike was impossible to resist when he got bossy.

Kate lifted up to make room for his shaft. She braced herself on his chest with one hand, the other reaching behind her blindly. Devon couldn't fault her for the lack of coordination that had her fishing for Mike's cock. The surfeit of sexy men would make anyone's system go haywire.

Kayla noticed Kate's dilemma and lent a helping hand. Cleaned of the cream, she rolled from her back and swiped at the last blob, which decorated the corner of Dave's mouth, with one finger. From where she perched on her hands and knees at the foot of the bed, she extended her left hand. Perpendicular to the three other couples, she easily encircled the base of Mike's shaft with her long fingers.

"I've got this, Kate." Kayla moaned when Dave couldn't resist the temptation of her ass on display before him. The broadest and most powerful of them all, he made sure not to crush anyone's legs when he scrambled to kneel behind his wife. The colorful design of her alluring tattoos flexed as she settled herself. They provided the perfect lines for Dave to trace with his tongue.

James, Morgan and Joe shuffled their feet and legs so they rested on top of Dave's calves, ankles and soles. They anchored him to the bed.

Each of them was connected in some way to the rest of the crew.

Kay still rode the same mental wavelength as Devon. She glanced up from her task, meeting Dev's stare.

How had they ended up as far away as possible from each other in the intertwined knot of lovers? Despite Kayla's lissome frame, enhanced by attending the early morning yoga sessions her resort offered, there was no way she and Devon could touch from opposite corners of the enormous bed.

Devon couldn't justify the sliver of disappointment prickling her heart.

James murmured, "What's wrong?"

"Nothing, really."

"You'll tell me later, right?" He whispered in her ear, so no one else heard.

She nodded.

He issued comfort in the form of a soft sweep of his lips down her cheek, along her jaw, then over her mouth. She reveled in the lingering taste of the whipped cream before shifting her attention to her friends once more.

Kayla had resumed her post, aligning the fat head of Mike's cock. Her hand slipped between Kate's thighs, ensuring she'd estimated the angle correctly. Kate and Mike both groaned at the flutter of skilled fingers over their aching genitals.

The constant pressure Neil imparted to Devon's channel as he filled her nudged her close to the edge of ecstasy. Devon could relate to the wild cries Kate unleashed when she slid down Mike's shaft, impaling herself on his full length. Kayla lowered her hand, fondling Mike's tight sac with a gentle caress that made Devon pretty damn sure her friend also remembered their conversation from the night before.

What if they all were together when Kate and Mike started their family?

"Shit, yes," the foreman hissed at the dual sensation of his wife sheathing him and their friend cupping his balls. He collapsed onto the mattress, his shoulders and head bouncing a little following the thud. His hands surrounded Kate's hips. Dinged, calloused fingers splayed across her ass.

He encouraged her to ride him, setting a demanding pace she eagerly complied with.

Kayla shouted when Dave distracted her from her ministrations by plunging his cock to the hilt in her welcoming body with one complete stroke. He covered her back, biting her shoulder as he fondled her breasts with his large hands. The graceful ripple of his body as he fucked Kay mesmerized Devon.

Did Neil look like that as he took her?

She looked into his wide eyes and flushed face. He must have read the desire there.

"That hot, huh?"

"Yeah," was all she could manage.

"Good thing I can't see them. I wouldn't last thirty seconds. It's hard enough listening to them. Sinking inside you. Christ. You feel so good."

Devon's legs spread as wide as they could, inviting him deeper, given her precarious spot on the edge of the bed and the pile of bodies to her left. James ducked his head to torture her breast. He sucked on her, bit her gently and plumped the modest mound with one hand while the other snaked lower to her pussy.

The industrious glide of Morgan's fingers over his cock freed him to pay the pleasure forward to Devon. His hand danced over her mound, glancing across her clit before measuring Neil's girth where he spread her pussy wide open.

James gathered moisture from the intersection of Devon and Neil's bodies. He used the slickness to draw frictionless circles around the hooded knot of her clit. Neil echoed her shudder when her pussy clamped tighter on his hard-on.

"You're strangling me," he rasped. "Come when you can, Dev."

"No." She thrashed her head on the pillow. "Not without the rest of you."

"You're so sweet." Joe reached past Morgan to pat Devon's tummy. "No one minds, munchkin. Hell. Likely to set us all off."

Devon scrunched her eyes closed, trying to regain a measure of control. It was no use. Neil descended. He trapped James's palm over her mound. The suction of Neil's mouth on the far side of her chest mimicked James's attention on her right breast, stealing the last of her reason.

She surrendered to pure sensation.

Devon relaxed, absorbing the pummeling of Neil's hips. The steady tap pressed James's wiggling fingers right where she needed the contact most. She resisted the initial wave of pleasure battering her senses. But when she made the mistake of opening her eyes, she caught sight of the admiration and lust in Kayla's.

The link was too much on top of all the other stimulation.

Devon's gaze winged frantically from person to person, trying to include them all in the moment. Each crew member focused on her as if they sensed her impending capitulation.

"Let go, Dev," Mike ordered. "We're with you."

An orgasm the likes of which she'd never experienced before wrung her dry from the inside out. It started as a buzz deep in her core and expanded until even her fingertips sang with ultimate pleasure. She'd swear her hair stood on end as electricity raced through her veins.

"Yes. Fuck." Neil threw his head back and roared. The tendons in his neck stood out in relief on the powerful column. They looked like the veins and ridges of his cock felt caressing her spasming tissue. "Me too."

"Fill her," James encouraged their lover. "Show her how you wouldn't let me take care of you while we were away. You tried to tease me. Backfired, didn't it? Give her everything you saved up."

If Neil wasn't the absolute picture of health, Devon might have worried about him keeling over. His heart hammered against her palm when she lifted it to his chest. Still she unraveled, and he rode her through the never-ending pulses of her climax.

"Yes. Yes. Yes," Neil chanted.

The first jet of his semen shot within her, splattering on the swollen walls of her pussy. He grunted and jerked between her thighs over and over, emptying himself with a ferocity she didn't often witness from her playful lover. The stakes had been raised again. Each person's rapture amplified as it fed off that of their neighbor, friend, paramour and confidant too.

"That's it." James cheered them both on. He tapped a secret code on her clit that never failed to set her ablaze. "Wring him dry."

Neil huffed as though he'd run an entire marathon in those sixty seconds. He rocked onto his haunches, looking unsteady and utterly wrecked. Dave put out a hand to steady his partner without pausing his beat as he fucked his wife. In fact, the contact might have been responsible for him speeding up his pace a tad.

Kayla moaned and lowered her cheek to Mike's shin. She gripped his ankle with her right hand. Head down, ass up, she accepted everything Dave had to give her. Still, the fingers of her left hand drew swirling patterns over Mike's balls, massaging them.

Kate bounced on her husband's shaft, somehow managing to look graceful as always despite the primal forces possessing her and obliterating all traces of the proper lady she pretended to be at times.

Aftershocks zinged through Devon, enhanced by the saturnalia around her and the calming strokes of Neil's palm over her arms, chest and belly. When she emerged from the daze of the most powerful climax of her life, she didn't waste any time. She yanked Neil toward her for a sloppy kiss before zeroing her focus on James.

"I like the way you think, Dev." Neil added his caresses to the exposed form of their lover.

Now petted by six hands, maybe more if she counted the occasional touches from Joe, James had no chance at resistance. He made a final stand, locking his jaw so tight she worried he'd crack a molar.

She grinned into his gorgeous eyes.

"Oh shit." He gasped at the dirty intentions in her gaze.

Devon reached over and rubbed his nipples with the sharp flicks destined to set him off. Sure enough, the scrape of her nails over the pebbled discs had him seizing in Morgan's embrace.

Come blasted from his cock, catching Devon and Neil with the spray. More fluid dripped from the head to coat Morgan's fingers as she stroked him slow and sweet after the initial rush had burst free. She massaged his softening flesh, bringing him down gently.

James sighed, welcoming first Neil's, then Devon's mouth on his. When they'd had their fill of his lips, he tipped his head, letting Morgan decide if she'd like to accept his invitation.

She did.

Devon smiled as the other woman moaned into James's mouth.

"Oh shit, yeah," Joe shouted as he fucked his wife harder. He examined her kissing James up close and personal. "You're going to make her come, James. She likes it when you suck on her tongue."

James must have obliged. His throat flexed, and a keening wail escaped from Morgan's chest. Devon stroked her hair while Mike crooned to her from behind the couple. Devon couldn't understand the individual words, but the tone conveyed all she needed to know.

Morgan bucked between James and Joe, surrendering to their spell. Joe stiffened and cursed a blue streak. He often did when he lost total control. Mike and Kate joined their friends, all four of them filling the loft with clear signs of their pleasure.

"That's so hot," Kayla panted from her front row seat. "I can see. Mike. Overflowing."

Devon couldn't quite tell what Kay did then. Both

Mike and Kate yelled, their orgasms extending at the contact. She figured it out soon enough when Dave groaned. He captured his wife's wrist, then tugged it behind her back. He lunged forward, enveloping her fingers in his mouth, sucking the combined flavor of Mike and Kate from them.

The restraint of her arm and the knowledge of how much Dave had shared seemed to push Kayla off the precipice. She clutched Mike's leg with her free hand and might have toppled beneath the force of Dave's enthusiastic fucking if it hadn't been for Joe, who sat up and braced her.

Dave tightened his grip on her ass, slamming home as Kayla shook and moaned. The periodic clenching of his glutes as he released inside his wife fascinated Devon. She wished she could pet his flank as he spilled his seed deep in Kayla's pussy. Neil reached out and did it for her.

For long minutes they all lay silent except for the rasp of their breathing and an occasional moan that refused to be muted. Content, Devon could have stayed floating in that cloud of mutual admiration and bliss for the rest of her life.

"Welcome home." Kayla nuzzled Dave, who'd sank on top of her, trapping her to their bed where she seemed perfectly happy remaining for the foreseeable future.

Devon adjusted to make room for Neil. She sat with her shoulders propped against the headboard, cradling Neil's and James's cheeks in her palms. They rested their heads on her thighs. Someone's stomach growled so loud she might have thought it was a truck in the driveway if she didn't know better.

She leaned to the side and plucked a slice of bacon from the tray. She held the strip between her guys, grinning when they ate it *Lady and the Tramp* style. Their lips locked when they reached the center, thrillingly close to her pussy.

"I could go for some of that too."

Devon passed the plate to Kate, who selected a waffle quarter. She ripped off a piece for herself, then another to pop into Mike's open mouth. He licked melted butter from her fingers before chewing his treat.

Soon, they all were indulging in a decadent breakfast in bed. Sporadic yawns ensured naptime was next on the agenda. Curled together, no one would be left in the cold as they dreamed of new ways to play with each other that would be hard pressed to surpass reality.

When they'd all settled in, satisfied, Joe announced to the room in general, "I take it back. We should definitely go away more often."

All four women bashed him with their pillows.

4

Morgan fiddled with the whisk attachment on the stand mixer she'd bought for Kayla's kitchen. She baked here often enough to justify the gadget. Meanwhile, Mike finished the last bite of his third helping of the passion-fruit crepes she'd whipped up in the aftermath of their sharing to help refuel the crew.

The extravagant breakfast for four she'd started out with seemed paltry when faced with the five bottomless pits the guys called stomachs. They could easily plow through enough food to keep her in business for eternity. They also loved helping her refine her experiments for Sweet Treats.

"What's the verdict?" She crossed her fingers.

"Fucking great." Mike thought for a minute, attempting to flesh out his description, as if knowing it'd help her understand the dish's potential. "Love how it's crunchy on the outside and squishy in the center. The plainer part helps temper the goo on top. It's crazy sweet. Love it."

Okay, so they had a little way to go yet before she'd claim to have trained them as panel tasters. She laughed. "Thanks."

He leaned against the cabinets, shooting the shit with her between delighting his tastebuds and complimenting the chef. Joe and Kate weren't quite ready to head back into town. Steam billowed from the bathroom where Kate showered, and Joe hadn't roused from his mandatory post-orgy nap. He loved the deep slumber following great sex so much, Morgan didn't have the heart to wake him just yet. Even if their pillow fight had aggravated the paring knife stabbing through her eye socket courtesy of her indulgence the night before. She smiled as she peeked at her husband, crashed on the couch in the adjoining room. When he was near, all her aches evaporated.

A hiss drew her attention back to Mike. He cleared his throat and attempted to disguise his wince as he swallowed the final morsel, complete with extra syrup from the edges of the plate.

Morgan crossed to him, relieving him of the dirty dish. "You know, that's only going to keep getting worse if you don't go to the dentist. Better have it taken care of before it turns into a fiasco."

"Shit." He massaged his jaw, as if that would help. "Don't mention it to Kate, okay? How could you tell?"

"When you drank the cold OJ with your first pass at breakfast, you flinched." She rubbed his shoulder, hoping to grant him some comfort. It seemed so natural to touch him, although the gesture had nothing sexual about it.

"Damn Joe's cousins." He scowled. "They're wild bastards, I swear. We need to find them some fine women to settle them down a bit."

She cocked her head, wondering what the Carter clan had to do with this.

"They were giving us shit about getting domesticated." He at least had the sense to look ashamed. "We'd had a *few* too many beers while waiting for nonexistent fish to bite."

"You got in a fist fight?" Morgan's eyes grew wide.

"It wasn't as barbaric as you make it sound." He shrugged. "Just a little roughhousing among friends. Except my boot slipped on the ice and I smacked my jaw pretty hard on Logan Carter's tackle box. I think I might have cracked one of my molars. Son of a bitch. I hate the dentist. *Really* hate it."

Morgan had never seen Mike like this before. His foot wiggled non-stop while his fingers beat an erratic tattoo on the counter.

Every superman had his kryptonite.

"Hey." She put her arms around his waist and hugged him. "I completely understand. I'm really afraid of the dentist too."

He shot her a look just short of rolling his eyes. "A lot of people dislike it. I get that, but I can't explain how it makes me feel. Something along the lines of a chick screaming on top of a table when a mouse invades her kitchen. It's irrational and stupid. I still can't help it."

"You mean how your heart seizes up like you're going to die, or how your vision narrows into tiny pinpricks of light, or how you can't draw a full breath into your lungs?" She shivered.

"Yeah. Like that." He frowned. "Didn't you get crowns on your front teeth last year? How the hell did you manage that if you're as scared as I am?"

"I didn't the first three times. I pulled into the lot and

drove right back home." She couldn't say which of them clutched the other tighter.

"Why the hell didn't you say something?" He hugged her to him and sighed.

"I was embarrassed." She grimaced.

"So how did you work up the guts to go through with it?" He paused. "Did it hurt this bad? And you suffered? Shit, better not tell Joe that. Soon I'm not going to be able to fall asleep. It throbs like a motherfucker."

"Yeah, there was that, although mine was more cosmetic at this stage. Plus, I went to school with a guy who's a dentist these days. Graduated at the top of his class, I swear. He has a fancy practice in the converted farmhouse on Werner Avenue. When I balked, he fetched me from the bakery."

"Nick Rocha?" Mike held her away a bit so he could meet her gaze.

"Yeah. You know him too?" She smiled.

"Sort of. We did the work on the building."

"I've always liked the way it turned out. The circular windows are my favorite."

"Blame your husband for that. He insisted they'd be perfect even though they were a pain in the ass to install and put us over budget." Mike smiled, some of his anxiety fading away.

"I wouldn't lie to you. He's good. Gentle. And he has lots of new-fangled gadgets to make procedures quicker and less painful than you're probably used to." She paused to consider. "He even offers oral sedation if you'd rather zone out while he's doing his thing. I don't mind driving you. Between both of us, I'm sure we could convince him to fit you in soon so you don't have to stress out."

Mike shuddered but nodded. "Fine. But I think I need you to make the call. Otherwise, I'll probably turn chickenshit again."

"No problem." She squeezed his hand, surprised by how sweaty yet icy it was. "Everyone's afraid of something, Mike."

"I guess." He wiped his palms on his jeans. "Thanks for noticing and for offering to hold my hand. Even though it'll be gross and slimy then too."

"What's the point of being a team if we don't each bring something to the game?" She smiled softly. "You're welcome."

"JOE?" Morgan sat up. She thought she'd heard a rattle from the general direction of the bathroom. Dusk permitted her a shadowy glimpse into the space adjoining their bedroom. "Everything okay?"

She didn't remember much of the ride home from Kayla and Dave's house this afternoon. She'd conked out before they'd emerged from the woods surrounding the resort's long, winding driveway. Head still pounding from the night before and their wild romp—though she wouldn't have missed out on that for the world—she'd surrendered to the utter relaxation suffusing her at having her man by her side again. Not to mention the boneless state their group session had put her in.

Grateful for the stress reduction, she'd embraced the floating sensation and let Joe's crooning duets with his favorite, Michael Bublé, via the streaming radio on his smartphone lull her into oblivion. A vague memory of him carrying her up the stairs to their apartment over the bakery, tucking her into their bed, inflated her heart to greater proportions.

The pressure had her chest aching when she remembered the bad news she had to tell him. No more excuses. It wasn't right to let him hang on to false hope.

Vile cursing followed a second, louder metallic clank.

She padded to the doorway, leaned on the jamb and admired the muscles in her husband's bare shoulders. They bunched and stretched from his place beside the toilet. He'd removed the lid of the tank to fiddle with something inside. He shook his hand, then mummified it in toilet paper. If she had to guess, she'd say he stanched blood welling from yet another gouge in his poor, battered fingers.

"What's up?"

"Damn. Tried not to wake you. Sorry." He swiped a bead of sweat from his brow with the side of his forearm. The motion left a grease streak that only enhanced his rugged charm. A spike of his golden hair stuck to the stain. "Thought I'd install the new valve and flange I picked up for this guy so it'll stop running in the middle of the night."

"Thanks, you know that drives me bonkers. Hate to waste water." Morgan frowned.

"Yeah, your Mother Earth act is cute even when it's a royal pain in the ass." Joe didn't flinch when she smacked his shoulder playfully.

"Hey, what's that?" She leaned in for a closer look, then clapped her hands. "You found a handle to match the sink hardware?"

"It was supposed to be a surprise." He grimaced. "I almost finished. But my hand slipped and I busted my knuckles on the nut. Hurt like a motherfucker."

"That's what *he* said," Morgan muttered under her breath.

"What?" Joe cocked his head.

"Nothing. Sorry. Kayla's a bad influence." She returned her attention to the vintage blue and white porcelain handle, admiring the intricate floral pattern all over again. Gorgeous. Classic. It matched the sink set she'd picked up at one of the antique malls she frequented with Kate. The embellishment couldn't have been easy to find. God only knew how many specialty websites he'd surfed or stores he'd called. What other man would pay attention to such a tiny detail?

"You like it?"

"It's perfect. Thank you." She looked up, admiring his bare chest and feet. She kissed his cheek, then daubed the perspiration trickling from his temple to his jaw with the tail of the long shirt he must have changed her into. "Your surprises will never get old."

"Even when they cut your nap short?" Joe finished tinkering with the guts of the tank, replaced the lid and waved to the handle. "Do the honors. Give it a test flush."

She did, raving over his upgrades.

"Thank you, thank you." He issued her a mock bow as he climbed to his feet. Suddenly the bathroom seemed to shrink. His heat and powerful build filled the space.

"And yes, being woken up is well worth it when it means a man as sexy as you is on his knees, servicing my appliances."

He leveled a searing stare in her direction.

Her legs went weak.

Joe scanned her from her tousled hair to the wrinkled flannel shirt she'd filched from his drawer and worn each night he was absent. He licked his lips.

"I don't think my wife would appreciate the way you're staring at me, ma'am." He returned her grin with interest.

Had any man ever been as fine as him? Playful yet smoking hot, he turned her insides as mushy as the fruit she'd macerated for the filling in tomorrow's daily special—a mixed berry pie.

"Give me ten minutes and I'll make you forget all about her." Morgan stalked the step or two to Joe, employing her best imitation of a sultry swagger. She ran the tip of one finger from the hollow of his neck through the smattering of his light chest hair, along the valley separating his rock-hard abs. When she landed on the waistband of his jeans, she skimmed his trim sides until she slipped her hands into his back pockets.

A double handful of his tight ass acted as a convenient grip to tug him closer. The ridge of his cock pressed into her belly. He stiffened a little, putting her at arm's length so he could stare point-blank into her eyes.

"You didn't answer my question, cupcake." He wiped his hands on his denim-clad thighs before he traced the dark circles beneath her eyes with his thumbs. "You were out like a light. Tired for a reason?"

She stared at the black and white tiled floor he'd installed last summer until he lifted her chin with one of his bandage-free knuckles.

"Morgan?"

"I got my period the morning you left. It was a false alarm." She bit the inside of her cheek. "I'm so sorry."

"Shush." He rubbed her lower back with his undamaged hand, which nearly spanned her waist, and kissed her nose. "Nothing to apologize for. I should have been here. I knew you were late... Hoping..."

"I'm sorry I didn't say so right away. I couldn't stand to

disappoint you again." She rested her head on his shoulder. Maybe he'd think the moisture tracking down his chest was the result of a few more droplets of sweat instead of the tears she shed.

"Never." He hugged her tight.

"And then last night, I got drunk. Really hammered." She hiccupped. So much for stealth weeping. "I couldn't bring myself to say it out loud. You know, like then it would be real. I had to forget about it for a while and I knew it was safe. I passed out because I was hungover, not because I'm pregnant. So sorry."

"Ah, honey, you should have called me home." He rocked her against his chest.

"Why?" She sighed. "Nothing you could do."

"You never have to suffer alone." He finger-combed her hair. "Seriously, Morgan, that's a major benefit of our crew. I'm sure they'll look after you if I can't for some reason. It's one of the things that makes me comfortable leaving. Why didn't you confide in Dev, Kate and Kayla? They would have been there for you."

"I know. I almost did last night. Then Kate told us that her and Mike are trying too."

"He mentioned it to us on the trip." Joe nodded.

"Well, you know how much trouble Kate's sister had. Another rocky experience wasn't what she needed to hear about." Morgan clung to her husband, so glad to have him home, here, in her arms. "Psyching her out isn't going to help."

"Maybe you need to take your own advice, Mo." He made a circuit up her spine, then down her sides with his sure fingers. "Getting upset isn't going to help matters. A bunch of the books we read said it's normal for it to take up to a year of trying. Let's enjoy each other. The rest will take care of itself."

"You're right." She drew a deep breath, then blurted, "But I think we should make an appointment to have some tests done. Fertility and genetics stuff."

"Okay, sure." He rubbed their noses together. "Probably not a bad idea in any case."

"You *hate* the doctor. Sor—"

"Don't you dare apologize again. I'd do anything for you." He kissed her long and slow until her toes curled in the bathmat and ten tons lifted off her shoulders. "I'd hope you'd understand that by now. Fucking *anything* to make you smile."

"No one does that as well as you." She encircled his waist with her arms and nuzzled her cheek against the hard planes of his chest. "I love you, Joe."

"Same goes." He ruffled her hair.

"So, how about we take a shower together and practice, huh?" She nipped his pec. "Another week or so and we'll be in primetime again."

"I'm not sure that's a good idea." He stared into her eyes with more seriousness than she could ever remember.

"You want to give up already? I can handle this. I thought—"

"I meant the wasted water." He covered her mouth with a searing kiss. After nibbling on her bottom lip, he retreated with a smirk. "This could be an awfully long shower if we do it right."

"Some things are worth the sacrifice." Morgan reached in to flip on the spray. "Oh my God. You found matching shower fixtures, too?"

"Nah." He shook his head. "They never produced them compatible with this type of plumbing."

"Then how?" She stared at him like he was her hero, because he was.

"My cousin Eli has some fabrication connections for the parts they use in fixing up classic cars." He grinned. "Probably the first time he's asked them to make shower handles and toilet hardware instead. Those bastards had a field day ripping on me."

"You really are full of surprises." She knelt before him to tear open his button fly.

His jeans pooled on the floor, and he stepped out of them, leaving his lanky frame nude. She couldn't stop herself from touching him. Her fingers explored his furry thighs before they wrapped around the base of his shaft, stroking him the few times it took to transform his cock from semi-hard to steely.

Morgan rubbed the head of his erection across her lips, then licked the slippery fluid from them while staring up into Joe's eyes. Could he read her devotion in the artless stare?

"Enough, I'd like to last more than three minutes."

She grinned. "I'm sure you can hold out for five at least. Just give me a taste."

Joe's hands cupped her face and guided her toward his cock. She parted her lips.

Drawing him inside, she traced every line and ridge of his shaft with the tip of her tongue. When she hit the spot on the underside that drove him bananas, he growled.

Joe reached beneath her arms to lift her. She hitched one thigh over his hip. He boosted her with a palm on her ass, allowing her to wrap her other leg tight around his waist. They made out while the water warmed.

After minutes of foreplay more delicious than the chocolate mousse cake she'd baked last week, steam billowed around them. She leaned back a bit to flick the buttons of Joe's borrowed shirt open one at a time, revealing herself to him inch by inch. Never before had she had so much self-confidence in her figure.

The hunger in his eyes never lied, though. He craved her as much as she did him. Something she would never stop being thankful for.

She tossed the well-worn flannel into the white wicker hamper. No need for that with him around to keep her toasty.

They groaned in unison when their bare chests met.

Joe shimmied against her, teasing her breasts with his pecs. As if he knew it would leave her breathless, he repeated the sinuous caress before she could beg for more. All the while his cock prodded her clit, poising her on the verge of climax before they'd truly gotten started.

They didn't pause their slow grind when he stepped into the enclosure. Gentle trickles from the rain shower showerhead cascaded over them.

Ever thoughtful, he angled the spray against the tile for a bit before pressing her to the heated surface. "I know I had you earlier, but I swear I'm about to explode all over you."

"I thought the idea was to come inside me. Again and again." She nipped his neck. "I'm no expert at this baby-making stuff, but I'm pretty sure that's how it works."

"Wench." He ripped the toilet paper from his hand and tossed it toward the trash. The slap he landed on the side of her wet ass with his now-bare palm reverberated off the tile surround.

"Come on, Joe." She wriggled, attempting to notch his cock in the opening of her pussy. "Fuck me."

Joe pinned her with his shoulders so he could wedge his hand between them. Pressing his cock down with two fingers on top of the shaft, he aimed the swollen purple head between her thighs. Slippery. He glided through her slit, coating himself with her arousal. Every pass poked her clit with the blunt cap of his erection.

She shivered.

"You're ready." He murmured into her neck, licking and nipping as he pressed against her, letting gravity do some of the work. She slid down, hugging the first couple inches of his cock even as he stretched her. No matter how many times they did this, he altered her, forcing her body to accommodate his.

"Always ready for you." She tipped her head back until her crown *thunked* against the tile and soothing drizzle misted her face.

Joe screwed deeper within her, each twitch of his hips merging them together more completely. Never once did she worry he might drop her. "You're so hot. Burning me. So sweet."

He sucked on her chin, then migrated to her mouth where he toyed with her tongue while he embedded himself completely. She hung, impaled on his shaft, rocking in order to rub the ache in her clit on the hard muscles above the base of his cock. He started to move inside her with nearly as much urgency as she felt. His balls tapped her ass when he really got going.

Counterparts—she took when he gave, and gave when he took.

Each round-trip of his taxiing cock had her channel tightening further. Soon, Joe could hardly move within her as every inch of her tissue clung to him, squeezing him. Undulations began at her core, sucking him in despite his attempts to retreat if only to slam home once more.

"Damn. Love it when you do that." He cupped her breasts, soothing the pressure caused by her diamond-tipped nipples. "More."

"Not voluntary. Happens when you fuck me just right." She realized her eyes had slid closed as she reveled in bliss. The lack of visual stimulation only encouraged her brain to detect other pleasurable sensations.

"Like this?" He swiveled his hips in a sinful figure eight.

"Yes!" She no longer felt the water on her face or the slight chill creeping in around the edge of the shower curtain. The only thing that mattered was bonding with her mate and maybe creating something new and wondrous, half her and half him.

The idea held so much appeal she unraveled in his arms.

She mouthed Joe's name, but couldn't hear any sound beyond the rush of blood in her veins and the pounding of her heart—so close to his. Strung tight, she arched in his rock-solid grip. Her heels drummed on his ass as rounds of spasms wracked her. She couldn't breathe, couldn't move, couldn't tell this man how much she adored him. Except by opening her eyes and putting her soul on display for him to read.

Joe stared straight into her eyes. Message received. He smiled and dropped his forehead to hers, allowing himself to fray around the edges. He rammed into her harder than he would consider appropriate when not at the height of passion. She loved every second.

He shouted, a guttural cry filled with jumbled babble that her heart translated into perfect sense.

Heat spread through her abdomen—whether she imagined it or she could really sense it remained a mystery. She cheered every grunt that accompanied a pulse of his cock and the resulting mess he made of her pussy.

Good luck, boys. She giggled when she realized she cheered on a bunch of sperm.

"What's...funny?" Joe didn't look nearly as amused. He panted between bites and kisses on her neck and shoulders. "Laughing because I didn't give you a dozen orgasms before I lost it? Give me a minute and I'll make it up to you."

"Not that at all." She worked his cock with her pussy, using the tricks Kayla had taught her and the rest of the crew women, even as Joe set her feet carefully on the tub floor without separating them. Erotic massage techniques came in handy, who knew?

Joe's eyes rolled back. "Jesus. That should be illegal. Wicked."

"I told you Kay is a bad influence."

"Pretty sure I like you corrupted." He groaned when she paused then flexed again. His legs trembled. She stood on her tiptoes, not willing to break the connection of their bodies just yet.

"I'm not ready to get out." No surprise, he articulated her thoughts. He held her hand to keep her from leaving, as if she would consider that option in a million years. "Stay in here. Where the world is made up of you and me. You're the only thing that matters."

He sank to the floor of the basin, sprawling on his back in the garden tub, another upgrade he'd insisted on undertaking for her. She could fully appreciate the benefits of his hard work.

"No, you are." Morgan followed him down. She cuddled against his humid skin, lapping at the nearest droplets dotting its surface. His salty flavor tasted like perfection to her. If only she could use him as the secret ingredient in her culinary creations, she'd be unstoppable.

They petted each other, touched, explored and soothed. It must have been a while because Morgan began to shiver despite their proximity and the still-warm spray spritzing them. The backup water heater he'd installed when she'd started serving customers in the bakery marked another point in his favor. She whimpered when Joe shifted, reluctant to end their snuggle session.

"Don't worry, I'm still not going anywhere." He leaned forward far enough to flip the drain closed and switch the water flow to the gorgeous new spigot he'd installed earlier. With one arm slung around her shoulders, he pumped some bubble bath beneath the stream, filling the tub. He grabbed a lighter and ignited the wick on the candle she kept on the surround for the nights she indulged in a proper soak while reading. She adored Sweet Treats, but being on her feet all day made the decadence part necessity.

"What would the crew think if they saw you taking a bubble bath?" Morgan licked his collarbone. Her hand wandered across his chest and down his washboard abs. His softened cock had long ago slipped from her. Half-hard, it bobbed with the rising tide.

Warmth suffused her as their bodies were submerged.

"They'd think I'm a lucky bastard to be sharing it with

you." He nuzzled her temple. "Especially once I get laid again."

"Awful sure of yourself, aren't you?"

"Am I wrong?"

"Hell, no." Morgan straddled his thighs. She gathered huge handfuls of the growing foam and spread it all over her chest and belly.

Joe cursed and reached for her.

She smacked his hands. "Put them on the sides of the tub and leave them there."

He complied, gritting his teeth all the while. "For how long?"

"Until I say so." She peeked at his fingers. They turned white from gripping the edge of the tub and the handle of the built-in soap dish on the other side. The corner of her mouth tipped up in an evil grin. "Remember when Kay gave us that nuru massage demonstration?"

"God, yes," he hissed.

"I've been thinking about asking her for some lessons." Morgan glopped more bubbles onto Joe's chest, then slithered across his frame. When she slid lower, she used her feet on the front wall of the tub to propel herself up his body once more.

"If we're not careful, I'm going to drown." He gurgled when her breasts and mound rubbed along his entire front.

"Imagine how much slipperier that seaweed goop is." She repeated her circuit, loving the contact of all his severe angles with her lush curves.

"Might make you too hard to hold on to." He grabbed her ass, spreading her cheeks as he tugged her where he wanted her. She rotated her hips to stroke his rejuvenated hard-on, trapped between them.

"I'm not trying to escape. Promise." She put her hands on his shoulders and boosted herself six inches higher. "But since you were bad and moved your hands, I think you should make it up to me by giving me your cock."

His cheeks flushed before her eyes. "I love it when you talk dirty."

"Really?" She lifted her brows. "Like when I say I need you to open me up and push your thick shaft inside my dripping pussy? Or when I say, I can't wait to feel you pumping your load inside me again, filling me with your come...?"

"Jesus. Yes. That." He shattered her illusion of control by plunging into her from below.

Thank God. She relaxed her thighs, allowing him to inhabit her fully. This time they had a tiny bit more restraint. They rippled together, gently for the most part, though surges punctuated the peace and tranquility of their joining.

She gave up attempting to articulate everything in her soul and relied on her body to speak his language. If his answering moans and caresses were any indication, he understood perfectly.

Their tender sharing escalated into something tinged with desperation and longing. Neither of them noticed the water and thick foam sloshing onto the floor. They wouldn't have cared if they had.

The waves they generated facilitated their rhythm, buffeting them and rocking them together with prurient insistence. Morgan bit her lip, hard.

"It's okay," Joe murmured. "There's plenty more of this. Come, Morgan. Never hold back. I'll always provide you as much as you need."

Her body obeyed his mastery. Nails sank into his

biceps as she came around him. He never flinched from her full-on display of passion. Instead, he pressed into her with long, strong glides that extended her pleasure until she nearly forgot her own name.

Only when the contractions lessened did he shout and release within her.

The rough seas they'd inspired calmed to a steady lap of waves that shook them both in the wake of their spent passion. Morgan sighed as they threatened to rock her to sleep. Probably not a great idea while still in the tub.

"Time for bed." Joe stifled a yawn. He flipped the drain with his foot, nodding when the valve opened smoothly even after the alterations he'd made.

"Already?" Despite the lassitude permeating her bones, it couldn't be past seven o'clock. "I just got up."

"I didn't say sleep." Joe grinned.

"Seriously? What were they feeding you up North?" She tried not to wince, imagining him invading her swollen pussy again so soon.

"Hey, I didn't say fool around either." He clutched her to him as he rose. Water sluiced from his cut frame. "I missed you. I'd like to catch up. Tell me how your weekend was. Did you try that new recipe I copied from my Aunt Bianca? She was thrilled and flattered you might use it."

"Oh! Yeah, it was as good as you remembered. Better than you said, even." Morgan poured out a detailed recounting of the tests she'd conducted to improve the balance of flavors.

Joe's stomach growled.

"Want me to run downstairs and check the fridge for leftovers?" She patted his flat belly.

"Nah. I'm sure I'll have a slice or five tomorrow." Joe

relinquished her to stand on her own long enough to towel off. He plucked her from the bathmat and carried her to their bed the instant she'd finished.

They burrowed under the covers together, exchanging stories and news. She shook her head at the antics of his Carter cousins. Together with the crew, the six guys—a collection of lost souls Joe's uncle had adopted after the untimely death of his wife—were rowdy enough to stir up trouble even in the middle of nowhere.

Eventually, they'd shared the peaceful evening together—though the time flew by—complete with a couple pieces of cold pizza and the remainder of her test creations, which Joe had inhaled, unable to restrain himself. A tough job, but someone had to do it. Having the foundation for her happiness nearby cleared her mind. She made her decision in a snap after debating all weekend.

"I'm going to tell the girls as soon as I have the chance." Morgan was grateful he nodded without her having to elaborate. She should have realized he'd be on the same page even hours later. It made it easier for her to continue, though she had to clear her throat before she could force the rest out. "They'll need to know to understand why I'm going to wear a diaphragm and insist on condoms next time we're together. The whole group, I mean."

"But—" Joe's jaw slackened. "Are you saying? What happened with James this morning? More of that? *Beyond* that?"

"Yeah, we discussed it and we'd like to try swapping." She wondered if he would love or hate the idea. "How do you feel about that?"

"Wow." He sank deeper into the pile of pillows. "You all *were* busy while we were gone."

"And..."

"Most of me says *hell yeah*." He scrubbed his hand through his not-quite-dry hair. "And part of me is unsure."

"Which part is which?" Morgan draped over his chest, relishing the strength of his arms, which came around her instantly.

"I think it would be smoking hot to watch the rest of the crew spoil you." He licked an imaginary crumb from her neck. "I'll never forget your birthday. I still remember how sweet that cake tasted when we all ate it off you."

She would cherish the memory until the day she died.

"But...you know...the other girls." He rubbed the back of his neck.

"Having sex with them?" she supplied, adoring his stumble considering the libertine delights she'd witnessed him and his friends indulge in.

"Yeah. That's a big step. Huge. You're like sisters. I couldn't stand it if we fucked that up." He sighed. "It took a while for the crew to find our balance with each other. It's not easy when all those connections linger. They can glue you together or trip you up. What if everyone gets tangled into a giant knot?"

"You've already been with Kate," she reminded him gently.

"True. But that was before you."

"I appreciate what you're saying. It's those worries exactly that made me hesitate. Still, I feel like we already have these crazy bonds. Do you really think we could ever drift apart?" They both considered in silence for a few moments.

"No." He reached the same conclusion she had after

she'd mulled it over. "We're one unit now. With that said, if something starts to happen and you decide it's not what you thought, or it makes you uncomfortable—"

"What if it turns me on to think of you with them?" She squirmed enough to admit exactly which part of her liked the proposition.

"Is that a hypothetical question?" He looked at her as if afraid this was some kind of sick trap.

"I'm willing to try just about anything once." She nibbled her bottom lip. "And I can think of a lot of things that would be lower on my list. We're so close. It feels unnatural to limit ourselves."

"My guess is the rest of the crew would agree with you. I do." Joe threaded their fingers together. "I would bet my share of the business that we're not the only ones having this discussion tonight either."

"I know how much I respect and love the other guys. I believe that goes both ways."

"Is that a bisexual crack?" He smirked, diffusing some of the tension simmering between them.

"No, but it would have been one hell of a that's-what-*he*-said joke if Kay were here to seize the opportunity." Morgan shook her head, clearing the distraction. "What I'm saying is this... Why would I want you or any of our circle of friends to have roadblocks to expressing our affection for each other?"

"How in the hell did I get so lucky?" Joe rolled, flipping her onto her back. He smothered her so well she wished she never had to draw another breath. "I have the best friends a guy could ask for. A sexy, sweet and dirty wife. And a collection of equally awesome women who all hope to get it on with me."

Morgan laughed. "That's a guy's perspective for sure, but... I suppose you do have it pretty damn good."

"And I'll never forget it." He lowered his face, bringing his lips down on hers, and blanketing her with his flaring heat. "I swear to you. I will always cherish you. And the crew. Our family. However big, small or unconventional."

With that, they *practiced* the whole night long.

5

Devon tucked a flat pencil behind her ear. She hauled the marked crown-molding to the compound miter saw in the corner, then flipped her safety glasses into place. The whir of the blade never ceased to impress and thrill her. In the blink of an eye, the long piece became two smaller ones.

Building something polished from raw materials, transforming an ordinary space into a home that met its full potential, had satisfied her since she first visited a job site with Ray. Her older half-brother, her mother's son from her first marriage, was a mason. He'd allowed her to wander freely between the various contractors as long as she kept out of his hair. Babysitting had never been his forte. At the end of the day, he'd found her crouched beside the foreman, who flipped through pictures of the house they worked on in various stages of its construction.

She'd discovered her professional passion when she was twelve years old. The fascination had grown over the past decade. But the crew elevated her craft to new levels. Though she'd been around the business forever, nothing had rivaled their attention to detail, flair for design or pride in their workmanship. Each man was held in high regard in his area of specialty. The friendship they shared enhanced their partnership. And now that dream team miraculously included her on its roster.

She grinned and bopped to Hot Chelle Rae's "Tonight, Tonight". The party anthem blasted through the beat-up radio they toted from site to site. It might rely on duct tape to hold it together, but it kept her entertained. Her shimmy punctuated the chorus. Dancing on the Hollywood sign couldn't match the euphoria her career and partners produced.

After checking the alignment of the angle, she dry-fitted the pieces on the ground before climbing her ladder to shoot a couple brads into the detail. With the finishing touches on the dining room as complete as she could make them, she hopped down to the hardwood floor, hands on hips, and surveyed the fruits of her labor. Pretty damn fine if she said so herself.

Devon rotated her wrists, which ached a bit from the awkward angle she'd had them at most of the morning. She peered through the plastic sheeting intended to confine dust to her workspace, into the living room. This house would make a great starter home for someone, complete with a smattering of furniture even.

Some of the pieces abandoned by the former residents, who'd moved suddenly following a job offer out of state, had great character. Devon planned to beg Kate to undertake some experimental reupholstering of Neil's hideous college-days sofa so she could apply the learning to sprucing up this set. She could picture the finished product in her mind.

Plus, it would be a handy skill, allowing her to bring

something new and different to the crew's capabilities. Win-win, it would also eliminate the burnt sienna plaid monstrosity from her home. Their home. James would definitely vote in her favor on this one.

A rustle from behind her had her glancing over her shoulder.

"Came to lend a hand. Doesn't look like you need our assistance, though." Neil ambled into the room with the rest of the guys in tow.

Dust clung to their holey jeans and T-shirts. Dirt streaked their arms. Exertion had their cheeks glowing. Rugged and filthy, they still managed to steal her breath. Maybe more than when they spruced themselves up.

They'd focused on demolition and the structural concerns rampant in the basement while she completed the more refined project on the main level. Worked for her, except she'd missed having them nearby. Okay, so one stinking floor below her didn't constitute a huge rift. Still, it was enough. Anywhere beyond her grasp seemed too far.

Their faith in her skills overwhelmed her with smugness. They wouldn't allow her to roam unbridled if they had any doubt about her capabilities.

Mike inspected her progress carefully. "This is good shit, Dev. I like how you built up the molding with the dental piece on top of the cove. Looks fantastic. Cost effective. Solid workmanship too. It's stuff like this buyers will notice and pay more for. They don't give a crap that we've made sure their foundation won't crack and sprayed enough insulation in this place to save them a boatload on energy bills. Nice work."

"Thanks, *boss*." She giggled when he smacked her ass

with one of his leather gloves. She couldn't resist teasing. "Was that my reward?"

"Careful or I'll put you over my knee, imp." Mike's warning held no heat, unless it was the kind borne of desire.

"Promise?" She would have liked to play more. If there wasn't one last thing she had to attend to. "Seriously, though, I couldn't reach the tray section, even with the ladder. Could one of you hammer this in for me?"

The twitch of Neil's lips guaranteed he'd caught her double entendre. "I suppose I could toss it a couple bangs, since I have such a big tool."

"Have a big tool or *are* a big tool?" Dave smirked.

"That's what *he* said," Devon said simultaneously. She groaned when none of the crew laughed along with her.

Mike imitated a sad trombone with a descending *waa waa waa*.

At least they didn't have any rotten tomatoes or rubber chickens on hand. Suddenly she had a lot more sympathy for Fozzie Bear. Devon stuck out her lower lip. "Aw, party poopers."

"Dave, you have to wrestle Kay under control." Joe smacked their friend in the gut with his knuckles. "She's got all of our girls doing it now."

"That's what *he* said," James quipped and high-fived Devon.

"I knew I loved you for a reason." She stole a kiss, aching for more than the tiny nibble. She hoped he understood how much she adored his infallible instincts, which ensured she was never the odd "man" out.

"Yeah, and let Kayla hear you talk about muffling her. She'll rip you a new one. Or better yet, maybe she'll tattle on you to Morgan." Mike shook his head.

"Oh please, no." Joe held his index fingers out in a cross as though warding off a clan of vampires on the attack. "I promise. I'll be good."

Devon's face hurt from smiling so huge, caught in the crossfire of their banter. She loved them so much tears pricked her eyes. Quickly, she put her back to the crew and shoved her safety glasses on top of her head like the least designer headband of all time. Kneeling as though tidying her workspace, she scrubbed surreptitiously at her cheeks.

James crouched by her side. His hand rubbed a soothing arc across her back. "What did we say?"

Only then did she realize the room had gone silent, her playlist complete.

She dropped her head on his shoulder and rooted her face into his neck. "You didn't do anything wrong."

"What's all this?" Neil bracketed her. With one hand on James's shoulder, he nudged her chin up so he could peer at her face.

"I can't believe how lucky I am." She sniffled. "Dumb, I know. But you make me so happy. Sometimes I'm afraid I'm dreaming and that I'll wake up and you'll all be gone. A figment of my imagination."

"That's kind of fucked up, Dev," Joe murmured from behind her where he, Dave and Mike stood shoulder to shoulder, guarding her back.

"Gee, thanks." She snorted. "Okay, now I know you're real men."

"We're in this for the long haul." Mike dropped a hand to her stubby ponytail and mussed the strands already flying free, since her hair was really too short for the 'do.

"You couldn't get rid of us if you tried." Dave towered

over her. His commanding presence reassured her. They all did.

She reached out to Neil and James. Neil nibbled on her trembling fingers, layering kisses along the digits he cradled as delicately as if they were a precisely calibrated set of calipers. He paid special attention to her ring finger and the stylized tattoo gracing it. They'd offered to buy her a ring. Fought with her over it, actually, until she convinced them the extravagance would go to waste. Safety prohibited her from wearing jewelry most of the time.

Truth be told, she preferred the indelible marking—a vine that wound around the base of her finger and cradled two flowers that mimicked center stones, one red and one yellow, the guys' favorite colors—as permanent as their residency in her heart. If the artwork bore traces of sawdust, Neil didn't seem to mind. More like his breath steamed harder against her wrist when his tongue traced the proof of their possession.

James captured her mouth. He coaxed her lips apart with skill and finesse that never ceased to amaze her. For a guy who claimed to prefer men most of the time, he sure as hell knew how to trip every single one of her passionate triggers.

He dazzled her with the thrill he inspired. Dizzy, she tipped into Neil's waiting embrace. He rose smoothly to his feet, lifting her too.

"Come here." He must have aimed the directive at James, because she had no choice except to go where he toted her. Not that she minded. Never would she have complained.

His gruff commands echoed through the space, which they'd cleared furniture from.

Devon closed her eyes as Neil ducked beneath the plastic shield they'd hung in the arched opening to the living room. When Mike, Dave and Joe evaluated his trajectory and guessed where Neil intended to place her, they jogged ahead.

Mike ripped the protective sheet from the worn leather couch and stripped the seat cushions off. He tossed one to Joe and another to Dave. Between the three of them, they converted the rustic coffee table into a padded dais faster than James's adopted kitty invaded the kitchen when he heard his savior rustling a bag of pricey organic kibble. Only the best for everything and everyone James loved.

Spoiled rotten and reveling in it, Devon winked up at the crew.

Neil swooped in to kiss her even as her legs were tugged from his grip. Her safety glasses clattered to the ground, skidding somewhere under the chair. Devon gasped when someone, James if the deft yet caressing hands were any indication, unclasped her tool belt, unlaced and disposed of her boots, then swiped her jeans off in no time flat. She wobbled on shaky legs when they shifted their attention to stripping her top half.

Thank God for the electric heaters they'd installed to keep the house cozy. They hadn't overhauled the plumbing yet and wouldn't take a chance on a busted pipe until they had.

She gulped for air like a fish out of water once her mouth ripped free of Neil's, their connection severed by the passing of her thermal top. One of the guys nudged her arms up while another whipped the cotton from her body. Left in her cute yet utilitarian cotton bra and panties, she didn't feel the least bit exposed.

"Your underwear is yellow." Neil traced the skin beside the cheery straps.

"With red hearts." James nipped at one cartoony symbol gracing the curve of her hip.

"What better to hug my lady parts all day than something that reminds me of you two?" Her whisper carried in the hush of the calm before the storm.

"*Nothing* would be pretty damn fine. Imagining you naked beneath those funky, patched overalls you wear sometimes gives me massive wood." Neil grimaced when several of them paused to consider that mental image. Dave cursed under his breath.

She laughed out loud. Too bad she hadn't known that before their Valentine's Day photo session. Although she doubted there'd be any complaints when he discovered the Victorian getup she'd stashed in the back of their closet. It *had* made her waist look tiny.

"What?" Neil shrugged. "I have to have something extra special to daydream about when I'm stuck worming around in dark, dingy crawlspaces to examine foundations, or evaluate attics, or check for mold, or whatever other duties these guys claim the skinniest of us should be on the hook for. If I thought about rats or spiders or asbestos monsters lurking in those tight spots, I'd flip out."

Devon laid her hand on his forearm. "I'll take inspection duty next time. You shouldn't have to if it makes you uncomfortable. I'm the littlest. Not afraid of bugs either. And claustrophobia has never been an issue. I kind of like being crowded."

As if by tacit understanding, each crew member took a step closer. Their heat and hunger blasted her from all sides as they encroached on her personal space. She closed her eyes and leaned toward Neil, trusting him to catch her.

Of course, he did. They guided her to the improvised bed they'd constructed. She yelped at the initial contact of the cool leather on her skin. Ten hands petted and soothed her until they abolished any hint of chill.

"Scoot over, Dev." James whipped his clothes off, then nudged her hip with his knee. She made room for him to join her. "I'm in the mood to share the bottom with you today."

"Or do you mean share *your* bottom?" She nipped his lip when he slipped his arm beneath her neck, supporting her.

"Either works for me." He pressed a delicate peck on the tip of her nose. "But I wouldn't dare steal your fun."

"There's plenty to go around." She switched her gaze from man to man to man to man, ringing them.

When she licked her lips, they shed chambray, denim and leather as if it were a race. Maybe it was. Dave finished first. Though Devon expected him to reach for James, or maybe the industrial-sized bottle of lube they kept in their tool chest, he didn't. Instead, he straddled the head of the coffee table, planting one foot on either side of her and James. He squatted until his thick cock hung between their faces.

"Ladies first." James rolled onto his side, and she mirrored him.

Devon reached upward to fondle the heavy sac swaying gently in the aftermath of Dave's gymnastics. It still felt new and somewhat taboo to be touching Kayla's husband. A thrill zinged through her, accompanied by a shiver that vibrated along her spine. The tremble had her hand retracting, severing her contact with Dave's electrified skin.

Did this adhere to their slumber party agreement? Or was she crossing the boundaries by indulging without her girlfriends?

She tried to work out the intricacies in her lust-hazed mind without much success. All she could say for sure was that her visceral response to the situation instilled a craving, the intensity of which she'd never known before. Or at least not since the first time she'd had James and Neil together.

"Trust your instincts." James came to her rescue. "He likes it like this."

He demonstrated a firmer grip than Dev would have been comfortable imparting on her own.

"Go ahead." Dave barked instructions. "Do me like he's showing you. It feels fucking great."

She hesitated, her hand a fraction of an inch away from her goal.

"Am I allowed to?" She hated the pale imitation of her voice. "I've never..."

"Kay confessed to me about your scheming the other night." He growled. "Time to put your mouth where your fantasies are. If you still want this. Me. Us."

The note of uncertainty in his gruff admission had Devon reaching out in a flash. Her insecurities would never affect the rest of the crew if she had anything to say about it.

He gasped and might have toppled if James hadn't braced the bigger man's bulging thigh. Devon didn't blink twice. They'd never allow her to be crushed. She focused on her prize, cupping his nuts in her palm. The heavy sac covered in soft skin nestled into her palm.

James lectured her on refining her technique. He offered subtle adjustments to her clutch. When she had Dave panting and groaning softly, they moved to phase two of their tandem attack.

Devon grinned across at James. He smacked his lips together while staring at the damp head of Dave's cock.

"There's enough to share," she whispered. "Probably can't fit him all in my mouth anyway. Suck him with me, James."

She twined her fingers in the neat strands of her mate's hair and used the clutch to coax him nearer. Not that he resisted much. When his tongue flicked from between his lips, she mimicked his technique. Together, they laved every inch of Dave's shaft from the base to just below the head. Veins grew in definition beneath each timid lap of her tongue.

From time to time, James would get carried away. His lips clashed with hers around the cylinder of Dave's cock. She gasped. Dave took advantage of the situation to poke his hard-on into her mouth. His girth stretched her lips into a wide O.

James traced the semi-circle closest to him with the tip of his tongue.

"Jesus. That's sexy, Dev." Neil leaned in to kiss her cheek. Although he had serviced James on special occasions more recently, it was a true act of love for him. He didn't derive pleasure from giving blowjobs. The crew respected his limits. Knowing his face lingered so near his friend's cock had Devon whimpering.

The vibration must have done wonderful things to Dave's shaft because the big man sighed and sank lower, feeding her more of his cock.

James took advantage of the opportunity. He stretched

his neck upward and engulfed Dave's balls. He sucked first one, then the other. The wet slurps and smacks inspired her to draw a few more inches of their friend inside her.

"Give me a break," Dave groaned. "Or I'm gonna shoot before we've really gotten started."

Devon giggled around his beast of a cock.

Neil cupped her cheeks in his palms and drew her off his friend's length. James rejoined her, abandoning his oral massage of the sensitive tissues between Dave's thighs. He tossed her a devilish grin, then nipped at Neil's restraining fingers.

"Ouch. That stung, asshole." Neil let go and shook his hand. His rebuke was hard to take seriously when he laughed through his curses.

"Just remember payback is a bitch." Mike slapped James's bare ass from his spot behind their lover. The crack reverberated off the hardwood floors gracing their latest project.

"Yeah. Except I fucking love that, you bastard." James hooked an arm around Devon's waist and tugged until their pelvises ground together. His erection never failed to impress her with its ultra-hardness. Though the rest of the guys had him in length and girth, he had more than enough to please her. After all, it was less about the tool and more about his proficiency in handling it.

James had skills beyond belief.

They bumped together until Devon was sure her panties had soaked through. Why wouldn't someone touch her?

"Is this what you want, little one?" Joe flicked his fingers over the catch of her bra. The pressure of the straps on her shoulders made it clear he planned to divest her of the extra-padded push-up. She lifted her arms, careful not to whack Dave in the family jewels. She might not have a lot to warrant the garment, but she was vain enough to enhance what little she had. Hopefully the guys didn't see it as false advertising. She'd never be as stacked as Kate or Morgan.

She shouldn't have worried.

Joe knelt on the floor behind her, cupping her chest in his calloused palms. The slight abrasion launched shafts of pleasure from her breasts to her pussy.

"Yes," she moaned. "More."

Neil released her, dragging his hands along the stretched column of her neck. He outlined the hold Joe had on her, making both of the guys' respiration grow ragged. Joe shifted his fingers to blanket Neil's for an instant before they continued their trek toward her belly. Neil paused to span her waist, as he often did. Both of them enjoyed how large he was compared to her diminutive form.

She lifted up when his hands tucked into the waistband of her panties. He peeled them from her so fast she was relieved she didn't get some kind of friction burn. At least he hadn't shredded this pair. She was rather fond of them. More so after today.

They cleared her matching red-painted toes, a remnant of the weekend photo shoot. He sling-shotted them at Mike. They all stared as the foreman brought the cotton to his face and breathed deep, like an alpha wolf memorizing the scent of a member of his pack.

"Sweet." He dropped the scrap of fabric onto the pile of clothes littering the floor. "Will you let me taste you too?"

Devon glanced between Neil and James. Neither of them objected. She squeaked when James reached down to hoist her knee toward her chest, opening her to their crewmates. "He's really good with his mouth, Dev. You don't want to miss out."

And there it was.

The truth. She didn't want to miss out anymore. This tension had zinged through them for months now. Every time the crew expressed their affection and relieved some stress on the job site, she cooled her heels on the sidelines. Granted, she already felt like she had an unfair advantage over some of the crew wives for her ringside seat to those glorious shows, but she'd longed to cross their unspoken boundaries and truly become one of the crew.

Today, there would be no stopping short. No embargos placed on the pure adoration in her heart. These men were hers and she was theirs. Though not many others would understand, she thanked the universe every single day that she'd found the family she'd never really had but always needed so desperately.

"Yes. Please, Mike." She would never forget the glitter in his eyes as he descended on her. It came close to the fire in her soul for the man who'd glued them all together.

The moment his lips brushed her core, she wilted, surrendering to his authority, which ordered her to relax and accept his gift. Once her eyes had stopped rolling back at the initial onslaught of pleasure, she realized Dave had cradled her head, granting her a clear view of Mike as he peppered her waxed mound with light, feathery kisses.

"So smooth," he rumbled against her sensitive flesh.

"Benefit of having a friend who owns a spa." She managed to force out the revelation between gritted teeth.

"Another reason I love my wife." Dave sighed dreamily. His cock lurched, rising up to paint a sticky trail across Devon's cheek with the dripping head. "I can't wait to tell her about this. She'll go crazy, begging me to fuck her, imagining she was the one to taste you. You know she wants that. Bad. Don't you, Dev? She cares for you. She'll be so happy you finally got what you've wanted."

When he put it so simply, Devon's lingering guilt evaporated. It would be impossible to deny the honesty of his rambling when desire acted like a truth serum, causing him to blurt out the deepest secrets in his heart.

"I dream about it too, Dave." She angled her head to kiss along the side of his thick shaft. James echoed her motion. They sandwiched Dave's cock between their hot, moist mouths, licking, sucking and sliding up and down his length again. Their dual blowjob was sloppy, but he didn't seem to mind. Some of his control restored, he helped them by rocking into their grip, fucking their faces relentlessly as Mike continued his reverent exploration.

"Damn, that's sexy." Joe stroked her back from his place behind her. "You're a natural, Dev. I always wondered what it'd be like to have shared you with the crew. Each of our girls is so different. Being with Kate the first time... Shit. I'll never forget that scorching afternoon. And seeing how much these guys could please Morgan, I would never deny her that. You either. I hope we can make it half as good for you."

While he continued his generous speech, he caressed her from head to toe. Neil moved out of his way, circling around the table to stand behind James instead. Joe stroked her hair, rubbed her shoulders and took over for James, supporting her knee so Mike had clear access to her pussy. James used his newly freed hand to reach behind him and connect with Neil. He didn't have to look to find their mate.

"Yeah," Neil groaned. "Go with it. Both of you."

Devon's lashes fluttered as she struggled to keep them open. She made direct eye contact with James. His gorgeous eyes seared a stare into hers and she knew she'd never feel lonely again. Not with him and the rest of these men surrounding her. His pupils dilated, and he gasped around Dave's shaft before releasing the plaintive whimper she'd come to associate with the initial burn of someone penetrating his ass.

She abandoned Dave's cock to soothe James instead. Distracting him with open-mouthed kisses, she helped him relax enough to accept the lubed fingers Neil surely worked into his ass.

"That's right, James," Neil whispered against James's neck. "Soon you'll have all of me. That's what you needed, isn't it?"

"Yes." He groaned when Neil massaged him from the inside out.

"And you, sweetheart?" Mike lifted his mouth from her long enough to ask. "What would you like?"

"Don't stop." She squirmed until her pussy aligned with his lips again. That talented, deceptively gentle mouth descended.

His chuckles buffeted her nerves. This time, he enhanced the sensation with his fingers. The pressure caused by two of his thick, blunt digits prodding at her entrance had her seeking James's hand.

"Holy shit." Mike paused the figure eight of his tongue to glare at Neil. "Why didn't you warn me? I might have hurt her, rushed her."

"We told you she was tight," they muttered together.

"She's tiny." He sighed and folded one of his fingers

against his palm, leaving only his index finger to penetrate her rippling channel.

No matter how she tried to relax, his decadent fondling had her tensed again in no time. "S-sorry."

"Shh. Only worried about causing you pain or frightening you away," Mike murmured against her mound. "Now that I've tasted you, I don't think I could be satisfied with a single serving."

"Want you inside me. Just do it. I don't mind." Her urging turned breathless when he lodged in her to the second knuckle.

"Not concerned about my fingers, cutie." He smiled against her mound. "More afraid of how you'll take my cock. I'm thicker than your guys. And Dave... Well, you might have to work up to him."

Joe groaned from behind her. She didn't like leaving him out of their circle. Devon squirmed, trying to roll over. Mike lifted his head, surveying her predicament.

"Good idea, Dev." The foreman flipped her as if she weighed nothing.

Lying on her back, she was able to wrap her fingers around Joe's shaft. She tugged several times, experimentally. A bead of pre-come dripped from the tip onto her forearm.

"Let me taste that." James drew her arm toward his mouth. He lapped at the slick streak there, making them all groan in appreciation. The wet heat on her skin had a shudder traveling down her body.

Mike cursed when she spasmed around his embedded fingers. When had he fit the other inside her? He scissored them, spreading her tissues gently. "I can't wait for you to hug my dick like that."

Devon whimpered. "Me either."

Joe caught her attention as he stroked himself, unable to wait for gratification. She winced. It would take some practice to service five men at once.

"Don't worry, Dev." Neil grunted. "It's up to us to find our own pleasure. You lay back and enjoy. Let them use you and the rest is our job, okay?"

She nodded.

"Fuck, that's hot." He stared between her thighs where Mike conditioned her pussy even as he nibbled on her lips and around her clit. "James, I need to be inside you."

"Do it." The smaller man huffed when Neil banded his arms around James's waist and used the hold to raise him to his knees.

From her position beside him, it was easy for Devon to reach beneath him and stroke his cock.

"Perfect, Dev." Mike hummed, vibrating her aching flesh. "Slow and easy, just like that. Help him forget about Neil sinking deep."

Devon met Neil's gaze. The cords in his neck stood out as he advanced. James's tight, hot hole must have clamped on his cock. Though they'd done this countless times before, he always had a look of wonder on his face when he mounted his lover. Devon hoped the same could be said for his liaisons with her.

James lifted his head. Breathing hard, his panting buffeted Dave's neatly trimmed pubic hair, which dusted the base of his monster hard-on. James didn't need to be asked. He opened his mouth and reached out with one arm to smack Dave's ass, goading him closer.

"You want it rough today?" Dave seemed eager to comply. He tugged on James's hair, positioning her mate's open mouth at the head of his cock. "I can fuck you as well as Neil can from here."

James's moan was all the encouragement he needed. Dave buried himself to the root in James's mouth. The shorter man choked a little, but held his place. He had nowhere to go, really. Pierced from behind by Neil and pinned in front by Dave, they skewered him.

The throb of his erection in her still-stroking hand reassured her he wouldn't have fled if he could. He'd be more likely to chase them down and beg them to fuck him.

"Shit. That's fucking hot." Joe used one hand to pinch his own nipple as he pulled on his cock with the other.

"Poor Joe." Mike *tsked* against her clit, making her mewl and beg for more. "You're not going to leave him hanging out there all alone, are you?"

Devon didn't have to be told twice. She swiveled her head, and Joe met her halfway. He ringed his erection with his fist at the base, ensuring she didn't attempt to take more than she could handle. She teased his head with flicks of her tongue, like James had taught her, interspersed with strong draws that hollowed her cheeks.

"Oh, Christ." He knelt, or half-folded, so his knees rested on the table beside her. From there he grounded himself with a palm on her breast. "She sucks as well as James."

"Good teacher." Her retort jumbled around the mass of his cock. But they got her point.

Mike admonished her. "Watch your teeth now."

She folded her lips over the sharp edges, although certain she hadn't nicked Joe. Only when the wide cap of Mike's erection prodded her saturated pussy did she realize what he'd meant. She froze as he began to enter her, a fraction of an inch at a time.

"Oh. Fuck." Dave grunted as he shuttled in and out of

James's mouth. "You should see this. He's opening her up and she's loving it."

James paused, removing his mouth with a slurp so he could tuck his head between his shoulders and witness Mike's progress for himself. "Are you okay, Dev?"

His wide eyes made her sure it looked as drastic as it felt. The invasion burned, stretched and caressed her in new and wonderful ways she hadn't expected.

"Love it. God, yes." She answered by increasing the pace of her hand, which jerked him with ungraceful passes now that sensations bombarded her from all angles. Neil helped when he fucked James harder, faster, thrusting James's cock through the ring of her fingers and eliminating the need for her to move at all.

"More, sweetheart?" Mike rode her with short strokes, bumping them together just enough for her to sample what he might really do if he pushed inside her to the hilt.

"All of you." She would have used her heels on his ass to try to force him deeper but she was no match for his strength.

"Not like that." He gritted his teeth. "I won't hurt you. No matter what you think you want, we'll take this slow. Neil, pass me the lube."

She was drenched, plenty slick to take him. Still, she didn't argue when she realized it meant his dexterous fingers would be slipping in and around her pussy beside his gorgeous cock. By thrusting upward, she captured another inch or two of his shaft.

Damn, it did sting. Not more than she could handle. And after a few heartbeats of stillness, the mild pain faded into something a hell of a lot more pleasurable.

"You pay attention here." Joe fed her more of his hard-on. "Let Mike handle that. He's really good at taking someone without hurting them. Especially if they're not used to getting fucked."

Devon glanced up in time to catch the flush spreading across Joe's chest and up his neck. He should know. She'd stared, fascinated, as Joe bent over for their foreman from time to time.

"Jealous?" She pulled off his tip long enough to taunt him.

"Be good or I'll think you don't deserve this treat." He ruffled her hair playfully.

She exacted revenge by relaxing her throat, taking him deeper than ever on the next pass. He traced her lips where they ringed his shaft. She swallowed around him, wriggling her tongue along the underside of his cock.

"Okay, I take it back." He choked. "This is just fine by me."

Devon relented, otherwise she could easily drain his orgasm before they were ready to shatter together. For some reason, it mattered to her. She had to share her climax with the crew in the ultimate wegasm or she wouldn't be satisfied.

"Better speed it up," Dave warned Mike. "She's getting that gleam in her eyes like Kay does when she's ready to rip me apart to have her way. You're not going to hurt her. She wants this. You."

Her stare flicked to Neil's. He read the desperation in her gaze even as he continued to ride their mate. One hand lifted from James's ass to rest on Mike's lower back. He prevented the foreman from retreating and instead, nudged him deeper within her.

Knowing Neil directed the action blew her arousal out of proportion. Logic fled. In its place was only sensation. The smell of men and sex and sweat. The sound of grunts, groans and sighs. The sight of muscles straining, flexing and bulging. The taste of Joe's pre-come, salty and sweet. And the feel...

Oh God, the feel of them.

Over her, under, around, inside... She couldn't help but sense them in every pore of her being. Every breath and heartbeat was filled with the crew.

She had never been happier in her life.

Mike nestled into the cradle of her thighs. Their abdomens met as they fused completely.

"You feel fucking amazing around me." He groaned into her neck as he fell forward for an instant, catching his breath before the sprint to the finish.

Her head lolled onto the cushion as she lost all sense of time and space. Joe's cock slipped from her mouth. Mike picked up her slack. He slurped the thick shaft between his lips, engulfing it in one long stroke.

As he began to move inside her, he fucked Joe with his face, plunging to the base of Joe's erection every time he bottomed out in her pussy. Devon traced the juncture of his lips and Joe's cock while reveling in the glide of Mike's broad, lightly furred chest across her mostly flat torso. They glued together from pelvis to shoulders, one of the few times she didn't mind her lack of endowment.

She pried her stare from the men before her, wanting to check in with her lovers. Her *other* lovers, she supposed. Neil pounded James in the unflinching rhythm they loved best. The smaller man's cock bulged in her grip as though he could sense her teetering on the edge of oblivion.

He met her gaze and smiled around Dave's cock. The tightening of his mouth was the final straw for the burly man. He growled, fisting his hands in James's hair as he slid deep and regular down James's throat.

Devon watched her mate's Adam's apple bob, no doubt wringing every possible drop of pleasure from Dave's cock. The release set off a chain reaction. She stiffened, every part of her—not least of all her mind, heart and soul—affected by the generous affection of the men surrounding her.

The sound that burst from her startled them all, herself included. They froze as they focused on her. The force of their attention guaranteed she'd reached the point of no return. Devon shattered around Mike. She clawed at his back with one hand while the other still clasped James.

Through delirious pleasure, the searing wetness coating her palm and wrist as James shuddered in her hold fueled the fire blazing through her veins. Neil roared, convulsing as he poured himself into James's ass.

Mike whipped his head off Joe's shaft just as the standing crewmate began to grunt and shake. Stream after stream of his ejaculate streaked Devon's chest. She wondered at Mike's choice, since she'd seen him gobble down come enough times to be certain he didn't mind, until he cleaned the evidence of Joe's orgasm from her one rivulet at a time.

Long laps of his tongue accompanied the hammering of his hips. He nailed her with a ferocity counterbalanced by the tenderness of his care. When he skimmed her nipple, she couldn't help but surrender to another climax. Her channel rippled around his cock, sucking semen straight from his balls.

He snarled, then bit her neck. Not enough to hurt. Enough to leave a faint bruise. As he deposited his come deep inside her, none of them could deny he'd staked his claim. As their leader, her mentor and a great friend, Mike had marked her as belonging to him. Them.

For the first time since she'd joined the crew, she felt fully a part of their unit. The bond she'd shared with her husbands expanded, including all five of the men in the radiance of her affection.

They looked at her, and she stared back. No words were necessary. They all understood. This kind of connection was forever.

What would their wives think of that?

6

"Morgan!" Kate shrieked and dodged the splash of suds from the sink when an earthenware bowl plunged below the surface.

"It was an accident. It slipped in, I swear." She held her wet, soapy hands up in front of her.

"That's what *he* said." Kayla wasn't about to let that one sneak past. She flipped a smirk over her shoulder, but Devon couldn't find the heart to return the cheeky grin.

Instead, she dropped a bomb. "I think I might have cheated on you. All of you."

Kate whipped her apron over her head and came to investigate immediately. She had to have been expecting the meltdown.

Devon wrung her hands in front of her churning guts. She shivered.

"Honey, isn't this kind of déjà vu?" Morgan joined the women where they huddled near the bar, which distinguished Kayla's kitchen from the rest of the open cabin.

"What do you mean?" Dev tipped her head.

"Remember when you came to us as an *intern*?" Kayla laughed. "And P.S., that was total bullshit. You already knew far too much about constructioning for that dumb title."

The fabrication had Devon cracking a smile as her friend had no doubt intended. "Right. I admit it. I lied on my resume by deleting a heck of a lot of experience. But I heard the crew was the best so I took my shot."

"And what happened then?" Kate arched one eyebrow. "The first time you came out here? When you were so afraid we'd hate you for watching the guys touch each other? As if any red-blooded woman could close her eyes to that."

"I didn't think I was so transparent." She scowled.

"Poker faces aren't your strength." Kayla patted her shoulder.

"Yeah well, if I was scared of losing the best thing I'd found in my life then, it's a million times worse now. I know what I'd be sacrificing if I fucked this up." Devon groaned. "They did tell you what happened, right? Please say they did."

"Of course." Kate propped her hand on her hip. It was a little hard to take her glare serious when she was naked. "If it's any consolation, I think Mike was more nervous than you are. I should kick both your asses."

Devon's heart plummeted through the floor. "I earned it."

"For doubting the experience you had? Yes. If it had been wrong, you would have stopped. Any of you. All of you." Kate glared at her. "Did it feel messed up?"

"God no." A wash of residual comfort and

homecoming knocked her on her ass on the kitchen stool. "I felt like I belonged."

"You do." Kate hugged her. "Mike told me they claimed you as soon as he burst through the door. Trust me…it takes more than that to satisfy him. If anything, he came home rock hard and ready to play. I think the pressure of the whole baby-making thing freaked him out a bit. It's been a while since I've seen him at the end of his leash like that."

"Honestly, Dev, I had horrible cramps that day." Kayla winced. "You guys did me a pretty big favor. Dave would never pressure me for sex when I'm not feeling good, but I walked in on him jerking off in the shower that morning. I admit it, I tiptoed out of there and he pretended he didn't see me through the steam. I couldn't bring myself to join him right then, and I felt pretty guilty about it until he told me what happened. I like knowing he's being taken care of."

"In that case…I'm glad to help." Devon chuckled when Kayla pinched her arm and called her a tart. "I guess I sort of got overwhelmed, you know? That's not an excuse. I should have thought it through first instead of following my instincts…"

"It's different when they're all together. I remember clearly that day in the pool." Kate's eyes glazed over a bit. "I'll dream about it until the day I die. It's like they're one person. Focused on you. I'd be lying if I said I didn't crave the power of that combined passion. Once Morgan came along, things changed. I'm not sure that was the right decision. Or maybe it was at the time. But we're stronger now. Sure of ourselves and our relationships. We've had time to sort out how our individual partnerships work and how we fit into the group. Maybe we should reevaluate."

"You just want to have them all to yourself again." Kayla winked.

"Maybe someday." Kate's eyes darkened. "I've been thinking about how to make this work. Because the reality is I'd also be lying if I ignored the flash of instinctual jealousy that pricked me when Mike first shared the news he claimed Devon. He told me she was hot, tight and delicate. For a blip, I wondered...would he prefer that all the time? Then he made sure I knew the answer."

"See, I guess I'm hyperaware of the fact that I have a different relationship with the crew." Devon winced. "I mean, I *am* part of them. I work with those assholes every day. I would hate if you thought I was taking advantage of the situation when you're not around. I've enjoyed watching when they would break for a long lunch or when things would heat up on the sites. I think we've been really clear that they'd end up watching me with James and Neil too. But the new touch-if-you-want rule... It changes things. Makes this something more. I just want to be sure that you're sure. Really, really sure. I couldn't stand to screw up what we have, since it's pretty damn amazing already."

Kayla sidled closer, levering herself halfway onto the last free stool at the bar. "The way I see it, you hit the nail on the head there. You *are* one of them. You spend the most time with them. I expect that you have a stronger bond with them. You have so much in common. You're on the border between friend, lover and co-worker. This is going to be harder on you, I think. You have no escape from them. No relief."

"It's true. You have a lot to juggle." Kate laid her hand over Devon's. "But when I start to get confused, I come back to this core truth. Mike's feelings for the crew didn't impact the formation of our love, unless it was to make it stronger. His attachment still doesn't harm our relationship now that our gang has grown beyond the five of them and me. It's the same for your guys and the rest of us."

"I totally agree. But some ground rules probably wouldn't hurt, right?" Morgan asked.

"You've been pretty quiet. What do you think about this?" Kate had clearly spent some time considering the possibilities and come prepared with a plan. "When we're all together, or a whole pair—trio, whatever—is present, it's anything goes as long as the couples involved consent."

"So if Dave and I are hanging out with Neil, James and Dev..." Kayla squinted her eyes as she puzzled through the scenario.

"It's your call." Kate nodded. "There shouldn't be any limits then. But for now, we'll reserve one person bonding with the crew for special occasions. You know, maybe each person's birthday. Sort of like, whoever is celebrating gets to be the centerpiece for the night. They can ask for whatever and whoever they want. No one will be excluded, though. Those not playing could still view if they wanted."

"Damn, who would choose not to?" Kayla shifted in her seat, fanning her rosy cheeks.

"I'm not making anyone else's decisions for them. I feel like if we're in it together, there's nothing seedy about it. When I saw Mike around you at dinner, Dev, I noticed a difference. It felt right to me. He seemed more natural when he interacted with you. He loves you. All the guys do, same as we love them. But it's something totally different than what he and I have as a pair. Hell, Morgan even wrangled him into seeing the dentist somehow! He still won't tell me how you did that."

Morgan didn't reveal their secret, though she and Kayla nodded their agreement.

"I admit, not being there when the guys took you screwed with my head a little. I started to wonder if Mike enjoyed himself more with you than me or if he might start to expect a new flavor every week. I don't think that's healthy for our relationship." Kate showed all her cards. "This way, it's not that different from what we talked about the other day, really. You know, swapping when we're together. Except every once in a while we'd take turns letting someone have all the attention. And that's putting it more simply than I mean to. I'm not trying to brush this off. Life is a constant jumble of priorities and unexpected shit. If we stick together, we can even out the peaks and valleys, make life better for all of us, you know?"

Morgan raised her hand sheepishly.

Devon whacked her on the butt with a dishtowel for the ridiculous propriety.

"I agree with you in theory." Morgan winced. "I'll never forget the heat in Joe's stare when he watched Dave, Neil and James playing with me. Hell, I retired that cake recipe. It could never taste as good as when I shared it with the crew. And Joe told me Mike was actually the one to suck him off at the end the other day. Damn do I regret not seeing that for myself, by the way. But for the first time, I got a little case of jitters. I think you're right. It's best if we reserve five-on-one for times we're all present. And...playing devil's advocate here...we haven't actually tried swapping yet. What if we do and someone finds out they can't handle it?"

"Then we'll discuss and reconsider." Kate made sure

to make eye contact with each of her friends. "I couldn't bear to break what we have now. It's a good thing. I think everyone has to know this is a risk-free environment. Everyone's in or no one is. Agreed?"

Each of the women nodded in turn.

When they got to Kayla, she nodded too. Still, Devon could tell the naturist had something else on her mind. "Spit it out, Kay."

"What if it's not five-on-one? What if it's eight-on-one?" The usually brash woman spoke so softly, Devon wasn't sure everyone had heard. "And I'm not just talking about the *guys'* birthdays either."

"To be frank, I'm not sure I'm ready for that, Kay." Morgan interjected before Devon could process the idea of such hedonistic gluttony. "I might never be. Like Neil and his no-BJ rule. But I would like to observe. And I don't begrudge you the request if it's something you're interested in and the other girls are too. Who knows, maybe after I see it for myself, I'll change my mind. I hope you don't count on that, though. Is that okay?"

Kayla hugged Morgan. "I would never pressure you into something you didn't enjoy. But thanks for understanding."

"This is exactly what I hoped for." Kate broke the lingering weight of the moment with a huge grin and a clap. Then she ticked off their agreements on her fingers. "When intact couples are together, like me and Mike over at Morgan and Joe's house or all nine of us here today, anything goes. Birthday girls and boys name their pleasure. Anyone who agrees is in. Anyone who doesn't feel like playing can stay and watch or leave, no hard feelings. None of us will ever judge. We swear to be open and honest if something makes us uncomfortable. What do you think?"

Each of them took time to really consider. This wasn't a fling or some crazy college experiment. These were their lives—their hearts, their soulmates, their futures—they were talking about.

"I think it sucks ass that my birthday was last month and I gotta wait a whole year for my turn." Kayla plumped out her lower lip.

"Ohh, good call." Kate grinned. "Mine is coming up soon. Neener neener."

"Lucky thing our birthdays happen to be distributed pretty evenly throughout the year. Otherwise we might develop some chaffage." Devon giggled.

The women linked hands with their neighbors until they made one continuous, unbroken ring. And with that, the promise was sealed.

"Time to celebrate." Kayla grinned.

"Does anyone have condoms?" Morgan confessed, "I'm wearing a diaphragm, like Kate said she's been doing when we play together, but I haven't been taking my birth control for a while. Mike and Kate aren't the only ones hoping for a miracle."

The friends squealed and fussed over each other. In the meantime, Kayla retrieved a jumbo box of rubbers in various colors and flavors from the bathroom and plunked it on the counter.

Devon raised her eyebrows at the mega-assortment.

"What?" Kay whistled innocently. "They're smart to have on hand for guests in the resort. Okay, plus I figured it wise to be prepared since we seem to gravitate toward my house for our sessions. I swear. Being a naturist is *not* about getting it on at every opportunity. That's your faults."

She wagged her finger at each of them, cracking up the whole time.

"Can I ask a favor?" Kate beamed when the women all nodded without reservation. "Mike is pretty far behind in the sharing space. The closest he came was granting Dev her wish the other day. Would you mind if we made his day?"

"You want to team up on him?" Morgan grinned.

"I'd love to see him speechless for once." Devon chaffed her hands together. "Let's do it."

"I'm in, too." Kayla winked at Kate. "Settle down, I think I see him coming in right now."

They giggled as they peeked through the kitchen window. Sure enough, he headed straight for their trap.

"Why do you ladies look like you're up to no good?" Mike crossed to the sink and filled a bottle with chilled well water. The filtration unit he'd helped Dave install ensured the taste was great direct from the tap.

All four of the women gawked as he slammed the refreshment. His throat flexed in time to his gulps. He sighed and placed the re-emptied container on the counter. When he turned and caught them staring, he swiped the back of his hand over his lips. "What? Did I drool on myself or something?"

He dusted at the front of his fitted T-shirt. Not a single droplet had escaped his mouth.

Pacing, he took a few steps one way, then a couple back. Their gazes tracked his every move.

"Oh. It's like that, is it?" The corners of his mouth kicked up in a self-assured smile that had Devon squirming in her seat. He locked his stare on his wife, who nodded. "Today's the day, huh? Where are the rest of your guys when I need them? Some crew. Abandoning me to the clutches of four horny women. Then again, maybe that's not a terrible fate."

He stalked toward their assembly, his eyes flicking from woman to woman to woman to woman. No one uttered a peep.

"Am I dreaming or do I really have you all to myself for a bit?" He stripped his shirt over his head and dropped it on the slate floor tiles.

Morgan began to clarify.

Mike waved her off. "The rest of them are about five minutes behind. They were wrapping up a few things and shooed me from helping. Let's teach them a lesson about keeping you waiting."

Devon couldn't deny his rugged grace and beauty. Neither could Morgan, apparently. She reached out and tentatively traced the ridge that stretched from his hipbone to disappear beneath the waistband of his low-riding jeans.

He trapped her fingers against his taut belly, then slid their joined hands into his pants. All the while, he never once glanced away from his wife. Kate used his belt to tug him closer. She kissed him as Morgan circled around to hover by his right side.

Mike groaned into Kate's mouth while Morgan unbuckled his belt. With the leather free, nothing held the fabric over his slim hips. Jeans crumpled at their feet. Devon couldn't stay still a moment longer. She abandoned her perch at the bar and stepped behind Mike.

She plastered herself against his back, her hands reaching around to roam over his defined chest while she hugged him from behind. If nothing else, she hoped he realized how much she appreciated the family he'd built and invited her to join. Because of this man, their construction foreman and the head of their gang, they'd each found a place where their individual and collective needs were met.

A row of kisses down his spine made him shiver in her hold. Or maybe his reaction was caused by Morgan and Kayla descending in front of him, stroking, licking and nibbling as they sank to their knees in unison. Having such a strong man in their clutches, causing his legs to wobble with their attention, sent a rush of adrenaline through Devon's veins.

She smacked his ass playfully yet hard enough to sting. She liked the evidence left behind in the form of her glowing handprint. It looked so small on his firm butt.

"Behave yourself, shorty." He grinned over his shoulder.

Whatever else he might have threatened dissolved into a gurgle. Devon craned her neck around his ribs to see what had caused such a guttural cry. Kate's lips were nestled against the base of his cock while Kayla massaged his balls.

When his wife pulled off his shaft, pressing a kiss to the tip, she wrapped her fist around it and aimed it toward Morgan. "Go ahead."

Kate's best friend whimpered. She looked at Kate, then Mike, then his cock.

They all held their breath.

"Now or never," she whispered before opening her mouth and leaning forward. Kate guided Mike's cock between her lips.

Tense, she choked a little. Devon laid a hand on her shoulder and kneaded the knot there. As Morgan relaxed, she took more of the foreman into her mouth. Soon her lips rested on Kate's knuckles.

Mike cursed. "Jesus, that's sweet. You're amazing. All of you. Hope you don't expect me to last like this."

Devon giggled as she angled herself more toward his side. He wrapped an arm around her shoulders. She suspected the gesture had more to do with keeping his balance than embracing her, though she didn't begrudge him the assistance.

Kate and Morgan took turns laving, sucking and stroking Mike's cock while Kayla perfected the motion of her relentless fingers over his sac. Devon felt like she should help, but even when Mike widened his stance, she didn't have any room to maneuver.

The next time Morgan descended on Mike, Kate glanced up. "Dev, let Kay suck on your fingers for a minute."

Turned on beyond belief, she wasn't about to argue. She extended her hand without question. Her friend smiled before taking the digits into her mouth. Devon couldn't help but squirm when Kay's wet tongue snaked around her knuckles, slathering them with saliva and making zillions of nerve endings stand at attention.

"Oh yeah, not so tough now, are you?" Mike squeezed her tight to his torso. "That's fucking hot. Shit."

She retaliated by scraping her teeth over his nipple. The tight disc couldn't have been in a better position for her to reach. He released a long, low moan. His head tipped back, and she saw his lips moving out of the corner of her eye as if he prayed for stamina or maybe thanked the stars for shining such good fortune on them.

Kate let him suffer while she relieved Morgan. In between their active duty, the women licked and nipped his abdomen or studied their friend as they imparted pleasure. Kayla never faltered in her dual manipulation of Mike's balls and Devon's fingers. She was an expert after all.

Next time Morgan nudged Kate from their shared treat, the foreman's wife developed an evil grin. "Enough, Kay. I think they're ready."

Devon glanced between Kayla, Kate and Mike. Could she mean...?

"Yeah." Kate nodded. "I'll let you in on a little secret. Mike might prefer to be the one doing the fucking, but when I use my fingers on him while blowing him... Let's just say the results are pretty spectacular."

"Fuck me." Mike swayed. Together they managed to brace him.

"Yeah, that's kind of the point." Kayla rubbed the side of his ass closest to her. She filled her palm with the solid muscle and gently pulled it toward her.

"You can find his prostate?" Kate smirked up at Devon.

"You have met my guys, right?" She rolled her eyes. "I might have done this once or twice before."

"I knew you were the right woman for the job." Kate entrusted her husband's satisfaction to Devon. She resumed licking him as if he were the best-tasting lollipop in the world.

"Be gentle with me," Mike half-teased. The corners of his mouth pinched at the first glancing contact of her fingertip sliding along his crack.

"Promise." She suckled his chest lightly while she traced his puckered hole with slow circles, painting Kayla's spit over the entrance.

"Her hands are miniature." Morgan petted his corded thigh. "You probably won't even realize she's inside you."

His huff when Devon pressed inward, breaching the tight ring of muscle guarding his ass, proclaimed otherwise.

"Or not." Morgan chuckled before engulfing him once more.

"That's right, Mike. Let Devon in. She's going to make you feel so good," Kate murmured to her husband.

"Already is." He grunted. "All of you are. Always do."

"We love you too." Kayla nuzzled his hip.

Devon took advantage of his distraction to penetrate completely. As she moved, he began to relax, loosen, allowing her to angle her hand. She stroked in and out, curling her fingers into the come-hither shape that usually did the trick for James and Neil.

She knew she had it right when he cursed a blue streak and twitched his hips first forward, then back hard. His cock slipped from Morgan's lips with a wet smack. Kate was quick to welcome him into her mouth again, sucking with enough pressure to hollow her cheeks.

Devon rubbed Mike's chest and belly to calm him as she continued to prod the chestnut-sized organ in time to his wife's quickening migrations up and down his solid shaft.

"Are you going to be a good boy and come for us?" Morgan impressed Devon with her schoolmarm act. "You know we like it when you show us how much we turn you on."

"Holy. Shit. Holy shit." Dave stutter-stepped as he entered the room, naked as always once inside. "Sign me up for the next turn. I know what I want for my birthday, and Christmas. Every year. Until I die."

"What the fu—" Joe crashed into him from behind. He

peeked over Dave's shoulder, then growled, "Son of a bitch. Me too."

James skirted around them for a better view of the action. "I could get into that. I think it should be a new crew tradition. Whoever's celebrating can be the center of attention."

"I wanna party. A lot." Neil didn't stop with the rest of his friends. He barreled toward the action like a young boy cannonballing into a lake on the first day of summer vacation.

"Funny you should say that." Kayla grinned up at them from her place at Mike's feet. "We sort of decided something similar."

"Can we...talk...about...it later?" Mike's chest heaved between each forced phrase.

Dave approached from behind. He looped his arms around Mike's middle, supporting his friend without interrupting Devon's devilish handiwork.

"That good, huh?" Dave grinned. "It's not every day you come apart like this, foreman. You've got quite an audience now. Why don't you show us what a fucking lucky bastard you are?"

Devon could feel energy sparking through the room, arcing in glowing connections between each of the nine of them in every possible permutation. She knew right then they'd made the right choice. Having all of them together made this so much...more.

Mike didn't stand a chance.

She tapped his prostate in a syncopated rhythm Neil had taught her to drive James wild. It worked just as well on their boss.

Neil and James chanted encouragement to her as the other guys did the same for their wives. In less than a minute, Mike shouted. His fists balled as though he struggled to keep from exploding. He thrust his hips into the air, his ass clenching around her fingers. Then he shook in Dave's hold like he'd grabbed the exposed end of a live 220 wire.

"Fuck, yes." Neil encouraged him. "Shoot all over them. Make them yours. Ours."

Only then did Devon realize Kate, Morgan and Kayla had huddled together, their faces side by side. Mike's cock had tugged from their lips with his involuntary shudders.

Slipping her hand from his body, she joined her friends in a semi-circle. Dave helped ensure each of them received at least one spurt of his come, adorning them with the results of their hard work.

When the foremen went limp, Dave allowed him to succumb to gravity, easing their weight onto the floor. He cradled his friend through the final throes of his rapture.

The rest of the crew descended on their women. Joe nearly tackled Morgan, who'd taken the brunt of Mike's orgasm. He snuffed the flicker of doubt Devon caught in her eyes when he kissed her madly, pausing only to lick her chin and neck clean.

James and Neil swarmed Devon. They had her feeling a little like a bone between two dogs when they both attempted to devour the droplets of Mike's semen on her cheeks.

The delicacy didn't last long. The guys had moved on, demonstrating exactly how much they'd enjoyed the scene they'd walked in on, when Kate's voice rose above the din caused by a cacophony of moans, sighs and pleas.

"Hang on a minute." She shushed their objections. "While you boys were outside playing, we decided it's time to take things up a notch."

The crew shot each other a round of worried looks.

"What could be more intense than that?" Neil nudged Mike with his foot. The foreman groaned, then shifted, his heavy eyelids rising slowly. "I think you might have killed him."

"Ladies, move over one couple to your right."

Devon kissed each of her guys on the cheek, laughing at the stunned expressions on their faces. "Have fun. See you in a bit."

She extricated herself from their limbs, regretting the loss of their heat, their touch, their love for a second. Until she sank into Joe's open arms, straddling his thighs. "Hi."

"Hi." He looked to Morgan for permission.

"It's all right." She smiled. "Probably only fair since I just gave your best friend a killer blowjob."

"Ohmigod." He clapped his hand over his mouth, but not before the rest of the guys ragged on him.

"What are you, a thirteen-year-old girl?" James cracked up.

"Hey, cut him some slack." Mike perked up as Kayla snuggled beside him on the carpet. "I can promise these ladies will make you forget your own name. Never mind that you're a grown man who should have some fucking pride."

"You held out longer than I thought you would, if that's any consolation," Morgan teased from her place in Dave's clutches.

Neil lifted Kate into his arms. "I hope you don't mind if I take you someplace a little more comfortable?"

"Suit up first." She jerked her chin toward the condom stash. "Anyone who's with Morgan has to wear one too."

"Are we supposed to use all of those?" His eyes got round.

"Maybe eventually." She laughed. "But hopefully we'll be pregnant long before then and we won't need to bother anymore."

"Good plan." Neil tossed two packets to each of the guys. He sheathed first James, then himself in record time. When he finished, he glanced over at Mike, who began to rouse from the daze they'd knocked him into. "Get on that, buddy, would you?"

"Sure, sure." He waved them off.

Kate giggled when Neil scooped her up once more. She trailed her fingers down his neck. "Coming, James?"

"I have a tiny bit more control than that, Katiebug."

Devon smiled as her guys toyed with her friend. James had told her once about how Kate had really cemented the crew together in the beginning. She would never forget that Kate had eased James's lingering worries about his sexuality and granted him acceptance to grow into the man he was today. Though they'd always been best friends, the guys had benefited from the women they'd pulled into their group, who had provided the extra emotional something they hadn't realized they were missing.

If it hadn't been for Kate, Devon suspected their group might have fractured or drifted apart. They'd grown so much. Shared so much. It was impossible to separate them anymore.

"Shh..." Joe's hush made her wonder if she'd actually whimpered for her pair. "We'll go with your guys. You can play voyeur if you want."

As if settling on a plan, the crewmembers each embraced their new partner and claimed a spot in the adjoining space. Neil and James had laid out Kate on the couch. James supported her shoulders while Neil pressed her knees apart with his shoulders. He burrowed between her thighs, intent on tasting her.

Dave sat in the loveseat with Morgan straddling his lap. She left room for him to roll purple latex over his thick erection. When he finished, she snuggled close to his broad chest. He kissed her cheek and spoke in a soothing murmur. Too low for Devon to make out exactly what he was saying, the general rumble of his bass sounded nice to her.

Joe opted to bend her over the coffee table in the center of the room. His warm chest blanketed her back, and his cock rode the furrow of her pussy when he reached beneath her to cup her breasts and prevent her belly from pressing to the cool surface of the furnishing. She couldn't say she minded when she had a panoramic view of the action around her.

Even Mike recovered enough to carry Kay and deposit her onto the rug in front of the fireplace. He stretched out behind her, caressing her from her shoulder along her ribs to the curve of her hip. He extended his arm for her to rest her head on, then snaked his other hand around her torso, sheltering her and keeping her close to his body.

They turned their faces toward each other to exchange a frisky kiss complete with Kayla nibbling on his bottom lip. "You know, you would look hot if you got this pierced. A little stud, right in the center."

"I think I'll leave that stuff to you and Dave." He laughed. "Though I have to say, I've always loved the way your hardware looks. It fits you perfectly."

As if to prove his point, he thumbed the silver in her breasts.

"They're not just for show, you know." She sighed.

"That feels twice as good as it used to. Tug on the hoops. Please."

Mike groaned. "Damn. I thought I'd never be hard again. It took you less than five minutes to prove me wrong."

He scanned the entire room as he proclaimed their victory.

Devon met his wandering gaze and smirked. Her smugness evaporated when Joe bounced his cock against her clit. She clutched the edges of the coffee table as though she might fly around the room like a rogue helium balloon if she didn't anchor herself.

"I always thought it would be fun to tease you, Dev." He dragged his fingertips from her shoulders to her ass in maddening, erratic patterns. "You're such an imp. And the pranks you pull... You're a disobedient pixie. It turns me on when your guys focus all that extra energy. I always wanted to try it and see if I could too."

"You're doing a pretty good job." Neil lifted his mouth from where he toyed with Kate's pussy. "Looks like you have her full attention now."

"Do I?" Joe covered her, nibbling at her ear.

"Yes," she mewled.

"Good." He gripped her hip easily with one hand, then reached between them with the other. "Because I want you to know who it is taking you, Dev. When we work together or when we hang out, you'll know that I've had you and you've had me. You can count on me. Come to me with anything. I'll always have your back like I do now. And if Morgan or I need to borrow some of your light and fun, you always know. You share your brightness with all of us around you. I love that about you."

Devon didn't expect the wash of emotion he inspired

in her. Not like this. Not so strong. She couldn't speak around the lump in her throat. So instead she reached down, between her legs, and lifted him to the threshold of her body. She held him there.

"Thank you," he whispered before he advanced.

The introduction of his flesh into hers shocked a gasp from her. Heat and pressure built until his head slipped inside. When she thought she might cry uncle and tell him he was too much, a familiar hand landed on her upper arm.

James.

"Give it a second." He promised, "You're going to love it. He's so smooth when he fucks. Just like he talks."

Morgan cried out from where she nestled tighter onto Dave's lap. Whether because their friend's large cock stretched her or because the discussion of her husband fueled the flames, Devon couldn't be sure.

"Damn, Mike wasn't exaggerating. You're so fucking tight." Joe huffed as he slowed his invasion. "You'd better go slow when you get to Dave. Maybe save him for another day."

Devon knew she wouldn't. After bonding with Joe and Mike, she couldn't leave the other man out in the cold.

Conversations flared, interspersed with moans, sighs and the slick slaps of good sex. The other women exchanged connections with their temporary partners the same as she had with Joe. They had so many of these compatible features—intertwined lives, hopes, interests and fantasies—that each combination resulted in something new and wonderful. Her heart glowed with serenity. She'd never felt as safe as she did surrounded by her eight best friends.

She looked up to see James kneeling above Kate, who

pampered him with what looked like one hell of a hummer. He played with his nipples and muttered encouragement while he stared at Neil. Their mate had climbed Kate's body and pressed inside. Devon's pussy clenched when the guys exchanged a sultry kiss, connecting all three of them in a lusty triangle.

Kayla cried out, drawing Devon's stare. The landscape was like a licentious feast, every course holding another delicious treat for her to devour. Mike held Kay's jaw at the perfect angle to grant himself access to her mouth. He kissed her hard and a little rough as he slid his other hand between her legs to play with her clit. She responded by opening herself to him, raising her leg to allow him to lunge deeper, faster, between her thighs.

Joe smacked Devon's ass and increased his pace. "Dirty girl. You like spying on them, don't you?"

"Yes." She squealed when he repeated the spank on the other side. The tingles left by his palm enhanced her arousal, making it effervesce like champagne.

"Keep watching." He stayed true to James's promise, gliding in her from root to tip, careful not to hurt her yet refusing to skimp on his thrusts. "I can feel your pussy fluttering around me. Getting stronger now. Especially when I rub my cock here."

He repeated the motion until they both were gasping for air.

Morgan shouted, "I'm going to come."

Joe froze for a second.

"Yeah, look." Devon figured he'd earned a little teasing of his own. "See how wild she is for your friend? Her hair looks gorgeous waving down her back while she rides him."

Joe landed another smack on her ass. And that was all it took.

Devon heard the escalating cries of the other women even as she surrendered to her climax. She stared into James's eyes as another man showered her with bliss. Except it didn't feel like that. Not really. Joe was part of the crew, same as Neil and James. An extension of her lovers, he treated her as his own.

Before she'd quite wrung all the possible rapture from his cock, Joe withdrew. "Sorry, sweetheart. I couldn't stay or I'd lose it. And somehow I don't think that's the plan."

She hadn't recovered enough to argue. Instead, when he traced her lips with his index finger, she sucked on the tip like a baby with a pacifier. The pulls of her mouth matched the aftershocks wringing her pussy. Before she could cool down, Mike took the reins.

"Trade women," he ordered.

Joe kissed her cheek, then smiled. "See you later."

Before she could figure out where she was supposed to be, Mike snatched her around the waist and yanked her to him. Lying on her side, she observed Kate slumped in Dave's lap. He changed his condom discretely while she recovered from the wreckage Devon knew James and Neil were capable of inflicting on a woman's reserve.

Morgan squealed when Neil got cozy between her legs and started the process of reawakening her arousal. As if they'd hit rewind, the guys seduced their new partners in the same manner they had the first. Devon could relate when Kayla yelped at the first tap of Joe's cock on her clit.

Unlike the day on the job site, Mike slid into her with relative ease. "Ah, that's better. I guess I should have had Joe work you open for me last time too."

Devon was used to being fucked twice in a row. There

were plenty of nights both James and Neil took a turn or two or three, one of them recovering while the other continued to raise her higher and higher. She concentrated on the spark of pleasure in her core and allowed Mike to fan it back to life. Apparently, the other women had similar experience.

Before long, a chorus of *fuck yeah* and *harder* and *right there* accompanied their moans. This round went faster, as the women had been primed by their previous lovers. They took pity on the men, who each managed to cling to their control long enough to grant his partner release.

Devon still floated when Mike called, "One more time. We can do it. Hurry."

Dave came to claim her. He flopped into the loveseat, draping her over him. "It's okay if you're not comfortable, Dev. Let me keep you close. That'll be enough. Rub your clit on my cock and I bet we'll both come in no time. Hell, I'll be lucky to last through a minute of outercourse at this point."

"I didn't know you were into frottage." She sighed at the mental movies that thought inspired, adding the demand to her birthday wish list. A fetish for another time.

The gentle giant held her as though she were made of spun glass. That wouldn't do at all.

"Stop talking, Dave." She put her hand over his mouth. He always rambled when nerves plagued him, which happened more often than she would have guessed in the early days of their friendship. Kayla calmed him with her easy acceptance, massage skills and naturist philosophy. It was a good match. No, a perfect one.

Somehow, Devon realized lately that of all the men, she could boss Dave around a bit. Not that she would manipulate him, or take advantage, but sometimes, it helped break him out of a mental rut. He bit his bottom lip and scrunched his eyes closed. His cock throbbed against her belly. She had no doubt he'd let guilt and fear keep him from the ultimate relief he so desperately needed if she didn't interject.

"Put your hands on the arms of the chair." She had never used such a stern tone before. With this man, in this time and place, it felt right. So she did it again. "Don't move them unless I tell you to."

"Dev?" He did as she asked despite the questions in his eyes.

"The biggest tamed by the smallest." Joe chuckled as he filled Kate. "Never thought I'd see the day. Son of a bitch, that's sexy."

"And so are you." Kate smiled up at Joe. They had such an easy friendship. Both of them people people. Both nurturers by nature. They loved to see their family happy and fed off the positive karma in the room. "I can't wait to hear you erupting inside me. I bet you flood that condom."

"Fuck." Neil skipped laving Kayla's engorged pussy and went straight to riding her. "I owe you a raincheck, hon. I can't wait."

"It's been too long since the last time we did this." She wrapped her legs around him, welcoming him inside.

"Won't make that mistake again." He tipped her face toward James's cock. Ruddy and painfully erect, it jutted into the air. "Now show James how much you missed him."

Kayla fulfilled his wish by entwining her fingers with James's. The two of them shared a bond so emotional it was almost spiritual. Devon had never seen two people be able to sit in comfortable silence as long as these two, whether it was on the deck, watching the lake or while listening to the rowdy crew at a dinner party.

"Same goes, Kay." James squeezed her hand. "But I'm dying here. Please?"

She opened her mouth and welcomed him inside before he'd finished asking.

Devon had to hurry or she wouldn't have time to recover and come with the others. It would hurt at least a little. She didn't mind. Rising onto her knees, she grabbed hold of Dave's cock and positioned it so she could slide onto the extra-thick shaft.

Fortunately, her two previous orgasms had generated a ton of lube.

Still he lodged in her, barely an inch deep.

"Dev, don't." Dave started to shift.

"Did I tell you to move?" She arrowed a disapproving frown in his direction.

"Sorry, sorry." His cock twitched between her stretched pussy lips. "And quit doing that if you want to have any hope at all of me finishing this race."

"Oh no, you're not allowed to surrender until I tell you." She had no idea this side of her even existed. But with him, it did. And now that she'd found it, she decided she liked it.

He nodded once.

"That's brilliant." Mike's awed murmur reached her ears as she hitched her hips to lift up a bit. Once she'd slicked Dave's shaft, she sank down, letting inertia force her onto him farther. It burned. She wouldn't deny that. But she kind of liked it.

Devon braced her hands behind her on Dave's knees.

She whimpered, then granted him permission to touch her. "Rub my clit."

He did, in such a perfect pattern she feared she'd come too soon.

"Not so fast."

He slowed instantly.

The rush of exhilaration his obedience brought helped her to work him deeper.

"You've almost got him, babe." Neil called reassurance as he rocked into Kayla. "Kay loves seeing it too. She's smothering my cock. Damn. So amazing. Both of you."

Their support gave her the strength to continue.

"I'm not going to break." She smiled into Dave's uncertain eyes. "Hold me. Kiss me."

He did. His broad hands covered most of her back as he tugged her to him. The more severe angle allowed her weight to press her the rest of the way onto his cock. White, searing pleasure mixed with pain flashed before her.

When it could easily have stolen her buzz, he neutralized the intensity with the cool, refreshing gentleness of his lips. Next to James, he was easily the best kisser of the crew. He made love to her mouth. Reverent and patient, he morphed her discomfort into ecstasy.

Once united, they hardly had to move to incite a riot of sensation in each other.

Dave went up for air.

She used the tiny separation to pat his chest. "Such a good boy."

"Not if you keep talking." His head dropped back against the cushion of the loveseat. "I'll break your don't-shoot edict pretty fucking fast."

If the desperate shouts behind her were any

indication, Devon figured the whole crew rowed in the same boat.

"Oh, really?" She tapped his cheek with her open palm. "Maybe you want me to punish you next time around."

"Serious, Dev." The cords in his neck stood out and the corner of his eye twitched. "On the edge."

And suddenly so was she. He filled her beyond belief yet handed over every ounce of authority without flinching. No one deferred to her that easily. Youthful and tiny, she was too easy to dismiss. Maybe that was what she loved about Dave. He'd never done that to her. His size probably made him all too aware of how much people assumed based on appearance.

How many people had expected him to be bold and in control simply because he was huge? She'd give him this if she could.

"I'll tie you up and ask Joe to teach me how to spank you properly." She bit his lip.

"No, no, no." He might have denied it, but his cock bulged. It said, *yes, yes, yes.*

"You're going to break. Do it." She set him free. "Come inside me. There's no room left. You're going to make us sloppy. Flood me. Force it out around us so it soaks your balls."

Devon had no idea where the stream of graphic portends came from. Dave seemed to appreciate it, though. He roared. His eyes flew open wider and his head snapped up. Across the room, Kayla screamed. James and Neil too. The cycle of shared desire paid forward to her as Dave capitulated.

He fucked upward with short jabs as he overflowed her pussy with gushes of semen. His hands locked on to her shoulders, pulling her tight. The juncture of their bodies ensured her clit strummed across his hard muscles.

An orgasm of epic proportions threatened to rip her apart.

Through the typhoon of emotion and sensation, she heard Mike, Morgan, Kate and Joe join them in release. Together they celebrated their bonds. To each other—their spouses, their friends and their lovers.

When Devon floated back to Earth, a long time later, she realized they'd ended up on the rug in front of the fire. Their heads all together, they lay in a circle with their bodies pointed out like the spokes on a wheel or maybe the rays of a glorious star.

James held her and Neil held him. Behind her guys was another couple and another and another. Or maybe that last one was in front of her. They snuggled in an infinite loop.

Someone whispered, "I love you."

They all echoed the sentiment.

7

———

The twenty-seventh of January came pretty damn quick. Dave hadn't looked forward to his birthday this much since he'd turned seven. That year, his father had promised him a red Schwinn if he was good—also known as staying quiet and fetching more beers whenever the jerk's current drink came close to empty. He always figured he must not have made the grade. Either that or the old man had been too hammered to remember his bribe by the time Dave's birthday rolled around.

But today had the potential to make up for all of that disappointment and then some.

The crew had shared his favorite dinner, then put candles on one of Morgan's sinful creations and even sang him a horribly off-key rendition of the birthday song. Still, he drummed his fingers on the table, barely containing his anticipation.

"I think somebody better suck this guy off before he explodes," Mike joked when he caught the raging hard-on pointing straight up on Dave's belly beneath the bar. "So what's it going to be, Davey-boy? An eight-person BJ?"

Since they'd held the party at his and Kay's house, everyone was already naked. Saved time too. He liked being efficient.

"What if I don't want to be the centerpiece?" He scrubbed his cheeks, unable to believe something so ridiculous would pop out of his mouth.

"Then I'd say there's a hospital twenty minutes down the mountain. We should take you to the emergency room and find out what's wrong." Joe's raised eyebrows would be comical if so much didn't ride on the line.

"It's *my* birthday. I think I should decide what I want my present to be." Dave tapped one finger on his cheek.

"Uh, you're turning down a chance to be ravaged like a dirty piñata at this soirée?" Neil looked at him like he'd gone crazy. "We're talking about four gorgeous, horny women and guys willing to suck, fuck or bend over for your beast of a cock."

Dave *thunked* his forehead onto his curled fist. "You're not helping."

"What *do* you want?" Mike stared at Dave, then smirked. "I can only think of one thing better than being the centerpiece."

"Yeah." He nodded. "That."

CREWMATES EXCHANGED GLANCES. Devon still didn't understand their silent communication. "Okay, stop with that spidey-sense shit. What's going on here?"

"I'd rather give my present to Kay." Dave slipped from the barstool to crouch next to Devon's chair. "I'd love to watch you and her together."

Caught off guard, Devon sputtered. Neil and James flanked her in an instant. Their erections seemed to second Dave's proposal.

"Are you positive?" Kayla tugged Dave to face her. "You've never seen me with another woman."

"Exactly. I'd sure as hell like to remedy that."

"No, seriously." Kay wouldn't let him misdirect her concern.

"I know what it's like when I need one of the guys. It's a fire that starts low and dim but builds until it's raging out of control. As much as I love you and want you with a ferocity that will never die, you can't give me that. Do you know what it's like to know there's something you need that I can't give you? Something you're not getting at all? It's been growing stronger lately. You wake me when you dream about it. You cry out in your sleep. I could tell how bad you wanted it the day we swapped partners. I'll help you however I can. You don't have to hide your needs from me."

Kayla didn't deny his claims.

He returned his focus to Devon, clasping her tiny hand between his. "*You* can do this for her. For both of you. I see it in your eyes when you're near her. You wonder...like I used to before I met Mike. Please. That's all I want for my birthday. Make my wife happy. Yourself too. Please."

"Dave..." Kayla might have said more if tears hadn't sheened her eyes and clogged her throat.

"It's okay, baby." He tugged her into his lap and nuzzled her neck. "I understand. Totally. I do. Let me give you this. And if Devon can't, we'll find someone else."

"I love you." Kayla smothered him with kisses.

Devon wondered if the couple would forget about the

rest of the crew, who admired their friends and shared in the harmony they generated. She stamped out the wave of jealousy that Dave's promise to Kay had instilled. She didn't care to think of someone outside their circle with her friend. Silly, yet true.

"I love you too." Dave finally broke their make out session, his forehead resting on Kay's as they both attempted to catch their breath. "Now get over there and seduce that girl before she balks again. You're so sexy you'll have her tripping over her own tongue if you quit holding back. I should know."

Kayla grinned. She hugged Dave tight, then climbed off his lap.

Air whooshed from Devon's lungs when the alluring naturist focused her attention on Dev like a laser beam.

"Holy shit," Mike cursed under his breath as Kay stalked closer. From the corner of her eye, Devon saw Kate and Morgan shove their men to the couch and kneel between their knees. If they were going to put on a show, she'd better make it good.

"Will you go easy on me because I'm a virgin?" Devon did her best imitation of a simper.

"Not likely." Kayla's feral grin shot adrenaline straight into Devon's heart. It beat a crazy tattoo against her ribs. "It's been too long."

Devon nodded. "I should have approached you after Kate's wedding, but we were tipsy and I didn't want it to go down like that. With readymade excuses, I mean. And then I got scared. I couldn't stand the idea of ruining our friendship. The more time that passed, the weirder it seemed to bring it up."

"You think too much." Kayla closed the last of the space between them. She wrapped Devon in a tender hug.

Softness to softness. That alone rocked her world, so different than the firm men who'd come up behind her.

Trapped between the heat and hardness of her men and the gentle warmth Kayla generated, Devon had no chance at escape, not that she wished for one. Dave couldn't resist approaching for a close-up view of the action. He cuddled up to his wife's back, supporting her as she embarked on a new adventure. The three men slung their arms over each other's shoulders, forming a larger ring around the two women who embraced at their center.

Utterly protected, Devon felt free to explore.

"Kiss me," Kayla whispered. "So I know you need this too. It's not my desire coloring the situation, is it?"

"You've worried you're imagining the chemistry between us?" Devon cursed. "I'm sorry. I didn't realize I put you through that kind of doubt. It's not one-sided, Kay. I've thought about doing this for a long time."

Devon stood on her tiptoes. She looped her hands around Kayla's neck and tugged until the statuesque woman bent. Their mouths lingered a hairsbreadth apart for the span of several heartbeats. Dev could smell Kay's signature organic cherry lip balm from this close. She reached out her tongue and stole a tiny taste.

Kayla's lips parted on a sigh.

That sweet, simple sound of relief was all it took to motivate Devon. She rocked forward, sealing her mouth over Kay's. The other woman responded immediately. Not with the vicious insistence of one of the crewmen when they were taunted beyond their control. Rather with an aching tenderness that inflamed Devon all the more for its affectionate restraint.

Kayla nestled their lips together with gentle caresses

that had goose bumps dotting Devon's skin and raising the blond hairs on her arms. Kissing a woman was nothing like kissing a guy. She couldn't tell if it was Neil, Dave, James or some combination of all three that chaffed her with consistent brushes of their hands that only revved her higher.

Pleasure suffused her being as she sank deeper into the fine, delicate kiss. It reminded her of the first time she'd framed a house and knew she'd become hopelessly addicted to the experience. Awe ran rampant through her system.

Kayla flirted with Devon's mouth, employing tiny licks and nips. When she sucked lightly on Devon's lower lip, she thought she might orgasm from kissing alone. So much attention was paid to each glance of tongue and teeth, the simple exchange mutated into a complex symphony of passion.

"Damn." The reverent curse sounded like it came from Joe. Devon peeked in his direction long enough to discern the slow bobbing of Morgan's head in his lap. Beside him, Mike enjoyed similar treatment as they watched the show. "That's *so* fucking sweet."

Devon agreed one-hundred percent. She found herself needing more. When she writhed against Kayla's lush frame, her friend grinned where their mouths were still joined.

"You're easy, Dev," she whispered. "I figured it'd take me at least five or ten minutes to have you begging."

"Bitch." Devon tweaked the nipple ring gracing her friend's breast. She'd often admired the jewelry, and wondered if it enhanced her pleasure as much as it seemed to when her husband flicked his tongue around the fittings and tugged them gently with his teeth.

If Kay's sharp inhalation was any indication, the answer was a resounding yes. She'd have to remember to ask Kay later who'd done them for her and if she'd accompany Devon for an appointment. She'd grown so much over the past year since she'd met the crew she could hardly believe how much of herself she'd hidden away. For the first time, she felt like she had come into her own.

The *real* Devon.

The complete woman was here to stay.

"Hey." Kayla stroked her cheek with the bent knuckle of her index finger. She separated their mouths long enough to ask, "Still with me? Too much?"

"No." Devon hated the tear that spilled over her friend's hand. "Perfect. Exactly right. I can't believe I wasted so much time."

"Maybe you weren't ready." James petted her back. "When you came to us, we pushed you hard. Fast. It was a lot to adjust to and you did great. You're sure now. Totally confident and so damn flawless I can't begin to deserve you. There's nothing to get in the way or trip you up. I'm so proud of you, Devon."

"We love you," Neil murmured in her other ear. "We're here for you. We have forever. No worries. Just enjoy the moment. No one could understand this better than James and me. It's not always easy to take what you need."

"What they said, runt." Dave propped his chin on Kayla's shoulder. "Everything we've shared has led to this moment. Go ahead. Claim your reward."

Devon smiled through her tears. Bundles of nerves unknotted in her gut. She savored Neil and James kissing her neck and the reassurance in Dave's gaze as he presented his wife for their shared pleasure.

This time when their lips collided, it was with greater urgency. The soft, sweet swipes still rocked her world, different completely from the fierce claim one of the men would make on her mouth. Devon shivered when Kayla advanced, pressing their torsos more tightly together. The mounds of her friend's breasts landed above hers.

Dev lowered her hands to Kayla's waist, her fingers grasping at Kay's tight ass, begging for what she wasn't sure.

Mike groaned from behind them. "Give me a minute, Kate, or I'm going to lose it. Let me grab the feather bed from the closet for them. If I can still walk with this monster hard-on."

Musical laughter accompanied the foreman's grumbling. Kate always told them how much she loved to torment her husband. Driving him wild was one of the highlights of her life.

Kayla reclaimed Devon's focus when the other woman planted her palms on Devon's ass. Dev slung one thigh as high on Kay's hip as she could, then hopped. The guys supported her as she clung to Kayla like a baby koala. Both of them moaned when their torsos aligned better.

"Shorty." Kay nipped her chin, then licked a trail down Devon's neck.

She might have been embarrassed about the slickness she painted across Kayla's belly if the other woman hadn't encouraged her to continue her gyrations with that unflinching grip on Devon's rear.

A cool breeze wafted over them, followed by a dull thump that could only come from a thick feather mattress. She'd know that sound anywhere since they'd each agreed to purchase one for their living rooms after their partner-swapping session. They'd had enough of bruised knees and rug burns in critical areas when an innocent movie night turned into one of their smoking group sessions.

The pad bounced a little, knocking into James's and Neil's ankles. The guys tumbled backward onto the puffy surface with matching grunts. Lacking their support, Kayla tipped forward. They landed in a tangle of limbs. Dave piled on for fun, squishing Neil. He also rubbed his rock hard cock against his friend in the process, if their sighs and lusty oaths were any indication.

Kayla and Devon giggled at their antics. They laughed together even as they writhed, their bodies connected from toes to fingertips. Devon spread her legs wider, welcoming Kayla into the cradle of her thighs. The pressure of Kay's pubic bone riding her mound surprised a whimper from her.

"Have you ever wondered about tribbing, Dev?" Kayla whispered in her ear.

"What?" She blushed. "I don't know what that is."

"Don't worry. I'll show you." Kayla rocked against her again. "It's my favorite. Like this. Or scissoring."

Devon didn't care what she called it as long as Kay continued to inject pure pleasure into her veins. They reveled in their clinch, using every part of their bodies to communicate their longing.

"She feels great, doesn't she?" James brushed stray hair from Devon's forehead and tucked it behind her ear. "I love it when your eyes turn dark like this."

"So amazing." She gasped, and dragged her nails from Kay's ass to her shoulders, begging her silently to move.

"More of that later," Kayla promised with another kiss. Each of her touches showcased an economy of motion that concentrated passion to its purest extract. "First, I want to taste you. All of you."

Devon's pussy quivered at the idea. If Kayla ate her out half as well as she kissed, Dev might die of ecstasy overload before the afternoon was over. Because she admitted James had been knocked from that coveted *best kisser* spot by Kay.

Would she expect Devon to return the favor?

She wasn't sure she was ready to be the aggressor yet. She had no skills. What if Kay had waited forever and Devon couldn't deliver a satisfying experience?

"No pressure, Dev." Kayla petted her belly. "It's your first time. Let me make it good for you. Believe me, I'll enjoy this as much as you."

Kay didn't hesitate. She licked a trail down Devon's neck, torturing her with the measured glide of her lips across Dev's collarbone. As though she had a map of all the most sensitive spots along her route, she detoured to every single one. One of the benefits to being with another woman, Devon supposed.

She recalled watching James suck Mike or how Joe could make Neil come in record time by jerking him off while riding him hard. It was clear the men fed off each other but also that they had a better understanding of how to push each other's buttons.

Kayla had the same intrinsic knowledge of Devon's anatomy. She put it to good use. Her fingertips fluttered over the peaks of Dev's breasts, teasing her nipples into hardened pebbles without pinching them too tight.

Kay's ideal manipulation had Devon's chest swollen and aching for more contact. She bucked her hips against Kayla's softly rounded tummy, moaning when her clit slid across the damp skin there.

"In good time, Dev." Kayla continued her unhurried assault. "There's no rush. Though, if you want to come, go ahead. We'll feed off each other's orgasms. It's not like being with a man. Climaxing isn't the end. It's just a peak on the journey to the summit. I bet I could give you a dozen. And the same for you to me."

"Jesus." Neil groaned from where he lounged above Devon's head on the mattress. James angled his face until he could suck their mate a few times from root to tip.

"They're so careful. Slower than molasses," Joe muttered to himself from the couch. He massaged Morgan's head, which lay in his lap as she observed her friends. None of the men would last if they kept up the stimulation. Somehow they all seemed to abstain by some collective order, wanting to share the women's ecstasy. "I would die if I had to hold myself to that pace."

"Nothing like savoring the moment," Kayla mumbled against Devon's breast. She spiraled kisses from the outside curve, growing ever closer to the center. All the while, they swayed against each other, brushing their clits across matching feminine softness.

"She's great. Placid. Precise." Devon forced herself to breathe through another wave of pleasure. They rolled over her rhythmically, each one more forceful than the last.

"Thank you." Kayla paused, lifting her head to make out with Devon again. Their tongues swirled around each other. Devon drew Kayla inside her mouth, twirling the tongue piercing she'd often admired. Kay shuddered.

Devon wrapped her arms around her friend, enfolding her in the steam they generated together. All the while blood rushed to her pussy, which only enhanced the periodic contact she made with Kayla's torso.

"More." She pressed on Kay's shoulders, desperate for relief.

"In time." The other woman smiled as she resumed her ministrations on Devon's other breast. While she dallied, her fingers walked down the flat expanse of Devon's belly. Need had her abdomen clenched tight. "Relax, Dev."

She tried. Nothing she did worked. Her appetite had grown too long. "Can't. Hurts. Help me."

"I will." Kayla drew figure eights over her stomach with the same unbreakable patience. The gesture soothed even as it inflamed. "You never have to lock this away again, Dev. You should have approached me. I would have given you what you needed."

Somehow Kay knew. Though she generally wallowed in the wild treatment of the crew, it would have shattered her today. Today, she needed calmness. Supple hands kneaded her knotted muscles. Kayla drew on her massage experience to blow Devon away.

When she added her lips to the steady manipulation of her magic fingers, Dev cried out. She arched, thrusting her hips at Kayla. Thankfully her friend didn't tease. She laid her mouth beside Devon's dripping flesh and blew a stream of cool, refreshing air over the puffy tissue.

If Kay had latched on to her steaming pussy directly, Devon would probably have rocketed through the roof. Kayla understood. She took care of Devon. The lush fall of her midnight hair brushed softness across Dev's leg.

Open-mouthed kisses started on the tops of her thighs and circled closer to the entrance of her pussy. When

Kayla lipped her mound, Devon's spine flexed, offering herself for whatever her friend chose to do to her.

In the background, a world away, Dave uttered a steady stream of encouragement to his wife. When Devon could tune in for more than the general buzz, she caught things like "yeah, you're driving her crazy" or "she's soaked, must taste delicious".

She hadn't realized she'd flung her hands out until Neil and James each claimed one. They twined their fingers with hers, lending her strength and enhancing her pleasure. With painstaking delicacy, Kayla extended her tongue toward Devon's pussy.

Everyone in the room held their breath.

Devon flexed her hips even as Kay descended. The moment they touched, both of them moaned. Kayla insinuated her wriggling muscle between Devon's saturated folds. She rimmed the opening of her pussy before lapping at the juices spilling freely from her core. Her nose nudged Devon's clit as she buried her face and ate as though she were seated at a five-star restaurant.

"Damn," Neil rasped. "She looks pretty fucking good at that."

"Agh!" Devon knew they'd interpret her unintelligible shout correctly.

"I want to learn how to do that flicky thing." Joe grunted from the couch. Devon looked up in time to see Morgan smack his hand when he reached for his own cock. She tormented him with a few more deep strokes on his erection before pulling off to observe.

"Can you see, Dev?" Neil released her hand to slide closer, propping her head on his ribs. "Watch how she makes each pass a work of art. She's relishing your taste.

Her lips are so shiny. I bet she'd taste so good if you kissed her again."

The thought alone was enough to cause shockwaves to radiate from Devon's overripe clit. She clawed the feather bed, trying to hold on. It was no use.

"It's okay. Plenty more, remember?" Kayla's permission vibrated through Devon's pussy, ensuring her surrender. She came harder than she expected. Wetness gushed from her channel, released by the dam breaking inside her. Though her men had treated her to unlimited delights, something about having this woman provide her satisfaction dialed the intensity up.

Kayla hummed as she drank every drop of the lust and satisfaction she'd inspired. She shifted, while Devon still shuddered and quaked. Not to abandon Dev at the height of her pleasure, but to raise her higher instead. The taller woman used her long limbs to spread Devon's knees as far as possible. Dave held one while James accepted the other. The men kept her spread while Kayla latched on to her pussy once more.

Devon expected overstimulation to hurt, stealing some of her glow. It didn't. Kayla sucked softly, easing Dev back to their joining. She fanned the passion before it had a chance to dim very much.

"Neil, do the honors here, would you?" Dave jerked his chin toward Devon's knee. Her partner shuffled until he rested by her side. James and Neil held her while Dave crawled somewhere behind Kay, out of Devon's range of vision.

The glassy-smooth motion of Kayla's licking stuttered. She groaned against Devon's pussy.

"Dave is playing with her," James informed Devon with a strained whisper. "He's dipping his fingers in her pussy and sucking on her clit. I've never seen her so eager before."

Devon couldn't believe it when another orgasm rushed her system. From nowhere, the intense relief sideswiped her, leaving her completely defenseless. She'd fantasized about this for so long that being here, with the woman and men they loved, was enough to set her over the edge again and again.

This time Kay joined her, if the broken cries bouncing off her tender flesh were any indication. True to her word, Kay didn't fall to the mattress, replete. If anything, the flood of passion encouraged her to amplify their rapture. She crawled up Devon's body like a lioness on the prowl. Her tattoos danced and rippled with the sinuous flexing of her body.

Devon was surprised when the taste of her own slick come on Kayla's mouth inflicted another aftershock instead of mild distaste. She devoured their mingled flavor. Where their kisses might have been rough if it had been woman to man or harsh if man to man, even at the height of their passion, they elected to meet with intensity over force.

Kayla stared directly into her eyes as they kissed.

Dev wrapped her hands around Kay's lush waist. She tried to guide the larger woman where she preferred. Kayla beat her to it, already in motion. She scissored their legs so that one of her knees landed between Devon's and she straddled one of Devon's thighs.

Two could play this game.

Devon planted the sole of her foot on the mattress, raising her leg until Kayla couldn't help but ride the sleek pillar of her body. At first it was enough to grind their pussies on each other's legs, searing heat to cool skin.

Their hips rotated as they rubbed themselves on their friend.

"Mother of God." Neil sounded as if he might pass out from excitement. "That's the sexiest thing I've ever seen."

Kayla slipped closer with each swing of her body over Devon until they'd knit as tight as could be. Slightly sideways, the position left Kayla rubbing her clit over Devon's mound. Another shift and they met, clit to clit.

Devon squealed and came again, each climax stretching into the next as her pleasure extended. Kayla glided above her, slipping against their joined, moist flesh. Devon knew she couldn't take much more before she overdosed on excitement. She lunged upward, latching on to Kayla's breast, sucking with enough force to transmit her sense of urgency.

Kay obeyed, convinced by the additional sensation. Their movements became choppy and desperate yet no less graceful. Kayla sat up straighter. She rode Devon, making sure to rub her pussy over as much of her delta as possible with each pass. When their stares collided, both women surrendered to the moment and the success of their experimental ardor.

They peaked together.

The release seemed to cascade in endless increments, lingering so long they rested in each other's arms. When Devon could open her eyes again, it was to a marvelous sight.

Dave, James and Neil attempted to match the passion their wives had generated. The three men locked together in a licentious chain that resembled a triple stack of Legos, each peg fasted to the hole in front of it. James in front, Dave in the middle, Neil behind them both. They fucked as if there was an award for most strokes per minute. Damn, Dave and James would be sore tomorrow.

A feminine cry from the couch drew Devon's attention. Morgan and Kate rode their guys. They'd opted for reverse cowgirl, seated so they faced out toward the group. A pair of naughty bookends. Four sets of eyes refused to blink as their owners joined in creating passion that radiated throughout the room.

Mike and Joe reached around their wives' waists to rub their clits or test the constricting rings of muscle hugging their cocks below. The guys thrust upward into their women with strokes so well timed they stayed in lockstep for as long as Devon could watch.

A strangled cry brought her attention back to the pile of men beside her and Kayla. She reached out to stroke James's cock, which bobbed and slapped his abdomen with every rough thrust from Dave. Each motion impaled James even as it withdrew Neil from Dave's ass. On the return journey, Dave shoved Neil deep in his own ass while granting James's prostate a moment of relief.

The cycle couldn't last forever. The men grunted and cursed as they fucked, already driven to the boundary of their restraint by the demonstration Kayla and Devon had given them.

"Oh, fuck." James didn't manage to give more warning than that before thick white strands shot from his erection. The first jet erupted with enough force to tag him in the chin. The purple head of his cock appeared even darker when pearly fluid streaked his olive skin. Blast after blast iced his pecs, abs and Devon's fingers.

He stared into her eyes as he surrendered, showing her how much he loved what he'd witnessed. All of her, as well as the men filling him. Dave jerked in Neil's hold, emptying himself in James's pulsing ass. Devon smiled. Guys never could resist the tug of his ring of muscles during orgasm. It yanked Neil with him every time.

The same was probably true for Dave. In a slutty domino fall, Neil caved while Dave's ass twitched and clamped around the long cock embedded in it. Neil fucked Dave, held his friend close, but never once did the big man's stare leave Kayla's face.

I love you, he mouthed to his wife as he shattered.

Kayla trembled in Devon's arms.

Dev rubbed the other woman's back, aware that they'd continued their subtle gyrations throughout the magnificent exchange their guys indulged in. As everyone turned to watch the two couples on the couch, they picked up the pace.

Devon moaned long and low when Kay added a swivel of her hips to every bump and grind. She'd thought they were through. It seemed they'd only rested. Passion flared again. She smacked Kayla's ass—whether to encourage or rebuke her, she didn't give a damn anymore.

They watched together as Mike and Joe rose from the couch without leaving their wives' bodies. They turned as one, lowering the women to their knees on the floor, bent over the seat of the couch they now faced. Kate looked toward Morgan and they both smiled as their husbands fucked them hard, fast and perfectly.

The best friends reached out, lacing their fingers on top of the center cushion.

As if they felt that connection, Joe and Mike growled in unison. Their knuckles turned white where they gripped their wives' asses. Buried to the hilt, they sprayed their semen as deep as possible into their women.

Devon sighed as she thought about how perfect it

would be if both women conceived after today's session. Being a part of building their family seemed fitting. After all, they'd shared one of the most personal experiences of her life and enhanced it with their presence.

The two couples stretched out, Mike and Kate lying on the couch and Joe and Morgan snuggled on the floor in front of it. Both men cradled their wives, angled toward the mattress where her and Kayla had interlocked.

"Have one more in you?" Kay sipped at the light perspiration sheening the skin behind her ear. "Come on, Dev. I know you do."

They writhed together, their pussies rubbing against each other as if they'd done this a million times before. The jewelry in Kayla's hood nudged Devon's clit. Metal beads ran across her hypersensitive flesh. The bar linking the nodules pressed and rolled her engorged nub.

Devon gasped.

"Now you see why I like them so much. They're not just pretty. They're functional." Kayla gathered her breasts and used them to paint circles over Devon's chest. When they both needed more, Kay stretched to her full length, proffering one of the mounds to Devon.

Without altering the flowing motion of her hips, she fed her breast into Dev's gaping mouth. Devon couldn't stop herself from suckling the tight peak or playing with the hoop piercing the darker tissue there. Having something soft yet heavy in her mouth while Kay stroked every inch of her body calmed her, allowing her to focus on the ecstasy spiraling higher inside her once more, enhanced the sensations.

"Yeah." Kayla grunted, then slid her hand beneath Devon's head. Her friend clasped her close to her heart, granting no quarter, though Devon would never have asked for any. She mashed their pelvises together faster and faster, her ass shaking in the seductive motion shared by all rutting animals.

Devon surrendered to Kayla, allowed herself to be used as a warm body for Kay to slake her lust on. In the process, she gleaned plenty of pleasure for herself.

She tried to warn Kayla that she was losing control. The breast filling her mouth with sweet warmth prevented her from uttering anything intelligible.

Kay seemed to understand regardless. "Yes. Yes. Come with me, Devon. One more time."

Kayla froze, then resumed her humping double-time. She came on top of Devon, her pussy kissing Devon's with the force of her orgasm. Dev feared she might have lost the thread of her arousal in the wake of the awe of beholding such a tremendous release.

Until she felt the stroking of six masculine hands over her arms, legs and anywhere else James, Neil and Dave could reach. Someone tapped the sweet spot on her neck and she was a goner. She spasmed beneath Kayla's weight, nearly throwing the limp woman across the room with the force of her seizing.

Passion overwhelmed her, leaving her nerves ragged and exposed. She whimpered, thrashing and caught in the throes of rapture so strong it scared her. When she cried out, a reassuring kiss landed on her mouth.

James gathered her to him, pacifying her as every muscle in her body twitched then died. Boneless, she allowed him and Neil to sandwich her between them. Kayla pressed between Neil's back and Dave's front. Their fingers still linked, they drifted for quite some time.

Minutes or maybe hours later, Devon heard rustling from the direction of the couch. When she lifted her head to check out the situation, her gaze met Kayla's. Her friend smiled, a little timid, then nuzzled into her husband's arm. "Still alive?"

"I think so." Devon couldn't stop her blush. Could things be normal between them? What would change in the aftermath of their exchange? "Are we good?"

"You're fucking terrific." Mike grunted following a smack, likely Kate reprimanding his smartassery in such a critical moment.

Devon couldn't thank him enough. Both women exchanged a grin.

"You know, I think he's right." Devon beamed. "We *were* amazing. Thank you."

"Anytime. I loved every minute. It's so different. Soft, gentle... I'd almost forgotten how good it could be." Kay sighed. "I was so afraid you'd freak. Change your mind. After that, I couldn't handle it if you were grossed out or things got weird."

"Me either." Tears stung Devon's eyes. Damn, she'd done enough of that lately.

"If it fits, it can't be wrong." James rained Eskimo kisses on her nose.

"That's what *he* said," Kayla murmured. Being half-asleep didn't thwart her bad joke.

"Yes. Yes, I did." Dave made her giggle as he cuddled her close, both of them resting in the arms of their beloved mate after sharing their needs and granting the other permission to find what they could not provide personally.

Devon couldn't imagine a deeper expression of love than that.

Unless it was the serenity she felt when her guys bundled her between them, whispering how well she did, how sexy she was and how much they adored her. Now and always.

Nothing she could say could communicate the love exploding from her heart.

"It's okay, baby." Neil kissed her temple. "We know. Same goes."

"Ditto." James laid his head on her shoulder and closed his eyes. "Love you. Even if you are going to give me a fucking heart attack if you keep getting me that worked up."

"I love you, too." She sighed into the dusk falling over their shared space. "All of you."

And much later, when they snacked on leftovers of the decadent birthday cake Morgan had slaved over, Mike didn't wince. Not even when he devoured the thickest section of the frosting.

EPILOGUE

Two and a half weeks later, Kate emerged from the bathroom of her renovated home with Mike so close he might be glued to her backside. She rubbed one hand in a circle low on her belly and grinned. It was the sort of shit-eating variety reserved for winning the lotto or telling someone you've just gotten engaged. Or...

Morgan perked up, wondering if she had it right. The rest of the crew had assumed the pair was in the powder room for a quickie, but she had a feeling...

Besides, they'd been *far* too quiet for that.

Everyone held their breath.

"I'm pregnant."

No one noticed the tight smile Morgan and Joe exchanged. If they caught the tears falling from the corner of her eyes, they would assume they were manufactured by joy, not sadness. Because she hadn't shared the news they'd received when their tests had come back from the doctor yesterday. Hadn't quite finished processing it really.

Joe was sterile.

No baby grew in her womb, and it never would. Unless...

She couldn't dare to think such things when her friends celebrated one of the most magnificent events of their life. She'd have time to grieve later. Until then, she'd be the best aunt this child could hope for and take comfort in her friends' bliss.

It wouldn't be all sunshine and roses. She'd help them every step of the way, as they would have done for her if the situation had been reversed. Her own upbringing had taught her that a family is what you make it, not what you're given genetically.

The crew was a perfect example of that.

Joe's hand shook when it landed on her waist. She smiled up at him, hoping to erase some of the tight crinkles around his eyes. He suffered too. Maybe more than her. She'd promised him it didn't change anything between them. She loved him as much today as yesterday, more as each day grew the miraculous bond between them.

Still, after hugging Kate and taking his turn at offering felicitations, he stumbled from the room.

"What's wrong with Joe?" Kate paused, searching Morgan's eyes for signs of trouble. If she wasn't careful, her best friend would ferret out the drama and have them swaddled in her mothering before they'd properly celebrated her revelation.

"He's not feeling well. Probably doesn't want to risk getting you sick." She squeezed Kate's hand, hating herself for the lie. "I'd better go check on him."

"Okay." Kate chewed her lip. "Let me know if there's anything you need. Either of you."

"We will." Morgan smiled without a hint of pretense.

"You're going to be the best mom in the history of the universe. I can't wait to spoil him or her."

"Him." Mike's arms folded across his chest. "I wouldn't know what the hell to do with a daughter. She'd be all gorgeous like her mom and I'd have to lock her up until she was seventy to keep boys from corrupting her."

"Oh, I can just see it now." Morgan patted the foreman on his puffed-up chest. "You're in so much trouble. A daughter it is."

"Shush." His face blanched a bit. "I could handle one little girl with my hands tied behind my back, right?"

"That's what *he* said," Kayla sing-songed. The eight friends cramped in the kitchen erupted into laughter at the horror in Mike's wide eyes. The raucous cheering still echoed in Morgan's ears as she burst from the house in search of her husband.

They would get through this. As long as they stuck together.

She scanned the deck and found it empty, so she jogged down the stairs and around the corner to the backyard. Joe leaned against a tree, his hands jammed in his pockets, head hanging, breathing hard.

Her heart broke all over again.

She slowed as she approached. As always, he knew when she was near. "Sorry. Just needed a minute."

Morgan threaded her hands between his bent elbows and his sides. She splayed one hand low on his flat abdomen and the other over his chest, infusing him with as much warmth as she could impart in the chilly afternoon air.

For a while they rested there together. She counted the beats of his heart as it slowed from pounding beneath her hand to a moderate thump. Eyes closed, she could have stayed there with him forever. Long before she was ready to let go, he roused, shifting in her hold.

He pivoted on his boot heel, turning to face her.

"That was really selfish. Shit." He scrubbed his hand through his hair, making it stick up in adorable disarray. She wondered if he'd remembered to make an appointment to get it cut.

"I don't think so." She reached up to cup his cheek. He leaned into her caress, heaving a sigh of relief or self-deprecation, she couldn't quite tell. "You're allowed to grieve. But don't shut me out. We're in this together, right?"

"Sorry for your luck." A rare fury entered his eyes, no doubt directed at himself.

Morgan had never had the urge to smack someone before. She yanked her hand away as if singed and took a hasty step back. She stumbled over a root from the gnarled old oak and would have fallen on her ass if he hadn't snagged her out of midair.

He buried his face in her hair, which she'd worn loose today just for him, and breathed deep. In the bakery, she always kept it in a bun. "I'm fucking this all to hell and back."

She separated them enough to grin long and slow. "Come on. You know you want to say it."

"No, I don't." How did he manage to be so fucking cute even when he pouted?

She chucked his chin. "Sure, you do. It's pretty fun once you get the hang of it."

"Fine. That's what *he* said." A ghost of a smile touched his extra-fine lips.

She couldn't help but smother it in a kiss until it blossomed into his radiant grin. "I love you, Joe. There are other ways. We can adopt. Something. Maybe being an aunt and uncle will be enough."

His grimace called her bluff.

The back door banged open hard enough to be a warning.

"Hey, are you all right, Joe?" Dave clomped along the deck, giving them plenty of heads up as he approached.

"Yeah," Joe called. He hugged Morgan. "I will be."

"In that case, the girls are pitching a fit because you booked it before they could unveil their big deal." Dave probably rolled his eyes. "You're going to have to be on your deathbed, or hurling at least, if you don't get your ass inside soon."

"I promise you'll enjoy this." Morgan stroked his cheek, surreptitiously swiping the lingering moisture at the corner of his eye before his crewmate could spot it. She hated keeping secrets, but this wasn't the right time to share their disappointment. "It's not very often that *I* get to surprise *you*."

"I don't deserve you." He dropped his head to her shoulder.

She would have ripped him a new one, then smothered him in affection until he couldn't deny the breadth of her love except Dave rounded the corner of the deck just then, spotting them.

"You sure everything's cool?" The big man chewed his lip.

"I love you." Morgan rubbed as much of his back as she could reach in their embrace.

"That's everything to me," Joe whispered in her ear. "We can survive anything as long as we have each other, right?"

"Right." She squeezed him tight.

"I'm sure." Joe enveloped her hand in his, then headed toward his friend. "We will be okay."

"If there's anything I can do…" Dave lost his jovial mask.

"Not right now." Joe shook his head.

Morgan's eyes burned when Dave hugged Joe and her husband didn't resist.

Then, as if by some Jedi mind trick, the two men snapped into their usual routine. "Probably have some pussy hangnail, is that it?"

"Yeah, just like that time you cried over the splinter." Joe socked Dave in his biceps. His loose fist bounced off a wall of muscle.

"Dude. That was a four-inch sliver of wood, and it went *through* my fucking hand."

Morgan had wondered how he'd earned the jagged scar. The crew had plenty of those.

"Flesh wound." Joe snugged Morgan tight to his torso as they climbed the deck stairs.

She wrapped her arm around his waist and rested her head near his heart. When they reentered the space, the whole crew looked up. Dave gave his head a barely discernible shake, so they all went about their business.

"Okay, ready?" Devon practically bounced next to a flat rectangle covered by a sheet.

Morgan took her place next to a similar package, the only one left that didn't have one of her best friends standing nearby. She fisted her hands in the soft, worn material draping it and winked up at Joe.

"We realize we're a day early, but since we all have plans tomorrow, we wanted to give you your gifts today. Together. Happy Valentine's Day," Kate said to Mike. The rest of them echoed the sentiment.

"One...two..."

They whipped the covers off the framed photos simultaneously.

Someone whistled, maybe James.

"Whoa." Joe crouched in front of the artwork. He trailed his finger over the likeness of her, reverence in every brush of his fingertip.

"I think I'm having a heart attack." Dave clutched his chest. "Please tell me you kept this outfit."

"I'll show you tomorrow." Kayla smirked.

The guys rushed to their wives, showing them exactly how much they loved their gifts—so much more than the physical presents the women had schemed to concoct. Mike swung Kate into his arms and twirled her around the kitchen while his best friends paired, or trebled, off to indulge in some one-on-one, or -two, affection.

"You know, our evil plot was to use these to take you as our horny hostages and issue tons of naughty demands..." Kate shrugged. "But you've already given us everything we wished for and more."

Mike pried his stare away from the likeness of his wife in her sexy lace catsuit long enough to glance over his shoulder at the rest of the crew and nod. He cleared his throat. "That's what *we* said."

HAMMER IT HOME

POWERTOOLS

JAYNE RYLON

NEW YORK TIMES BESTSELLING AUTHOR

For all my readers.
You have made this a landmark year in my writing career.
By helping me reach several major milestones—like hitting the
New York Times Bestseller list with my great friend and co-
author, Mari Carr, and winning an RT Reviewer's Choice
Award for Best Erotic Romance of the year—you've propelled
me several giant steps closer to my dream of one day being able
to proudly declare that I am full-time writer.
Thank you for your support.

1

"Awwww." Morgan's three best friends melted as Kate withdrew her latest purchases from the pink-and-blue-striped, lamb-dotted Cutie Patootie shopping bag to display for their approval. They passed around the itty bittiest pajama set Morgan had ever seen.

"I love the matching fuzzy socks." Kayla grinned.

"So soft." Devon sighed as she ran the tip of her index finger across the plush fabric.

"Do you think they'll be warm enough?" Kate nibbled at the inside of her cheek, highlighting her dimples. "Or maybe too thick?"

"Don't worry so much, Katiebug," Neil chimed in from where he—along with the other four guys in the crew—slathered cheery green paint on one wall of the nursery. "Your girl's probably going to kick them off anyway. My sister's kids always seemed to strip and have their toes in their mouth in half a second flat."

"Look, it could be a boy. There's no telling yet." Mike paused with his roller in the middle of the patch of color he'd focused on. His lack of typical gusto made it seem as if even he didn't believe the mantra he'd recited for nearly three months now.

"How much longer do we have to wait to say, 'I told you so'?" Dave dodged a half-hearted swipe from Mike. Not fast enough to avoid minty splatters on his already Pollock-esque coveralls. "The ultrasound is next week, right?"

"Whoa. Stop that right there." Kate wagged her finger at the guys. "No paint fights today. The baby will not be happy if you mess up her gorgeous new hardwood floors. A little drop cloth is no match for you when you get riled up."

"Last time I checked, you liked it when I got riled up." Mike smirked until her admonishment sank in. "Hold up. *Her* floor? No. No. No. Whose side are you on?"

He pouted, the roller forgotten in his hand, which dangled by his knee as his shoulders slumped.

"The one that gives us a healthy baby of either gender." She rolled her eyes at his exaggerated antics.

"You know I am too." Mike cleared his throat, drawing her attention to the lump of emotion he struggled to swallow around, making Morgan wonder what it would be like to see such awe on her husband, Joe's, face. "It scares me a little, that's all. A baby is so tiny already. So delicate. The thought of a girl half as beautiful as you and the hell I'll have keeping her safe from teenaged horn-dogs..."

James snorted and clasped his middle. "Oh, karma. Gotta love that bitch."

"Seriously, though..." Mike squinted down at his wife, who rubbed her rounded belly in cathartic circles. "What made you say that?"

"I don't know." Kate practically glowed, despite her shrug. "I just...have a feeling. And I keep dreaming about her. I see you sitting there in the corner, on a white rocking chair with a frilly pink cushion, holding our daughter while she sleeps. It feels so real."

Mike set the roller in the tray and crossed to his wife. He wiped his hands on his pants before cupping her cheeks in his trembling fingers. "You saw her?"

"Yeah." Tears tracked down the slightly puffy cheeks of Morgan's best friend. "Both of you together, and knew I could never be more in love."

Morgan couldn't stand upright another moment. The precious outfit she'd crumpled in her fist fluttered to the floor as her fingers went numb. She realized Kate didn't intend for every word to eviscerate her as viciously as if she'd slashed Morgan with a thousand paring knives simultaneously. Still, the ragged cries clawing at her vocal cords threatened to rip free of her throat if she didn't escape the reminder of all she'd never have.

She squeezed past the couple, lost in each other.

When Kate's full abdomen brushed Morgan, she flinched as if scorched. The drop cloth twisted around her foot and she stumbled. Joe reached for her. She couldn't bear to look her husband in the eye, afraid he might recognize her pain. Never would she add to his burdens.

Except it seemed even without intending to, she had. Their relationship had grown strained lately. The more she tried to protect him, the more he seemed to blame himself, and today was no different.

"I'm sorry, Mo," his ragged whisper chased her as she fled the scene of adorable bliss.

Lousy friend.

Horrible partner.

Failure of a wife.

"Morgan." Mike's command boomed from the top of the stairs she clattered down. "Stop. Right now. You're going to hurt yourself."

Something in her obeyed the foreman instinctively. Still, she couldn't force herself to turn and face him. Ashamed, she dashed tears from her cheeks with the heels of her hands. Before she figured out what direction to go next, strong arms surrounded her, lifted her.

She scrunched her lids closed and buried her face in the chest supporting her, too broad to be her husband's or Mike's. Definitely too big for James or Neil. "Dave."

"I've got you, doll." The gentle giant had reached her first. He carried her into the living room where she soon found herself surrounded by friends and lovers.

At times like this, she couldn't have been more certain the crew had evolved into something beyond a gang of friends who doubled as fuck buddies. These eight people —five construction workers and the women they'd made their life partners—shared a bond stronger than sex.

When she peeked from the shelter of Dave's embrace, her gaze locked on her husband as if drawn by a rare-earth magnet. The rest of the group closed rank around them, shuffling Joe to the center of the semi-circle flanking the couch.

Hands guided him, pressing on his shoulders until he sank beside her.

Acid ate holes in her stomach when he sat, stiff. Leaning away from her, he was careful not to touch a single molecule of her legs, bare beneath the hem of her flirty sundress.

"Enough." Mike shattered their perpetual cycle of guilt, pain and self-loathing. "This is insane. I refuse to watch two of my best friends ruining the most amazing thing in their lives. Dave, give her back to Joe."

When the big man kissed her forehead and shifted to transfer her, Joe sighed. "I'm not sure you should force her, Mike. I wouldn't want me either. I'm defective. Useless."

Then no one needed to prod her.

Morgan launched herself at her husband. In her peripheral vision, she caught a glimpse of Kayla hugging Dave, since her mate had been left empty-handed. Morgan and Joe weren't the only ones suffering. Their agony and disappointment radiated outward, tainting everyone who loved them.

How selfish had she been?

"Joe." She straddled his lap. Still he refused to lift his stare from his limp hands. They rested, palms up, on the cushions beside his powerful thighs and her pale knees. "Please, look at me."

When he granted her request, the torment in his stare stole her breath. Ten times more potent than the loss and regret she harbored because he couldn't get her pregnant, his misery ripped her heart from shreds into tatters.

"I'm so sorry," they murmured in unison.

A multitude of hands rubbed Morgan's back and Joe's arms, which banded around her. She spied her friends stroking her husband's powerful shoulders from either side of him, where they had crowded beside and behind the couple on the couch.

"You have nothing to apologize for. *Nothing.* You hear me?" Morgan shook her man, though he barely budged.

"Sure, right. Then why are you pulling away from me?" The laugh lines at the corner of his eyes had all but vanished from disuse. Tension drew them tight, repurposing them into deep gouges in the planes of his usually affable visage. "You can't even bear to be in the same room as me most of the time. I don't remember the last night I fell asleep with you in my arms, or woke to you snuggled next to me. You think I don't know you're stalling when you're downstairs baking until two in the morning? Napping on the couch for a few hours before preparing for the early rush? This is bullshit. I can't take anymore. Just cut me loose already. I can't survive another day wondering if it's the last. The one when you finally admit you deserve better. This resentment is going to poison everything we shared. I don't hold it against you. I understand, cupcake. I can't give you what you need."

Her guts roiled.

She jerked as if he'd slapped her.

And still she wished she could flay herself a million times over for giving him the wrong impression. All that time suffering alone, for nothing.

"No." She smothered his face with butterfly kisses. "You have it all backwards. It's me that's the problem. I'm greedy. Selfish. So angry at myself. How can I be disappointed when I'm so damn lucky?"

"What?" Joe blinked up at her as if she'd lost her marbles.

"I tried to keep busy so you wouldn't see my grief. I didn't want to hurt you." She sobbed. "I think I made a big mistake."

"Shush, both of you." Mike plopped beside them. He nudged the couple with his shoulder, rocking them with his gentle pressure, and infusing them with his heat. "No one is winning here. I let this go on too long. I think because I felt like shit, knowing Kate and I have what you want. I let that fuck with my perspective. This is nuts. You love each other. Nothing should matter more than that."

Morgan glanced up to see Devon, James and Neil nodding their agreement.

Dave stood with his feet spread, his arms crossed over his chest.

"Is this some kind of intervention?" She attempted to deflect the concerned disapproval with levity. Her attempt flopped.

"I guess you could say that." Kate mirrored her husband, sitting on the couch on Morgan and Joe's other side. She cleared her throat, then scanned the gathering. No one spoke up when she paused, so she continued, "We've discussed the matter."

"Who's *we*?" Joe tensed again beneath Morgan. She rubbed his chest, reminding him the crew meant well. "All of you? Talked about us behind our backs?"

His cheeks flamed.

"There was nothing sinister about it," Mike growled. Rare displeasure rolled off the foreman, making Morgan blink. "If I didn't know how rocky these past few months have been, I'd kick your ass for thinking such stupid shit. We're trying to help."

"Oh yeah, and how do you propose to do that?" Joe harrumphed. "Wave your *magic wand* over my cock? Implant some healthy swimmers in my nutsack when I'm sleeping? They said the chance is next to nothing. No hope, Mike. None. Not all of us can be Captain Fertility like you, knocking up your wife on the first try."

"Don't you see...?" Kate tilted her head, curious yet stern. She would make one hell of a mom.

"See what?" The hairs dusting the nape of Morgan's

neck began to rise. She shifted her stare from one friend to the next.

"Dev, grab the folder from the sideboard, would you?" Mike gestured with his chin.

The cute construction worker, the only girl on the crew, dashed for the requested item and delivered it to Mike's outstretched hand in a flash. She smiled softly, then squeezed Joe and Morgan's linked fingers.

When had that happened? Morgan wasn't sure, but she'd missed the warmth of his partnership recently. Only herself to fault for that, really.

"What's all that?" Joe's hostility morphed into curiosity.

"*We* have a surprise for *you* this time." Mike flipped open the manila cardstock and thumbed through the papers inside. "Me, Dave, James and Neil all got tested. You know, for genetic markers and a bunch of other shit I didn't understand much about."

"Why?" Joe squawked. His body vibrated beneath Morgan.

She smothered him with affection as best as she knew how. Because surely, there was only one reason the guys would subject themselves to that kind of medical scrutiny.

Mike looked to his wife for help. Fancy talk had never been his strength. Morgan felt pretty sure what they were about to say might change all of their lives forever.

"They wanted to see which of them would have the best shot of giving you a baby." Kate stuck to direct yet sympathetic. "We also did a lot of research on adoption. We've scraped together some money if you'd rather try that route. But lots of people use sperm banks. You wouldn't have to stick with our guys if the idea makes you uncomfortable. We just thought...you might want some options."

"And you're all willing to make a charitable donation, is that what you're saying?" Joe sneered. "Great, I love being the dude all my friends pity."

"Quit being so defensive." Mike socked him in the shoulder. "This isn't the Joe I know. Pull your head out of your ass and think about this for a second. Look at what you're doing to your wife. Your marriage. Are you willing to throw that all away for pride? If so, then you're not the man I thought I respected enough to suggest this to."

When Joe's stare winged to her, Morgan tried not to flinch. She took a deep breath and held still, afraid to tend the seed of hope Mike had just planted. If it sprouted then withered, she might not survive. Blank, she allowed Joe to form his own impressions.

"Oh, fuck." His head crashed to the cushion behind him. "You're right."

"It's not too late to fix things." Kate finger-combed his hair from his brow. "Tell her what's in your heart. Right now, before the moment's gone."

Joe took a breath so deep his lungs rattled. He sat upright, pressing close. For the first time in months, he donned the confident, sexy swagger he'd always worn as well as his favorite ripped old pair of jeans. "I never want to see that guarded look on your face again, Mo. That's not the girl I love. I can't believe I've done this to you. To us. There were other ways. Other choices. I just... I felt so much like I'd let you down."

"Leave the past alone." Mike kept them on track. "You can only change the future. Where do you want to go from here?"

"Who had the best chance?" Joe didn't hesitate.

"Neil." Mike's smile turned wry. "Apparently, he's pretty lucky he hasn't done it by accident at this rate. Dev should probably double the dosage of her birth control shots."

"You're welcome." James pinched his longtime lover on the ass. Devon, James and Neil laughed as they hugged each other. "Seems like my ass might have saved yours."

"Okay." Joe nodded before returning his gaze to Morgan. "What do you say? Want a tall, pain-in-the-ass kid with blond hair? I bet Neil can rub one out in the doctor's office in thirty seconds or less and we can be on our way. No muss, no fuss, right, Mikey?"

"Something like that." Their foreman sounded wary. "It doesn't have to be so crude."

The clinical nature of the deed frightened Morgan. She imagined bright whitish-blue lights, doctors poking and prodding her, and antiseptic smells corroding what should have been one of the happiest moments of her life. Suddenly she didn't know if she could sign up for such a sterile origin for her child. Then again, what choice did she have?

The pressure of her friends' regard bore down on her until she thought she might be squished flatter than a pancake. They were trying to help. Offering a solution.

"Morgan?" Joe narrowed his eyes as he observed her pulse speeding in her neck.

She had to escape their scrutiny. She couldn't hide anything from the crew. But she didn't know if she was ready to be totally honest yet—either with them...or herself.

"I..." No matter how many times she swallowed, she couldn't manage to clear the lump in her throat. "Thank you. Really. I just... It's a lot. Need some time. To think."

Scrambling off Joe's lap, she rushed for the door.

Heavy booted footsteps trailed close behind her. Their owner didn't try to stop her, but followed at a safe distance instead.

By the time she'd run to the passenger side of Joe's truck, she'd calmed enough to lift her head. Through two panes of glass and the chasm of the cab between, she watched her husband monitoring her reaction. "Let's go home, Mo. We can figure it out together."

The truck separating them distorted his reassurance. Still, she could decipher the movement of his lips. Not hard to understand him. After all, it was as though he read her wishes straight from her soul. If nothing else, she promised him silently right then, she'd quit letting this baby fiasco ruin their relationship.

No matter what she had to do, she'd fix things.

For them both.

Joe climbed inside. He reached across the bench seat to unlock and open her door. Then he extended a green-speckled hand, which she latched on to as if it were a lifeline, and used it to tug her into the vehicle. Without letting go, he backed out of the driveway. His fingers never abandoned hers, not even to wave to the cluster of seven worried friends huddled on Kate and Mike's porch.

She stared at the rest of the crew until they were specks in the side mirror, wondering—with each foot of distance that they added between them and their friends —if she'd dug this yawning pit deeper than it had already been.

2

Morgan didn't object when Joe told her to sit tight before jogging around to her side of the truck. She slid willingly into his open arms when he invited her. All her energy had drained away as she mulled over their options on the short ride home. She clutched the manila folder he handed her to her chest and allowed him to carry her up the stairs to their apartment over her bakery, Sweet Treats.

He didn't pause to check the mail or snag some of the leftovers from yesterday's special. Instead, he marched directly to their bedroom and settled her on the bed. Deft fingers swiped her sneakers from her feet, then tucked her beneath the thick strata of covers they preferred.

Joe joined her moments later, gathering her to his chest.

"Mo."

"Joe." They initialized conversation at the same instant. She giggled. "I never noticed before that we rhyme."

"Me either." He grinned, then trailed a knuckle along

her cheek. "Guess it's no surprise, though. We were meant to go together. I still believe that."

"So do I." A wince tugged at her lips. "I'm so sorry I let you think otherwise."

"It's in the past." He angled his chin toward the papers clasped between them. "Let's work on the future."

Morgan worried her lip between her front teeth.

"Their offer obviously upset you." He traced the shell of her ear, tucking loose strands of hair off her face. "Why don't we start with why? Do you not want a child if it can't be conceived the traditional way?"

"No. That's not the problem." She shook her head, pushing up a little with one palm on his chest so she could meet him eye to eye. "I admit I hadn't thought of alternate arrangements after they told us it wouldn't be successful to implant your sperm in me artificially. But it's not like I haven't embraced some unconventional practices in the past few years."

"No one's questioning that, cupcake." Joe smiled, then nuzzled their noses together. "Especially after the shit your ex pulled on you, I'm still amazed you gave me and the crew a shot. Grateful every day that you were brave enough to try again."

"Thank you for being so patient with me." She stared into his warm, dark eyes.

"So if it's not that you object to..." He spoke slowly, as if selecting each word carefully. "You think there could be issues with asking one of the guys to do the job?"

A cringe compressed her spine at his blunt description of what should be a miraculous event. "It does worry me that we'd be risking an awful lot. Let's say Neil did...*donate*. What if he can't let go? What if he wants a deeper relationship with the baby? How will we all feel about that? You, me, Devon and James. Will we be able to cope?"

"Shit. That's a good question." Joe sighed. "I didn't really think of it that way. I know the three of them aren't interested in kids. How many times have they told Katiebug they're glad to spoil her baby temporarily, as long as they get to give it back?"

They both chuckled at the memory. The trio had promised to adore their honorary niece or nephew—though of course they'd said niece—lavishing her with obnoxious toys and hopping her up on sugar before returning her to her parents.

"That's what they've said, but Devon is young. She could change her mind yet. And what if it hurts her to see her husband's child raised as someone else's?" The familiar sting of tears prickled Morgan's eyes. "I couldn't stand to injure one of them just to appease my own desires."

"We can talk to them, double check they're certain." Joe tipped her face toward his. "But I know my friends. They don't say or do shit they don't mean. You can bet Mike and Kate had these discussions with them long before they agreed to hand us that folder. They wouldn't risk disappointing us by rescinding an offer like that."

"And if they're not sure. Really, *really* sure, we can look at adopting." Morgan picked at a string on the edge of the duvet. "It's just so expensive. And it won't be fast. I thought maybe in a few years, when Sweet Treats was more stable and we weren't reinvesting all the profits in growth, maybe then... This gift from the crew is more than we can accept."

"Can I be real honest, Mo?" Joe levered up onto one elbow and leaned his forehead on hers. "I'll do whatever makes you happy, I swear. But if it can't be me who gives this to you... It feels right to have it be one of the crew. They're closer than brothers. More than friends. They're part of me. And if one of them can do this, it's almost like I did in some fashion. Easier to be excited about than if a stranger were to be mixed with you. Though I swear to you, I will love any child we raise together. I swear I'll be the best dad I can be. The best husband and friend."

"I know." She didn't hesitate to grant him reassurance. His decency and commitment were qualities she'd never had reason to question. "Even when I've treated you horribly these past few months—been so self-absorbed, I'm ashamed of myself—you never once wavered. I love you, Joe. And if this is the path you prefer, I'll walk it. I'm so thrilled they offered, humbled really. It's just..."

Panic chilled her as she thought of cold steel tables and instruments beeping in the background instead of warm embraces, flickering candlelight and the soft sighs of great sex. It was a ridiculously small thing to endure. And when they came home, Joe would make love to her. It would be easy to convince herself the magic had happened then.

"That." Joe zeroed in on her reaction as if she'd advertised her discomfort on the Times Square JumboTron instead of attempting to mask it. She could conceal nothing from him. "There it is again. What was that hesitation?"

"It's silly." She shook her head.

"Nothing is trivial if it affects you or our family." Joe flashed the steely core he seldom unveiled. "Tell me what you were thinking just then."

She breathed in, then released the air in a steady stream.

"You can share anything with me. Don't you believe that?" Pain darkened his eyes, drawing his brows lower on his handsome face.

"Yes, of course." Morgan refused to hurt him anymore. "It's just that those procedures are so *sterile*. Formal. Surrounded by strangers. It's not how I would choose to create a new life. I wish it could be borne of our shared joy and pleasure. Instilled with all the love and hope and gratitude I feel when we're together."

"Oh." He sat up, leaning his shoulders against the headboard. "I guess I didn't think that far ahead, cupcake. When you put it like that..."

"It's ridiculous. So many other couples have done the same. If anything, our child will know how much we fought to have him or her in our life. No accidents here." She patted his chest as he stared into the bathroom he'd remodeled for her. The blue and white of the custom handles infused color and style to the small space. "We'll do this our way, however that turns out to be."

"What if—"

"Yes?" She prodded as she enfolded his hand in hers. "Finish your thought."

"We already share." Joe faced her, determination and a wicked smile on his lips. "No reason we can't get you pregnant the old-fashioned way. Just not by me."

"Are you saying...?" Morgan shivered, every pore of her body opening to the idea. Heat flooded her where chill had seeped in before.

"Uh-huh." He nodded. "I'm gonna go out on a limb and say none of the other guys will object. Their ladies either, since we all agreed to be each other's birthday presents. No reason we can't all try together. Would that make it special enough for you?"

"Hell yes." A wave of excitement rolled over her. "I wonder if they'd really be okay with that?"

"Why don't we call a crew meeting and find out?" Joe tugged her over until she straddled him. "As soon as we celebrate our kickass friends and genius brainstorming session. I've missed you a hell of a lot, Morgan."

"Same goes." The kiss they shared started out slowly and gently. Her lips grazed his smile. Settling onto his lap more fully, she ground against his erection, plastering herself to his torso so she could revel in the beat of his heart, which resonated through her chest.

"No matter what happens, we'll always sort it out if we're willing to work together." He murmured against her neck, "I'll never give up on us. On this. I swear."

Two weeks after the painting party, Morgan hovered at the edge of her closet, a discarded pile of not-quite-right outfits littering the floor. Maybe the lavender skirt and rich purple sweater Kayla had given her for Christmas would be appropriate.

"Mo, what's the holdup?" Joe paused in the middle of their bedroom. "You're changing? Again? Cupcake..."

"Ug. I know." The thud of her palm smacking her forehead didn't do much good. "It's not like I'm going to be wearing this for very long. I guess I'm pretty nervous."

"I'm not." His smile spread, slow and wide. "I have the easy part. Just watch and wait. Maybe snag a blowjob in the meantime. Way better than shitty coffee in a Styrofoam cup at a clinic or something."

The strained laugh she surrendered only highlighted her tenseness.

Joe crowded behind her, bundling her into his arms so

her back rested on his chest. His chin perched on her crown. "You know I'm yanking your chain, right? Well, maybe not about the BJ part. I'm not going to be able to resist when I see you unravel for the crew as usual. Everyone was in favor. Pretend it's your birthday. That you're getting your present a couple months early. If all goes according to plan, you might not enjoy it quite as much then."

The crew had voted to allow each member to be the centerpiece of their libertine sessions, all pleasure focused on them, for their birthday. Helping Dave and, a few weeks later, James indulge in their annual decadence had been highlights she wouldn't soon forget. Somehow, all the power of their attraction focused on her seemed a little more intimidating.

Pressure built as she considered the possibility they wouldn't be successful tonight. What then? Would they have a rematch? How many orgies would it take? After nearly a year of trying to conceive, she worried Joe's condition wasn't the only factor inhibiting their success.

"I can practically hear the gears spinning in your mind. Stress isn't going to help, you know?" Heat combatted some of her chill when Joe's palms traversed her bare arms. "Your ovulation thingy said the timing is right. The setting is right. The people, the love, the intent—everything about this feels fucking perfect. So relax. Enjoy. That's all you have to do. No worries. Come on, now. How about this? I love this color on you. So pretty."

Joe selected the exact ensemble she'd considered. A sign, she thought.

She pivoted in his grasp, wishing she were tall enough to nail him to the wall and kiss the shit out of him. Instead, she settled for wrapping her hands around the back of his neck and encouraging him to bend. She almost forgot about the clothes, the crew and their plans for the evening when they exchanged a fierce yet seductive kiss.

"That's better." He nipped her lip before separating them.

"Maybe we should take the edge off before we go?" Morgan squeezed the thick shaft distorting the crotch of his jeans.

"I think I like you a tad desperate." He cupped her breast in his palm, smirking when she rubbed against his hold like a cat on the corner of a coffee table. "Get dressed. We're leaving in five minutes."

It took her less than three to change into the luxurious fabric, then check her hair and makeup. No sense in delaying any longer. Joe whistled when she emerged into their living room. He swooped in for another kiss, not caring that she'd slathered on a layer of gloss.

"Gorgeous."

"Thank you." The jacket he held out to her slipped easily over her clothes. "I feel like I'm going to a wedding. It all seems so...pivotal."

"It is." Joe kissed her cheek. "I got you something to remember tonight by."

"What?" She glanced up at him, her eyes widening. "You don't know yet if it'll work. Maybe we shouldn't jinx it."

"I'm certain." After fishing in his jacket pocket, he withdrew a tiny velvet box. "I saw it, and I knew you were meant to have it. Tonight is the start of a new era in our lives. I'd like you to wear this, carry something of mine with you."

A gasp escaped her when he flipped the lid open. A

dark purple gem set in swirled silver wire winked up at her in the light from their kitchen chandelier. A thin chain ran through a tiny heart at the top of the pendant.

"The jeweler told me amethyst and moonstone are good luck for women trying to conceive. Balances feminine something or other. Not sure I believe that, but I thought it was pretty and it reminded me of you. Can't hurt, right?"

"Right." Tears pooled in her eyes. His genuine and thoughtful surprises always made her day. He couldn't show her in more ways how much he loved her. She'd never felt so valued in all her life as when he was near.

"Joe, I need you to understand." She waited until he finished latching the clasp so it held his gift around her neck. "Even if this doesn't work out. If we never have a child...you are enough for me. You're more than I have a right to hope for."

Raising her knuckles to his lips, he dusted soft kisses there before linking their fingers and guiding her from their home. "I want to give you everything."

"You already have." She squeezed his hand as he boosted her into the truck, tucked her inside, then shut the door carefully.

They rode to Kayla's resort in contented silence, their hands joined again as soon as he took his place behind the wheel. By the time they bumped through the woods, along the twisted path that led to the secluded property hosting Kayla and Dave's house as well as their naturist retreat, stars dotted the sky like glitter set on fire.

She expected Joe to take the fork to the right, which led to the private cabin where their friends lived and most of the crew's interludes took place. Instead, he veered left. Toward the cute bungalows the crew had recently expanded on in response to the initial success of Kay's venture.

Several of them hadn't even opened to guests yet.

Morgan didn't ask where they were going. She trusted Joe to take her where she needed to be. As long as he was by her side, it didn't much matter where they ended up. Good thing her faith in him thrived. The truck slowed in the middle of nowhere until they rolled to a stop in the center of the rustic road.

When he removed a strip of black silk from his back pocket, she knew what he expected. Her lashes rested against her cheeks as she closed her eyes, leaning toward her husband.

"Sweet girl." He fastened the fabric around her head tight enough that she couldn't peek even if she'd tried to open her eyes, yet loose enough to be comfortable.

"For now." The hint of naughty she added to her response had the desired effect.

Joe's voice turned husky. "I like you spicy too."

The anticipated kiss she craved never arrived. The truck started off down the road. She threw her hand out, searching for the handle on the door or the edge of the seat. Joe's fingers landed high on her thigh. "I've got you."

"I know."

"Almost there." He crooned to her in soft, steady murmurs, never letting her forget he sat by her side. "I see lights now. And there's the crew. They're waiting for you."

"For us."

"True, for us." After a quick squeeze, his hand abandoned her leg long enough to unfasten her seatbelt. "Go with Dave. I'm right behind you."

Before she could respond, the truck door opened.

Huge hands engulfed her waist. She floated into their grasp. "You look really nice tonight, Morgan."

Thank goodness she hadn't worn a dress with a short skirt or she'd be flashing her ass to the entire forest. Not that the eight people she couldn't see but knew were there hadn't gotten an eyeful of every inch of her already. Soon they'd be doing a whole lot more than looking too.

Dave's boots thudded on what sounded like wooden treads as they ascended together. The new buildings had adorable porches complete with swings. That must be where they were. She hadn't observed the progress personally, though Joe had told her the crew had decided to take a couple weeks off before starting their next project to help Kay out.

Someone cursed softly. A subtle creak made her sure they'd opened a door for her and Dave. "So sexy, Morgan."

"Thank you, James."

"I'm going to set you down." Dave murmured to her as he lowered her feet to the floor. He braced her shoulders. Scuffles and whispers surrounded her as her friends all assembled as they saw fit. "Joe's got you now."

The big man's hand swapped out for her husband's familiar grasp. Dotted kisses at her temple had her sighing while he worked the knot on her blindfold loose. A steady white noise piqued her curiosity. What could that be? "Tonight is special. For all of us. We wanted you to know how much. Live in the moment, Mo. Take what we're giving."

He whipped the silk from her, letting it slither to the floor unnoticed.

Blinking against the sudden light, she tried to focus. When she did, a sheen of tears immediately turned the flickering candles into glittering sparkles, dazzling her.

She reached out. Joe held one hand while Dave collected the other.

"You did all this for me?" The whisper cut through the hush of her eight best friends, who awaited her reaction. Behind the naked, oiled men who stood shoulder to shoulder and their wives—adorned in gossamer togas that hid the bare essentials, proclaiming their intent to sit the festivities out—sheer panels of iridescent fabric draped from exposed wooden rafters.

Zillions of tiny clear lights, like the ones hugging their tree at Christmas, hung behind the soft falls. She felt as though she'd taken up residence in an enchanted snow globe, or maybe a cloud way, way out in some ethereal paradise on the edge of the universe. Romantic touches overflowed the space. Pale silk flowers, warm vanilla candles on wrought iron stands and the largest canopied bed she'd ever seen were just a few of the details bombarding her senses.

"We did it for both you and Joe." Kate smiled from her post with a fluffy white towel draped over her forearm. What the heck?

The guys stepped aside, chiseled bodies parting like a fleshy curtain at the most alluring opera she'd ever attended. Behind them, a waterfall trickled from what could have been a loft. A tiny stream bounced next to vines that looked as real as the ones Kayla had cultivated in the gardens outside. Maybe they were.

Splashes drew her eye from expertly crafted faux stone to faux stone until droplets rained into an elaborate whirlpool fashioned from river rock on the outside and something natural yet smooth-looking in the basin. A gradual slope led up to the dais supporting the magical indoor pond. Lush greenery surrounded the pool. She suspected the window on the other side would grant glorious views of the lake if it were daytime.

A fireplace made from the same cut stone chased away any chill emanating from the glass.

"Whoa." Nothing more elaborate formed in her mind.

Awestruck, she allowed Joe to manipulate her, stripping her sweater over her head and freeing her from her lacey bra before she'd recovered. Next he slid her skirt from her hips, then lifted her from the puddle of gorgeous fabric. He swiped her shoes from her feet and patted her bare ass. No need to remove underwear. She hadn't bothered with panties.

"Nice touch, Mo."

She grinned over her shoulder at her husband. "Glad you approve."

"Now run along and play." A gentle shove inspired her to put one foot in front of the other, heading in the direction of the crew.

"You're not joining us?" She paused.

"Told you." Mike put his hands on his hips. The motion drew Morgan's gaze to his stiff cock, which jutted from the shadow of his trimmed hair. "You can catch up. Wouldn't dare let our girl get a chill waiting for you to undress."

The foreman took a few steps forward, extending his arm as though they really were out for a ritzy night on the town instead of embarking on a procreational interlude of sordid proportions.

"Whatever you're thinking, I don't like it," he hissed. "You got that look. You know the one. Quit it."

A laugh bubbled up from somewhere beneath her nerves. It reminded her of the water in the spa and how it seemed to effervesce from an unknown source. "Yes, sir."

"That's better." He grunted as he led her up the incline then into the water, one step at a time. Miniature waves sloshed against her ankles, then her shins, then her knees. Warm and silky—probably loaded with rejuvenating minerals, if she knew Kayla— the bath felt heavenly. "We figured you might go a little Type A on us, so we decided to help you relax a bit."

"So far it's working." Tension drained from her muscles as she settled into the seat he directed her to. Water flowed around her shoulders, encouraging her to lean her head back against the contour of the tub, which provided a perfect rest.

"Good." Mike sat next to her. He massaged her hand then her arm until her eyelids fluttered closed. It shouldn't have surprised her when someone took up a similar exploration on her opposite side. Soon after, a third pair of sure fingers cupped her foot, kneading the pad beneath her toes.

She couldn't help but moan.

Finally another set of hands plucked her other foot from the waves and echoed the caresses. A smile tugged at her mouth. Joe's four crewmates pampered her.

"Yeah, lift up one sec. Now lay your head here." Kayla guided her to a folded towel at the edge of the hot tub.

Morgan opened her eyes, reassured to see her friend, upside down and above her. The affectionate smile ensured Kayla didn't begrudge Morgan her indulgence. The women kneeling on either side of Kay grinned too.

"You're doing great." Kate patted her shoulder.

"And I love your necklace. It suits you." Devon nodded.

Morgan wondered if she imagined the heat that seemed to pulse from the pendant where it nestled in the hollow of her collarbones. "Thanks. All Joe, as usual."

Further conversation became impossible when Kayla dipped her fingers in the warm water then laid them on Morgan's cheeks. She began a massage that leeched stress, which Morgan hadn't realized she'd harbored, from her facial muscles. Kayla's gift for soothing others impressed her, as always. Masterful, complex motions loosened every last holdout of tension.

The guys progressed from her extremities to her core, their continuing massage lessons with Kayla evident in their handling. Morgan was glad for their support. Otherwise, she might have drifted away on a swirl of fragrant mist.

"I think she's ready." Kayla spoke low and gently. "The switch is behind you, Joe."

"What—?" Morgan didn't have a chance to finish her question.

With a low rumble, the pattern of the jets in the tub changed. Where they'd been unfocused and random before, several direct flows added impact to the gentle swirl of fluid. Paired columns of water focused on the muscles flanking her spine. A few more pummeled the cheeks of her ass, digging deep into the muscles there to eliminate any knots. Finally, a burst fluttered over her pussy in a maddening oscillation that aroused her instantly.

"Ohmigod."

"Works as advertised, I guess." Dave chuckled from her side. He skipped along his path up her left arm to pet her belly a few times.

"They say having orgasms increases the likelihood of conception." Mike nibbled on her earlobe. "Have no idea if that's a fact. Figured we should give it a whirl just to be safe."

In unison, each of the men rubbing her limbs advanced, stroking her calves, knees, forearms and elbows. She lifted her head, pleased to find Joe had joined them, and was rewarded with a vision of him rising from the steamy water like Neptune, his hand stroking slow and sure over his generous erection.

"No peeking." Kayla draped a washcloth over Morgan's eyes and returned her head to its reclined position, continuing to heighten the sensual trance the men were working her into. "Don't you worry. Your guy is right here. He can't stop staring at you."

"Want him." It didn't matter to her that the statement sounded a bit like a whine given the erotic luxuries her friends lavished on her.

"We can make room." James shifted the angle of her leg. Neil mimicked the motion, splaying her wider, granting the jet more direct access to her swollen pussy.

Joe braced his hands on her thighs, lighting up her nerve endings with his comforting touch. His torso nudged her legs apart as he settled between them, probably kneeling in the deeper water beyond the ledge her ass rested on.

His hand glided across her pussy, making her shriek and squirm. The touch poised her on the edge of orgasm, far too soon. "Wow. The current is pronounced. It's rippling across my hand."

"That's not all it's doing." She gritted her teeth.

"Don't tense up." The pads of Kayla's thumbs prodded Morgan's jaw until she turned pliant once more.

"Or fight us." Mike had progressed to her shoulder.

His fingers teased the top swell of her breast. "Feel free to come as often as you like. This isn't some starvation diet."

Kayla's hand seemed cool in the wake of the flush that raced across Morgan's cheeks. She couldn't believe how quickly they'd revved her up. Her ridiculous objections earlier dissolved in the warm water steeped with the care of her friends. If she could have hugged each and every one of them right then, she would have.

"Time to get serious, boys," Devon called out to her mates. They advanced, walking their fingers up Morgan's thighs, swirling and teasing as they rubbed her down.

"You too, Dave," Kayla encouraged her husband. He matched Mike's fondling, which grew bolder by the instant.

Morgan's abdomen undulated, raising her pussy toward the elusive ripple of the continually evolving current. Just when she thought she'd homed in on it, the spray would change.

"More?" Joe slipped his hand between her lips until he was on the verge of penetrating her. "Does your pussy need to be filled?"

She cried out as he fed her the tip of a finger, then two.

"No worries about that," Neil rasped from where he now rubbed her ass and hip. "Soon enough you'll be stuffed. All of us, Morgan. Have you thought about that? Taking four cocks in your pussy in one night?"

"Five." Mike's tone brooked no argument. "Joe will have her last."

"Damn straight he will." Kate clearly approved, from her dulcet tone. "No matter which of you has the winning swimmer, this child is his. Theirs."

"Ours." Joe and Morgan uttered the promise in unison.

She didn't doubt for one second he meant the entire crew. She had too.

She squeezed his fingers with her pussy as he insinuated himself more completely within her. Careful to keep his hand low, he allowed the water to continue to caress her clit. Her toes curled.

"Shit, yes." Joe called out to his buddies. "She's close. I can feel her rippling around my hand. Dave, suck on her nipple."

The whoosh of the big man sinking below the surface was followed in short order by his mouth applying pressure on the tip of her breast. Mike mimicked the action from his post on her other side. The dual sensation —combined with Joe stroking her from the inside out, James and Neil petting her flanks and Kayla massaging her face—crescendoed until Morgan had no chance at resistance.

She capitulated to their care, allowing them to cradle her through an orgasm strong enough to burn away the last vestiges of her nerves and replace them with newborn hunger. Mike and Dave broke the surface of the indoor oasis. They dragged mass quantities of oxygen into their lungs. She felt as if they were breathing for her as she gasped and struggled to force enough air into her body to keep her from passing out with the pleasure they'd imparted.

Joe and Kayla anchored her, keeping her from drowning as her entire body thrashed and spasmed. Mike cupped the nape of her neck to quiet her. His reassurance —in conjunction with the long, loving strokes from the four other guys' hands, which roved across her body— granted her the serenity to maximize her enjoyment.

Dave lifted her fingers to press a kiss to her knuckles

and *tsked*. "You're getting all wrinkly. Time to get out, I think."

Her eyes fluttered open, unfocused. Lights flickered in her vision like errant fireflies. Joe kissed her softly before climbing over her. Water sluiced from his lithe frame. The three women nearby rushed to dry him with their plush towels. When they'd done their best, he crouched, arms extended.

Mike and Dave scooped their hands beneath her. They lifted her to her husband. He plucked her from the whirlpool, then held her out for Dev, Kayla and Kate to care for. Softness enveloped her as they rubbed her down.

"Next." Devon winked and moved on to Neil.

"Go ahead, Joe." Mike directed traffic. "Make your wife comfortable. We'll be there in a minute."

3

———

Morgan couldn't believe how completely the crew had transformed a simple cottage into a fairy tale hideaway. Everywhere she looked, touched, something delighted her senses. Yards upon yards of eyelet fabric draped from the rafters, making the space around the bed seem like a cocoon spun of seduction, love and wistful dreams.

Pinned in spots to form a luscious canopy, the airy cloth fluttered in the light breeze circulating through the intimate space, courtesy of the wide-bladed ceiling fan. It spun idly to keep the heat from absconding to the apex of the peaked ceiling. Joe ducked beneath yet more netting, this batch complete with fine silver filaments that coruscated in the glow of the twinkling lights. She trailed her fingers along the gauze as he delivered her to the platform bed.

"This is..." She had no words.

"I know." Joe nuzzled her neck as he settled over her. "When Kayla showed me the design inspiration pictures, I had my doubts she could pull it off. Now, when I see this, it's far beyond what I had envisioned. She's going to keep it staged. A honeymoon suite for the resort."

"Think we could get married a few dozen times?" she sighed.

"That can probably be arranged." Joe pressed a kiss to each corner of the smile she hadn't even realized her mouth had curved into. "I do know the owner pretty well, you know?"

Morgan giggled. "So I've heard."

"And there's so much more yet to come, Mo." Her husband rubbed their noses together, staring deep into her eyes. "Are you ready? Are you sure?"

"Absolutely." She didn't have a doubt left in her mind or heart. "Are you?"

"Hundred percent." He smothered her in a kiss so rich she knew she'd never forget this moment and the connection burning between them. She wrapped her arms and legs around him and returned the fervor of his lips, tongue and teeth.

Morgan didn't acknowledge the shifting of the mattress beneath her until someone pried Joe from her clasp.

"Excuse me. I believe I have this dance." Mike tapped Joe on the shoulder as though he were part of a naughty tag team.

Joe licked his lips. He shook his head, clearing the haze generated when they met soul on soul. *Later*, he mouthed to her while drawing a cross over his heart.

She blew him a kiss.

"You're making me jealous." Mike issued a mock growl. "I get some of that sugar too, right?"

"Of course." Morgan put her arms up and welcomed

him into her embrace. Over his shoulder, Joe nodded before he smacked the foreman on the rump.

Mike didn't flinch. Instead, he continued to impress himself on her from his toes to his hot and ready cock to his mouth. He laughed between her parted lips. "Yeah, sweetie, that's all for you tonight."

When he'd slowly and thoroughly delved to the far recesses of her mouth, he retreated enough to rasp into her hair. "Do you realize how much I've dreamt about taking you like this? All the way? It'll be our first time with no condom between us. No diaphragm either. What the hell were we thinking?"

"I don't know anymore. This feels good." She ran her hands up his powerful back, enthralled and appreciative of his presence in her life. She'd been ecstatic when her best friend found this man, and now she got to share in the wealth of rapture and security he provided for Kate, as well as the rest of the crew.

"I'm glad tonight is special for us." He kissed along her brow line. "I hope I can give you what you wish for. If not, I'm still gonna enjoy the hell out of this opportunity to show you how much I respect you and how lucky I think Joe is to have you. We all are. I've hated seeing you both suffer. No more. Only happiness from here on out."

All the while, he touched her. Skilled hands roamed her body—down her ribs, over her face, along the sides of her breasts. When he lifted a tiny fraction, putting minimal space between their torsos, she whimpered.

"Don't worry. I'll take care of you. One second." He brushed his thumb across her damp mouth as he reached for a couple pillows. "We have to make this count, huh? Gravity will aid and abet these little guys in their escape if we're not careful to make you a one-way avenue."

Someone off to the side snorted when he manhandled his junk. "Classy, babe."

"Hey, I am what I am." Mike tossed a wry grin at his wife. "Haven't heard any complaints from you before."

"Never will." Kate had curled up in a divine wingback chair. She slung one arm over her full belly and tucked her feet onto the pad by her ass. "I love you, Mike."

Morgan tried twice to speak when he propped up her hips then sank so that his cock rode the furrow of her pussy. "Kate."

She couldn't bear it if her friend changed her mind later and decided this had been over the line. They'd been BFFs since they'd hidden beneath their bunk beds with a deck of Go Fish cards and a stash of stale Thin Mints to avoid traipsing through mosquito-infested woods at the Girl Scout camp from hell in seventh grade. Wonder if there was a merit badge that covered helping your best friend get pregnant?

That was a lot of history to risk.

Kate leaned forward enough to squeeze Morgan's hand. "It's the right thing for us. Enjoy. Tire him out, would you? I haven't been feeling up to much lately."

Morgan laughed. Mike didn't. She licked the lines of strain bracketing his mouth. "You really are strung tight tonight, aren't you?"

"Yeah. Sorry. I worry when she's not feeling well. And this is a ton of responsibility. Plus, I'm afraid I'm not going to last that long." He scrunched his eyes closed for a moment. "It's been a while. You feel great beneath me. Soft. Hot. The idea of making a baby...another baby... It's powerful."

He adjusted his hips. With his hands tangled in her hair, he attempted to penetrate using just the motion of their pelvises. Newish to each other, they couldn't quite get lined up right.

"James, give him a hand." Devon coached one of her husbands from a similar chair to Kate's, which sat at the foot of the bed. She must have had one hell of a view despite the three men lounging beyond the tangle of Morgan and Mike's toes. Dave and Neil each rested their shoulders against a bedpost, while James had been cradled with his back to Neil's chest. Kayla sighed from her vantage point at Morgan's right, her thighs splayed over the arms of her matching seat.

"You two are sexy together." She whimpered as she drew circles over the damp crotch of her sheer panties.

Morgan would have responded, except James chose right then to tip forward far enough to insert the head of Mike's cock into her dripping pussy. All three of them strangled groans.

"I'll try to go slow." Mike huffed as though he'd sprinted around the resort a few times.

"Please don't." Morgan clutched his shoulders, aware of her nails sinking into the thick pads of muscle there. "I can't wait either. Been thinking about this for almost two weeks. Damn ovulation cycle."

"Tell me about it," Joe grumbled. "Those months we waited then did it on command a hundred times in a row... I don't know how gigolos do it. I swear my cock was sore afterward."

He stretched out on his side next to the temporary couple, positioning himself so he could peel one of Morgan's hands from Mike and enfold it in his own. He kissed her palm, then held on tight.

"Oh, sure. We feel so damn sorry for you." Kayla

kicked him lightly in the ass. "Like you didn't love every moment."

"You know I did," he answered Kay, yet he never deflected his stare from Morgan.

"Me too." She squeezed his fingers tighter than she intended when Mike plunged a bit deeper.

"Damn. Sorry." He cursed below his breath. "You're killing me with all this talk."

"Do it, Mike." Her attempt to wrap her leg around his hip was less than successful given the incline of her torso. Hell, he really had her hiked up. The thought of his come pooling inside her while his friends added to the mix sent a bolt of lightning from her brain straight to her pussy. She clenched around him.

"Not going anywhere when you're tighter than a fist." He attempted to work through her rings of muscle. Soaked, her body still had to be cajoled to permit him entry. "You sure I'm not hurting you, sweetheart."

"Uh-huh." She didn't care that the affirmation held no ladylike grace, only desperate craving. "More."

Mike concentrated then. They all knew when he set his mind to something... Well, you'd better look out. He whipped up his charm along with his persistence, plying her breasts with deceptively tender ministrations while he forced his shaft deep inside her.

Each crewmember fucked differently. They had their own styles. With her eyes wide open, she assembled visual memories she'd snipped while studying him with the other guys—and more recently the women, herself included.

"My favorite thing about you is when you get bossy. You're a natural leader, Mike." She couldn't believe she found her focus long enough to share the admiration in her heart for him. "Your children will have that spark. I would be lucky to foster that brand of bravery."

His stride hitched with him seated almost fully.

"Thank you." He blinked several times as though to clear away the moisture threatening there. "Now stop talking and put that pretty mouth to better use."

Lips descended on hers, preventing her from injecting some smartass remark into the heat of the moment. Honestly, that was more Devon's thing anyway. Morgan preferred to be honest and open in her affections. Mike sucked her bottom lip into his mouth, nibbling on the plumped flesh. The man could kiss, that was for sure. Maybe not with all the finesse of James or the caring of Joe, but with heat and drive and pure passion. *Yes.*

"Do that again." Joe directed Mike. "You just made the muscle in her jaw twitch like it does before she loses it."

What was her husband talking about? She'd have to ask him later. Way later.

"Don't worry. Felt it straight through my cock." Mike rocked inside her, rubbing himself on every swollen inch of her pussy. "You didn't tell me Mo was so submissive. Why haven't I noticed before? You're going to have to let us tie her up soon."

This time she couldn't deny half her face practically seized. How could it not when she clenched her jaw to keep from begging him to try it without hesitation? Every time she shared herself with the crew, she learned more about her inner core—who she really was and who they could be together.

Mike pursued the lead like a pitbull with a juicy bone. He bracketed her wrist, the one not already captured in Joe's hold, and pinned it to the pillow beside her cheek. His hips hammered into her, driving him home to the full extent within her moist channel. She swore she could feel his blunt head tucking directly against her cervix each time he bottomed out.

"You want us to rule you? Make you take what we're giving you? You will because you trust us to love you and bring you only the greatest of pleasure along with a twinge of pain." He uncovered a fantasy she hadn't realized she'd buried. So deep she had never admitted the curiosity even to herself. Maybe she'd never trusted anyone with absolute faith before. "I won't forget, Morgan. How much you like this."

Before she could figure out what he meant, he released her wrist. His hand snaked between them, his fingertips pinching her nipple.

Not gently.

Not brutally.

Just right.

At the same time, he ground himself between her thighs in a sinful figure eight that kept him buried balls deep yet stimulated every possible area of her pussy, inside and out. Her clit mashed against the flat, taut plane of his torso, just above his cock. The veins and ridges of his shaft aggravated the lining of her channel, which fluttered around the embedded cock that nudged, nudged, nudged her in all the right places.

Morgan tried to warn him, but it was no use. She shouldn't have bothered.

"Damn, I can see her coming around you." Dave groaned.

"Better keep your hand off your hard-on, buddy," Kayla chided her husband. "Wouldn't want you wasting the good stuff before it's your turn."

The steady commentary of her friends and lovers spurred Morgan to greater heights. She loved sharing this moment with all of them. At one time, she might have been self-conscious about surrendering so completely before their eyes. Now having them with her only magnified her pleasure. Her orgasm grew in intensity until she would have sworn she would hurt Mike with the force of her clamping.

The strangled cry he emitted seemed to support that theory.

Until the flood of desire rushed out of his cock and poured inside her as thick and hot as a lava flow. He pumped into her in time to the spurts blasting her unprotected pussy. Milking him deliberately, Morgan concentrated on obeying Kayla's calm yet clear instructions for wringing every last drop of semen from his balls.

"Jesus." His arms shook as he held himself up enough to prevent crushing her.

Joe reached out, steadying his friend. When the imminent threat of her being turned into a pancake by a smoking hot construction worker had passed, he petted Morgan with loving caresses, allowing his hand to wander between her and Mike until his fingers ringed his best friend's softening shaft. "Pull out."

The foreman kissed her cheek, then slipped from her body. Pearlescent fluid clung to his cock. She whimpered at the reminder of their purpose.

"Wait." Joe collected the remnants, stroking along Mike's length with his index finger. Mike shuddered and cursed. Dave leaned forward to brace him while Joe finished his thorough cleaning.

"I realize it probably doesn't make a difference." Joe

smiled softly when she would have interjected. "Still, I like the idea of you taking it all."

Morgan's eyes rolled back when he spread the lips of her pussy and smeared the thick cream along her opening.

"There, that's better." He hummed his approval.

"I've got to be next." Dave shouldered Mike aside, trusting Neil and James to situate the nearly comatose man in the corner of the bed, propped as Dave had so recently been to ensure he didn't miss a moment of the action. "Unless…"

Dave paused, his hand idly traversing the bold thickness of his erection.

"You're not too much for me." Morgan held her arms up and open again. "I've had you before. You fit me just fine, remember?"

The concern clouding his eyes cleared up in the wake of his smile. "Oh, hell yeah. I thought you might rocket into space the day you rode me in our living room chair, when we all swapped partners."

Blushing was ridiculous. It didn't matter, Morgan's cheeks heated at the reminder of the first time they'd gone round robin with each other. She'd come again and again with hardly any effort, turned on by living out a longtime fantasy and discovering the real thing to be a million times better than her imagination had proclaimed it would be.

"You're cute when you turn shy." He nudged her legs wide enough to accommodate his huge, though fit, frame. Burrowing close, he kissed her softly, then stroked her hair, helping her recover from the ecstasy Mike had inspired while keeping the embers of her desire glowing.

His bulk sheltered her from anything beyond their embrace.

"A child of yours would have a kind and accepting nature. I promise Joe and I will protect the baby, and allow him or her to blossom into a person as generous and loving as you are. It would be an honor." She trailed her fingertips over his ripped muscles. Just because he was stronger than an ox didn't mean he didn't need to be cared for. She would never make that mistake, not knowing him as well as she did.

Joe cleared his throat from beside her. Proving her point, Dave extended his hand and tapped Joe on the cheek, roughly scrubbing over the five o'clock shadow Morgan adored. "I wouldn't trust very many people with my legacy. You know Kay and I aren't planning to have kids of our own, so I hope you don't mind me saying I really pray this works out. I'd like to know some part of me will live on after I check out, and I couldn't think of any better people to nurture that seed than you."

Dave glanced at his wife. She flashed a watery smile in their direction. Neil leaned over to rub her shoulder and she tipped her cheek onto his knuckles. Kayla whispered, "Good luck."

With her blessing, Dave notched the tip of his fat cock in the vestibule of Morgan's pussy. Pressure built. He rocked until the head penetrated, breaching her initial resistance. They both gasped when she hugged his engorged cap.

"I love watching you surrender to him." Joe traced the taut tissue of her inner lips around his friend's intrusion. "It seems impossible, until it's not. It makes me wish I could give you more."

"You've given me everything." Morgan laid her fingers

on Joe's chest, over his heart. "Everything that matters. Home, family, friends and your love. What else is there?"

They exchanged an entire conversation with one look. Reassurance she could never find him lacking. Oaths to continue to provide unfailing support for each other, no matter what obstacles the future flung in their paths. All with the security provided by the crew woven throughout. Together they were unbreakable.

She'd nearly forgotten Dave existed as she and Joe locked lips. Or perhaps he simply became an extension of the man she loved. Her husband plied her mouth with tender nips and flicks of his tongue across the sensitive underside of her own, distracting her from the discomfort caused by the advancement of his burly friend. Until Dave bucked and groaned, igniting a conflagration that burned her nerve endings from the inside out.

"Sorry, sorry." He panted, though he froze between her legs, his cock fully impaling her. "It's just, you're so... squishy. Warm and wet. Mike must have been saving that up for a few days."

Kate whimpered, cutting through Dave's awe.

The foreman abandoned the bed. He scooped his wife into his arms and settled himself in the oversized armchair, tucking her to his glistening chest. Reminding Morgan of a horse, steaming in the winner's circle after a mad dash to the finish, tired yet proud, he stroked Kate's hair. "It's fine. I'm a big boy. I can take care of myself. You haven't been feeling well. Concentrate on staying healthy and helping my *son* grow strong. I've got the rest. Hell, it's not like I'm going to be horny for a solid year after tonight."

"Promise?" Kate blinked up at her man.

"Yeah, I'm good. Perfect."

"Shit. Didn't think..." Dave's cock lost some of its steeliness.

"It's impossible to hang on to reason when you're visiting paradise that sweet." James mediated the potential awkwardness, as usual. "I can't wait to feel her for myself. Though after you, I'm afraid I'm not going to be very impressive."

"I've got an idea." Neil whispered in James's ear, pausing to nibble on his lover's lobe.

"You dirty bastard." James shivered. "Pour on the speed, Dave. I'm in a hurry to try this deviant's latest scheme."

Morgan chuckled when Dave looked from guy to guy surrounding them. Distracted, he lost a little of his focus. Kayla unfurled herself from her chair and climbed onto the elevated bed. She sidled up behind her husband and brushed her almost-bare breasts across his back.

Though her hands weren't visible, Morgan could guess what kind of magic they worked when Dave shuddered between her legs. The other woman spoke, low and wicked, to her husband. "Remember what I told you before? How it turns me on to see you lose yourself to giving one of our friends pleasure? How I'm going to reward you later? Too bad I didn't think to bring my strap-on or we could have been a little more efficient. I'm a fan of multi-tasking."

Dave jerked forward, his cock firming with every pounding beat of his heart. Buried as deep as possible, he inflated within Morgan, stretching her until she swore she'd never been so full in all her life.

Indentations made by Kayla's dark purple nails on Dave's pecs caught Morgan's attention. The prickle they caused only seemed to rile him further. His nostrils flared, and muscles ticked beneath the ink swirling across his olive skin, making him look like a bull ready to charge. His wife waved the red cape of his turn-ons like a world champion matador.

Morgan didn't mind being pierced by his horns.

"There you go." Kayla spanked Dave several times in rapid succession. Morgan imagined flaming handprints appearing on his tight ass. "Give it to her nice and we'll play rough later."

"Looks like Mo isn't the only one exploring lately." Mike raised an eyebrow from his place at the head of the bed.

"Devon gave me the idea." Kay beamed at her friend. She sank onto the arm of Dev's chair instead of returning to her outpost. "I love that we learn from each other. Constant progression. Getting old together will never be boring when we're changing and growing all the time."

Dev patted the cushion beside her hip as she scooted to one side of the oversized seat. Kayla slipped beside her friend, gathering the smaller woman close so their legs braided. She kissed Devon with the soft yet fierce passion the crew had come to expect from the pair on occasion. "Thank you."

"Anytime." Devon winked, then got comfy, resting her head on Kayla's shoulder.

"Oh, shit. They're making out, aren't they?" Dave clenched his jaw. He retreated only long enough to advance again, less carefully this time.

"Shit yeah," Joe teased. "With lots of tongue and even some boob fondling."

"Really?"

Morgan didn't blame Dave for looking over his

shoulder. She giggled at the epic pout that crossed his face when he realized Joe was pulling his leg.

"We'll save the show for later. You need to focus." Devon ratcheted up her stern inner minx. She was getting pretty damn proficient at playing the part. "If you do a good job, maybe I'll help Kayla teach you a lesson after we're done here."

"Don't fuck this up." Neil added another swat to Dave's ass. "I want to watch."

"Morgan…" Wide eyes implored her to help.

"Nobody's stopping you." She ran her fingers through his hair. "Fuck me, Dave. You don't have to go slow."

"Want it to be special." His face lowered enough so he could capture her mouth beneath his. The soothing kiss he imparted had little in common with the jacking of his hips. An apology transmitted through every soft caress of his tongue. Tenderness offset by the power of his thrusts between her quivering thighs.

Heat and wonder built inside her like steam in a pressure cooker. Weight compressed her chest as he descended, trying to close any lingering gaps between them. Their perspiration-coated skin adhered where they collided. The insides of her knees stuck on his ribs as he folded her practically in half.

Metal brushed her nipple. The warmed bar of his piercings glanced across her pebbled flesh, inciting a riot in the primed tissue of her breasts. How could he be so tough and yet so sweet? So huge and yet maybe the most delicate of all the men?

Morgan hugged him to her, sheltering him in a welcoming grasp. The discomfort of his oversized cock and heavy body were nothing compared to the bliss of granting him safe harbor and an outlet for the glorious energy he'd obviously pent up.

"It is. Perfect." She encouraged him to abandon the last of his inhibitions by dragging her nails down the bunched sinew on either side of his spine hard enough to leave proof of the claim she staked. Her heels drummed on his ass when he rutted in earnest.

Morgan scooted toward the headboard as he plowed into her, over and over.

Joe shifted, draping one arm beneath her head, around her shoulders, to anchor her through the storm of Dave's unleashed fervor.

She couldn't do more than hang on and enjoy the ride. Tingles spread throughout her body, electrifying her from her fingers to her toes. Focusing on the absolute pleasure, she cultivated the sensation, fertilizing it until it bloomed out of control.

"It won't be much longer." James murmured in the background. "Are you almost ready, Neil?"

"Been waiting our turn for at least nine million years, haven't we?"

"Just feels that way." Mike shushed the pair. "Don't distract Morgan."

As if she could think of anything but the force of the man driving inside her, pushing her tighter to her husband with every surge of precise momentum Dave instilled in her. His scrunched lids flew open, revealing the clear honesty in his bright eyes. "Want this. So badly. Both of you. Deserve it. To have what you need."

The intensity of his desires percolated through every pore of Morgan's body. She absorbed each droplet of the genuine compassion oozing from him while hoping she deserved such gallantry. Her body responded to the emotions barraging her heart and soul. It squeezed him tight, enhancing the effort he dedicated to pleasing her in this moment as well as the greater scheme of their lives.

She hadn't imagined she could come with each man this evening. In the recesses of her mind, she remembered Mike's advice—orgasms improved the odds of conception. Thank God it wasn't the other way around or she'd stand no chance at all.

Her toes curled as ripples began to undulate her swollen channel around the constant invasion of Dave's shaft. Balls slapped against her ass each time he ground deep within her. They both shouted as they escalated each other's pleasure through the natural expression of their own rapture.

"I'm going to come," Dave bellowed. He threw his head back and impressed her all over again with the magnitude of his strength. Muscles twitched as he restricted the range of their flexing.

Morgan looked to Joe. No speech was possible, or necessary.

Greedy. If she was going to climax, she required everything Dave had to give.

"Fuck her harder." Joe spanked Dave. A crack rang through the room as his palm met bunched muscle. "Give her all of you. She can handle it. Wants it. *Needs* it."

The plaintive mewling that erupted from her throat might have been embarrassing if she hadn't been so desperate to shatter with her husband's friend. Instead, the sound seemed to infiltrate Dave's resistance.

Roaring in a primal display she'd never witnessed from him before, Dave grasped her hips, tilted her to optimize the angle of his invasion, then dug deep. He rammed inside her, reaching magical spots she'd only heard clinical discussions about in the past. The fringes of her vision grew smoky as she held her breath in anticipation of the climax about to burst through her.

Flares danced in front of her eyes when she shattered. Though she squirmed and thrashed, Dave never let go. He rode her with the single-minded purpose of a man driven beyond sanity, boundaries or polite considerations. When the clenching of her muscles prohibited him from plunging as fast as he preferred, he locked deep instead.

Intermittent grunts rained over her like the plop of thick cake batter from the wire attachment of her favorite mixer. Dave bit her neck and trapped her. Utterly helpless to move, she was forced to endure every blinding sensation, on the verge of too intense. Too amazing.

And then she felt it.

Scalding heat flooded her pussy.

Dave emptied himself inside her one stream at a time. He jerked in synch with the spasms gripping him, cursing and praising her with every wrenching wave of his orgasm. Their hips banged together at each involuntary buck that enhanced the natural range of his spurts inside her. A wash of liquid lust drenched her.

His climax seemed to last forever, renewing hers with each additional seizure of his muscles and the strangled groans accompanying them. The final two or three pulses of his cock tapered off, leaving him moaning and chanting her name in reverent sighs.

Morgan floated, completely dazed. She tried to cling to his sweaty shoulders when he retreated, but he slipped between her fingers. Strong hands pinned her to the mattress, preventing her from following. "Shh. Don't sit up yet, cupcake."

"Joe."

"I've got you. Stay still. Catch your breath. God, that looked incredible." He kissed her brow so sweetly tears stung her eyes. "You're so gorgeous when you unravel like that."

Half-entranced, she started to roll toward him.

"Keep that ass in the air." Mike's command knifed through the fog in her brain, reminding her of their purpose. How could she have forgotten, even for a moment?

Joe began to rearrange the pillows beneath her hips, enhancing the incline to guarantee the mingled fluids of two of his best friends remained deep in the well of her pussy.

She couldn't say if her whimper had more to do with the thought of their deposits or the ecstasy still gripping her mercilessly or the blinding love her husband inspired or the pressure the awkward angle put on her neck. Probably a bit of each.

"Let me help." James crawled beside her. He motioned with his chin. Neil and Joe complied, lifting her high enough for their lover to worm beneath her body and prop his own pelvis on the feather-stuffed ramp they'd constructed ad hoc. The two men lowered her into the comforting cradle of his mass. James cushioned her while maintaining the optimum angle. The nape of her neck rested comfortably on the curve of his shoulder.

"Much better," she sighed.

"I aim to please." James cupped her breasts. "Plus, this is a great spot for copping a feel."

Morgan laughed, trying to keep her eyes open despite the lassitude barraging her.

The entire bed shook, jostling them all, when Dave crashed—completely limp—onto his face at the foot of the mattress. Kayla and Devon reached out to soothe him with long, smooth glides of their hands. Murmured praise babbled in soft tones Morgan couldn't decipher. She strained for a glimpse of the contented smirk on his face.

"Don't worry about him," Neil flashed his asymmetrical grin. "He'll survive. He just needs some time to recover after that wild ride."

"Me too." She hid her flaming cheeks in the crook of James's neck.

Why did she feel like everything changed by the moment? It was as if her chemical makeup had been irrevocably altered by the radiant emission of their love and the attempts they'd made on her and Joe's behalf.

How could she take more when she'd already been given so much?

"I don't know, feels like your pussy is still begging," James rasped in her ear.

"You're inside me?" She wished she could rescind the question the moment Joe choked at her side. It wasn't that she hadn't felt anything *down there*, but rather that she'd felt too much. Assumed it was an aftereffect of Dave's possession.

"Well, that'll make a guy try harder." James flexed beneath her in a sinuous motion that left no doubt as to the accuracy of his claims.

"Urg." A contented gurgle served as her only reply.

"That's better." His smile warmed his tone. "No hard feelings, love. Dave is huge. I imagine it's hard to discern anything aside from extra happy tingles, considering the way that orgasm looked from where I was sitting."

Dave grunted his agreement, his finger idly drawing swirls over her anklebone from where he splayed.

"So maybe I better do this before she recovers?" Neil

knelt between two sets of spread thighs. He looked not at them, but at Joe when he made his suggestion.

"You're the expert at tandem fucking, not me." Joe sat on his haunches, close to her and James's heads as though monitoring her reactions with strict observation and intention to shut down the operation at the slightest hint of trouble.

Morgan didn't pay much attention to their banter. With her eyes closed, she drifted through euphoria, sturdy arms around her and rhythmic breaths lulling her with their metered rise and fall. What could they have in mind? She decided to relax and grant them complete control. Not one fiber of her being lacked trust in them, either singly or as a whole.

"Right." Neil's determination had her prying her lids open in time to catch his grimace. "Hold her tight, boys. She's going to be sensitive at first."

James's arms banded around her waist. Joe cupped her jaw in his hand, angling her face so she met his stare. He crooned encouragement when Neil advanced, sliding into her still-throbbing sheath beside his life partner.

"Ohmigod!" She didn't mean to wriggle, but she couldn't help herself.

"Joe..." Neil paused, checking in with her husband.

"Don't stop, it was a good OMG."

She'd never been so glad he could read her mind. If Neil had changed his course then she'd have wept with frustration. How could they continue to elevate her enjoyment?

Part of the pleasure came from realizing she was a conduit for the two men to love each other. James shivered beneath her as his mate's cock rode along his ultra-firm length. An involuntary flex compressed them within her.

The idea of pleasing them both, pressing them together, sent aftershocks racing along her pussy.

"Feel that?" Neil cursed.

"She's still coming." Rough breath stirred the hairs at her temple, tickling her cheek. James simultaneously melted and stiffened beneath and inside her. "From Mike. From Dave."

"All of you." She combed the sheets and covers with a widespread hand until her knuckles knocked into Joe's knee. Unfocused eyes prevented her from reading his expression. When she walked her fingers up his corded thighs and surrounded his impressive erection in her palm, there was no denying how her wanton display impacted him.

Several uncoordinated passes along his length had her frustrated she couldn't maneuver as she pleased. "Come closer."

"Don't have much choice when you tug on it like that. It's not a leash, Mo." His grumble mixed with a chortle.

"Seems pretty effective to me." Kate stuck up for her best friend.

"Let me taste you." Morgan licked her lips, then parted them as she strained her neck toward his bobbing cock.

The brush of his silky head over her mouth had her drawing him inside instinctively. Positioned so that he could feed her his entire length, Joe dangled his balls across James's jaw.

"Help yourself." Neil glided inside her as he encouraged his mate to add the salty tang of Joe's nuts to the stimuli driving him inevitably toward total annihilation.

Another shockwave passed through Morgan when James's full lips met hers at the base of Joe's cock. Abs bunched and released beneath her lower back as he fucked up into her. Each thrust was timed to James laving her husband's delicate sac.

"Oh, shit." Joe's hand tangled in her hair, adding a bite to the gentle massage of his fingertips on her scalp. If James's purr were any indication, he received similar treatment.

"You weren't joking, Dave. She's fucking soaked. Feels so damn good. Slippery." Of all the things Neil had on his long list of personal accolades, stamina had never ranked very high. It seemed he already bordered on the edge. "So slick when I rub over James. He feels like satin inside her. But hard. Fuck. So hard."

Waves of rapture battered Morgan, increasing in frequency and intensity until she couldn't tell where one ended and the next began. The two men shuttling inside her passed each other with each return journey, their counterpoint voyages generating delicious bumps as their heads lodged within her tunnel at different points.

Subtle variations in timing kept her guessing as to when the largest knot of them would form. The combination of their crowns created a bulge that massaged her tensed muscles from within. Joe took advantage of her slack jaw to bury himself to the root. He poked into her throat. She swallowed around him, wishing he could feel even a sliver of the miraculous attention his friends lavished.

"Careful," Mike warned from his post beside them. "Too much more of that and Joe is going to forget to add his load to the rest. Deep inside Morgan. Remember the plan?"

They'd strategized the best way to fuck her tonight?

Morgan couldn't restrain the full-body shiver of delight

that coursed through her at that revelation. She wondered what tricks they kept secret in their playbook for another time. Nothing could surpass this moment. Glorious, pure and perfect, she couldn't have loved each of them more.

"Just a minute, Joe." Neil panted as he redoubled his strokes. "Hang on a tiny bit longer. I can't wait. Not much more."

James laughed at the desperation in his lover's declaration. Not out of cruelty, but because he adored the moment the man of his dreams reached fulfillment.

"And you'll be right there with him." Mike reminded James. "You never can resist him coming on you. Sorry, but tonight you're going to have to give up your favorite dessert. Mo gets to keep it this time."

James pulled off Joe's testicles with a slurp. Probably for the best, as her husband's shaft had taken on the defined ridges that proclaimed him ready to explode. "There's always later."

"Ah, God. Yes. Later." Neil shorted the amplitude of his strokes. He fucked fast and furious. The motion declared his imminent breakage. "You. Devon. You'll suck me together. Later."

Before he'd finished issuing the prophecy, Morgan's best chance at conceiving was realized. She hugged Neil to her as tight as she could, given the frantic pace of his fucking. Granting him as much comfort as possible, she clung to him while come jettisoned from his balls.

"Arghh." James turned hard as a stone slab beneath her. He froze, then shouted, "Feel it. Shooting on my cock. Right on the head. Oh. Damn. Right there. Right there."

Then Morgan could no longer discern the individual sensations bombarding her. Two men pumped within her, drenching her folds with their semen. The idea alone, maybe aided by the erratic press of Neil's pelvis bone on her clit, triggered yet another pulse of orgasm in her. Shudders wracked her body.

She must have thrashed hard enough to dislodge James, because next thing she knew, Dave and Mike were helping the longtime pair disentangle themselves from her. Only Joe remained in her field of vision. He fixed her pillows, though she slumped, as floppy as a rag doll wherever he placed her.

"Even like this, I can see their come about to spill from you." He dipped his finger in the pool of thick fluid, then held it out to James, who gladly cleaned the work-roughened digit. "You're brimming with all they've given you. Us. It's as much as we can do."

Morgan tried to lift her hand when his voice crackled. Utterly wrecked, she couldn't.

Mike held Kate in his arms as he stood. He leaned close to Joe to whisper something in his ear. Kate took the opportunity to kiss Joe's cheek. She licked at his cheekbone as though clearing away a rogue tear. Soon Devon, Kayla and their men huddled close. They petted Joe, offering him comfort when Morgan could not.

Each crew member spoke softly to him, rubbing his back, patting his ass, hugging him from behind. And when the flurry of male and female reassurance alike had swarmed over him, he knelt just a little taller between Morgan's thighs. The buzz of affection and praise traveled over her as well.

She closed her eyes, enjoying the soothing of her husband and their seven best friends. And that's when she felt Joe—she'd know him anywhere, no matter how many other lovers she took—press inside her. Careful, gentle and reverent, he fused their bodies.

Her lids fluttered open.

Stares locked. She didn't have to glance around the room to realize they were alone. The crew had left them to bond. To claim the new life she felt sure they had created. Endless disappointments flashed through her mind. Month after month of periods coming to shame her with their failure.

Somehow she knew... Those days were gone.

The universe couldn't be so cruel as to mock the union they'd joined in tonight.

At the heart of everything, was this.

Joe.

"Hi," he whispered against her lips as he moved the barest bit within her tender pussy.

"Hi."

"Not sure where you went just now, but I missed you." Gentle strokes of his fingers through her tangled hair swelled her heart to unimaginable proportions. "Must have been somewhere good to put those stars in your eyes though."

"Those are all because of you, Joe."

They traded languorous kisses and ground against each other, more interested in feeling every inch of skin on skin than the acute pressure of his cock in her pussy or a finger on her clit.

Morgan explored his back, ribs and ass, as much of him as she could reach. She loved him as best she knew how. With everything she had, primarily her heart and soul. Without words, without vigorous motion, without carefully placed touches on pressure points, they idled in bliss.

And still the energy they generated lifted them inexorably toward a pinnacle they reached together.

Instead of an explosion, their synchronized release was a cleansing spring shower. They came in unison. Hope, love and unending happiness stole away the pain they'd unintentionally inflicted on each other over the past year and replaced it with optimism. Along with the certainty that the moment marked a new beginning for them, their family and a love that would never die.

Joe overflowed her pussy with come though only the clench of his ass and the subtle tightening of his jaw gave any hint of his surrender.

They came in silence.

Staring into each other's eyes.

At the beginning of everything important.

4

Kayla spied Morgan fanning herself with the lovely straw hat she'd purchased from a kiosk at the trendy, open-air mall they enjoyed frequenting on nice days. Unusual for the woman who ordinarily basked in the heat of summer, always trying to talk the gang into tanning by Kate and Mike's pool, not that it was a hard sell.

So what if Kayla attended more for the cocktails and girl talk, preferring the contrast of her pale, unwrinkled skin to the bold swirls of colored ink decorating it? That's what SPF 80 was for. They hung out and Morgan toasted herself golden, sans lines. Which fairly often led to the guys coming home from a job site to snarfle dessert before grilling out. Exactly how their wives liked it.

Today Morgan had complained at least fifty times that the glorious temperature seemed oppressive, even after a double helping of fresh berry sorbet, which Kayla was more than happy to indulge in as well. Protesting the humidity in a whine, Morgan had actually started to annoy Kayla, a nearly impossible task.

Which might explain why Kayla had strutted more quickly than usual down the cobblestone lane. Well, that and the fact that they approached the shop housing the dress she'd been lusting after for weeks. Their pace certainly couldn't account for the fatigue plaguing Morgan, though. Unfortunately, the other woman slowed to a near crawl, then paused in the shade of a tree at exactly the worst possible place for Kayla's self-control. "Can we cross the street at least, Mo? It's on the way to our cars. There's a bench over by the fountain there if you want to re—people watch for a few minutes."

She'd almost said *rest*.

The instinctive denial Kayla expected didn't bubble from Morgan. Odd, since the woman was on the go all day, every day, running her bakery. A stroll through the mall should not have warranted a break. Typical Mondays, when Sweet Treats stayed closed, meant recipe research, epicurean experiments, buying supplies or component prep for the week ahead. Still, Morgan never seemed to lose her focus or her drive.

Kay had been pleasantly surprised when her friend had texted and begged her to play hooky from the resort for a few hours. Everything, including that mid-morning message, had convinced her aliens had abducted the real Morgan and left this lookalike in her place. Heavy circles marred the golden skin beneath her eyes. Crankiness didn't suit her generally lighthearted nature.

The only other time Kayla had seen Morgan so sullen...

She swallowed hard, afraid to ask. It'd been almost three weeks since the night in the honeymoon suite. Shouldn't she know by now? Maybe it hadn't worked.

What else could sap Morgan's infinite energy and perky spirit?

"Using me as an excuse to avoid your dream dress?" Morgan raised one eyebrow at a jaunty angle, distracting Kay from her mental investigations.

"Hell yes." Kayla scowled. She'd successfully resisted the seductive design, hand-painted in gold and plum on lapis silk, during the prior two trips she'd made to the shops with various assortments of the crew ladies.

"Just try it on already. Please." Her friend rolled her eyes.

"We both know if I do, it's going home with me." Kay glanced over her shoulder at the temptation in the window, then to Morgan, then back at the dress.

"Maybe you'll be extra picky, as usual, and delude yourself into believing it's unflattering or some crap. Though I bet you the Boston cream pie in my case right now it would look fabulous. Worthy of the annual award ceremony for the Independent Business Alliance. You know, 'cause I've heard rumors you're about to be nominated for owner of the Best New Venture of the year."

"What?" Kayla's jaw hung open. "Are you freaking kidding me?"

Morgan would know. She'd chaired the committee in her ridiculously sparse free time after scoring the honor the prior year. Her sincere smile wiped some of the fatigue from her eyes. "I can't tell you anything officially, but...congratulations. You'd be better off snagging that now than hunting for something in a few weeks. It'll be gorgeous with your tattoos."

Kayla took two steps toward the shop door before hesitating.

"Go on." Morgan shooed her. "Maybe it's not as expensive as it looks."

They both laughed at that one.

"Okay, okay." Morgan sighed. "How about this... I'm sure it's worth every penny."

It would be a splurge and a half considering the reputation of the boutique, which featured the latest summer fashions in the ornate window display. Still, she couldn't help herself. "I'm telling Dave this is all your fault."

"He's going to thank me when he sees you wearing that masterpiece." Morgan lagged behind as Kayla dashed up the handful of stairs leading into the store.

Miracles did happen. They had her very un-Devon-petite size right there on the front of the rack. Kayla slipped her head through the trapezoid formed by a wooden hanger as well as the straps and bodice of the stunning handkerchief dress she'd drooled over from afar. Up close, it stole her breath.

She giggled as she spun around in search of a changing room, loving the flare of the airy material. Brilliant colors flashed in several mirrors, which hung on the backs of open doors nearby, causing a kaleidoscope effect.

In one of the frames, Kayla glimpsed Morgan sinking to her knees.

"Mo!" She rushed to her friend's side. "Are you all right? What's going on?"

From a foot away, she detected the shaking of Morgan's hands and the unnatural sheen of sweat on her greenish-gray skin. Clamminess greeted her fingers when she laid them on her friend's brow.

Eyelids scrunched shut, Morgan leaned on the

shoulder Kayla lent her. "Sorry. Crap. I thought my dizziness was fading away."

"You're not well." Kayla conducted a mental inventory of the homeopathic remedies lining the shelves in the apothecary at her resort. "How long have you felt like trash? Why didn't you tell me?"

"I'm scared," she whimpered.

The plaintive wisp of audible agony broke Kayla's heart. "It's going to be fine. I'll take you to the doctor. Right now, if you're good to stand up."

"Can I help you?" the salesperson hovering over them asked from more than ritual this time. "Should I call security? There's a nurse's station in the main building."

"No, no." Morgan rose to wobbly legs. She clutched Kayla's arm hard enough to leave bruises. "I'm fine, really. Just...a spell."

The shopkeeper ignored the protest, flicking her concerned glance to Kayla for a ruling.

"Mo... Have you missed your period yet?" The time for pussyfooting around had passed. "Are you..."

"She's pregnant! Of course." The helpful woman perked up, her face illuminating as she clasped her hands over her heart. "Oh, dear, don't worry. This is perfectly normal. Is this your first?"

"Well, I'm not sure yet." Moisture gathered at the corners of her eyes. "I...I hope."

"Honey, I have five brats of my own." The loving tone belied her disparagement of the kids. "The glow in your cheeks is like a neon sign flashing *Preggers! Preggers!* I should have spotted it right off. Here, breathe deep. The heat isn't going to be your friend for a while. Make sure you're eating regularly too."

Kayla stripped the dress from where it'd nearly

strangled her in her mad dash. She sighed as she pivoted, intending to replace the garment. There were more important things than the most beautiful outfit in the world.

"Wait." Morgan looked as if she'd fight the kind woman dishing out conventional wisdom like turkey at Thanksgiving. "We'll take the dress."

"I didn't even try it on."

The shopkeeper exchanged a conspiratorial eye roll with Morgan. "It might as well have been made for you."

"Please." Morgan didn't often beg. "It's the very least I can do after ruining your day off. You take even less of them then I do."

"You didn't—"

"I did."

Kayla was stunned into silence. Right there in the middle of the boutique, Morgan—practical, fierce, independent, tough, Morgan—burst into tears. "I'm sorry. Was a bitch all day. You should have slapped me. But instead you bought me ice cream. Twice."

A hiccup interrupted the mangled admission.

"Now that's a friend." The shopkeeper plucked the dress from Kayla. She floated behind the furniture-quality display case supporting a gilded, old-fashioned cash register as if hysterical women had epic meltdowns in the middle of her sophisticated showroom all the time. "This one is on me. You two are the highlight of my Monday. When you wear it, just make sure people know where you found it. Better than a billboard, I swear. Women everywhere will want to emulate your style."

Before Kayla could protest, the woman had swaddled the dress in impressive tissue paper origami and tucked it into an artsy box. She wrapped the package in a bow of some organic material then pressed it into Kayla's hands.

"Wow. I don't know what to say." Her brows climbed.

"Th-thank you." Morgan sniffled.

"You're very welcome, dear." The woman joined them once more, this time extending a wire and bead box concealing mundane Kleenexes. "Go ahead, blow your nose. Take a few spares. The weepy phase can snap back on you."

Morgan accepted her advice with an exceptionally unladylike noise that reminded Kayla of something she'd heard during a show Dave had watched about rhinoceroses on National Geographic. Probably best to keep that thought private.

"Best of luck." The owner ushered them to the door. "Mind the stairs. And come back soon. I'd like to know if you're having a boy or a girl. I'm guessing boy. They always wreaked havoc on my system. What else is new?"

Kayla wrapped her arm around Morgan's waist and took the stairs slowly, in lock-step with her friend. When she looked up, she caught the shopkeeper waving to them and smiled.

"See, there are benefits to having a hormonal, decrepit, freakazoid pal, huh?" Morgan rested her head on Kayla's shoulder as they wound their way to the parking lot. They stopped at the bench Kayla had indicated earlier and two others along their route so Morgan could catch her breath.

"Mo, you're not driving like this." Kay broke the silence that had stretched between them. She couldn't forget her friend's earlier admission... *I'm scared.*

"Okay."

"And when we get to your place, you're going to take a pregnancy test." She squeezed the other woman's hand. "I'll stay with you. Or we can wait for Joe if you'd rather him be there. I know you're afraid of bad news, but you have to be sure. There are things your baby needs from you—"

"*If* there's a baby," Morgan whispered.

"Yes, if..." Kayla wouldn't hurt her friend unintentionally if things didn't turn out like she was almost positive they would. She honestly couldn't believe Joe hadn't made his wife take the test already. True, they'd both been damaged by the disappointments of the past year. Neither was eager to hurt themselves, or the other, again. Still, the insanity had to end.

"I think all the tests I have are expired by now." Morgan sighed as Kayla handed her into the passenger side of her hybrid sedan. "I'd rather not detour on the way home. Not feeling so great. Need to lie down. Somewhere quiet, dark, cool. Please, Kay. Can we hurry? Maybe one of the guys could make a run?"

"No problem. They're going to have to pick up your car anyway. Let me give them a call. I'll have them stop then meet us at your apartment, okay? You can take a little nap while we wait."

"Good idea." Morgan's eyes were already closed, her head tipped back against the rest.

Kayla shut the door, then whipped her phone out of her purse. She monitored Morgan through the glass. Speed dial had her connected to her husband in less than a second.

"Hey, sexy."

"Dave."

"Ah shit. It's not *that* kind of call, huh?" He laughed. When she didn't, he caught on. "What's wrong?"

"It's Morgan." She tried to explain quickly so he didn't panic. "She's all right. But we went to the mall, and she's acting... Well, like Kate did at first, I guess. Crazy emotions. Tired. Sick. Cranky. Just off. I'm taking her home."

"Joe! You'd better come down here." Dave's shout was muffled, as though he held the heel of his hand over the mouthpiece.

They arranged for the guys to swing by to collect Morgan's car and the supplies. Kayla pressed her hand to the butterflies in her stomach. If she felt this unsteady, Morgan must be a mess. She said goodbye and wrapped their call quickly, jogging to the driver's side and slipping in. Only then did she realize she hadn't told Dave she loved him like she usually did when they spoke. There'd be plenty of time tonight to make sure he realized how much she appreciated his reliability. No matter what, he always made her feel safe.

"Okay, everything's set. A half hour or so, and all will be just fine. You'll see." Kayla rambled the rest of the way home though Morgan never once responded. Dozing or not, she seemed to relax at the news of her husband's impending arrival.

Kayla could definitely relate.

Joe dodged the headlock Dave attempted to put him in. Noogies wouldn't relieve the knots in his guts.

"Looks like you're going to be a dad, buddy. Your wild days are done."

"Huh. Not if I have anything to say about that." Mike saved Joe from Dave and Neil, who danced around him, whooping, tossing light punches and hollering. "Guys. Tone it down until we know something for sure."

"Thanks." Joe bit the inside of his cheek and nodded. He couldn't stand it if they all had to go through the disappointment he'd endured for close to a year. Too many false alarms had him on edge. Could this be the time? Terrified to hope, he couldn't squash the spark of optimism catching fire inside him.

"You got it." Mike slapped him on the shoulder. "You and Dave head out. We'll be right behind you as soon as we stash the supplies inside. Don't need any of this lumber walking off before we get back tomorrow morning."

Sounding like a broken record but not caring, Joe said, "Thanks," again.

His lips were numb and his fingers beat an irregular rhythm on his ripped jeans as he loped to Dave's truck. His wingman never strayed from his side. The rest of the crew cheered them on, shouting good luck in their wake.

Joe reached Dave's monster black pickup first. He didn't ask before opening the driver's side door. Without something to do he'd go crazy by the time they reached their wives. The pair piled into the cab. Dave tossed the keys across the bench seat. Joe snagged them in one hand, jammed them in the ignition and backed out of the new paver driveway they'd laid last week fast enough to chirp the tires. "Whoa there buddy, no sense in wrecking now. Things are finally going your way, remember?"

The click of Dave's seatbelt echoed in the space between them.

Joe nodded, taking a shaky breath. He fastened his

own harness, then moderated his speed to something he wouldn't go to jail for if a cop spotted him.

"It's gonna work out, Joe." Dave slapped Joe's thigh hard enough to leave a bold handprint beneath the denim. "This time next year, you're gonna be exhausted, broke and wrapped around your kid's eensy-weensy finger. I have a feeling."

The big man had pulled his psychic shit one too many times for his friends to dismiss his intuition easily. Somehow that only accelerated the pounding of Joe's heart. What if... "Dave?"

"Yeah, man."

"Am I ready?"

Raucous laughter ricocheted around the truck. "Kind of late to wonder that isn't it?"

Joe couldn't answer past the tightness of his lips.

"Shit, shit. Sorry." Dave rubbed his flat belly. "Right. You're not joking. This is like me freaking out at my wedding, remember?"

"No. I mean, yes. I remember. But they're nothing alike." Joe took his eyes from the road long enough to laser a stare at Dave. "That was ridiculous bullshit. Standing there at the edge of the resort, waiting for Kayla, you lost your mind. Babbled like a crazy man. Not good enough, not rich enough, not hung enough. Whatever. That last one killed me, by the way. How much bigger could one cock get?"

"Exactly." Dave shifted his muddy boots on the thick rubber mat. "Not my finest moment. Don't pull that shit on me now. You're going to be a kickass father. And if you're really lucky, you'll have a son so you can rub it in Mike's face."

Joe couldn't help but laugh. As usual, his friends knew

exactly the right thing to do to shake things into perspective. He flipped on the turn signal, taking the exit to the artsy-fartsy mall the girls preferred over the department stores he'd have frequented. In, out, done—unless he was picking out something special for Morgan.

Maybe he should have gotten her a present just in case. He'd work on a surprise for her after they verified... After it was really real.

But in his heart, he knew Dave was right.

He hoped they had halfway decent flowers at the drugstore.

"Okay, I'll stop somewhere and get the stuff." He slipped from the truck, leaving it running as Dave came around the hood. "I know where they keep the tests in each store in a ten mile radius at this point. I'll run in, and be right behind you. Tell Morgan I love her."

Dave grinned and saluted. "Sure will. I'll probably beat you by an hour or two with you driving that recycled tin can."

Joe shook his head as he bent to move the seat back at least a foot in Morgan's hybrid sedan. She loved the miniature neon green car so much he didn't have the heart to suggest she upgrade to something a little more peppy or spacious. Though she might have to soon. He was finding out from Mike that a baby required a ton of shit they'd never considered.

The rumble of Dave's truck pulling away yanked Joe from his vision of a cute toddler with Morgan's eyes, who smashed a plastic toy hammer against his car seat, and everything else he could reach.

With a smile, he slid behind the wheel, then puttered off to the drugstore.

"You've got to be kidding me." Joe stared at the empty slot on the shelf where the pregnancy tests should have been piled fourteen boxes high.

"Sorry, sir." A zit-faced teen in a smock with a giant store logo printed on it looked up from where he was slashing tape with his box cutter. "There was a recall on the store brand and the others sold out. I heard they have some down at the supermarket on the corner."

"Right. Damn. Okay, thanks." He jammed his hands in his jeans and turned Morgan's keys over and over across his knuckles. This was the third unsuccessful stop he'd made so far. What were the odds of that?

Rather than waste time with the lights and fighting soccer moms in enormous SUVs for spots, he dashed out of the store and down the block. He zoomed around displays, a motorized cart blocking most of the walkway and a pallet of two-liters temporarily parked at the entrance to the feminine hygiene aisle. It was like some bizarre nightmare, trying to swim upstream to a place every man dreads being sentenced to in the first place.

There at the end of the aisle, he spotted the purple and white box of the test brand Morgan preferred. He stood on the bottom shelf, ignoring its ominous creaking, and reached to the back of the top row, snagging the lone survivor.

Score!

He grinned as he sprinted for the check out. Of course, when he got there, it seemed only one lane had anyone working and that cashier had a huge yellow *In Training* ribbon on her apron. The line looked long enough to stretch the whole length of the Great Wall of China. Twice.

Joe worked hard to never in his life be *that* guy. The asshole his dad had been so many times he could recall. It took every ounce of his patience to keep from growling until shoppers scattered and cleared the way.

The lady in front of him turned her head. Blue-gray curls bounced as she not-so-subtly eyed the package in his hand. With the brashness only age could generate, she peered up at him from somewhere near belly button height and shook her finger. "I hope you intend to take care of your girl."

He tried not to grin, but couldn't help it. "I swear, ma'am. My *wife* is the most amazing woman on the planet. I'm lucky to have her."

"Good boy." She patted his arm.

Some punk chose then to squeeze past, so intent on texting on his iPhone or posting a picture of the outrageous line on Facebook, accompanied by some smartass caption, that he bumped into the lady. She stumbled, but Joe kept her upright.

"Watch where you're going, kid." Joe's bass had the boy turning, eyes wide, before he hustled off into the crowd.

"I didn't think there were gentlemen like you left in the world." The granny beamed. "I'd say your wife is pretty lucky herself, son."

"Ma'am." A manager approached them. "I can take you over here so you don't have to stand in line."

"Thank you." She nodded once, then swiped the pregnancy test from Joe more deftly than he would have imagined possible. "My son and I appreciate that."

The wink she tossed in his direction caught him off guard. He laughed, then hurried to keep up with her surprisingly swift pace. In the end, she even refused to let him pay for his item or the single red rose he'd selected from the checkout station.

"Best of luck." Mildred, his new BFF, blew him a kiss when he finished packing her groceries in her trunk.

"Thanks!" He smiled as he trotted back to Mo's car. He glanced at his watch. Holy crap, that had taken about a decade longer than he'd hoped. Thank God for Mildred.

He hopped the guardrail dividing the lots, only to find a three-wheeled, blue-and-white meter-maid-mobile, light flashing, parallel to Morgan's ride. "No, no, no."

"I'm afraid so." The petite woman spiked one hand onto her hip as though to ward off a verbal assault he didn't intend to launch. "This lot is for customers of the Drug Shop only."

"I don't suppose it would do me any good to tell you about how I tried to buy a pregnancy test there except they were all out, so I had to go to the supermarket instead?" He sighed, resigned to his fate. If he had to endure the shitstorm of a lifetime in order to find a rainbow at the end of this day, he'd do it a million times over.

Hell, this would make a good story to tell his kid someday.

"Don't waste your breath." She shook her head. "Want to pay this here and now or through the mail?"

"Does it take longer to pay now or for you to give me some kind of voucher?" He reached for his wallet.

"Normally, I'd say paying now is faster, but our wireless credit card doohickey's been on the fritz." She shrugged. "You can take your chances. Heh. Maybe you already did that. Doesn't look like your luck is so great."

Joe tried not to glare. "Not that it's any of your

business... I'm praying this test is positive. Write me the ticket. Quickly. Please."

She snagged a pen from her clipboard and scratched away at the triplicate forms. Joe's teeth gritted with each swipe of her pen. How much info could there be on that damn paper?

He peered over her shoulder. Only halfway finished. Shit!

"Quit breathing down my neck, buddy." It might have been his imagination, but her writing seemed to slow. He shuffled backward, tapping his foot when he reached his new outpost.

In a few seconds, she was scribbling along the line on the bottom, some indecipherable signature worthy of a doctor. "Here you go. Have a nice day."

"I'm trying," he snarled.

"Never any love for the meter maid." She shook her head in chagrin.

Joe paused, half-crumpled into Mo's tiny car. "You're right. I'm sorry. That was shitty of me. Enjoy the rest of your day too."

"Hope your girl has a bun in the oven." She tucked herself into the mini-wagon, outrageously blanketed with flower stickers and pastel stripes, then toodled off down the street. It had to suck having a job no one appreciated. He'd give her that.

Banging his head on the steering wheel, he hauled out his cell and dialed Dave. After the third beep, he gave up. Either the guy was driving on the highway and didn't hear the AC/DC ringer he refused to give up or he was already at the house, taking care of their women.

Probably the later.

I'm coming, Mo. Hang in there. Joe flipped on the radio

as he merged into traffic on the side street, debating whether or not to risk the beginnings of rush hour on the freeway or stick to ground roads. He checked the flow of traffic over the railing of the bridge heading out of the main part of the city, toward Sweet Treats and the small yet lush apartment he shared with the love of his life, and maybe their child.

Red lights snaked along the pavement like a bold satin ribbon. He swore and jerked the wheel with a cursory glance in the side mirror, avoiding getting trapped in the jam. Holy hell, that had been close. In his rearview, he caught sight of emergency vehicles. Their sirens ballooned then wailed, distorting as they passed him by.

Joe cursed the delay, but stopped to let another batch of emergency trucks, these heading from the other direction, join the ambulance. Probably some douchebag —on his cell phone, not paying attention—jacking everyone up. They should fine dumbasses like that for imposing on everyone else. How many times had he been snagged in the aftermath of a senseless collision on his way home from a job site?

Joe eased off the shoulder, still shaking his head.

Finally, finally, *finally* he swung onto their cute little street with its adorable row houses. Most of them hosted businesses on the first level. He zipped around to the garage in the back, then took the stairs two at a time with the paper bag crumpled in his fist and Morgan's rose tucked into the front pocket of his work shirt.

Kayla met him in the entryway with a smile and a big hug. He almost crushed his friend's wife. Relief at finally being here, home, spread through him. They could survive anything as long as they stood together. The crew. His family.

"Morgan's napping," she kept her voice low. "It won't hurt to wait another hour or so until she wakes up, will it?"

Joe laughed. After all that. All his rushing. All his stress and the hijinks of his journey. Just to wait some more. If he could lie beside his lover—friend and wife—hold her and hang on to her, nothing else mattered. He'd delay an eternity as long as he had her.

"No. No rush." He rubbed Kayla's shoulders. "Thanks so much for helping her. I can't tell you what it means to know you're watching out for her."

"No different than she would do for me. Any of the crew, you know." She smiled.

"Speaking of, where's Dave hiding?"

"I thought he was with you." Kayla tilted her head, her brows drawing together.

"Nope. He dropped me off at the mall. Long story. Way long. It took forever to get the test and..." Unease tingled at the base of Joe's neck. "Wait, he's really not here yet?"

The delays had cost Joe at least half an hour, maybe more.

"Joe?" Kayla's hands trembled where the clenched his arms.

His cell phone already halfway to his ear, he pasted on his best imitation of calmness. "Probably just stuck in traffic. I heard the highway is snarled."

It seemed as if years passed while he listening to ringing. Once, twice...

Then a man who was definitely not Dave answered. "This is North Side Emergency Crew #157. Are you a direct family member of Mr. David Rosewood?"

The flashing lights.

The backed-up traffic.

The accident on the highway.

It all came together with sick certainty in Joe's heart. He flashed cold as ice. Terrified, he bent in half. The white paper bag holding the pregnancy test fell to the floor, forgotten. Joe braced himself with one hand on his knee while the other clutched his cell.

Kayla screamed in the background.

"Yes." He whispered something close to the truth. "I'm his brother."

"There's been an accident." The no-nonsense voice barked out instructions that resonated through the panic in Joe's soul. He noted the hospital the man indicated, repeating it back as commanded.

"Is Dave okay? What happened?" Joe probed for details.

"I can't give you that information over the phone. Hell, I'm not even supposed to have answered. But I got a family too. Meet your brother over at the hospital. Get there fast as you can. And if you believe in praying, you might want to try that. We're doing everything we can."

Joe still held the disconnected phone, staring at the screen while Kayla alternated biting the knuckles of her fist and pummeling his shoulders. No matter the pain she inflicted, he couldn't seem to unfreeze. Until a tired, weak imitation of Morgan's voice called from their bedroom doorway. He peered over his shoulder at her, scrambling to stretch himself upright.

"What's happening?" She pressed her hands to her stomach. "I thought I heard yelling."

"It's Dave." Joe couldn't believe he got the two syllables past the bile and terror swirling in his throat. "There's been an accident. It's bad."

"Oh, God." Morgan reached out to steady herself on the jamb, but Joe saw her losing the battle with gravity.

He dove toward his wife, cradling her against his chest as she fainted. But the motion left Kayla alone. Without him to block her, she charged out the door. He couldn't be in two places at once. Refusing to fail his friend in this too, he deposited Morgan gently on the sofa, then chased after Kay.

5

Kayla's world instantly leeched of all color, life and happiness. Black and white shapes swirled around her. She could think of nothing but closing the distance between her and her soul mate.

Dave needed her. She should never have ignored the discordant rumblings in her gut when he hadn't answered her call or texts. He never failed to know when she needed him.

Horror the likes of which she'd never experienced before drove her to fly down the stairs. She didn't care that she slipped on one of the risers. The descent went quicker as she slid, twisting her ankle just a bit.

"Whoa, there." Neil absorbed the full impact of her weight and the momentum she'd gathered as she tumbled. He staggered a few steps, but didn't fall. Instead, he blanketed her in the warmth of his sinewy arms. "Where's the fire?"

James and Devon giggled from behind their partner.

The lighthearted tinkle didn't linger when they caught

sight of her face. Tears streamed down her cheeks. She wouldn't have known except Devon tucked in beside her mate and reached up, brushing them away with her thumb. "Oh no, Morgan wasn't really pregnant?"

"No," Kayla sobbed.

"Shit." Neil brushed his chin over her head, trying to comfort her. "That blows, but we can try again. It'll be fun."

No amount of thrashing could break Kay free of the prison of his embrace. Too strong for his own good, he didn't realize he trapped her. She wasn't proud, but she bit him. Hard.

"Ouch! Damn." He let go, buffing the ache she'd inflicted. "What—?"

"It's not that." Devon understood. She lunged for Kayla's wrist, wrapping her fingers around it. "Something else is fucked up. Wait. Kay. Let us help you. Tell us how. Anything. Just not on your own."

James approached from the other side, speaking calmly, his hands held palms-out as though she were a wild animal. "We're not stopping you. Just want to go with you. We'll drive. You're too upset. Where are we going?"

"H-hos-pital." She surrendered an undignified screech.

"Oh, no." James encroached on her space. "Dave. His truck isn't here."

"Acc—" Her teeth chattered so hard she couldn't say the rest. She didn't have to.

"Okay, okay. In the car, honey." James ushered her into the backseat while Neil bolted for the apartment to snag the keys. Joe collided with him at the top of the landing. They discussed for two seconds before disappearing into the apartment.

Soft hands angled Kayla's face toward Devon, who snuggled up to her side on the bench seat. "Focus on me for a second. We're going to get through this together. I'm going to ask you some questions, yes or no. Just nod if you can, okay?"

Kay's nod came out more like a jerk.

"Good, good." Devon petted her all over. She might have enjoyed the bold caresses from the usually timid woman any other time. Her system was attuned to the touch. Comfort permeated the shell of ragged emotions hardening around her.

"We're going to the hospital, right?"

Kayla bobbed her head hard enough to fling tears onto her shirt. She didn't worry for one second about what Devon would think of that. The other woman offered unconditional support, and Kayla intended to seize it with both trembling hands.

"Which one, sweetheart?" Devon might have been the smaller of the two, but she still managed to rock Kayla, hugging her tight.

"S-Sa..."

"Shit, sorry. St. Anthony's?" Dev supplied the missing link.

Kayla nodded again. Before she could get frustrated by the delay, the door beside her opened. Joe stood there with a floppy Morgan in his arms.

"Ah, crap." Devon tugged on Kayla's belt loops, dragging her to the center of the backseat. "Looks like we need to make some room. Squeeze in next to me, Kay. We can fit. Not much different than piling into your bed that time after the guys went ice fishing."

All Kayla could remember was the heat and pressure of Dave, riding her from behind, sheltering her after the storm of their passion had rained out. Oh God. What would she do without that? He had to be okay. She would know if he wasn't. Surely if the bright flame of his spirit had extinguished, she would have died along with him, their hearts so entangled that a visceral bond had formed.

She buried her face in Devon's neck and sobbed. Huddled close as could be, they sank when the seat dipped behind her as Joe somehow must have contorted himself into the backseat, still cradling his groggy, though conscious, wife. James and Neil claimed the front.

"St. Anthony's," Devon muttered to one of her men.

Kayla couldn't bother to look up long enough to see which drove them to find out her fate. She guessed it was Neil when James spoke low, yet urgently, into his phone. "Mike. Yeah, not good. No. We don't know about the baby yet. But... It's Dave. There's been an accident. It's serious. No other news. Meet us at St. Anthony's."

Devon reached around to buckle herself in then help Kayla with her seatbelt. Dave was always so conscious of safety. She could only hope today had been no exception. This extended family of hers was her world, but without Dave, there was no universe to exist in.

She hiccupped, struggling to draw in a breath despite the stars dancing behind her lids. Dave needed her, she had to be strong for him.

Don't give up, Dave.

I'll be with you soon, I promise.

I would take your pain if I could.

You're not alone. Never.

I swear I'll do everything I can to help you.

Just don't surrender.

I can't live without you.

Please. Please. Please.

Thoughts rolled through her mind. Rapid, strong and endless, her litany drowned out anything her friends attempted to communicate. All she understood was that they were there. By her side.

Dev squeezed her fingers and Joe did his best to shelter both Morgan and her with the angle of his broad body. James shifted in his seat to lay a palm on her knee. She didn't look up again until the car screeched to a halt under the portico of the emergency ward of the hospital.

Then she practically climbed over Devon to exit first.

James and Dev each grabbed one of her hands. They ran beside her through the automatic doors and skidded to the first nurse's station in sight, relieved to find Mike and Kate playing good cop, bad cop with the harried woman behind the polished glass island.

"Here. See." Mike held out his arms for Kay. "This is his wife."

"And the rest of you are his *brothers*? Short, tall, blond, brunette, skinny and ripped?" She *hurrumphed* as she scanned their features. Neil and Joe straggled in. "What do we have here? A long-lost sister too? What's wrong with that girl?"

Joe held Morgan so the nurse could inspect her. Despite her weak protests, he didn't seem like he planned to set her down any time soon. "My wife fainted. And I think she might be pregnant. Please help?"

"Oh, you kids are just making my day." The thick, older woman shook her head. Her cheeks might have gotten more colorful. The sexy café-au-lait shade of her skin made it more difficult to tell. She shouted over her shoulder. "Mel, we need a bed. Pronto. As soon as we send the rest of this gang to the trauma waiting room."

"Trauma? What does that mean? Somebody please tell

me something." Kayla begged for more information. She peeked at the nurse's nametag. "Anything, Ms. Ofelia."

"Your guy is in surgery, honey." Her gruff exterior melted around the edges. "This is where I'm supposed to say I don't know squat and tell you to wait it out, but I'm not going to bullshit you. I chatted up one of the EMTs in the break room. He looked as if he'd spent a day digging a ditch with his bare hands. Exhausted, you know? Sometimes we give everything we have to this place, to our patients, and it's not enough. He had that look. Things are grim. They almost lost your husband a few times in the ambulance on the way here."

Kate cried out. Mike drew her close to his side, chaffing her arms until she nodded, inhaling slow and deep through her nose.

"He bled a ton. If he weren't such a beast of a man, he probably wouldn't have stood a chance at all. They got him patched up as best they could. His left leg is causing the most concern right now. They might not be able to save it. And if they can, it won't be pretty. I'm sorry."

His leg? Kayla couldn't give a shit right then. "But Dave? He..."

"You're going to have to wait and see. Even after all that, they're gonna have to run a battery of tests. No telling what else got banged up that they can't see straight off. We can't issue guarantees here, I'm sorry. It was a horrible accident. They're giving him every chance they can. Now he has to fight."

"He will." Mike spun from Kate to brace Kayla with one hand on each of her shoulders, his elbows locked. "You hear me? He will battle with every breath to stay with you. Do not give up on him. He's stubborn and strong. You'll see."

"Listen to your friend. Errr, brother-in-law." Ofelia scrunched up her nose. "Whatever you want to call him. I've been around long enough to know a person's soul makes all the difference. And if you're part of our patient's, then you fight with him."

"I will. I am." Kayla nodded, straightening her spine. Neil, James, and Devon flanked her.

"Good." The nurse pointed down a long hall glowing with florescent lights. "Third left, follow the signs. The surgeon will come find you as soon as he's finished. Don't get antsy. If things go well, it's gonna take quite a while. Quick news is bad news in this case."

Kayla gulped, then nodded.

The crew led her away.

"Not you." Ofelia's arm shot out, stopping Joe. "Bring your girl in here. We'll straighten her out and see if you're going to be a dad. Sound like fun?"

"Yeah." Joe didn't try to hide the tear that plopped onto Morgan's forehead, rousing her a bit more.

"Oh, Joe." She alarmed him when she couldn't seem to say more than that.

"Was that a happy one, or the scared shitless variety?" Ofelia asked him quietly.

"Maybe some of both." He sniffed discretely. "Hoping to grow our family. Not shrink it."

"I'm rooting for you too." The nurse patted his shoulder as they veered off from the rest of the crew. "You kids seem like you deserve to catch a break. But you're a hell of a lot luckier than most I encounter. You've got some crazy thing between you. Not everyone has a support group that tight. You're going to be okay, no matter what happens here today. Trust me."

Joe swallowed hard. "I'm trying."

He set Morgan gently on the gurney, sighing as Ofelia shooed him back a few paces. Morgan's fingers slipped through his, barely clinging when he withdrew. He winced when he watched Ofelia hook Morgan to all kinds of machines and swallowed hard when she inserted the needle with the IV beneath Morgan's delicate skin, though she didn't even flinch.

"Oh, sweet stuff. You're gonna have to toughen up. If she's preggo, you'll see a hell of a lot worse than that in the next nine months." The nurse chuckled. "Nothing we can't fix here, kids. Fatigue, dehydration and likely some wacky hormone crapola. Look at how I can pinch the skin on her hand and it stays. I'm guessing she's been suffering a few bouts of sickness and hasn't wanted to worry your fine ass."

"Is that true?" Joe canted his head.

Morgan didn't deny it. Her lids fluttered closed instead.

Joe didn't bother pursuing the topic. Especially not when she visibly relaxed, her breathing evened out and some of the lines around her eyes vanished.

Another woman entered the room, wheeling a cart of supplies. She was young, pretty, blonde, and something about her niggled Joe's memory. *Please, don't let her be a chick the crew played with.* He honestly couldn't remember some of them. They hadn't been Mo. That's all he knew.

"Oh, Morgan!" The woman rushed to the bed and started flipping through the mostly blank charts, assessing the situation for herself.

"You know this girl?" Ofelia perked up. She snatched

a few items off the cart, then worked efficiently doing things Joe couldn't quite see. "Today just gets better and better."

"I went to school with her." She waved smelling salts beneath Morgan's nose, then began to talk low and sweet. "Hey there, Mo. It's Melody Cramer."

Melody. Oh, yeah. Joe had met her at a barbecue once.

"Mel?" Morgan's lashes fluttered as she struggled to stay awake. "Where am I? What are you doing here?"

"Your sexy husband brought you to see me. Seems like you might have passed out on him." She smiled at Morgan. "I thought you told me he was treating you right, huh? Is that any way to repay him?"

"Joe." Morgan reached out.

He clasped her fingers, trying not to disturb the tube protruding from her hand. Ofelia seemed too engrossed in her fiddling on the cart to chide him for interfering. "Right here, baby."

"*Baby.* Accident. Dave." Morgan gasped. Clarity returned to her eyes in a flash. She tried to sit up. The three of them restrained her.

"One thing at a time, girly." Ofelia petted Morgan's hair. She filled in Melody as well as reassuring Morgan. "Your friend is in surgery. There's nothing to know yet. He's strong and he has the rest of his *brothers* to watch out for him. You gotta work on yourself here a bit so you can help and not hinder. Got it?"

Morgan nodded, tears sliding down her cheeks. "Dave."

"You know, I've seen a lot of families in my time here. Not everyone loves their in-laws like you." Ofelia leveled a stare between Joe and Morgan.

Melody saved them from explaining when she

presented Morgan with the infamous pee stick. "I assume you know what to do with this?"

"Yeah," Morgan sighed. "We've been trying for a long time."

Joe helped his wife to the restroom. She clutched the pole on her IV bag, and they awkwardly trundled off to take care of business. Once they'd suffered through the ordeal and toddled back to the hospital bed, both of them had grown silent. Afraid to see the giant magic negative on the test they'd become so familiar with.

A minute or two passed while they resettled Morgan, adjusting her and helping her get comfortable once more. "Melody." Morgan cleared her throat. "Can I ask you a favor?"

"Oh Lord." Ofelia slapped her forehead with her hand. "Do I have to leave the room? Why does indulging patients always mean breaking the rules?"

"Maybe you'd better." Joe had a feeling he knew what Morgan was after.

"Shush." Melody flapped her hand at Ofelia. "You're the first in line to buck tradition around here."

"Good." Joe nodded. "Because I think my wife is about to ask you..."

"*If* I'm pregnant—"

"You are." Ofelia whipped the test with a bright, cheery plus sign out for them to see, clasped between her gloved fingers. "Congratulations."

Joe couldn't help himself. He knocked the nurses aside and smothered Mo in hugs and kisses worthy of a homecoming after a decade absence. "I love you, cupcake."

"Love you too." She sniffled.

He laid his hand on her belly. "And mini cupcake."

Melody bawled at their display, and in his peripheral vision, even Ofelia seemed to knuckle away a tear.

"So...since I *am* pregnant." Pride resonated from Morgan's triumphant declaration. "What I wanted to know—"

"Yes?" Melody glanced from Morgan to Joe to Ofelia and back.

"—is when are you able to determine paternity? Can you tell me who the father of the child is?"

Melody opened and closed her mouth. Twice.

Even Ofelia seemed speechless.

They both looked at Joe as if they expected him to render the hospital to rubble, leveling the whole place right down to its foundation.

"It's okay." He laughed ruefully at their shock. "I...sort of... I can't. My brothers. Dave. The one in the accident. It could be him."

"Whoo doggies." Ofelia flopped into one of the chairs near the window. "Are you trying to give me a heart attack?"

"I'm sorry, Morgan." Melody shook her head. "Absolute earliest would be ten weeks in. A few more if you can hold out for a less risky procedure."

"Okay. It doesn't matter to me, you know." Morgan squeezed Joe's hand. "This baby is ours. I just thought..."

"I understand, Mo." Joe kissed her forehead. "Anything to keep him fighting."

The beeping of the machines escalated.

"Oh no, none of that." Ofelia scolded Morgan. "Your blood pressure has to stay nice and steady to keep your little guy happy. You've got more to consider now than you or your husband or even your brother-in-law. Got it?"

Morgan nodded. She peeked up at Joe.

Despite everything, they both wore identical, shit-eating grins.

KAYLA PACED the length of the twenty-seven-and-a-half-tile-wide space. Precaution along with a healthy dose of superstition led her to avoid stepping on the black linoleum sprinkled in a mostly random pattern between the beige monotony of the rest of the flooring.

Would that make a difference in the long run? Probably not, but she would try anything at this point. Maybe she should dodge the cracks too.

She swore at least three days should have passed since they'd arrived, every racing heartbeat seeming to pump in ultra-slow motion. The clock hanging crooked on the wall proclaimed it hadn't even been four hours yet.

It killed her to be so close to Dave and yet so far away. If only she could see him, hold his hand, tell him she was there. Lend him whatever strength she could. Maybe then she wouldn't feel like she'd chugged an entire bottle of bleach. Her stomach churned when she considered how minor that pain would be compared to what Dave likely faced.

A rhythmic squeak interrupted the now familiar soundtrack of the waiting room—the crunch of Styrofoam coffee cups, people tapping their fingers or toes, snores from the elderly man in the corner and the soft murmurs of various crew members fortifying each other. Heads turned in unison toward the new stimulus.

"Hey." Morgan lifted her fingers from the arm of a wheelchair, pushed by Joe. The plastic hospital bracelet around her wrist slid higher on her thin arm. Rosy cheeks and alert eyes unwound one small tendril of anxiety from Kayla's heart.

"Feeling better?" Mike crossed to the chair and crouched so he could evaluate her up close and personal.

"Much." She leaned forward until her forehead rested on his. "Any updates?"

"Nothing." Neil joined them.

"Remember, Ofelia said that's a good sign." Joe laid one of his broad hands on Morgan's shoulder when she slumped. Kayla, James and Devon circled around their friends.

Kate approached to stand right in front of Morgan. She rubbed her own slightly rounded belly, then said softly, "Can you give us something to smile about?"

"It doesn't feel right." Morgan stared at her socked feet on the metal rests of the wheelchair.

Kayla marched over, taking up a post on the opposite side from Mike. She ordered, "Look at me."

A watery gaze lifted. Tears bulged at the corner of Morgan's eyes, threatening to fall.

"If you're pregnant, no one would be happier for you than Dave." Kayla shivered. "He's talked about it almost every night while we were falling asleep. How much he was hoping for you. How much longer we'd have to wait to find out. Please, tell me it's true. Tell me something wonderful is happening today."

James and Devon wrapped Kayla in their protective embraces. Still, everyone alternated staring at Morgan and Joe.

The tears suspended in her eyes fell, tracing silvery tracks down her cheeks. She bit her lip. Then nodded. "It's true. This time. I'm *pregnant*. It's really true."

Joe leaned forward, burying his face in his wife's neck.

If the shaking of his wide shoulders was any indication, he joined her in emotional release. His arms folded over her chest as he hugged her from behind. The guys took turns slugging him in the shoulder, slapping his back and ruffling his hair before nudging Mike out of the way to kiss Morgan's cheek.

They finally cleared away. Even Joe stood upright, giving Kayla room to approach. She leaned in and hugged her friend. "Congratulations. You're going to be a great mom. I'm so thrilled for you."

"And I'm here for you." Morgan clasped her tight enough to border on painful. "Both of you. Dave is tough. We're going to make it through. Him. And all of us too."

"Excuse me. Is Mrs. Rosewood in the room?" A doctor stood in the entryway that had only been empty—and empty and empty some more—for an eternity.

Mike threaded Kayla's arm around his elbow and escorted her to the rumpled man. His scrubs were askew, hair sticking up on end, and his face seemed pale in the harsh lights. Dark stains smattered his clothing.

After the interminable torture of not knowing, the truth suddenly frightened Kayla. She stutter-stepped. The foreman dragged her forward with his momentum. She must have whimpered.

"Come on, Kay." He squeezed her arm. "We have to find out. Hearing the truth isn't going to change anything. It is what it is. We're going to cope with it together."

"This is Kayla Rosewood." Mike presented her to the doctor. "I'm Dave's brother. We're all his brothers."

The rest of the crew huddled close behind them. Morgan and Joe tucked in the rear.

"Big family." The doctor nodded slowly. "I'm not surprised he has so much support. Ma'am, your husband is stubborn as hell. I don't think I've ever seen someone quite so determined not to give up. There were a couple very close calls. Both according to the rescue workers and from what I saw myself. I'm thrilled to be standing in front of you right now and to be able to say your husband is being moved to the ICU for recovery."

"So he's going to be fine?" She struggled to translate each phrase that drifted from the doctor's lips and decipher the repercussions his pronouncement had on her and Dave's lives. Her heart soared with hope and relief.

"I wouldn't say it like that." The surgeon sobered. He ground his hands over his face. "I assume the police haven't been in yet, since he wasn't conscious to answer questions."

Kayla shook her head no.

"Then you don't know anything about the accident?" The surgeon sighed.

Several shallow, quick breaths threatened to choke Kayla.

"You're scaring her." Mike rubbed circles on her back.

"I looked it up on the local news." James spoke up from the rear. A green cast infused his typically bronzed skin.

"You did?" She whipped her head around to stare at him. "Why didn't you show me?"

He didn't answer.

"It's that bad?" She looked between Mike and the doctor.

"All I know is he took on a semi and lost." The surgeon shook his head. "Or maybe he won. I'll let you be the judge. This I'm sure of. It's going to be a long, hard road from here. Your husband was pinned inside his car. His left leg was shattered. Tibia, fibula, kneecap—you name it. A large chunk of his calf muscle was...missing. I did all I could to save the limb. We'll have to wait until he's awake and healing to see if it worked."

"There's still the possibility—"

"I'm afraid so." He grimaced.

"Okay, okay." Kay had spent the last several hours preparing herself for this, based on the tips Ofelia had given them. "It's horrible. Terrifying. Going to be so difficult for him to not be active—"

She didn't realize she'd cut off until Mike hugged her tight and someone petted her hair from behind. She cleared her throat. "But other than his leg. He's okay, right?"

"I'm not trying to be evasive, Mrs. Rosewood. I'm sorry. The reality is we just can't be sure yet. They'll run more tests in the morning. A lot of him is too swollen for accurate imaging right now, but we think we've addressed the bleeding and isolated all the critical issues. He's banged up pretty much everywhere. A piece of the door gashed his belly. He had stitches in his face, arms, chest and... Well, there's no part of him we didn't work on except his back."

Her knees buckled.

Strong arms surrounded her, keeping her afloat through the storm of fear and pain.

"I know it may not seem like it. Not today and not six months from now, but your husband is lucky. So very fortunate to still be with us, given the situation. A few inches more of that door bending or a couple inches higher on the crushing pressure that mangled his leg or... any number of *almosts*, and we would not have been able to help him."

"Dave." Kayla cried his name over and over.

"Can we see him?" Mike asked for her.

"Once they have him in the ICU, we'll let Mrs. Rosewood in for five minutes. You—only you—can go with her. After that, you might as well go home and get some rest. You won't be able to see him again until tomorrow after his exams, and he's going to need you when he wakes up. He's stayed strong for you all, now you're going to have to carry him."

"That won't be a problem." Neil crossed his arms over his chest as if storing up his energy. "We're a crew. We stick together. That's what we're here for."

"I sort of got that sense." The surgeon smiled wanly. "You all hang tight a little while longer and a nurse will come for you. I'm heading home now. Days like today make me wish I had more time to spend with my family."

Kayla's hand shot out, latching on to the doctor. "Thank you."

"You're very welcome." He nodded.

JOE WATCHED Mike and Kayla march down the hall behind the nurse who'd come to collect them and lead them to Dave. They trundled off as if headed to the gallows, bracing themselves for whatever they might find at the other end of the journey. He wished he could get just a glimpse of his crewmate. As if that tiny contact might help one of his best friends rest more peacefully.

Tomorrow.

His pocket vibrated. He jumped. Almost anyone who would bother calling him was already in this room. After considering ignoring it, he figured what the hell? It wasn't like the tension was doing him any good without distractions. He slipped the device from his jeans and winced at the contact picture of his cousin Eli, who wore a smug grin while he held up a monster, twenty-two-inch rainbow trout he'd caught on their last ice-fishing trip.

Eli and his gang of adopted brothers plus one sister had grown close to Dave over the years, despite sporadic contact. How would Joe tell them what had happened?

"Hey." He choked out a greeting, hoping the rest came easier.

"You weren't even gonna call me with the news, dirtbag?" Laughter, not heat, infused the accusation with lightheartedness Joe couldn't comprehend.

"How'd you hear about Dave?" He plopped onto one of the molded plastic bucket seats that made him feel like a giant in a kindergarten class. With his back turned to the rest of the crew, Joe pitched his question low to avoid upsetting them any more than they already were. He dropped his head into one hand, his elbow propped on his knee, and scrubbed his fingers through his hair. "Is the footage so bad it hit the regional news? We don't know much other than that he tangoed with a semi."

"What?" Eli's tone morphed from cajoling to serious in no time flat. The hot-rodder might have mastered his cool facade, but Joe didn't have to be told Eli led his gang of mechanics with the same natural instinct Mike used to glue their crew together. The rest of Eli's shop was comprised of a motley assortment of kids from rocky pasts. His dad had rescued each of them after getting involved in his wife's community outreach program following her untimely death. They'd stuck together ever since. A blend of family, yet not. It was scary how much they reminded Joe of the crew when he got to hang out with them, which wasn't as often as he'd like, being a couple states away and all. "I was talking about Neil's fucking Facebook post that claimed he was gonna be an honorary uncle again. And James's comment that Morgan was going to kick his ass for spilling the beans. Assumed that had to be all you. Congratulations, daddy-o."

Joe glanced over his shoulder to where the youngest guy in the crew fiddled with his smartphone. Devon curled under one of his arms, reading off the screen too. Joe had assumed they were playing some brainiac word game together, as usual, to pass the time and keep themselves from going insane with worry.

"Ah, right. Yes. Dad-to-be. That's me." How could one man be so damn happy and so torn up at the same time?

He glanced over to where Morgan had dozed off on a bench, her head resting on Neil's thigh. The tall blond man stroked her hair idly, calming himself along with Joe's wife. Purple smudges still stained the skin beneath her eyes, and she huddled beneath two flannel shirts the guys had sacrificed for her. He felt as though he wanted to laugh until he cried. Again.

"Dude?"

"Ah, thank you. I can hardly believe it's finally real."

"So, not to cut the celebration short, but what the fuck did you mean about Dave?"

Rocketing to his feet, Joe stormed around the corner, frustration bubbling to the surface. "It's bad. We're in the mother fucking hospital trauma center. The waiting room. We've been here for fucking ever. Like, six hours at least. We don't know jack shit. Except that we're all about to fucking go nuts. Long story short, Dave and I left work about the same time. I had to stop and pick up the pregnancy test. It took *way* longer than I thought. When I got home, he hadn't made it yet."

A horrible noise, maybe something like a sob, tangled in his throat.

"Calm down. Deep breaths, man." Eli waited him out until he got his shit together.

"He never made it."

"Holy shit." Eli sounded like he might be running. Breath huffed from him. A heavy metallic crash could have come from the thick fire door, which separated the auto body restoration offices from the garage, slamming into the cinderblock wall.

A chorus of cheers burst through the receiver.

"Woot woot!"

"Congrats, man."

"Way to knock her up!"

Eli tried to shush them. They clearly didn't understand.

"It's not true?" That sounded like Sally, the lone girl Eli's dad had brought into their fold. Tough as nails on the outside, Joe suspected she had a gooey core not so far below the surface, if only she met the right person to crack her shell.

"It is, it is." Eli reassured them. "Alanso, clear my schedule and yours for a couple days. We're heading out there."

"What's wrong, boss?" The guys loved to rile Eli by calling him that. They'd realize things were serious when he didn't bother protesting. No time to waste.

"It's Dave. There's been an accident. Don't know much yet. At the very least we can deal with his truck, get the insurance under control and take the paperwork off their hands. We know that shit inside and out."

"You don't have to—" Joe tried to interrupt. He shouldn't have bothered.

Eli railroaded right over him. "Dude. Let us help. That's what family is for. You're going to have other shit on your plate. Double now. How is Mo, anyway?"

"Up and down." Tension crept along his neck, infusing a dull ache in the base of his skull. "The whole reason we headed home in the first place was 'cause she was acting funny at the mall. Kay called us to give us a head's up. Oh, fuck. I was so pissed off there was an accident, cursing and raving like a road-raging lunatic because it was going to make me five minutes later getting back to Morgan. I detoured. Took the back way. And all that time he was lying there, hurt. If I'd gone the other way, maybe..."

"You'd have been stuck in the miles of traffic behind him. You couldn't have helped. Not even to stand by his side. Quit it, Joe." Eli broke him from the destructive line of reasoning. "There's enough legitimate stuff to freak out about here."

"No kidding. Morgan fucking passed out when she heard the news and spent several hours getting fluids at the hospital before we joined the rest of the crew. I'm worried. The stress isn't good for her or the baby."

"See, see." Eli dropped to a hush. The background clanks and ratchet whirs died down, telling Joe he must have stepped outside. "Too much at once. We've got your back. Look, Joe. I'll never forget the summer after my mom died when you quit your league to come out here. Baseball is everything to a fourteen-year-old, especially one as good as you were. You never blinked twice. For my dad and me. You pumped gas at the station, cooked those horrible meals and did whatever you could to keep me from going crazy. Let me do this for you."

Joe swallowed hard. The times he'd sat shoulder to shoulder with his cousin while silent tears streaked down his cheeks were as vivid as if they'd happened yesterday. He hoped they didn't have to repeat those sessions in reverse. Still, it'd be nice to have that kind of support, one step removed from the pain. "Yeah. Yeah, okay."

"Great." Eli sighed. "We'll be there tomorrow around lunch. I'll call when we're closing in so you can tell us where to meet you."

"Thank you.

"You got it. Call us if...anything changes." Eli didn't have to spell it out.

They both knew what he meant.

"Will do." Joe couldn't manage more than that. He disconnected then slammed his fist into the wall. Bruised knuckles wouldn't help the situation. Still, they gave him something else to focus on. "Son of a bitch."

6

"We'll see you first thing tomorrow, okay?" Kate hugged Kayla tight enough that the bulge of her baby belly bumped into Kay noticeably.

"There's not going to be a lot for you to do. You should sleep in as long as you can." She patted Kate's back. "Don't want your little princess getting upset. Same goes for you, Mo."

Joe didn't argue. In the shadows of the hospital parking lot, she thought she detected frown lines around his sexy pout. He tucked his wife close to his chest.

"Okay." Morgan nodded before glancing at James. "As long as somebody promises to text us any updates."

"I'm on that." He tossed her a mock salute.

"Agreed then." Mike and Joe boosted their wives into Mike's extended-cab pickup. Despite everything, Kay smiled softly at the picture they made. Two young families. Everything in front of them potential.

"Sweet dreams." Kate's wish for Kayla escaped before the door shut. The women waved as they pulled away.

"Come on, sweetheart. We were thinking we'd take you to our place since it's closer. Just in case. Unless you'd be more comfortable at your cabin?"

"No. You're right, Neil." She allowed him to entwine their fingers and direct her to Morgan's car. "It's smarter to stay nearby. Plus, I just don't think I could sleep in our bed knowing he's up there…"

Neil broke her line of sight with the ultra-modern glass and chrome building, so unlike their craftsman cottage in the woods. Everything about the cold, concrete structure would repulse Dave. Neil picked her up and carried her across the remaining few steps to the vehicle. Even in the blackest hour of the night, its cheery neon paint glowed. He slid into the backseat and buckled her in before attending to his own restraint. He used his sleeve to wipe rogue tears from her face.

"S-sorry." She couldn't believe she hadn't noticed them herself. "Didn't think I had any of those left."

"You don't worry about that." Neil held her hand. "I'm sure we're all going to be taking turns with the tissues. When someone's down, the rest of us will shoulder the load for a while, okay?"

She nodded, with the pathetic amount of affirmation she could muster in opposition to the millions of inner voices shouting nothing would ever be all right again.

"Good night, Dave," she whispered, craning her neck to keep his window, or one as near as she could guess, in sight as long as possible.

Devon and James occupied the front seats. The four passengers kept quiet the entire drive to her friends' house. No one uttered a peep. Not even when they pulled in the driveway and shut off the engine. It seemed to her they all took a breath in unison, then sat, trying to muster the energy to move. Kayla might have thought she was asleep except her eyes were open and her body was quasi-responsive to her commands, if a bit sluggish and delayed. She reached for the door handle when James took action first, leaving the vehicle.

It was his turn to scoop her into his arms, surprising her as always with his deceptive strength. Though she was far from Devon's petite build, he had zero trouble subduing her token protest and toting her up to their bedroom in no time flat.

While he held her, Devon and Neil stripped out of their work clothes.

"Do you want a shower?" James paused as they neared the bathroom.

"No. Just a warm, soft bed, please." She hurt all over. Tension locked her muscles stiff enough to give the Tin Man a run for his money. Hours of gritting her teeth, endless bouts of crying and the uncomfortable furniture at the hospital hadn't helped either.

"That can be arranged." Neil smiled. Devon ran her fingers along Kayla's shoulders as she and Neil headed for the adjoining space. "We'll be back lickety-split. We were dry-walling earlier, gotta get this dust off before mussing up James's fancy sheets or he'll spank us."

Kayla nodded, though she only listened to half of what they said.

"Damn." James let her legs down gently. "You're done in. Can you stand just a minute? This will go quicker if you do. I know how much you hate clothes. These have to be bugging the shit out of you after all this time."

She wobbled but stayed upright when he released her torso and reached for the hem of her sweater.

"Lift up, honey." He nudged her into the position

required to slip her shirt over her head. Before she knew it, he'd knelt at her feet to unbutton her jeans and peel them off too. From there he probably had a great perspective on her bare essentials. She couldn't stand binding herself with underwear in addition to the rest of the garments. Unlike any other day, he didn't comment on her nudity. "There you go. Better?"

"Much." She heaved a huge sigh of relief before scratching at the dent left by the button on her jeans. When she did, something funny twinged in her shoulder. A wince tugged the corners of her mouth further south.

"Sore?" James focused on her with unflinching intensity.

"Hell, yes." She had to lie down or fall. Reaching out with one hand, she searched for the bed behind her.

James put his arm around her waist, then guided her to the lush duvet. "Roll over onto your front. I'm nowhere near as good as you, but I'll try to work out some of the knots."

"Mmph," was all she could muster. He impressed her by running his hands lightly across the surface of her skin, averaging their temperatures and assessing the greatest areas of tension to target. Maybe he had been paying attention when she'd given him lessons. Usually he practiced on Neil or Devon, which led to a lot of fooling around and not so much serious massage technique acquisition. Or so she'd thought.

The pressure of his fingers increased as he threw a thigh over her torso. Heat and softness assured her that he'd joined her in the clothes-free club for the evening. Kayla closed her eyes and took a deep breath, let it out then drew another.

"That's right." He crooned to her as he alternated

caresses with real rubbing on either side of her spine. "You're here with us, safe. We've got your back, Kayla. No matter how long or hard this journey is, we'll be with you both."

The gentle rush of water in the shower cut off. Kay drifted. Sometime after, probably not too long, the bed shifted and more hands joined James's. Damp fingers traced the caricature of Dave she'd added to her back piece as a wedding gift to the man who'd already indelibly marked her soul.

A keening whimper ripped from her throat.

"It's okay," Devon whispered in her ear. "We have you. We love you. Go ahead and cry if you want."

"Don't. Want." But still she couldn't seem to halt the steady stream of agony driving moisture from her eyes and sobs from her lugs.

Six hands roamed her body, petting her, soothing her, untangling her. Someone concentrated on her back and ass while the others paid attention to her arms starting at the top and progressing to her fingers. When they'd turned her mostly to jelly they began again, this time on her legs.

The more her body deflated, the easier the agony tore free of her. It poured out all over the soaking pillowcase like an infection draining from her core. Without them, it would have festered, eating her alive from inside.

Instead, one of her friends focused on her neck and scalp while the others erased the debilitating tautness from her thighs, knees and calves. By the time they'd touched her everywhere, imparting healing, she had cried her heart out and was left wasted.

Gasps faded to hiccups and then to sniffles. Someone wiped her nose and kissed her cheek. They had to be as exhausted as her. She reached out, surrounding a wrist with her grasp. Gauging by how her fingers wrapped around the delicate bones, it could only belong to Devon.

With a tug, she invited her friend and sometimes lover to lie beside her.

The women curled together, Devon wrapping around Kayla as she entwined them completely. James and Neil bracketed them. James snuggled up behind Devon, hugging the joined pair tight to his chest. Neil blanketed Kayla's back. He layered his long arm over all three of the people in his bed, keeping them close. The girls, at the center of their snugglefest, were protected from anything outside their tiny sphere.

"We always promised each other we'd take care of our own if it came to that." Neil kissed her cheek. "This is what Dave wanted for you. We've got you. We love you. You won't do this on your own."

"Thanks." Kayla could hardly get the whisper out. "Love you too."

She accepted Devon's tender, reassuring goodnight kiss as the world faded to black.

Together, they managed to find some solace and rest.

THE NEXT MORNING brought more endless waiting, ambiguous test results and a shitload of frustration. Dave remained unconscious. Doctors granted each of the crew members five minutes to make a quick pit stop by his bedside. Neil, James and Devon had gone in first, followed by Kate, Mike and Kayla.

Joe and Morgan waited their turn.

After precisely the prescribed visitation, Mike led Kate

and Kayla from Dave's room, one arm around each of the women. Tears streamed down his wife's cheeks.

"He had more color this morning." Kayla sniffled.

"I thought so too." Mike agreed. He rubbed his Kate's shoulder when she sobbed again.

"How could he have looked worse than that? He was so still. So different from his usual self." She slumped against Mike.

"It's okay, sweetheart. They're keeping him sedated so he can't feel anything or aggravate his injuries." Mike glanced from Kate to Joe. "Maybe you'd better hold off. It can't be good for the babies for their moms to be so upset."

"No." Morgan gripped Joe's hand hard enough to be uncomfortable. "I need to see him. To talk to him, just for a minute. I'll be okay. I swear."

"If you're not, I'm hauling you out." Joe didn't give a shit if that pissed her off. Her safety, and their child's, came first.

"Deal." Her throat flexed as she swallowed hard.

Joe braced himself for a horrifying sight. A deep breath expanded his ribcage before he consciously relaxed his muscles. Tension wouldn't help any of them. He laced his fingers tight with Morgan's, then turned the corner into Dave's room. Reality exceeded the worst nightmares his imagination had cooked up. Tubes formed macabre spaghetti that threatened to choke Dave, machines blipped in a symphony of discordant electronic music and wires attached to a sling supported Dave's left thigh in mid-air, transforming him into a ghastly marionette.

Joe had overheard the surgeon tell Kayla something about pre-operative traction for proximal femoral something-or-other fractures. He'd lost track about twenty-seven syllables in. All he'd caught was blah blah blah, multiple surgeries to correct, blah blah blah.

This...this looked bad. He hadn't ever seen something so horrific outside of a movie screen. "Holy shit."

"Oh, Dave." Morgan rushed to his side. The big man nearly overflowed the hospital bed, yet the bruises and bandages covering his face and jaw detracted from the aura of strength and vitality that usually surrounded him. She kissed her fingers, then laid them lightly on his shoulder, which appeared free of obvious damage. "I'm *so* sorry."

"What?" Joe whipped his gaze to his wife when she began muttering apology after apology to his best friend.

"If I hadn't been so afraid of taking that stupid test, none of this would have happened. I should have bucked up and done it a week ago, when I first started to suspect. I ignored the signs. I didn't rest enough. Didn't drink enough either, I guess. If I had just been responsible, you wouldn't have been driving right there, right then. I'm *so* sorry. I'll never forgive myself for doing this to you."

"Mo." Joe closed his eyes and wrapped an arm around his wife from behind, snugging her to his chest. "Don't say shit like that. It's life. Chance. If he'd stayed at the site, maybe he'd have fallen off the roof instead. No one can know what the future holds. Dave wouldn't like to hear you talking such crap."

It might have been his imagination, but Joe thought he saw Dave's eyelid twitch.

"Fine." Morgan didn't sound convinced. Still, they only had a few more minutes. They could argue later. In private. Regardless of Dave's state, Joe believed their tone of voice and any strain they harbored could affect his friend. Dave had always been very sensitive to those sorts of things. Trouble between crewmembers would set him on edge until they'd resolved their differences.

"Tell him the good news, cupcake." Joe nuzzled Morgan's hair. Their joy generated powerful positive energy, sparked by the new life embedded in Morgan's womb. Pride and tenderness swamped him.

His wife leaned in even closer, perching delicately on the edge of the bed. She took Dave's hand and, with infinite gentleness, scooted it the inch or two necessary to close the gap between his fingers and her lower abdomen. "It's true, Dave. I'm pregnant."

Neither of them had managed to say the words without shedding a tear yet. This reiteration was no exception. Morgan pressed Dave's palm to the fullness of her belly. "Thank you for all your sacrifices for me and my family. I love you. I swear I will be here every step of the way. Whatever Joe and I can do for you, we will. I hope you know that. You're strong. And you have the most gorgeous woman on Earth to come home to. Sleep tight, sweet dreams. Naughty ones too."

Joe sniffled when his wife leaned forward to kiss the man he'd considered his best friend for nearly a decade. He hadn't imagined it possible, but his adoration multiplied.

"We'll be in again as soon as they let us," Joe promised Dave. "Until then, we'll take care of Kay. Don't you worry about a thing. We've got her. Just like we always swore we would. You concentrate on healing up. Okay? See you later, masturbator."

The only response was the beep of a timer.

A nurse popped her head in the door. "I'm sorry. Mr.

Rosewood needs his rest now. You may rejoin your friends in the waiting room."

Joe nodded. "Please take good care of my brother."

"You got it, sugar." She smiled.

He collected Morgan's hand, granting her a moment to toss a lingering glance over her shoulder before they ambled along the linoleum channel toward the rest of the crew.

"You shouldn't lie to a man just because he's injured." Joe *tsked* at Morgan.

"What'd I say?" She tipped her head to the side. "You don't think he's going to be okay? Eventually, I mean. It's going to be hell. But if we don't have faith in him..."

"Not that, cupcake. You told him Kay was the most gorgeous woman on Earth. Clearly that title belongs to you." Joe tugged on her wrist until she tottered to a halt. He surrounded her in his arms, squeezing tight. "I can't believe you thought this was in any way your fault. You bottled that all up and didn't tell me? I'm disappointed, Mo. I thought we were beyond that stage. Look what happened when we avoided our emotions on the baby junk."

"Sorry." She had the decency to look ashamed. "I didn't really understand myself. The grief overwhelmed me. I just felt this horrible dread in my gut. The instant I saw him, it all unlocked, then came pouring out."

"From now on, you tell me when something's bothering you, and we'll work through it together." He wiggled his brows. "I know a great way to reduce your stress."

"Joe. Morgan." Devon waved to them from the end of the hall. "Could you come here? The police would like to ask you a few questions."

Morgan's arm tensed in his grip. "I know hearing about it won't change anything. It scares me, though. To know. To speculate about just how close we came to losing him. Plus I'm sorry, I do still feel responsible."

"We'll get to that in a minute." Joe kissed her knuckles. "If you'd rather go to the cafeteria, I can come find you when this is finished."

"Being away from you is worse." She laid her head on his shoulder even as they picked up their pace. "Let's get through this, then maybe we can go find some lunch. Even though we slept in late, I'm really wishing I could take a nap right about now."

"Remember what Ofelia said." Joe evaluated the dark rings under Morgan's eyes. "Everything about your body is different. Listen to what it's telling you. We'll take some time out. Catch a rest, okay?"

She bit her lip, then nodded.

When they rounded the corner, they found the rest of the crew, along with Joe's cousin Eli and one of his mechanics, Alanso Diaz, gathered around a young police officer. His explanation was already in process. Even he brushed a hand over his close-shaved hair before he got to the meat of the matter.

Grimacing, he turned toward Kayla. James and Neil flanked her, each man cupping one of her elbows in their dinged up hands. "Eyewitnesses corroborate the report from the skid analysis. The brakes went out on a semi. We're verifying the records now, but his rig hadn't maintained inspections. After what I saw in the field yesterday, I'd be glad to testify as an expert witness for your family. The truck hopped the barrier and came at your husband head-on. The tracks on the road show he attempted to avoid the collision and probably mitigated the impact as much as possible, but the bumper of the eighteen-wheeler caught the bed of his pickup and spun it around. The guys I talked to said they think three or maybe four cars hit him as he veered off the road."

Kayla didn't utter a single word. Her face went ashen.

Alanso cursed violently in Spanish from the rear of the group.

"What about everyone else?" Devon asked in a whisper.

The cop shook his head. "There were five fatalities. I haven't been at this all that long, four years now, but this is the worst I've seen. Hopefully for a long time. The truck jackknifed, then rolled. Driver was killed instantly. The trailer crushed a car being driven by an elderly couple who had no chance. Two of the cars that careened into your friend's truck also didn't fare as well. His skilled driving, the safe following distance the witnesses said he maintained and an epic stroke of good luck helped your friend make the best of a nasty situation. About a half dozen other people are seriously to critically injured, though it looks like all of them will pull through now. I would have been here last night, but it's been a total cluster getting this all sorted out."

Joe had to stop his train of thought when it imagined, all too vividly, those horrifying moments Dave had spent wrestling his truck through the chaos.

"When you have a chance, we'll need you to come down to the lot, take some pictures for insurance and let us know what to do with your husband's vehicle." The officer didn't sound as though there were anything to salvage.

"We can take care of that." Eli nodded when Mike looked to him and Alanso. "No problem."

Morgan trembled beneath Joe's arm. He gazed down at his wife, alarmed to find her unsteady on her feet, hooded eyes half closed. "I think Mo's had enough for now. Mike, you mind if we crash at your place for lunch and a nap since you're closest? We'll come back this afternoon for a shift with Kay."

"Really, you should all take a break." Kayla's monotone hurt Joe's heart. "There's nothing we can do now. They've declared him stable. Go ahead, Mike. Take Kate too. Eli and Alanso can meet you back there to catch up. No reason this should be all doom and gloom. You don't get to see each other often, and I can tell this is draining everyone."

"What about you?" Kate tried to protest.

"We're here. We'll stay." Neil looked to Devon and James for confirmation. The three of them stood united, keeping Kayla strong.

"Thank you," Morgan mumbled. "You're right. I feel like a wimp, not able to be a rock for you. Right now, it's just...too much."

Joe followed as she lurched for the bathroom. He didn't give a fuck about the sign marked *Ladies*. He held his wife as she lost her breakfast, rubbing her back and wiping her face with cool paper towels after the bout had passed.

"Come on, cupcake." He lifted her in his arms. "You're okay now. We're gonna go take a nice nap together."

"So sorry. Love you." She was asleep before they reached the parking lot, Mike and Kate close on their heels. The couple's identical grimaces matched Joe's.

MORGAN STRETCHED, basking in the late afternoon sun

that poured through the oversized windows in Kate and Mike's living room. Sparkles danced across the surface of the pool outside, making the walls glitter. Thank God for the privacy fence the crew had installed pronto after Mike moved in.

Someone had laid out the sprawling feather mattress in the middle of the floor. She'd pit stopped only to use the restroom, brush her teeth and strip down before collapsing onto the soft nest complete with the cozy patchwork quilt Kayla had sewn for their friends' Christmas gifts last year.

Beside her, Joe snuffled, then rolled to his side, enveloping her in the shelter of his embrace. The furnace of his chest alleviated the need for any covers. She kicked them off. Naked felt more and more comfortable to her. The crew had changed her irrevocably.

A smile spread across her face when she reached out blindly behind her. Hard, hot muscle filled her palm.

"Watch what you're grabbing there, girly. The good stuff is down and to the left." Mike's sleep-roughened drawl had her cracking up. She couldn't stop giggling. Especially not when the foreman took advantage of her sprawl to tickle the spot on her hip that set her off every time. The crew hadn't let her off the hook since they'd discovered the sensitive area.

She shrieked. Jerking around, she retaliated by pinching his nipple with just enough twist thrown in that it couldn't be entirely pleasurable.

"What's wrong?" Joe bolted upright. Fight or flight kicked in. He grabbed Morgan, tucked her beneath his arm, and searched for imminent danger.

"Calm down, tiger." Kate half-smiled around a yawn as she reached across the pile from the far side of Mike to pat

Joe's calf. A soothing litany poured from her as easily as if she'd rehearsed it a million times. "No one's coming after Morgan. You're safe. We all are. Even Dave is pulling through. There's nothing to be afraid of."

"Dave!" Morgan clutched her hands over her heart, afraid her chest might rip open when a spear of agony pierced it. Breath locked in her lungs.

"Quit it, you two. He's hanging in there." Mike switched from playful to serious in an instant. "That stubborn motherfucker is not going to quit on us. It won't be easy, but I honestly think he's going to be okay. I know it. Deep down. Don't you give up on him, okay? He deserves better from us."

"You're right, he does. So much better." Tears dripped off Morgan's jaw onto her bare breasts. "I'm a horrible damn friend. I didn't remember. I forgot he was hurt. Alone. In that awful room."

"You just woke up, Mo." Joe tipped her face toward him with two fingers beneath her chin. "After being sick and exhausted and scared shitless. Your mind is probably trying to protect you. You should let it."

Kate and Mike huddled closer, coming to kneel beside her. "Dave is never by himself. None of the crew is. We're all there with him. Thinking about him. Loving him. Even if we're not touching."

"I know you ladies probably going to rip my balls off for saying this..." Mike angled away from Kate and Morgan just a bit. Enough to put his impressive family jewels out of clawing distance when he continued, "But these pregnancy hormone jobbies... They're making you temporarily insane. I mean that in the nicest way possible. We won't hold it against you, seeing as how we adore you and all. Holy shit, though. What purpose could this possibly serve in nature? Kate's kind of coming around now. You're in the thick of it, Morgan. Right at the worst possible time. Believe me, this is not the calm, rational woman I know and love. You even said damn. You *never* curse."

"Tell them what you told me at the hospital." Joe dropped his forehead on her quivering shoulder. "I could see you didn't believe me. Get some more opinions."

"What is he talking about?" Kate took Morgan's hand. None of them were fazed by their lack of clothing anymore. They had nothing to hide from each other, she reminded herself.

A confession lodged in Morgan's throat. She had to try to several times to spit it out. "If it weren't for me, Dave never would have gotten hurt in the first place. And now I'm so fucking self-centered, all I thought when I woke up was *thank goodness I feel better*. Dave isn't going to be okay any time soon. He's not going to wake up pain-free for...a *very* long time."

A hiccup interrupted her. Mike, Joe and Kate stared. Mike sputtered but didn't formulate a response quick enough to keep her from unburdening herself. "I put him there, and I didn't even remember. He could be the man who gave us a child. Look how I repay him. Not by caring for his wife—by detracting from her support, by letting some mild discomfort take me out of the loop, by even forgetting *he* needs *me* this time!"

By the end of her tirade, she was shouting like the guy outside the sketchy gas station in the heart of downtown, who ranted that civilization was doomed because people drank too many Slurpees. Waving her hands and foaming at the mouth would be the next stop. As if having an out of body experience, she could see it happening, yet couldn't stop herself from escalating.

"Shh. Cupcake, calm down." Joe tried to avert disaster. It was far too late for sensibility.

"You're not listening to me! I fucking nearly got our friend killed and then FORGOT he was alive and suffering!" Every dog in a three-block radius barked and howled when she really hit her stride.

"Oooo-kay." Mike abandoned logic. "Enough is enough."

The men exchanged a look over her head. Joe nodded.

"Oh, no. Whatever you're doing with that mind-meld bull, you just quit it right now." She wagged her finger at them. "It isn't going to work, misters."

"We'll see about that." Mike pounced. He ensnared her legs, keeping her from thrashing when Joe pressed her backward. Neither of them treated her roughly. Their infinite care couldn't be confused for leniency though.

"Do you know how adorable you are when you're pissed?" Joe's placating murmurs only riled her further.

"This isn't a joke, guys."

"It's hard to take you seriously when you spout such nonsense." Mike shook his head. "If you weren't pregnant, I'd already have you over my knee."

Morgan shivered.

"Yeah, that's right. You like being spanked, don't you?" He pinned her legs with one arm so that he could stroke himself a few times. Then he turned to his wife with a wink. "Do you want in on this or are you still feeling this morning?"

"Go, have fun." Kate patted his cheek. "Help her relax before she shatters."

The foreman kissed his wife. His hands roamed until she winced into his mouth. "Sorry, babe."

She retreated, sitting with her shoulder blades propped on the coffee table, which they'd shoved aside to make room for their bed. "No, it's me that should be sorry. It's just that everything is super-sensitive right now. Morgan, you'd better enjoy this while you can. I think I'm going to watch from over here."

Mike lunged for Morgan, devouring her mouth in a heated kiss. The intensity with which they joined had Morgan forgetting about her desire to break free and continue her rant. Some of the steam bled from her as Joe grounded her in reality. Sensing her surrender, his hands on her wrists loosened, then travelled up her arms. He cupped her breasts, massaging in the lingering moisture from her tears.

She groaned. Kate was right. The light touch already felt a million times more potent than usual. Soon it would be overwhelming.

The sound brought Mike's attention back to her. His eyes shone when he saw what Joe did to her, how she'd splayed her legs and arched her spine at the barest beginnings of contact.

"It's been a little bit now since Kate could enjoy me going down on her." He licked his lips. "Can you handle it, Morgan?"

"Let's find out." She abandoned everything other than the bliss the two men above her bestowed. They knew exactly how to distract her from life's worries. How could she say no?

Mike started at her knee, nibbling a trail up her thigh. Joe held her shoulders at an angle so she could watch. She wanted more. Wanted to give him something in return.

She reached for his hard-on with a clumsy grab, close enough Mike caught her intention. He paused his journey to instruct Joe. "Give her your cock. She wants to taste you."

Joe grabbed several pillows. He arranged them beneath her, then shuffled closer to her side on his knees. She angled her head toward him, opening her mouth and stretching her neck until he fed himself to her inch by inch.

The head of his cock felt warm and soft against her tongue. She flicked the muscle over his firm shaft, savoring every curse, sigh and groan that dropped from his lips. When Mike reached the apex of her thighs, she gasped, allowing Joe to advance further into her mouth.

As if he could sense her desperation, Mike didn't screw around. He buried his face in her pussy and ate as though she were his favorite meal. One of his broad fingers followed quickly, burrowing inside her drenched pussy.

"Love watching him play with you." Joe groaned. "Almost as much as I love the way you suck me, cupcake. Having him here means we both get what we want. That's right, just like that."

Morgan hollowed her checks, enjoying the taste of her husband. He was right. Not many women could relish the thrill of pleasuring their men without sacrificing some ecstasy of their own.

The rhythmic flick of Mike's tongue zeroed in on her favorite spot. She aided him by wriggling her hips until his mouth aligned perfectly. He hit the bulls-eye. Her eyes flew open wide.

When they did, she caught sight of something she hadn't expected. Two men stood above their playground, arms crossed, legs spread. She squealed and attempted to dive for the covers. With Mike between her legs and Joe supporting her head, she didn't get very far.

Kate gasped.

The distress was enough to shake the guys from their ministrations. But they didn't panic. Joe laughed when he recognized his cousin and Alanso, peering down at them.

"I'm positive I locked our damn doors," Mike growled at the duo of sexy mechanics. Still, he didn't release Morgan. Joe kept her impaled on his cock. Knowing the men couldn't help but stare, she should have been embarrassed. Instead, she couldn't deny a fresh gush of wetness bathed Mike's still-embedded fingers.

Eli, who looked enough like Joe to really rev Morgan's engine, grinned wickedly. "Minor details, friend. We heard some suspicious sounds and thought maybe you needed a hand."

Alanso might actually have blushed. "Not like, a hand in this. Like, it sounded like maybe Morgan was hurt. Though, I think you all have been holding some info out on us."

Mike looked to Joe. They were his family. Morgan knew the foreman was leaving the call to her husband. Would he be ashamed they'd caught him allowing his wife to fuck around with another man? She couldn't stand to dishonor him.

"Shh, Mo." He didn't have to look at her to feel the difference in her posture. "I love you and I don't give a fuck who knows about the crew. It's not like we're hiding our relationship. But guys, we're kind of in the middle of something here. So if you don't mind..."

Tall, dark-haired and devilishly handsome, Eli turned serious. "Will you share your story with us later? I think we might…benefit from hearing your experiences. Sorry to have interrupted your fun, kids. See you back at the hospital."

When he turned to leave, Alanso lingered, unable to stop his gaze from flicking between Morgan, Kate, Mike and Joe.

"Diaz," Eli barked. "Move it."

"Coming, Cobra," he answered yet didn't budge.

Joe peered down at Morgan. She knew instantly what he was asking. Something about the uncertainty in Alanso's naked gaze had hit her low and hard too. She nodded.

They looked to Mike and Kate together. Both of them added their assent.

"Wait!" Joe halted both men with his command.

Eli spun on his heel. Morgan had never seen the feral gleam lighting his dark eyes before. "What are you saying?"

"Talking could never have the same impact as seeing for yourself. Stay. Watch. Learn."

Morgan adored the inherent control Joe wielded. Mike slapped her husband on the shoulder, transmitting his approval with two hard claps.

"Come here, boys." Kate patted the seat she'd made for herself. Plenty of room remained for the two newcomers to share. "Might as well strip down too. I'd bet a hundred bucks you can't keep your hands off your junk once you see… No sense in getting all messy, huh?"

Alanso glanced between Eli and Mike as though afraid they lured him into a trap.

"I'm not going to kill for you for looking at my naked wife." Mike's laugh boomed through the room. "If I didn't trust you, you wouldn't still be here. Go ahead. Do what she says. Let her coach you through your first time."

"It's been a hell of a long time since I was a virgin." Eli stopped just short of rolling his eyes.

"This is a different league," Joe assured the men.

They didn't waste any more time debating.

Morgan sighed when Eli whipped his fitted black T-shirt over his head. Similarly built to Joe, his muscles rippled while he dispatched his jeans in the next instant. Alanso seemed stuck. His body froze as his stare winged to Eli.

"Don't make me undress you like a child," Eli growled at his mechanic.

If Morgan wasn't mistaken, the man might enjoy such treatment. She whimpered.

"Shh, sweetheart." Mike settled deeper between her legs, returning his focus to her saturated folds. "Commercials are over. Now back to our program…"

Eli snorted.

The contact of Mike's soft laps around her clit had Morgan arching in his hold. She grabbed Joe's ass and tugged him closer so she could devour his erection. If she wasn't mistaken, he'd gone harder knowing the other two guys watched her servicing him.

Lyrical muttering in Spanish had her smiling around Joe. In her peripheral vision, she saw Alanso practically rip his black sleeveless tank from dark tan skin. The colorful tattoos covering his arms continued across most of his torso.

Damn. He was gorgeous.

Kate would make out today. Her friend grinned, then reached up to unbutton Alanso's black cargo pants. He didn't protest when she stripped them down to his ankles along with sexy, bright blue briefs that looked amazing in contrast to his complexion.

"Come on, honey." Kate purred, "Take a seat next to me and get comfy. You too, Eli."

Mike increased the pace of his tongue before withdrawing his finger to trace Morgan's opening. When his hand returned, he inserted two fingers, stretching her with little scissoring motions of the digits.

"Christ." Eli didn't screw around. The instant he settled, his hand wrapped around his shaft. He winced, then looked as though he might spit in his palm.

"Hang on." Kate stopped him. "That's not necessary."

She reached into a drawer in the coffee table and withdrew some lube. Ever a gracious host, she went as far as to drizzle some of the cool gel onto her fingers to heat it. She rubbed her palms together, smearing the slippery substance between her hands. When satisfied, she reached out.

Alanso flinched when she would have grasped his straining cock in her hand. "Is that okay? Will Mike care?"

The foreman lifted his head long enough to reassure their visitors. "She's free to do what feels right in the moment. It's how we roll. Quit worrying. Enjoy."

Kate smiled. "I won't bite unless you ask. Promise."

Eli puffed out a breath. Color stained his cheeks as arousal overran logic. "Give me some of that please, baby."

"My pleasure." Kate went for broke. She reached out with both hands simultaneously, filling each with a steely cock. She giggled when the men jerked, shoving themselves deeper into her hold. "That's nice. I like the way you feel. So hard. You like seeing Morgan laid out like this, don't you?"

"Fuck, yeah." Alanso's hips flexed, straining to get closer to her grip.

"She's pretty when she comes. Of all the crew's women, she's always girly and cute. It's kind of sickening, really. That bitch." Kate laughed.

"You fuckers have been living in paradise all this time and you didn't bother to tell us?" Eli growled. "We're going to talk about this later, Joe. When I can think again. I might have to kick your ass."

"Is that any way to treat my husband's best friend?" Kate paused in her stroking, teasing the men.

"Shut up, Cobra." Alanso panted. "If she stops now, I'll die."

Morgan lost track of their banter when Mike redoubled his efforts. Getting serious, he sucked on her clit. For every increase in pressure, she matched his motion on Joe. Her husband began to shake in her hold.

"Oh, Joe's going to lose it soon. He loves to come in Morgan's mouth." Kate glanced over her shoulder.

Just hearing the effect she had on the man of her dreams was enough to ratchet Morgan's enjoyment through the roof. She shuddered, then clenched on Mike's embedded fingers.

"Morgan's right there, Joe. It's okay. Stop holding back. Take her over the edge with you." Mike helped Joe gauge the timing. They would shatter together.

She switched her stare to her husband. The desperation in his gaze motivated her to let him off the hook. She concentrated on Mike's mouth and the wonderful sensations he imparted. Then she reached up and fondled Joe's balls.

They came together.

Pleasure erupted through her mind. Colors danced

like a kaleidoscope in front of her eyes. She moaned, though with her mouth full the shouts were muffled. Her heels drummed on the mattress. Every muscle in her body went taut, shuddered, then melted, utterly relaxed.

Joe took a similar journey. Throughout the storm of her passion, Morgan suckled his cock, draining him dry even as her pussy nearly crushed Mike's fingers.

"You're right, she's so sweet when she surrenders." Alanso's reverent whisper cut through the haze of Morgan's lingering arousal. She felt relaxed for the first time in weeks.

Joe crashed, face down, to the mattress beside her. His body ended up perpendicular to hers. She cradled his head on her chest.

But with Kate out of the game, Morgan felt compelled to help Mike reach the same rapture he'd given her. She reached for him, but he shook his head.

"Not this time, Morgan." His nostrils flared as he focused on Joe instead. "Joe, I need something more. I need to fuck. I want to be in control of life for five damn minutes before we go back to that piece of shit hospital. I won't be rough with our girls. Not now. Will you do this for me?"

Eli grunted. "Does he mean what I think he means?"

"That I bend over for my foreman on occasion?" Joe looked up from his place at Morgan's side. The slightest hint of vulnerability etched onto his face had her burying her fingers in his hair. "Yeah. He does."

"I'm not going to fucking bash you, dickhead." Eli shook his head.

Alanso whipped his head to Eli. "You're not?"

"Why do you all suddenly think I'm a tool?" He

snorted. "Hell, no. If that's what you like... I've just never. You know."

Joe nodded and sighed. He didn't say anything else. Instead, he rose to his knees, spreading them wide while leaving his cheek pressed to Morgan's torso. "Take what you need, Mike. It sounds good to me too, giving up control for a while. To let you worry about everything. I trust you."

Morgan gripped her husband tight. The strain of the past twenty-four hours had affected him more than he let on.

Mike grunted, then looked to Kate. "Toss me the lube, babe."

"My pleasure." She winked at her husband.

He snatched the tube from the air with one hand. Wasting no time, he slathered himself with the gel, then began to prepare Joe. He grunted, nipping Morgan's breast lightly when Mike reached between his cheeks to spread more slickness there.

"Son of a bitch." He hissed. "Remember, I'm not James over here. I haven't done this in a while."

"You can take it." Mike unleashed a powerful side of him they didn't often get to see unrestrained. "Open up. Spread your legs wider, then relax."

Morgan glanced between Mike, her husband and the trio of friends on her other side. The guys synchronized their stroking on their cocks to the pace Mike set, penetrating Joe's tight hole with his finger. Now two fingers—or was it three?—when she looked to the foreman again.

Another Spanish curse had her peeking at the hot-rodders.

Kate was getting devious. She clasped Eli and Alanso's

wrists, one in each of her much smaller hands. Then she crossed her arms. No way could she force the powerful men to move if they would rather resist.

Eli and Alanso exchanged a heated glance, then allowed Kate to curl their fingers around each other's erections. Alanso didn't hesitate. He picked up right where he'd left off massaging his own hard-on.

A grunt exploded from Eli's chest. He flushed, then breathed hard as his friend stroked his cock. "Shit. It feels so much different when you do it."

"Do you like it?" Alanso swallowed.

Eli paused.

Morgan could tell Kate was preparing to smack him upside the head if he squashed the fragile experiment blossoming between the pair. At least, if he wasn't into it, he should let Alanso down easy. They shouldn't have worried.

"Should I stop, Cobra?" Alanso looked up at the garage owner.

"Fuck yes," he panted.

Kate glared at Eli when Alanso tried to yank his hand back as if burned. Instead, Eli trapped his friend's palm over his cock.

"Not so fast. I meant, fuck yeah I like it. Don't stop or I might deck you." He laughed at the shock on Alanso's face. Then he did one better and began to jerk off the guy sitting muscular shoulder to muscular shoulder with him.

Morgan shivered at the raw lust on their faces. She could only bring herself to look away when Joe tensed. A moment later, he groaned. The sound morphed into a hiss as Mike pushed him forward on her torso, sinking deep with one unrelenting thrust.

"This isn't going to be a long ride, Joe." Mike grunted.

He withdrew slowly, then slammed forward once more. "You'd better hang on tight."

Morgan stroked Joe's face and finger combed his hair, helping him relax while Mike invaded his ass. She didn't miss the sigh he released when he surrendered completely to the foreman. "You're doing great, Joe. Let him have you. Give him what he needs. Take too."

Mike squirted more lube onto his shaft before tossing the bottle aside. He leaned forward, getting leverage on his side to work his cock deeper, harder into Joe's welcoming hole. Joe tensed his arms beside her, keeping Mike's momentum from smashing him into her. The show of his strength, in so many different ways, made her love him just a little more. If that were possible.

Morgan basked in the energy created by the four smoking-hot guys surrounding her. Each of them used another to find his release. Sexual, spiritual or mental— maybe all three. She felt honored to be part of their exchange.

Slick slaps echoed from Alanso and Eli, who had lost their initial hesitance. They pumped each other with the sureness only another man could manage when handling cock. Cords stood out in Eli's neck as he flexed his hips upward. His erection bulged in Alanso's hold.

Mike laughed even as he pummeled Joe. "You're never going to be the same again. Trust me. Don't freak when you go back to that damn garage, Eli. It's going to be like fire in your veins. Trying to stop it is stupid."

"Sounds like experience talking," Eli grunted.

"It's been so long. Almost don't remember." Mike increased the intensity of his strokes. "But yeah. Wasn't always...like this."

Joe didn't bother to try and speak. He hung on and

offered himself to Mike, lifting his ass higher to meet the increasing pressure of Mike's fucking.

"Thank you." Mike growled as he blanketed Joe's back. He sheltered his friend even as he drilled his ass. "Needed this. Christ. So bad."

Sweat glistened on the skin of both men. Morgan couldn't have adored them more in that moment. Powerful, graceful and a little brutal. They held nothing back.

At the last possible second, Mike lifted his head and stared directly at Kate.

"I love you." The foreman's wife encouraged him, "Go ahead. Come in his ass. Fill him up."

Morgan couldn't say if it was that little speech or the spectacle before them, maybe the combination, but something proved too much for Alanso. He threw his head back and muttered a stream of broken Spanish and English she couldn't understand. Eli must have, though. He tore his gaze from Mike and Joe to observe as he pumped stream after stream of come from his mechanic.

Mike roared. He jerked several times as he too came. His fingers gripped Joe's hips hard enough to leave bruises, but her husband didn't seem to mind. Only when the last drop of fluid leaked from Alanso's cock did Eli surrender. He glanced between his friend and the two men, panting from where they'd collapsed near Morgan, before shattering.

The force of Eli's orgasm impressed Morgan. After all this time with the crew, that was saying something. How long had he hidden his desires? Only a forbidden fantasy could draw that kind of response.

When he shuddered against the coffee table, his cock spent, Alanso developed a wicked grin. He lifted his messy hand to his mouth and licked a swath through the delicacy there. Had James been there, he'd have come in his pants at the sight.

Eli didn't fare much better. He groaned, then slung one arm over his eyes as his seizing renewed. "Stop, stop. I can't take anymore. Holy shit."

Mike and Joe cracked up. They separated with sighs mingled with grunts.

While Kate and Morgan looked on, Mike crossed to Eli and extended his hand. Eli took it with his clean one and allowed Mike to lever him to his feet. Mike banded one arm around his back and squeezed tight. "You've got this. You'll know what the right thing is for your gang."

"And we're always here if you need to talk." Kate kissed Alanso on the cheek.

"Thank you." He turned away, but Morgan caught the shimmer in his delicious chocolate eyes first.

She hoped they were able to fashion a relationship even half as strong as the one she was so fortunate to be part of. Rejuvenated, she couldn't wait to get back to the hospital and the rest of the crew.

7

—————

Dave stared up at the thick wooden beams of the cathedral ceiling in the living room of Kayla's cabin. Thinking of it as her home, a place he merely lived, helped him cope with the possibility of leaving sometime soon. Really soon.

He swore he'd memorized every knot and streak of grain in the timbers during the past three months. It was a big upgrade from counting creepy birds in the wallpaper of the antiseptic hospital room he'd occupied for almost seven weeks. Still, he'd spent a hell of a lot of time right here, flat on his worthless back. If he never saw another episode of *Dr. Phil* or *Judge Mathis*, it'd be too soon. On the plus side, he did have a better idea of what constituted a good deal at the grocery store after about a million viewings of *The Price Is Right*.

He rolled his eyes. The cluster of dark spots near the ceiling fan caught his attention. They'd started reminding him of the profile of his childhood dog, Barker, lately.

"Jesus. I need to get out of here," he grumbled, shifting to his side on the bed, which the guys had *temporarily* lugged down from the loft ages ago. Careful to keep the dead weight of his bad leg on top, he pushed up to half-sitting.

"Hmm?" Kate moaned from her spot, where she'd crashed beside him. He hadn't meant to rouse the ultra-preggers woman. As much as he loved her and Morgan, who snuggled against his other side, he struggled to draw in a breath.

Suffocation seemed like a very real possibility.

"Nothing. Sorry. Gotta get up." He did his best not to jostle either of the exhausted women, who'd elected to stay home and nap with him rather than join their friends in picking blueberries for Morgan to incorporate in upcoming seasonal specials. The untamed section of the property, which contained masses of fruit bushes, was too rough for Dave's wheelchair.

He was coming to hate the contraption. His doctors wouldn't let him switch to crutches until he regained feeling in his limb. Rightly so, they feared he'd put pressure on it or bang into things, causing more damage unintentionally. The specialists hadn't said so yet, but their frowns and dampening reassurances led him to believe he was getting close to being written off.

What if he *never* recovered fully?

It seemed he should face the possibility. This could be the new him. His new life. What the hell use was he to the crew like this? He wanted to run, but he had nowhere to go and a leg that wouldn't support him regardless.

"Need help getting to the bathroom?" Morgan scooted aside, giving him a wide berth.

"No!" He hated how she flinched. Yet he couldn't stop the frustration boiling inside him from erupting in a roar.

"I do not want help taking a goddamned piss. You might almost be a mother, but I'm no fucking baby."

She raised a single brow from where she lounged. Kate scrubbed her eyes, blinked a few times, then huddled closer to Morgan as if to protect her.

Bile rose in his throat. He tried to escape faster, nearly capsizing his wheelchair in his haste to climb over the arm and haul his leg into position. A vision of his dumb ass, sprawled helpless—and completely devoid of the last scraps of his pride—across the plank flooring rushed into his brain.

Before it became reality, someone snagged the handles of the chair and returned his prison to level. Dave plopped into place none too gently. Footsteps on the hardwood confirmed the rest of the crew had returned from their outing.

"I admit I missed the beginning of that tirade..." Joe's menacing rumble rose goosebumps on Dave's skin. "But you sure as shit sounded like a child just then, douchebag. Don't you *ever* talk to my wife like that again. Bum leg or not, I'll bury my steel-toed boot up your ass."

"He likes that sometimes." James strutted into view, trying to disperse the tension between the two men. "In fact, maybe that's part of his problem. It's been a while, huh? You've dodged every one of our sessions since the accident. Sex is a great way to blow off some steam, you know?"

Dave's gaze flicked to Kayla. His wife tried to pretend everything was normal, putting away the berries with the same determination she'd harnessed to forge on with their lives the past several months. Even turning her back to set buckets in the refrigerator couldn't disguise the stiffness with which she carried herself.

James had hammered a sore spot, hitting a little too close to home.

"Holy shit." Neil jammed his foot in front of the wheel of Dave's chair when he would have rolled away and locked himself in the bathroom. "Look at your face. You really aren't getting any, are you? Did the accident affect—"

"What? Jesus! No." He sputtered, "I can still get it up."

Mike ushered Kayla from the kitchen. She crumpled onto the end of the bed, with Devon close beside her. Dave was grateful for the bond the two women had formed. He hoped his wife could take solace in that since he'd fucked up their perfect relationship. Maybe it was time to cut her loose so she could find a real man. How long could they go on like this?

"Then why is your wife crying?" Devon bristled on behalf of her friend. "What are you doing? To both of you?"

"Ah, damn. Kay, I'm so sorry." He paused to gather his courage before ripping his heart out of his chest. Losing her would be a hell of a lot worse than losing the use of his leg and that had just about killed him. He'd never survive. But as long as she was happy, able to find someone who deserved her, that's all that mattered.

"You are?" She went very still. When she faced him, a glimmer of hope danced in her eyes. "Does that mean you're ready to quit shutting me out? I miss you, Dave."

"No, it means I'm ready to leave." He shoved Neil at crotch level, forcing the tall man away so he could roll. "You deserve better than taking care of me. All of you do."

Fury contorted Kayla's features beyond recognition. She never got angry, never mind exhibiting this unholy rage. "How dare you!"

If Joe hadn't braced the chair, they both would have summersaulted backward at the force of her impact when she flew from the bed and onto his chair. She wasn't careful of his leg when she straddled him. Fists balled in his shirt, and seams popped as she shook him, rattling his teeth. He could do nothing more than stare, his jaw hanging wide open, when she went ballistic.

And still some part of him registered the feel of his naked wife in his arms.

Mainly the part hardening between them.

Jerking off in the shower every morning and a couple times during the day hadn't brought him a fraction of the satisfaction she had without even trying.

"You swore to love me for better or worse. This is pretty fucking awful, and you're stranding me on my own?" Rage evaporated from her, passing as quickly as a violent summer storm. It morphed into something more insidious and painful. Kayla deflated in his arms. She molded perfectly to his chest, then begged, "Please, don't do this to me. Please don't *choose* to leave me. I cried every night you were unconscious in that hospital because I was afraid death would steal you from me. But this...this is worse. You're a ghost of my husband. A shadow of my best friend. Don't do this. Please."

He gulped, unable to argue against her raw agony.

"I can feel you. Your body responds even if your brain is trying to fuck you all up." She kissed the trails of synchronized tears he hadn't realized he shed. "Stop doing this to yourself. Stop thinking for two damn seconds and listen to your body."

"The mangled one? The broken one? Great idea, babe." He snorted.

"I need you," Kayla whispered. "Don't make me suffer alone."

"I know you're hurting, but enough is enough." Devon looked horrified. "Dave, pay attention."

"You're about to make the biggest mistake of your life." Mike dropped a hand on his shoulder and squeezed. "We won't let you do this. Fix it while you still can."

"Why do you want me?" He couldn't stand the rasp his voice had transformed into. Weakness infiltrated every part of him.

"Because I love you." Kayla kissed him gently. She tasted divine. Like blueberries and sunshine and promises.

"I'm useless." He closed his eyes. "I'm not getting better, Kay. How long are we going to act like things are just fine? I'm not. May never be again."

"Do you think I fell in love with you for your leg?" She bit his earlobe hard enough to sting. "Maybe you hit your head harder than they thought in that crash. If this is how things are, that's fine. I love you, Dave. However you are."

He wished he could believe her. What job would he have? A pity role on the crew? Desk jockey for their company? He'd rather not be involved. Living half alive seemed worse than finding a new place.

"Quit thinking so hard." Morgan laid a hand on his arm despite how he'd treated her.

"The doctors can find nothing wrong with your leg, Dave." Kayla peppered his face with kisses. "Tests are all positive. Maybe one or two more surgeries will get the nerves talking again."

"And maybe they won't." Dave shook his head.

"Okay, so what?" Joe jiggled the wheelchair. "You've

already lost enough, without adding your soul mate to that list, haven't you?"

Dave wanted to argue, but Kayla warmed him. Her body heat penetrated the ice he'd packed around his heart. She rubbed against him like a cat, fuzzing his logic and stealing his arguments. What if this was the last time he ever held her?

Something primal in him roared, wanting to make it count.

He opened his eyes and met her stare. Point blank, they assessed each other.

Kayla raised up enough that she stole the soft pressure from his cock, which had tucked against her through his pants like a tracking missile locked on its target.

"Get him naked. Someone. Anyone. Hurry." She surprised him with her desperate plea.

"Don't!" Dave barked at the same time Neil reached for the waistband of Dave's sweats.

The crewmember didn't hesitate. He worked the cotton beneath Dave's ass then off his legs, despite the fact that Dave hadn't allowed himself to roam his own home, part of a naturist resort, nude since the accident.

"Oh, Dave." Devon knelt on the floor beside his chair. Her fingers wandered along the length of his disfigurement.

"Don't touch it." He tried to focus, but Kayla returned, sinking over his bare flesh, spreading her wetness on his aching shaft. They were torturing him, and he didn't know if he wanted to survive. "I'm so weak. Lame."

"When I look at this, I see how strong you were to fight through the pain. What the hell was all that for if you're going to quit now?" James joined his mate in petting the wounded leg. Dave couldn't feel their hands, but he imagined what such tender touches would have done to him.

His cock flexed, brushing Kayla's belly.

She shifted, causing the chair to creak. Joe made sure it didn't tip.

Kate, Morgan and Mike observed with eagle eyes.

"Put him inside me," Kay ordered Neil.

"This isn't smart." Dave couldn't bring himself to say no outright.

"But you want it as much as I do." His wife rested her forehead on his.

"More. God, you have no idea how bad." More squeaking followed in time to his trembling. He gripped the arms of the chair so hard he didn't understand how they didn't buckle. It was the only way he could keep himself from wrapping Kayla in his arms and begging her to keep him, injury and all, even though he knew how selfish that request would be, unfair to the woman he loved beyond measure.

"That's all I need to know." Long, gentle fingers cupped his cheeks and angled his face so he couldn't help but observe the devotion in her eyes a moment before she settled her lips on his.

The unique taste of Kayla nourished him. Starving without her, he'd started to lose touch with sanity. After whetting his appetite with the sweet appetizer, he devoured her offering. Engrossed in their lip lock, he didn't notice when she began to squirm, aligning her pussy with his steely erection.

Neil assisted her in taking Dave inside.

The moan he unleashed came straight from the pit of his belly. He'd abstained for months because he could never turn away from this. Knowing he might need to leave for her own good, he'd refused to bind himself tighter to her warmth. The ecstasy, the rightness and the comfort Kayla bestowed, as if her gifts were ordinary. Fuck that.

"Go slow," Neil instructed Kayla. "I can see how tight you are around him. I can't believe you've waited so long. Both of you."

Mike stepped closer to Kayla's side to see for himself. "I should have realized something was broken. I thought you just were avoiding the group, not your own wife too. Dumb bastard."

Dave barely grunted when Mike smacked him upside the head. He deserved it. Besides, the light impact shoved him closer to his wife. She seated herself on him, taking him completely inside her, surrounding him with her light and love.

"Am I hurting you?" She broke their lip lock to pant out a status check. "There's not a lot of room in here for how I want to ride you. It's been way too long to take this slow."

"Here, let us help." Neil put his hands around Kayla's waist. "Let him go just for a moment."

She whimpered when he lifted her. The plump head of Dave's cock locked in the ring of muscles at her entrance. A wail broke from her chest when he slipped free.

"I promise we'll give him right back." Neil kissed her cheek as he laid her on the bed. Mike and Joe each grabbed one of Dave's arms, ducking under them as they had so many times over the past months. Neil and James each held one of his thighs, careful with his injured leg.

Together, his four best friends lifted him, raising him from the wheelchair and depositing him on the mattress where his immobility didn't seem to matter so much. It's not like he could have moved anyway, what with four women piling on top of him, hugging him, kissing him, petting him everywhere they could reach.

Kayla straddled his hips and guided him home once more. She didn't stop until she'd fused them completely. And this time she had plenty of space to operate. Her hips rocked in a sensual arc that stroked all the most sensitive parts of his cock with the lush tissues of her pussy. Leaning forward, she assaulted his lips while she used him for her own pleasure.

He loved every second of her erotic torment.

Dave couldn't last. Not with the brilliance of her energy blinding him to his worries and fears. He couldn't restrain the desperate rapture creeping up inside him, bringing unwise hope with it. "Guys. Help her. Close. Fuck."

They didn't have to be asked twice. Insinuating themselves between their women, the crew guys focused on Kayla with every bit of intensity their wives applied to blowing his mind. They sucked on the silver rings in her nipples, smacked her ass in the playful way she adored, kissed trails up her spine, and he swore he felt someone's hand nudging his balls as they teased her from behind.

It was too much. For Kayla as well as Dave. She ripped her mouth from his, sitting up to drive him as deep as possible. She bucked a few more times, then stilled. Dave held his breath in the moments before she shattered. And when she clenched on him, wringing him tighter than his own fist had so many times lately, his balls churned. They drew tight to his body the instant before he came, shooting an impossible number of blasts inside his wife. His lover. His mate.

It felt so right, he knew he could never leave her without killing them both.

Harming her was something he vowed never to do again.

"Kayla." He stroked her hair and the long lines of her back. He held her so tight she squeaked.

But when she separated their chests, just enough to peer into his eyes, it wasn't pain he saw there. It was love.

"Are you okay?" She panted the question, still catching her breath.

"Perfect. That was amazing." He relaxed for the first time in months. "Thank you for rescuing me from that black hole. Christ. I can't promise I won't go there again but I'll try my best."

"We'll be here to kick your ass and fuck some sense into you." James patted his chest. "Don't you get your panties in a wad about that."

"Right now, I'm not worrying about anything." And it was true. Since the accident, his mind hadn't once been quiet. Constant babbling terror had coursed through his brain. Telling him he'd never heal, never satisfy his wife, never be the man he'd promised to be.

In the wake of passion, silence reigned supreme.

Welcome quiet.

Calm.

Peace with whatever might come next.

"I love you, Dave." Kayla hugged him tight before pulling off, allowing him to slip from her body. "Please never forget that again."

"I promise." He grunted. "But...is someone crushing my leg? Can you move over, please?"

He couldn't lift his head very far, being the bottom of

the pile of crewmembers. Still, it was far enough to catch the glances that winged from person to person.

"No one's touching your leg, Dave. We were all careful not to hurt you."

"Shit. Then why is it burning so bad?" He clawed at the sheets as tingles spread from his toes, up the sole of his foot to his ankle then along his calf. "Holy fuck. It hurts."

He laughed and laughed and laughed—with a generous amount of crying, cursing and gasping mixed in.

"Should I call 911?" Devon got to her hands and knees, poised to scramble for a phone.

"No." He chuckled some more. Relief flooded his veins, making him believe he could dance a jig like Uncle Joe with his golden ticket in *Charlie and the Chocolate Factory,* despite the pain. "Don't you see? It hurts. I can feel it. Finally, I can feel it."

Kayla buried her face in his neck and sobbed.

The rest of the crew stroked him over every exposed portion of his body. Fingers combed his hair, held his hands and rubbed his chest. They comforted him through the initial blaze of returning sensation. When the stabbing tingles began to abate, he puffed out a huge sigh.

"Okay, big guy. Let's get you to your doctor's office. Pronto." Mike put an arm around Dave's shoulders, as though he would lift his hulking carcass from the bed singlehandedly. Even with one withered leg, he still weighed a ton. Physical therapy had seen to that.

"Wait a minute." Dave brushed him off. "I want to try something."

The eight faces ringing him looked at him in unison. Devon tilted her head.

He stared at his toes—afraid to do it, afraid not to.

When they realized what he was about to attempt, they switched their stares to his foot.

"It's okay if nothing happens." Kate stroked his bad knee...and he felt it.

"Don't push yourself." James clasped Dave's good ankle. "This is a big step already."

Dave reached out blindly, finding Kayla's hand and clutching it in his.

"I love you no matter what." She kissed his knuckles. The contact sent a jolt of blissful electricity into his system, lighting up his nerve endings. He twitched.

And the toes on his left foot wiggled.

EPILOGUE

"What the hell was so urgent you couldn't wait for the end of the game?" Dave grumbled to Joe as he navigated the half a flight of porch stairs on his crutches. He was getting damn good on the things and cheating a bit, putting pressure on his bad leg when he thought no one was watching.

Joe didn't blame the guy. He'd be going stir crazy by now too. Six months was a hell of a long time to be benched, doomed to rely on others for most everything. Hopefully, today would help Dave regain even more independence.

"Is that any way to greet your best friend's favorite cousin?" Eli shouted from around the corner of the house, intentionally out of sight.

Dave swung out, then back, as he stopped abruptly. "Holy fuck."

Joe sidestepped in time to avoid knocking him over. The rest of the crew and their women scrambled to join them once they realized their friend had spied his surprise.

"What's going on?" The hesitation in Dave's voice might have been amusing if circumstances had been different. Kayla joined him, laying a hand on his ass from a step behind.

"Seeing as your truck wasn't quite as indestructible as your hard head, we thought maybe you'd like a new set of wheels." Eli sat on a gleaming chrome bumper, muscular arms crossed over his built chest. Apparently working on classic cars was about as much exercise as construction jobs. All of his hot-rodders were lean, mean and not dudes Joe would want to scrap with in a dark alley.

"Well, an old set of wheels, really. She's a 1934 Ford Model A." Alanso winked from his spot beside Eli. He patted the enormous red ribbon tied into a bow on the hood of the retro delivery truck. The glossy black paint job, complete with flames on the front, gleamed along with chrome in the fall sunlight.

"She's gorgeous." Dave crossed the rest of the driveway in three swings. He trailed a finger lovingly along the contour of the oval side mirror. "This is way, way too much. I could never accept this kind of gift."

"Look, Joe isn't the only guy in my family who gets off on surprising people. You wouldn't steal all my fun, now would you? Besides, the gang worked their asses off on this beast. They've been dying hear about your reaction. Don't make me say you rejected their efforts."

Dave didn't respond. His face fell a bit, and he looked kind of pale.

"What's wrong?" Kayla whispered to her husband. "Do you need to sit down for a minute?"

"No. Shit. Sorry." He held his crutch in the juncture of

his arm long enough to wipe his face. "It's just that... I'm not really to a place where I can drive. I mean, it's better, but the doctor said it could be months still."

"Dude." Eli shook his head. "No worries. We heard that too. Figured you could use a little freedom. Come here."

Eli stood, crossing to the driver's side door. The motion caused his midnight spikes, accompanied by a smattering of neon blue locks, to bob. Dave joined him, still picking at the foam rests on his crutches.

"We modified more than just the exterior for you. It's got hand controls. No foot action necessary." He slapped Dave on the shoulder, then dangled a key with chrome dice for a keychain in front of their friend. "You're ready to blow this joint."

"I. Uh. Wow." Dave froze for a few seconds. "I don't know how I'll ever repay you for this, but...thank you."

His crutches clattered to the ground as he balanced on his good leg. He smashed Eli in a bear hug that seemed to rattle even the sturdy mechanic. Alanso cracked up and snapped a picture with his smartphone of the two men with the truck in the background alongside Eli's pristine Shelby Cobra. "The gang is going to love this shit. I think his eyes bugged out."

Dave put one hand on the frame above the door, then hopped, pulling himself into the driver's seat of the lowered vehicle. He fiddled with the chrome shifter and admired the extensive detailing Eli and his hot-rodders had crafted in the cabin of the truck. Even from a distance, Joe could tell the vehicle was a masterpiece. Maybe Dave would let him have a turn sometime in the next decade.

Dave shut the door then rolled down the window,

wiggling his eyebrows at Kayla. "Want to go for a ride, sexy?"

Alanso turned his head, his eyes looking misty, even as a punch hit Joe's gut. *This* was the Dave he knew and loved. The confident, optimistic man who had been missing since that fateful day, eight months earlier.

Thank God.

Kayla squealed. She bolted for the other side of the truck. With her tattoos and new eyebrow piercing, she looked right at home in the stylish ride. The engine roared as Dave turned his key in the ignition. If Joe knew his cousin, he wouldn't have settled for any reasonable amount of horsepower.

Eli did everything full throttle.

The head mechanic snagged the crutches from the driveway, carefully lowered them into the bed, then leaned in to give Dave a one-minute tutorial on operating the modified controls. "Have fun. Don't do anything I wouldn't do."

Dave grinned. "That leaves a hell of a lot on the table, doesn't it?"

"Damn straight." Eli waved as Dave put it in reverse and carefully navigated the open space, three-pointing it until he could pull forward through the winding drive. He seemed to have no problem with the new driving technique, not that the crew limited themselves to traditional methods in any situation. He honked before rounding the bend and cruised out of sight.

"That was fucking awesome." Mike strode up to Eli and slapped him on the back. "Thank you so much."

"Anytime." Eli and Alanso stood shoulder to shoulder, facing the rest of the crew and their women. "I have a feeling we owe you just as much. For showing us...what you did."

Joe grinned. "So, have you shared your sordid knowledge with the rest of your group? How'd that go?"

"It didn't. Not yet." Alanso cursed in Spanish. "Cobra's too damn cautious. Soon, though. If he doesn't, I will. Things are getting tense at the shop."

Eli glared at Alanso. "We have to be careful. When the time is right..."

"Sometimes, things just happen." Kate crossed the gap. She shifted a bundle swaddled in bright pink blankets to one arm, then hugged Eli. "If this past year has taught us nothing else, it's that time is precious. I know you get that too. We never know how long we have. Don't waste your chances. I was scared at first. I almost waited too long. What if I hadn't taken that leap? Told Mike my fantasy about him and his crew? Where would I be today? Certainly not here, with my family."

Alanso grunted his agreement.

"I hear you. I do." Eli nodded. "I'm working on it. Now let me see this daughter of yours. I hope she gets her looks from you, gorgeous."

Mike growled, "Abby's too damn beautiful for her own good. I'm hoping she'll grow out of it. Maybe we'll get lucky and she'll need braces. And some really thick glasses."

"Payback is a bitch, my friend." Eli cooed for the infant, wiggling his fingers and turning to jelly, pretty much the same as all the rest of the crew inevitably did around the minx. It was pitiful how easily one tiny baby could rule them all.

Especially when she giggled and smiled, like now.

"And you, *mamacita*?" Alanso gathered Morgan to his

side carefully. His accent always seemed to thicken when he talked to women. Most of them melted beneath the force of his Latin lover routine. Even Joe's wife wasn't immune. "How are you doing? You're glowing and...huge."

She laughed as she patted his rock-hard abs. "Thanks, I think. Things are great. I'm ready to meet our son though. Any time now. The guys keep teasing he must be Dave's to be so damn big. My back is ready for a break."

"It isn't your back I'd be worried about." Alanso's rich skin couldn't hide his blush.

Eli smacked him upside his sexy bald head. "Will you ever learn to think before you speak?"

The crew laughed. Except Morgan's chuckle sounded strained. She grabbed her middle, then bent in half.

"*Joder*! Lo siento. Didn't mean to upset you. He's right. My mouth has no filter. I'm sure it's stretchy—"

"Alanso. Shut it," Morgan hissed. "Not mad. Having a contraction. Sort of been having them all day. Not like this, though. I think it's time. Now."

Before the startled man could recover, Kayla, Devon and several other crew members swarmed Morgan, helping her to sit on the grass by the driveway. James shook Joe from his daze. "Where are you bags? In the car?"

"Yes. Morgan's been packed for a couple days. We're ready." Somehow it sounded like he was trying to convince himself.

"You'd better be." Eli grinned. "Go ahead. Take her to the hospital. Unless you plan to deliver that baby yourself on the way down the mountain. Al and I will wait for Dave and Kay. We'll come as soon as we can."

"Right. Yeah. Okay." Joe could hardly catch his breath when Morgan shrieked again. Kate tossed him a look that said they should get to the hospital *fast*. It was going to be a long night. Somehow, though, he knew by morning his world would be forever changed. For the better.

Kate handed Abby to Mike, then sank to her knees beside Morgan. She coached her best friend through the now-familiar breathing routine. When Morgan relaxed, Kate looked up. "Carry her to her car. Neil can drive for you. I'll come in the backseat too. Okay?"

"Yes. Thank you." He smiled, unable to believe the day had finally come. He scooped up Morgan and cradled her to his chest. After contorting himself into her tiny backseat, while wishing he'd talked to Eli about finding them something more practical, he reached into the front pocket of his jeans.

"I know they're going to make you take off all your jewelry, but I wanted you to have something to hold. Something to remind you of how far we've come," he murmured to Morgan, love radiating from his heart. Every particle of hope, care and concern was returned to him a million times over in her doe-eyed stare. "So I brought this."

He handed her a pebble. The edges were worn smooth and the stone had turned glossy in spots from him handling it so often.

"What is this?" Her brows arched as she looked back to him.

"Just a rock." He shrugged. "I picked it up from the pumpkin patch on our first date. Kind of kept it as my good luck charm. Maybe if things get rough, you could squeeze it in your fist and remember, I'll always be there for you and our son. You're not alone. We'll do this together."

"All of us," Neil and James added simultaneously from the front seat.

"I love you, Morgan." Joe kissed her, then tucked her head against his shoulder as they pulled out of Dave and Kayla's yard. Close behind them, Mike and Devon followed. He caught Eli and Alanso waving as they passed by.

Lifting his hand to say thank you and goodbye, Joe knew it was really the beginning of so much more.

WANT TO READ MORE ABOUT THE CREW?

If you've enjoyed the Powertools Crew so far, don't wait to find out what happens to them and their mechanic cousins next in the Hot Rods series, which begins with King Cobra.

If the sexy construction crew were Powertools, their cousin mechanics are sure to be Hot Rods. Nothing's sexier than seven men with hot rods.

Hot Rods, Book 1

After Eli's mother died, his father honored her life's mission as a social worker by taking in several kids from the wrong side of the tracks. Not all of them stuck, but those who did became Eli's quasi family.

Their bonds, forged in fires set by their personal demons, are unbreakable—or so Eli wants to believe. Especially since he and Alanso, his best friend and head mechanic, witnessed the overpowering allure of polyamory while visiting the Powertools crew.

Much as Eli would like to deepen the relationships among his foster brothers and sister in the Hot Rods Restoration Team, he's hesitant to risk everything on a quick romp behind a stack of tires.

But when Eli catches Alanso exploring their mutual fantasy at a known hookup spot in a public park, all bets are off. And Eli must decide if it's time to jump in full throttle—and trust his instincts to guide him through the night. If the pair of mechanics can dodge the potholes in their own relationship, maybe they can race together toward the unconventional arrangement with Mustang Sally they both desire.

Warning: Fasten your seatbelts, this is going to be a wild (and naughty) ride!

An Excerpt From King Cobra:

Chapter One

Eli London stared at the drop of sweat gathering on the shoulder of one of his mechanics, Alanso. He flexed his fingers around the torque wrench he'd retrieved for the man, refusing to let go and trace the path perspiration took over deceptively wiry muscles.

Inked artwork brightened as the bead dampened several tattoos. First a tribal scribble, then a portrait of Al's long-lost mom, and finally the top of an intricate cross that disappeared beneath the bunched fabric clinging around his waist. Torn and oil-stained coveralls hugged a high, tight ass.

All Eli could think of these days was that goddamned ass, which Alanso now shoved out in his direction while the bastard tuned some rich kid's engine. With hardly any effort at all, Eli could smack it. Or bite it. Or fuck it.

Son of a bitch.

Nothing good could come of this obsession. Damn his cousin Joe for putting crazy thoughts in his brain. The guy was a member of a construction crew that liked to work hard and play harder together. Their polyamorous bedroom gymnastics had become obvious when Eli and Alanso had walked in on a scene he couldn't forget. But just because that bastard had been lucky enough to find a whole team of fuck buddies his wife adored—no, loved—

didn't mean such a wild arrangement could work for everybody in the world.

Eli had no right to wish for the same. Yet lately, each time he looked at the half dozen guys and girl he considered his grease monkey family, he found himself sporting a hard-on stiff enough to jack up a tank with. Thankfully, the oblivious gang hadn't identified the source of his recent frustration. Though they certainly had borne the brunt of his bad temper, adding guilt to the unslakable arousal stripping his gears, leaving him spinning his wheels.

Stuck and stranded. Alone with his dirty little secret.

Except for Alanso

Why had that mechanic been the one to witness Joe and his crew's alternative loving along with Eli? Probably because they went most everywhere together. Eli shoved the memory of his right-hand man's right hand from his mind. Or at least he tried. The guy had tortured Eli's cock with greedy pumps of his trembling fist while the crew's foreman, Mike, demonstrated just how hot it could be to take on one of his own. By fucking Joe while the mechanics had stared, in awe of the power exchange.

Grunts had spilled from Joe's mouth, which knocked against his wife's breast as he took everything Mike gave him then begged for more. The audible decadence echoed through Eli's mind day in and day out. In perfect harmony with the memory of Alanso's answering cries as he witnessed the undeniable claiming.

Eli knew that if he slammed Alanso against the 426 inch engine block of that 1970 Dodge Challenger R/T coupe, the man would spread and welcome him.

Boss, friend...brother.

And that's where the fantasy turned to battery acid,

burning Eli's insides with the bitter taste of responsibility and logic.

How could he want a guy he considered family? How could he violate that trust?

He couldn't afford to lose Alanso.

Not from his business, definitely not from his life.

So he could never seize what he craved. Frustration bubbled over.

"What's taking so long, Diaz?" Eli knocked thick, bunched biceps with the tool he carried.

"We're trying to make a profit here, you know?"

Alanso couldn't seem to wipe his glare away as easily as he rid his brow of the moisture dotting it. He snatched the wrench from Eli and returned to his task without taking the bait. If Eli couldn't fuck, the least the guy could do was give him the courtesy of engaging in a decent fight. His teeth ground together.

"You hear me, huevón? This isn't some charity case. Hot Rods is a business. Don't spend all day on a five-hundred-dollar job." Eli thumped the hood, knowing how the impact would reverberate.

Alanso's shoulders tensed. The clench of muscles along his spine altered the shape of his tattoos. Still, he said nothing about the low blow—or how he'd repaid the Londons a million times over for their hand-up through a solid decade of friendship and loyalty—and continued about his job. One he was damn fine at performing. No one could make an engine purr like Alanso.

"You want half-assed, go hire a motorman from the chain in town." He didn't bother to acknowledge Eli with a look.

Still, as Alanso's boss and best friend, Eli knew that

tone well enough. It'd be accompanied by Al's tattooed middle finger sticking up along that wrench, he'd bet.

The defiance made Eli long to grab the other man's chin and force him to gaze up. Maybe then Alanso would see the desperation making Eli more unhinged than Mustang Sally during a particularly bad bout of PMS. God help them all.

He'd never wanted something he couldn't have so badly before. Except maybe to heal his mom during those horrid weeks she'd spent dying.

Terror and a soul-deep pain that never entirely faded turned him into something no better than a cornered animal. Eli lashed out. "Good idea. Maybe they'd spend less time checking me out and do their goddamned work."

A clang surprised him. He didn't quite realize what had happened until a spark flew from the metal tool where it connected with the concrete floor of the garage. Alanso had winged the thing an inch or less from Eli's thankfully steel-toed boot when he spun around.

He wouldn't have missed by accident.

"Para el carajo! Maybe I should've done more than look. You're obviously too hardheaded to man up and come for me. So the deal's off the table. I've wasted too much time on a dude who's in denial. You're right about that." Alanso sneered. "I'm tired of waiting for you to grow some cojones."

"Keep your voice down." Eli checked over his shoulder. Kaige and Carver didn't so much as glance in their direction, but the stillness of their bodies made it clear they caught at least wisps of the conversation. Years of tough living had taught the men to tread lightly in conflict. At least until swinging a punch became necessary. Then it was likely to become a free-for-all.

"Joder! Now you want to shut me up. Come mierda." Alanso scrubbed a hand over his bald head, leaving a streak of oil that tempted Eli to buff it away, maybe with his five o'clock shadow. "Wouldn't want the rest of the Hot Rods hearing about the good life and how we're not living it, right? They might revolt."

"Hey, I've never kept anyone against their will. You all chose to stay here. With me. The door's open." Eli waved toward the enormous rolling metal sheets that protected the garage bays at night or when the weather turned cold. Through them, the pumps of the service station his dad had started were visible.

A flash of something miserable twisted Alanso's usually smiling lips into a grimace. The gesture had Eli thinking of something other than what it would feel like to get a blowjob from the man. That was a first after weeks of studying that mouth.

He reached out, but it was too late. Alanso dodged, taking a step back and then another.

"You know what, Cobra." He grabbed his crotch hard enough to make Eli wince. "You can suck it. Or, then again... No, you can't. That fucking checkered flag has dropped, amigo."

Reflex, instinct, dread—something—inspired Eli to lunge for the man who turned away.

Warm, moist skin met his palm.

"Get your fucking hands off me." When the engine guru pivoted, the unusual chill in his brown eyes froze Eli in his tracks. "You had your chance. You blew it. For us both. I'm out of here."

"You're quitting?" Eli gaped as the bottom fell out of his stomach. "Wait—"

"Hell no. I told you I'm over that bus-stop phase."

Alanso sliced his hand through the air between them. His knuckles skimmed Eli's chest. They left a slash of fire across his heart. "I've got places to go and people to do. There are things I gotta learn about myself. And for the first time since we were fifteen, you're not going to be a part of that with me. Your loss."

"Shit. I-I'm sorry." Eli couldn't find a way to say what for. For violating their friendship, for wanting to destroy what they had or for acting like an ass by postponing the inevitable—he couldn't make up his mind. "Don't go."

They'd drawn a crowd. Even Roman inched closer now. The tough yet quiet guy stared openly at their spectacle. Charged air had somehow tipped off Sally too. She emerged from the painting booth, crossing the bays at an alarming rate. If she got tangled up in this, Eli would never forgive himself. Of all their gang, he knew better than to trample on her emotions. Her heart would rip in two if she had any idea of the rift opening at his feet right now.

Just like his chest was hewn.

"I'm not leaving leaving, Cobra." Alanso lowered his voice. "This is my home. I hope some things haven't changed. Let me know if I'm no longer welcome and I'll pack my shit. But I can't fucking do this anymore. Not for another damn minute. I have to know what it's like. To be honest about who I am and what I want. Before I lose any more respect for either of us."

"Fine then." Eli leaned forward before he could stop himself. The awful sensations sliding through his guts had to stop. Fast. Before the rest of the garage got caught in their crossfire. He shoved Alanso hard enough the man stumbled across the threshold before catching his balance. It felt like forcing a baby bird from the nest. He only hoped Al spread his wings fast enough. "Get the hell out. Do what you gotta do."

Alanso mouthed a plea out of sight of the guys now wiping hands on coveralls and milling near in a semi-circle. "Come with me."

Eli slammed his fist on the big red button on the doorframe beside him. With an ominous rattle, the metal door began to lower between them, severing all communication as completely as if the aluminum were a drawbridge over a monster-filled moat.

The scream of a crotch rocket taking off at an unwise speed ricocheted through their space. Gravel pinged when it slung against the barrier he'd erected.

"What the fuck did you do to him, Cobra?" Sally canted her head as she laid into Eli.

"You've really been acting like a snake lately, ever since Dave's accident. Hissing at anyone who comes near. We get that you're afraid of losing people important to you. The crew's near miss seems to have scared you stupid. I get it, I do."

He closed his eyes, trying to block out the concern she voiced for all the rest of the guys staring at him.

"But keep going like you are and you'll drive him away."

"Stop talking, Salome." He knew better than to tell her to shut up, even if she didn't understand how her insight cut him. Hopefully using her full name would be enough to convey how serious he was. He couldn't dive into the details.

No way could he admit what he and Alanso had seen. What they'd done.

"You better not have let your fear hurt him. Tell me

you didn't." Her emerald eyes begged much more softly than her steely tone.

Eli didn't bother to lie.

The hand she let fly didn't catch him by surprise. She loved Alanso. They all did.

Which was why he didn't bother to duck. He deserved the stinging impact of her open palm on his cheek. That and more. Because even as his head whipped to the side, he admired the stretch of her petite frame when she stood on her tiptoes, her raven hair and the glint of her fancy-painted fingernails, one of her pride and joys.

If he'd only wanted Alanso, maybe the two of them could have explored the possibility. But he was going to hell because he lusted after all of the Hot Rods.

The gang held their collective breath, waiting to see how he would react to Sally's uncharacteristic act of violence. Roman stiffened, prepared to spring to her defense.

All the fight leeched out of Eli.

No matter how bad it got, they didn't have to be afraid he'd attack one of their own. Then again, hadn't he done just that?

The damage he'd wrought would be far worse than the impact of a fist.

His shoulders dropped and his head hung. "I'll get him back."

"You'd fucking better." Mustang Sally shook her hand before propping it on her hip and pointing to the door. "Don't come home without him."

The five remaining guys closed rank around their littlest member. They knew she'd hate for Eli to see her tears or her alarm. He didn't waste any time offering comfort she wouldn't welcome. Kaige, Carver, Holden, Roman and Bryce would take good care of her.

They didn't need him.

But Alanso might.

To keep reading **King Cobra, click here**.

NAUGHTY NEWS

Want to win cool stuff? Get sneak peeks of upcoming books? How about being the first to know what's in the pipeline or where Jayne will be making appearances near you? If any of that stuff sounds good then sign up for Jayne's newsletter, the Naughty News. She never shares you information, pinky swear!

www.jaynerylon.com/newsletter

WHAT WAS YOUR FAVORITE PART?

Did you enjoy this book? If so, please leave a review and tell your friends about it. Word of mouth and online reviews are immensely helpful and greatly appreciated.

JAYNE'S SHOP

Check out Jayne's online shop for autographed print books, direct download ebooks, reading-themed apparel up to size 5XL, mugs, tote bags, notebooks, Mr. Rylon's wood (you'll have to see it for yourself!) and more.
www.jaynerylon.com/shop

LISTEN UP!

The majority of Jayne's books are also available in audio format on Audible, Amazon and iTunes.

ABOUT THE AUTHOR

Jayne Rylon is a New York Times and USA Today bestselling author. She received the 2011 Romantic Times Reviewers' Choice Award for Best Indie Erotic Romance. Her stories used to begin as daydreams in seemingly endless business meetings, but now she is a full time author, who employs the skills she learned from her straight-laced corporate existence in the business of writing. She lives in Ohio with two cats and her husband, the infamous Mr. Rylon. When she can escape her purple office, she loves to travel the world, avoid speeding tickets in her beloved Sky, and–of course–read.

Jayne Loves To Hear From Readers

www.jaynerylon.com

contact@jaynerylon.com

ALSO BY JAYNE RYLON

MEN IN BLUE

Hot Cops Save Women In Danger

Night is Darkest

Razor's Edge

Mistress's Master

Spread Your Wings

Wounded Hearts

Bound For You

DIVEMASTERS

Sexy SCUBA Instructors By Day, Doms On A Mega-Yacht By Night

Going Down

Going Deep

Going Hard

POWERTOOLS

Five Guys Who Get It On With Each Other & One Girl.
Enough Said?

Kate's Crew

Morgan's Surprise

Kayla's Gift

Devon's Pair

Nailed to the Wall

Hammer it Home

HOT RODS

Powertools Spin Off. Keep up with the Crew plus...

Seven Guys & One Girl. Enough Said?

King Cobra

Mustang Sally

Super Nova

Rebel on the Run

Swinger Style

Barracuda's Heart

Touch of Amber

Long Time Coming

STANDALONE

Menage

Middleman

4-Ever Theirs

Nice & Naughty

Contemporary

Where There's Smoke

Report For Booty

COMPASS BROTHERS

Modern Western Family Drama Plus Lots Of Steamy Sex

Northern Exposure

Southern Comfort

Eastern Ambitions

Western Ties

COMPASS GIRLS

*Daughters Of The Compass Brothers Drive Their Dads Crazy And
Fall In Love*

Winter's Thaw

Hope Springs

Summer Fling

Falling Softly

PLAY DOCTOR

Naughty Sexual Psychology Experiments Anyone?

Dream Machine

Healing Touch

RED LIGHT

A Hooker Who Loves Her Job

Complete Red Light Series Boxset

FREE - Through My Window - FREE

Star

Can't Buy Love

Free For All

PICK YOUR PLEASURES

Choose Your Own Adventure Romances!

Pick Your Pleasure

Pick Your Pleasure 2

RACING FOR LOVE

MMF Menages With Race-Car Driver Heroes

Complete Series Boxset

Driven

Shifting Gears

PARANORMALS

Vampires, Witches, And A Man Trapped In A Painting

Paranormal Double Pack Boxset

Picture Perfect

Reborn